Reau Campbell

Campbell's Complete Guide and Descriptive Book of Mexico

Volume 1

Reau Campbell

Campbell's Complete Guide and Descriptive Book of Mexico
Volume 1

ISBN/EAN: 9783337426835

Printed in Europe, USA, Canada, Australia, Japan

Cover: Foto ©Andreas Hilbeck / pixelio.de

More available books at **www.hansebooks.com**

CAMPBELL'S

Complete Guide and Descriptive Book

OF

MEXICO

POOLE BROS. PRESS,
CHICAGO.

J. MANZ & CO., ENGRAVERS,
CHICAGO.

PHOTOGRAPHS BY
W. H. JACKSON, DENVER.
ROCHESTER CAMERA CO'S POCO.

PREFACE

IT IS the early traveler in a country who knows the real need of a guide and descriptive book, from the fact that his journeys are made, perforce, without one, and he is compelled to find the places and things as best he can.

To find these places and things, of which one may have only heard, is not unattended by difficulties. The native does not always regard them as out of the ordinary, or of special interest, and, however courteous and willing he may be, is not always able to show the way to objects of even considerable importance.

I have known these difficulties as an early traveler in Mexico, and, while I rejoiced in seeing what others had not seen, I have wished for the book that might guide me over untraveled roads, till I have come to believe that he who writes the book leaves a legacy to him who comes after.

The Guide and Descriptive Book of Mexico is written after the experiences of a decade of travel in that country, which have given a knowledge of its cities and towns, of its mountains, valleys and spreading plains, and of its history and legend, impossible from reading or hearsay.

The Historical and Clerical data have been carefully culled from the best authorities and from the records of Church and State.

The Legends are from the country's books and from the fascinating folk-lore of its people.

Statistical and tabulated information is compiled from the latest data and from the most reliable sources.

The Maps are from the latest surveys, comprising the extension of railways and routes of travel to the year of the date of the book.

The Descriptions have been written under the spell; in the presence of an atmosphere of romantic adventure ; during the loiterings in the fields of the Conquest; under the shadows of ruined temples, whose describing by the ancient chronicler suffices, and of which no more is known to-day than then, when it was written by him that those temples were, "the work of a people which had passed away, under the assaults of barbarism, at a period prior to all traditions, leaving no name, and no trace of their existence save those monuments, which, neglected and forgotten by their successors, have become the riddle of later generations."

The Illustrations are from photographs taken during a tour in the early months of the year 1894, and engraved directly from those photographs, without redrawing. The tour of exploration was made for the express purpose of the publication of a guide and descriptive book, that should guide and describe for the traveler or reader of Mexico.

Every date and place of the story of Mexico, from the Grand River of the North to Tehuantepec, is noted compactly and with all the accuracy possible. Every city and town of note which has been written of elsewhere has its place here; there are some not found in other books which are in these pages, and none are more important or more interesting than the pre-historic Ruins of Mitla, visited first by my exploring expedition of 1894, and which are here written of for the first time since the earlier chronicles of the country.

To the courteous citizens of the country I traveled in, to the strangers of America, England, France, Spain and Germany abiding there, to the Railway officials especially, and to my co-travelers and explorers I am indebted; to the expert artists of the engravers craft, and of the art preservative, who have made a culmination so devoutly wished, I am deeply grateful.

REAU CAMPBELL.

CHICAGO, January 1, 1895.

CONTENTS

Geographical.

Between the Pacific Ocean on the west, the Gulf of Mexico on the east, the United States on the north and Guatemala on the south, lies the Republic of Mexico, extending from the 15th to the 32d degree of north latitude, and from the 86th to the 116th degree of longitude west from Greenwich. From north to south the length is nearly 2,000 miles; from east to west about 800 at the widest part, with an area of 772,652 square miles. Along the Gulf coast the low ground extends a distance into the interior, called the *tierra caliente*, or hot land; then it rises in terraces to the table-lands called the *tierra templada*, temperate land, and still to the regions of higher elevation, to the *tierra fria*, or cold land. In the *tierra caliente* it is summer always; in the *tierra templada* eternal spring; in the *tierra fria* it is rarely cold enough for snow or ice.

It is an erroneous idea that it is not safe or pleasant to travel in Mexico in summer; in the interior the summer time is the most delightful. The only difference between summer and winter is that it rains in the summer and does not in the winter. The altitude, the showers, the cooling breezes from the snow mountains make a perfect summer climate, and a healthful one. Fevers peculiar to the tropics are known only in the hot lands of the coast, and never experienced on the elevated table-lands. The mean temperature of the hot lands is about 80°; of the interior table-lands, as in the capital and principal cities, 70°, and the higher elevations 60°. A more perfectly delightful climate is hardly possible to imagine, and possibly exists in few other countries.

Rivers—The rivers of Mexico are more dignified by the appellation than from the amount of water flowing within their banks. They are little more than creeks, but as to length they are entitled to be called rivers. With the exception of the Rio Panuco, and one or two others, the rivers of Mexico are not navigable, and then only for a short distance from their mouths. The lack of tributaries, and the immense amount of water drawn off for irrigating purposes, is the reason given for the small size of the streams. For the most part they are, during the winter, but straggling brooks, but in the rainy season become raging torrents. The Lerma is the longest river in Mexico, running its whole length within that country, being nearly 700 miles long. The Rio Grande, which rises in the United States, is over 1500 miles long. The Panuco, at Tampico, is a beautiful stream, navigable some score of miles or more through a tropical country, the banks fringed with that verdure so often described by travelers in the tropics. The navigation of these few miles of deep water in Mexico is to be one of the attractions for tourists in that section. The jetties at the mouth of the Panuco make the harbor at Tampico one of deep water.

The Rio Lerma rises on the west slope of the Sierra Madres, not far from Toluca, and runs in a northwesterly course till it empties into Lake Chapala, and, curiously enough, leaves the lake again, only a few miles from its mouth, and becomes another river, the Santiago, flowing on to the Pacific Ocean. The Mexican National Railroad crosses the Lerma near its source, east of Toluca, and at Acámbaro, running along its course between the two points. The Central crosses it, or the Santiago, as it is called after passing through Lake Chapala, just east of Guadalajara, and also follows along the valley for some miles before reaching Lake Chapala. Humboldt said that the Lerma could be made a navigable river, and he also said he could drive a carriage on the table-lands from the capital to El Paso; in either case there would be many ups and downs to be encountered. The Santiago, or Lerma, empties into the Pacific near San Blas. The river at Morelia, along which the National Railroad runs near that city, is called the Morelia River, though there are other names. The Grijalva River, named for the commander of the Spanish fleet, who was the first white man who ever saw it, rises in Guatemala, and empties into the Gulf at Frontera. The Rio Uzumacinta also has its source in Guatemala, and empties into the Gulf at Frontera. The Rio Balsas, also called Mescala and Zacatula, rises in the State

A WAYSIDE SHRINE.

of Tlaxcala and flows westward, and empties into the Pacific at Zacatula. The Papaloapan rises in the mountains and empties into the Gulf at Alvarado. The Rio Coatzacoalcos rises in Oaxaca and empties into the Gulf at the town of the same name. Atoyac is a favorite name for rivers; there are several of them in the States of Puebla and Vera Cruz.

The Rio Nazas is one of the rivers that loses its waters in the marshes of the great Bolson de Mapimí. The Sonora, Yaqui and Mayo rise in the mountains of western Mexico and empty into the Gulf of California.

Lakes—The lakes of Mexico are of exceeding great beauty. Than those of Chapala and Patzcuaro no prettier waters are anywhere in the world—not even the romantic Como, the tales of whose beauties are so eloquently told, can surpass their islands and wooded shores, and only the villas are lacking to make them as picturesque as Como or Killarney. Lake Patzcuaro is the highest navigable water on the continent, being some thousands of feet greater altitude than Chautauqua of New York, that so long enjoyed that reputation. The islands look like the peaks of submerged mountains with only the tops above the water; on their rugged sides, seeming to cling to them, are some huts of the fishermen of the lake, and up near the top of one the square white tower of a church rises above the trees, the sonorous sounds of whose bell floats over the waters.

There are canoes for freight and passengers, and a few rude sail boats making voyages between Patzcuaro and the islands and mainland ports up the lake, and to Tzintzuntzan, where the celebrated picture of Titian is, in a ruined church. Lake Patzcuaro is near the city of that name on the western division of the Mexican National Railroad; it is about thirty miles long and twelve miles wide.

Lake Cuitzeo is also on the same division of the National, thirty miles west of Acámbaro, the junction point with the main line. Lake Cuitzeo is forty-five miles long and ten wide. The islands are very much like those in Lake Patzcuaro; some of them are inhabited. One, "La Isla de los Burros," is the objective point of a very interesting voyage from the station at Queréndaro, where canoes may be obtained. The island is inhabited by a hardy tribe of Indian fishermen, who know little of the main land, and care less—a happy, contented lot, living off of what they can catch, the little white fish about the size of a minnow or whitebait, which, when they are dried in the sun, are ready for the table, if there was one on the island. The lake is literally alive with water fowl, and so unused to the gun that many a good shot may be had.

RAILWAY CONSTRUCTION CAMP, MEXICAN SOUTHERN RAILROAD.

On the eastern shore there are some old salt works, and near the station of Queréndaro some hot springs, the steam rising from the marsh in white columns. Near the track, where one of the largest springs rises, is a pool so arranged that the waters can be turned in or out, as the water may be too cold or hot. On the bushes, on the trees, on the rocks, and stuck in the ground, are rude crosses made of sticks and twigs, left there by grateful bathers whose ills have been cured by the genial waters.

Lake Chapala is the largest lake in Mexico. It is nearly a 100 miles long and is thirty-three miles at the widest point. It is on the Guadalajara division of the Mexican Central Railway near the city of that name. The station of La Barca is at the head of the lake. The River Lerma empties into Lake Chapala, and the same river under another name, Santiago, but some authorities use the same name, is the outlet.

"Libertad" was the name of Lake Chapala's first steamboat. She ran from La Barca to the towns and villages up the lake, and the voyage was one of the most delightful in Mexico, through the "floating islands" to the towering cliffs with sparkling cascades tumbling into the lake from far up the rocks, by the picturesque towns and villages, of which the town of Chapala is a resort of ancient renown, from its pure and healthful climate, its hot springs and most picturesque scenery.

The steamer "Libertad" had her machinery built in California, and was transported by piecemeal on burros over the mountains from San Blas.

In the Bolson de Mapimí are several lakes, of which Mayran and Parras are the largest—twenty to thirty miles long by ten to fifteen wide. In the Valley of Mexico and near the City are Zumpango, Xaltocan and San Cristobal on the north,

Lake Texcoco on the east and Xochimilco and Chalco on the south, La Viga and the other canals connecting them with the City. All are very shallow and without an outlet, except what may result from the great drainage ditches and tunnels. The steamboat has not made its advent on the lakes of the Plain of Mexico; transportation is carried on by long flat-bottom boats propelled by poles in the hands of strong men. There are regular packets between the City and the towns and villages on the lake shores, some of them of capacity for fifty or sixty passengers, and where voyages cover many miles and two or three days' time, they have accommodations for eating or sleeping in the most primitive style. The passengers are mostly country folk bringing their wares or garden truck to the city markets. The burros and dogs lend their presence to make up a picturesque ship's company.

Cortéz came across Texcoco in some such flat-bottom boats from the eastern shore when he laid siege to tne City of Mexico; but there was deeper water in those days, and the feat was not without its merits.

Mountains—To describe or even name them would be to write over all the face of the country. Ask a native, "What mountains are those?" His answer—no matter where he is or where the mountains are—is "Las Madres." There seems to be no other name except certain peaks here and there, that take names from their fantastic shape, curious color, or from an incident of history or legend, as Ixtaccihuatl is the "White Woman;" Malintzi, called "Malinche," was named from an appellation of La Marina, the guide, interpreter and wife of Cortéz. La Bufa, at Zacatecas, is so called from the resemblance of the rocky crest to a Buffalo. There is no mistaking the Saddle Mountain at Monterey, as a perfect saddle is on its crest; and so all over this country are mountains and romance.

Above ranges high peaks are raised to the line of perpetual snow, and volcanoes still throw out fire and brimstone. The following are the most important:

Ajusco, Federal District	13,612
Cerro de Culiacan, State of Guanajuato	10,640
Cerro del Proaño, State of Zacatecas	7,762
Cerro de Patamban, State of Michoacan	12,290
Cofre de Perote, or Nauchampatepetl, State of Vera Cruz.	13,403
Cumbre de Jesus María, State of Chihuahua	8,230
Gigante, State of Guanajuato	10,653
Ixtaccíhuatl, States of Mexico and Puebla	16,060
Las Navajas, State of Hidalgo	10,528
Los Llanitos, State of Guanajuato	11,013
Matlalcueyatl, or Malintzi, State of Tlaxcala	13,462
Nevado de Colima, State of Jalisco	14,350
Nevado de Toluca, or Xinantecatl, State of Mexico	15,000
Orizaba, or Citlaltepetl, State of Vera Cruz	17,356
Pico de Quincéo, State of Michoacan	10,895
Pico de Tancítaro, State of Michoacan	12,653
Popocatepetl, States of Mexico and Vera Cruz	17,782
Veta Grande, State of Zacatecas	9,965
Volcan de Colima, State of Jalisco	12,728
Zempoaltepec, State of Oaxaca	11,965

Table-lands—The plains of Mexico vary in extent from a score of square miles to many thousands; they are arid and they are fertile, they are as a desert and as a marsh. The Bajío, in the State of Guanajuato, is a very fertile district well watered, and near to it the Cazadero (hunting place), in Querétaro, a district of grazing. The Plains of Apam are noted for the growth of the maguey and its production of pulque; on one side of these fertile lands is the arid Plain of San

Juan; to the north and east, just on the edge of the terrace, are great marshes almost covered with water. In the State of San Luis Potosí a desert extends from a few miles north of the capital nearly to Saltillo. In the States of Coahuila, Durango and Chihuahua are the lagoons and marshes of the Bolson de Mapimí.

A GLIMPSE OF OAXACA.

The Coast is almost devoid of harbors and safe roadsteads except at Tampico, where the mouth of the Rio Panuco has been jettied over a thousand feet out into the Gulf. The outward scour of the river cleans the sands from the bar, affording an entrance for the largest ships and a safe harbor large enough for all purposes. At Vera Cruz ships anchor opposite the city and discharge cargoes and passengers by lighters; harbor improvements are being made. At Coatzacoalcos, the Gulf terminus of the Tehuantepec Railway, a deep water harbor will be provided, as the physical advantages of the port are capable of great improvement by jetties. On the Pacific Coast the harbor of Salina Cruz, near Tehuantepec, will be improved for the entrance of big ships.

At Acapulco is one of the finest harbors in the world; at Manzanillo, Mazatlan, San Blas and Guaymas are very fine harbors. The mountains on this coast are washed by the sea while on the Gulf are wide expanses of lowlands with the hills farther to the interior.

Agriculture and Forests—The lands of Mexico, with its diversified climate, grow the vegetable products of the world—corn, wheat, rye and barley, of the temperate zone, on the uplands; sugar cane, coffee, the finest in the world, vanilla, cotton, indigo, tobacco, jalap and cocoa in the hot lands, while every variety of cactus produces something of use, from the fibre of the ixtle to the *pulque* of the maguey. In the forests are all the hardwoods, mahogany, rosewood, ebony, as well as the oak, pine and cedar of less value. In a great extent of country, in the interior, wood of any kind is scarce, and timbers for manufacturing purposes are freighted from distant points. The possibilities for agricultural improvement are unbounded.

Mines and Mining—This subject may be treated in one word, *silver*. It is everywhere, in every state, in every hill and mountain. It is probable that the total production of silver in Mexico, since the opening of the mines to date, would reach $4,000,000,000. Gold exists in small quantities. It is a curious fact that the ornaments found by the Spaniards in the houses of the native kings and nobles were all of gold; silver was hardly mentioned among the trophies taken to Spain. There is little iron, except at Durango, where there is a mountain of it that is from 75 to 90 per cent. of pure metal. Coal of fair quality is mined extensively. Lead there is, and some copper; also quicksilver, cinnabar, salt, bismuth, alum, asphalt, naphtha and petroleum; sulphur is taken in huge blocks—pure sulphur from the crater of Popocatepetl.

Manufactures—Mexico has advanced wonderfully in manufactures in the last decade, till, within herself, she could supply all wants of her people without the imports from the outside world, could clothe them from head to foot, feed them, give them wine to drink and houses to live in. Statistical information as to manufactures is not expected here. The percentage of increase is not easily calculated. The advance has been from the primitive hand loom of reeds to the factory of the most improved machinery. The lack of the important factor of fuel will necessarily relegate the manufactories to the timbered regions, or to the line of the water-powers of the country, where fuel is not needed. The forests are for the most part in remote sections and in the hot lands. Coal is not yet mined in sufficient quantities, though it exists in many parts of the Republic, and there are evidences of petroleum.

The water-powers have never been utilized to their fullest capacity, and there are great possibilities in this direction, as at Juanacatlan, near Guadalajara, where a wide river makes a sheer fall of seventy-one feet. This immense power is almost wasted. It is used only for an electric light plant, and a mill that is idle the most of the time.

Carpets and woolen cloths are made at Soria, near Celaya, at Salvatierra, and several other points; calicoes and cotton goods in the Federal District and in many of the larger cities; blankets and zerapes at Durango, Saltillo, San Miguel de Allende, Aguas Calientes, Guadalajara and San Luis Potosí; saddles, bridles, shoes and leather goods at Leon, Maravatio and the City of Mexico; cigars and cigarettes at Vera Cruz, the City of Mexico, and the larger cities; breweries are at Monterey and Toluca; foundry and rolling mill near the iron mountain at Durango. Chihuahua and Monterey are the largest manufacturing centres of the country; the factories include almost every branch of trade. Smelters and reduction works for getting out silver are located in all the great mining towns. Sugar mills are in the cane country, but as yet the refineries are very few. Crockery and pottery are made at Puebla, Guadalajara, and in very many smaller towns and villages. The onyx of Puebla is famous for its delicate beauty. It is manufactured into very handsome ornaments and used extensively in the manufacture of tops for stands and tables, altars,

SAN JUAN VALLEY, MEXICAN SOUTHERN RAILROAD.

fonts, etc., for shrines and churches. All of Mexico's manufactures are infant industries, but growing very rapidly.

Railroads—THE MEXICAN RAILWAY was the first completed line in Mexico. It extends from Vera Cruz to the City of Mexico, 263 miles, passing through a very rich region, both in the tropics and the table-lands. Córdoba and Orizaba are the principal cities in the *tierra caliente*. The line is famous the world over for the beauty of its scenery, and that between Maltrata and Esperanza is beautiful beyond all description. From Esperanza the line runs through a succession of fertile plains; the most noted are the famous pulque Plains of Apam. The tramroad from Tejeria to Jalapa has been abandoned. A tramway extends from Esperanza to Tehuacan. A branch from Apizaco to Puebla and from Ometusco to Pachuca.

THE MEXICAN CENTRAL RAILWAY from El Paso, Texas, crossing the Rio Grande to the old town of Paso del Norte, now called the City of Juarez, runs almost due south 1224 miles to the City of Mexico. Passing the cities of Chihuahua, Jimenez, Lerdo, Fresnillo, Calera, Zacatecas, Aguas Calientes, Lagos, Leon, Silao, Irapuato, Salamanca, Celaya, Querétaro and Cazadero on the main line.

Torreon is the junction point with the International Railroad. From Aguas Calientes a branch line extends to San Luis Potosí and Tampico. From Silao a branch runs to Guanajuato. From Irapuato a line runs west to Guadalajara. At Celaya the main line crosses the Mexican National Railroad. From Tula a branch extends to Pachuca.

The ride over the Mexican Central is an interesting one, both as to main line and branches—varied in valley and mountain scenery, broad plain and rocky chasm; and the going and returning schedules should be arranged so that part of the line passed at night southward should be traveled in daylight going north.

It is impossible to enumerate the points of interest; they are in almost every mile. The most important are: the view of Chihuahua on the west side; San Pedro Bridge; Bolson de Mapimí on the east side; approach to and passing of Zacatecas and Guadalupe, seen from the east windows; Barranca de La Encarnacion; approach to Lagos and Leon; Irapuato for strawberries and Celaya for *dulces*, both every day in the year; Querétaro for opals; and just south of the city the road passes under the great stone aqueduct of the city's water supply and into a fine valley, and afterwards to the Plain of the Cazadero to Leña, the point of highest altitude, 8,140 feet. At Tula are the ruins of Toltec temples; the road, continuing, runs through a beautiful valley to the great Nochistongo Canal, seen on the west side. From Huehuetoca may be obtained the first view of the great volcanoes of Popocatepetl and Ixtaccihuatl, and the plain, valley and City of Mexico.

The scenery on the line from San Luis to Tampico, is unsurpassed in Mexico, and the branch roads to Guadalajara and Guanajuato are rich in scenic beauty.

THE MEXICO, CUERNAVACA & PACIFIC RAILWAY extends fifty miles from the City of Mexico to Cuernavaca, with an ultimate destination on the Pacific Coast. The road crosses the broad plain of the Valley of Mexico, passing historic points, Molino del Rey, Chapultepec, Padierna and Contreras. The scenic beauty of the line, as it passes up the hills on the southern border of the plain, is magnificent.

THE MEXICAN INTERNATIONAL RAILROAD enters the Republic of Mexico at the city of Porfirio Diaz, crossing the Rio Grande from Eagle Pass, Texas, and runs 383 miles westward to its junction with the Central at Torreon. Connection is made at Treviño for Monterey. The principal cities and towns are Monclova, Jaral and Paila; near the latter are the famous vineyards of Parras. The road skirts the southern border of the Bolson de Mapimí, and all along the line are fine views of mountain scenery, making the ride an interesting one.

After Torreon the road enters the San Juan Valley, and extends, southwesterly, 157 miles across the plains, over a fine roadway to the beautiful city of Durango.

THE MEXICAN INTEROCEANIC RAILROAD has its main line from the City of Mexico to Vera Cruz, and is under construction to Acapulco on the Pacific Coast. On the eastern division the principal points of interest are Texcoco, Puebla, Perote, Jalapa and Vera Cruz. On the western division are La Compañia, Tlalmanalco,

Amecameca, Ozumba, Napantla, Cuautla and Yautepec. The scenery is pleasing beyond description; the great volcanoes are in full view for many miles, in fact scarcely out of sight during the entire journey. Leaving Mexico, the road passes along the shores of Lake Texcoco, seen from the east windows, while Lake Xochimilco and Chalco can be seen from the other side. At Los Reyes is the junction of the east and west lines. On the east line the points of interest are the Hacienda of General Gonzales—Texcoco—Molino de Flores—the Arcos de Zempoala, an aqueduct thirty-seven miles long, with arches nearly 100 feet high—the pulque Plains of Apam, Puebla, Pyramid of Cholula, Volcano of Orizaba, Perote and beautiful Jalapa.

On the west line the interesting points are Amecameca, the nearest view of Popocatepetl and Ixtaccihuatl, Sacro Monte, Nepantla, Cuautla and Yautepec, Hacienda de Santa Inez and many others.

THE MEXICAN NATIONAL RAILROAD has its northern terminus at Laredo, Texas, Nuevo Laredo being the city in Mexico on the opposite bank of the Rio Grande. The line runs in a southwesterly direction, 840 miles, to the City of Mexico, passing the cities of Monterey, Saltillo, Catorce, San Luis Potosí, San Miguel de Allende, Celaya, Salvatierra, Acámbaro, Maravatio and Toluca on the main line.

At Monterey the road crosses the Monterey & Mexican Gulf Railroad. At Vanegas connection is made with the Vanegas, Matehuala & Rio Verde Railroad. At San Luis Potosí is the crossing of the Tampico division, and at Celaya the main line of the Mexican Central. Acámbaro is the junction of the western division for Morelia and Patzcuaro.

At Maravatio connection is made with the Michoacan & Pacific. At Tacuba is the junction of the El Salto branch.

All roads lead to the capital, and all have their points of interest. These are not lacking on the National, and daylight schedules are to be chosen whenever it is possible. To be especially noted are the following: the beautiful Monterey Valley, the City, Saddle Mountain, Mitre Mountain, Bishop's Palace, on the east side; the ride through the cañons to Saltillo; on the east side see the mountain peak with a hole in the top, as if made with a monster cannon shot; Hacienda Ramos Arispe and approach to Saltillo; battlefield of Buena Vista, just south of Saltillo; Catorce, station for the great mining town of the same name; Bocas, with

TRAVELING

its beautiful hacienda (on the east side) and village; San Luis Potosí, on the west side; Dolores Hidalgo, once the home of the patriot priest; San Miguel de Allende, the city on the hill, seen from the east windows; the cañon and valley of the Laja; the cotton mills at Soria; cañon near Maravatio; cañon of the Zopilote, south of

Solis, where is shown the rock of El Salto de Juan Medina, where the famous bandit leaped his horse from the top to the chasm below, rather than be captured; Zirizícuaro, on the east side; valley and city of Toluca; ascent of the Sierra Madres to a point 10,000 feet above the sea; passing around the village of Ocoyocac, and a few minutes later a thousand feet above it; grand view of valley and volcano of Toluca; mill and aqueduct of Jalapa; battlefield of Las Cruces; grand view from the mountain top after passing La Cima; the

A MOUNTAIN PATH.

plain and valley of Mexico; the City and the volcanoes on the east side; descent of the eastern slope; the "Moonstone" near Rio Hondo; Naucaulpan; Los Remedios on the west; Chapultepec on the east; old aqueduct on the east side. These are on the main line. On the western division the attractions are no less, as it passes through the beautiful lake region of Mexico, Lake Cuitseo and Lake Patzcuaro, and to the cities of Morelia and Patzcuaro.

THE MEXICAN NORTHERN RAILWAY extends from Escalon to Sierra Mojada, 78 miles.

THE MEXICAN SOUTHERN RAILROAD runs from Puebla to Oaxaca, 228 miles, passing through the important towns of Tecomavaca and Tehuacan, with an ultimate destination at a Pacific port in the State of Tehuantepec. The road has a splendid passenger equipment, and runs through a country wildly picturesque, where primitive Mexico may be seen as nowhere else. Convenient schedules are operated to and from Puebla, connecting with those of the lines from the capital. The line runs at the bottom of the cañons, instead of on the cliffs, as in the case of almost all the other lines, presenting views unlike those seen anywhere else. Just below the beautiful city of Oaxaca, reached by a broad, level carriage road, are the big trees of Santa Maria del Tule and the wonderful Ruins of Mitla.

THE HIDALGO RAILROAD runs from the City of Mexico to Pachuca and the mining cities beyond; the road runs through a country rich in scenic beauty. There is a branch line to Irolo.

THE MICHOACAN & PACIFIC RAILWAY runs from Maravatio, on the Mexican National, to Ocampo, with an ultimate destination on the Pacific Coast.

THE MONTEREY & MEXICAN GULF RAILROAD extends from Tampico, on the Gulf, 387 miles to Treviño, on the International Railroad, crossing the Mexican National Railroad at Monterey, with an ultimate destination on the Pacific Coast, passing the cities of Victoria, Linares, Montemorelos and numerous smaller towns and villages of more or less interest to the traveler, in the newly opened country through which the line passes.

The constantly changing scenes in the mountains and valleys from Treviño and Monterey to Linares and Victoria make the journey over the Monterey & Mexican Gulf road a pleasing one, to which is added those of tropical beauty on the southern division of the line south of Victoria and all the way down to Tampico. The road passes near virgin forests where all the woods of tropics grow and from which the builders took cross ties and bridge timbers of ebony and mahogany; here are, also, the fruits and flowers, the birds and beasts peculiar to the torrid zone, offering attractions to the touring traveler not found on every railroad, even in Mexico. Tampico is the chief seaport on the east coast of Mexico, an interesting city and a most charming winter resort. Branch lines are projected from San Juan to Camargo on the Rio Grande, and from Linares to Soto La Marina.

THE SONORA RAILROAD runs from Benson, in Arizona Territory, to Guaymas, on the Gulf of California, 353 miles, passing Hermosillo, the capital of the State of Sonora, and through a country intensely interesting and possessing a wealth of scenery. The harbor of Guaymas is one of the finest on the Pacific Coast, landlocked by high mountains that make it very beautiful as well as a very safe one.

THE VANEGAS, CEDRAL & MATEHUALA RAILROAD runs from Vanegas to Cedral, Matehuala and Rio Verde.

TEHUANTEPEC RAILWAY—The completion of the Tehuantepec Railway makes the shortest possible transcontinental line north of the Isthmus of Panama. The road runs from the fine harbor of Coatzacoalcos, on the Gulf, to that of Salina Cruz, on the Pacific Coast. Both harbors are amply protected and possessed of sufficient water for all practical purposes. The harbor of Coatzacoalcos was discovered by a band of Cortéz explorers. As there was no safe road where his ships could ride off the coast of Vera Cruz, he sent an exploring party down the coast, and Coatzacoalcos was the harbor they looked for. Tehuantepec is a few miles inland from Salina Cruz. The importance of this railroad is realized in the immense sailing distance saved on both sides, which is from 1,500 to 2,000 miles on the Gulf, and about the same on the Pacific. The Tehuantepec Railway is about 140 miles long, while the Panama road is only forty miles, but this difference does not count; when freight or passengers have to be transferred it is as well to travel 140 miles as forty, when the saving of sea voyage is considered.

FIRST SHRINE OF MEXICO.

Steamer Lines—The principal steamer lines to and from Mexican ports are the Ward Line, New York & Cuba Mail Steamship Company, with weekly steamers between Vera Cruz, Tampico, New York and Havana, touching at Progreso, Campeche, Tuxpan and Frontera.

The Ceballos or Spanish Line steamers make the same ports. A railroad is in operation from Progreso to Merida, and other interior points in Yucatan.

The Pacific Mail steamers, between San Francisco and Panama, touch at Acapulco, Mazatlan, Manzanillo and San Blas.

Inland navigation in Mexico is at present very limited; small steamers are run on Lakes Patzcuaro and Chapala, and on some of the smaller rivers of the States of Tabasco, Yucatan and Vera Cruz, and up the coast to the ports of Vera Cruz and Tampico, touching intermediate ports. The Ward Line has a coastwise steamer in the same waters. The Rio Panuco and Tampico Rivers are also navigated a short distance into the interior. But every one of these lines have their attractions that do not obtain on any other waters of the western world.

Historical.

 What might have served to enlighten upon the history of the earlier races that inhabited the land, was destroyed by the fanatics, who saw in the temples they found, evidences of a civilization almost superior to their own, and of a religion so nearly identical, that it seemed only a creed of the one they professed; the jealous bigotry that threw down the graven stones, and tore the pictured parchments to fragments, wiped out volumes of history and placed bloody chapters in their stead. The bigots pulled down that which in their day and generation they could not build up, placed a period and a finis to the story of the races that were there for centuries before they brought their bloody banners to these shores, till there is only here and there a sculptured wall, with mosaics more intricate than any builded since, or massive monoliths set up in pillars to grace a corridor of grander proportions than their own, and, if they could, they would have destroyed all of these works of a people who had passed away under the assaults of barbarism, at a period prior to all traditions, leaving no name, and no trace of their existence save these monuments, which, neglected and forgotten by their successors have become the riddle of later generations.

There was a survival of the fittest. The bigot and fanatic passed away in the fire of his own kindling. The good men and true saved, as brands from the burning, some scrolls of picture writings, and from destruction saved the marvelous carvings, that hung up for ornaments, and set as treasures within our modern walls, tell us of a departed civilization, but with only a drop of the knowledge of it.

It is to be regretted that from the wreck of this primitive civilization some of the arts peculiar to it were not saved. The methods by which its astronomers succeeded in determining the apparent motion of the sun and the length of the solar year; of working and polishing crystal and other stones; of manufacturing delicate articles of use and ornament of obsidian; of casting figures of gold and of silver in one piece; of making filigree ornaments without soldering; of applying to pottery even and transparent glazes, such as are used by makers of fine ware, with colors that, after remaining for centuries under ground, still are fresh and brilliant; of weaving extremely delicate tissues of cotton mixed with silky feathers and rabbit's fur.

The earliest data of record is in the coming of the Toltecs to Auahuac, A. D., 648, and the movements of the various tribes in the succeeding centuries till the foundation of Tenochtitlan in 1325, nearly 200 years before its destroyers came. But these dates are determined by tradition only, on which no two of the ancient chroniclers agree, but their differences are not material.

The Conquest. The name of Cortéz is synonymous with the conquest, but it was not his privilege to be the first of his race to reach the shores of the land of his brilliant adventures.

Francisco Hernandez de Córdoba discovered the coast of Yucatan, March 4, 1517. A year later another expedition was sent out by Velasquez, the governor of Cuba, under command of Don Juan de Grijálva, who came to the shores of Mexico and landed on the island of San Juan de Ulúa, opposite the present city of Vera Cruz. A good report of the land was sent back to Cuba by one of the captains, Pedro de Alvarado, later a famous officer under Cortéz, and still another fleet, larger than the others, was fitted out and placed under the command of Hernando Cortéz. Before the fleet was ready to sail the governor determined to remove Cortéz from command, which coming to the ears of the Conqueror, he prepared his ships for sea and sailed before his removal could be accomplished, on the night of November 18, 1518, from Santiago de Cuba, touching at several other ports on the island for supplies. Cortéz finally sailed for Mexico February 18, 1519. The fleet consisted of eleven ships, carrying 110 sailors, sixteen cavalry men with their horses, 553 foot soldiers, 200 Cuban Indians, a battery of ten small cannon and four falconets; with this army went two Indians as interpreters, captured by Córdoba in Yucatan two years previous.

On his ship Cortéz raised the standard of the conquest, a black ensign, emblazoned with the arms of Charles V., bearing the crimson cross borne in clouds, with the motto: *Amici, sequamen crucem et si nos fidem habemus vere in hoc signo vincemus*—" Friends, let us follow the cross, and if we have faith we will conquer." Under this flag and the patronage of St. Peter, Cortéz sailed. On the island of Cozumel a shipwrecked Spaniard, Geronimo de Aguilar, was picked up; having been there for nearly nine years he had acquired the language and was a valuable acquisition as an interpreter.

The first landing was on March 20, 1519, near the Rio Tabasco, where there was fighting with the natives and a number made captives, among whom was La Marina, a native of Jalisco, sold here as a slave. She understood the language of the uplands as well as the coast, and thus, through her and Aguilar, Cortéz could communicate with the people. La Marina soon learned the Spanish language and became the interpreter, ally and wife of the conqueror, and bore him a son, who was called Martin, as was another son by his Spanish wife.

Leaving the River Grijalva, Cortéz sailed up the coast and dropped his anchors off Vera Cruz, April 21, 1519. Efforts to secure a peaceful reception on the part of the natives were unavailing. Discontent arose among the Spaniards. Cortéz, acting with his customary decision, burned his ships, and on the 16th of August began his march toward the capital of the Aztecs.

With little incident or opposition the brave band of adventurers reached the table-lands and after a fight with the Tlaxcalans made them their allies. At Cholula, Cortéz put down a conspiracy reported to him by La Marina, attended by a great massacre of the Cholulans. The natives were completely terrorized by the cannon and fire-arms, and the horse and rider of the cavalry were regarded as almost a god, or at least one being, as they had never seen a horse, so the invaders proceeded on their march, unopposed, passed over the causeways of Tenochtitlan, and entered the present City of Mexico, Tuesday, November 8, 1519; the Aztec

King, Montezuma, came out to meet Cortéz, tradition says, on the site of the present Hospital de Jesus, founded by him in commemoration of this meeting.

The aggressions of the Spaniards, and their oppression of the Mexicans soon turned their apparent friendship to hatred, and they drove them out of the City over the Tlacópan causeway, now called Tacuba, on the night of July 1, 1520, called *la noche triste*, the Dismal Night; retreating, Cortéz fought another battle at Otumba on the 8th of July, where the Tlaxcalans came to his rescue and turned the tide of war in his favor, and he halted in the city of these allies. While at Tlaxcala reinforcements came from Cuba; powder for the cannon and small arms were made from the sulphur taken from the crater of Popocatepetl. The *bergantines*, small flat-bottomed boats, were built, to be put together and launched on Lake Texcoco, when Cortéz returned and commenced the siege of Tenochtitlan, December 31, 1520, operating from the town of Texcoco with a force of forty cavalry, eighty arquebusiers and cross-bowmen, 450 infantry, armed with lances and swords, and a battery of nine small cannon. This was the Spanish contingent. The native allies numbered about 125,000.

Montezuma died on the 30th of June, the day before the Noche Triste, and his nephew, Guatemotzin, called also Cuautemoc, who, it is said, shot the first arrow that caused Montezuma's death, was placed in command. The siege continued till the native garrison was starved into submission, and the Spaniards made their second and triumphal entry into the City of Mexico, August 13, 1521; but they found a different city than when the meek Montezuma met them at the city gates. Almost all the treasure had been destroyed or concealed, and to extort the secret from Guatemotzin, Cortéz cruelly put him to torture, but without avail; the wealth of jewels, gold and precious stones had been thrown into the lake.

Cortéz was born in the town of Medellin, Province of Estramadura, in 1485, the son of Don Martin Cortéz de Monroy. He came to Cuba before he was twenty years of age, and later married Doña Catalina Juarez under compulsion, whom he murdered in the garden at Coyoacan. During the conquest La Marina took the place of Doña Catalina, by whom no children were borne. A son, Don Martin, was born of La Marina, and three daughters by other Indian women of rank.

After the conquest Cortéz married Doña Juana de Zúñiga, who was called his second wife, and by whom he had three daughters and one son, also named Martin, who was heir to the conqueror's titles and estates. There was a son, Don Luis, by Antonia Hermosillo.

The two sons, both named Martin, entered into a conspiracy to secure the rulership of the province to Don Martin, the son of Doña Juana. For this his estates were confiscated, but finally restored to him. He married and left a son, Hernando, the third Marques of the Valley, whose son, Don Pedro, the fourth Marques, lived on the estates until 1629, dying in that year without male issue. Through the daughters the property passed to the Neapolitan Dukes of Monteleone, which family still controls the vast estates. The sons, Luis and Martin, by La Marina, were recognized by their father. There is no record of the descendants of the latter. Those of Don Luis are known as Cortéz Hermosillo.

Hernando Cortéz, the Conqueror, died in the town of Castelleja de la Questa, in Spain, December 2, 1547.

The Viceroys—Mexico was under the dominion of Spain for 300 years, during which time there were five Governors, two Audencias and sixty-two Viceroys. Cortéz was the first Governor; the others were military commanders of the time. The Audencias, composed of three to five members each, were torn by envies and jealousies and proved entirely unsatisfactory, so the government by the Viceroys was resorted to. The most prominent, with the important incidents of their administrations, are recorded here. Don Antonio de Mendoza was the first Viceroy, continuing in office from 1535 to 1550. He brought the first printing press and printed the first book in Mexico. He extended the domain to Morelia and Guadalajara, and opened the mines of Zacatecas and Guanajuato, and during his administration the first money of Mexico was coined.

Don Luis de Velasco, the second Viceroy, held the office from 1550 to 1564, and extended the territory of the province northward to Durango. He freed 150,000 Indians held as slaves by the Spaniards, and founded many important institutions, among them Hospital Real and the University. During his time the *patio* process for the reduction of silver was invented at Pachuca by Bartolomé de Medina. He built the dyke of San Lazaro after the first inundation of the city in 1552. Loved and lamented, he died in the City of Mexico, July 31, 1564.

Don Martin Enriquez de Almanza was the fourth Viceroy, from 1568 to 1580. The first stone of the Cathedral was laid during his reign and the Inquisition established.

The seventh Viceroy was Don Alonzo Manrique de Zúñiga, 1585 to 1590 ; he was instrumental in extending the commerce of the country.

The eighth Viceroy was Don Luis de Velasco, son of the second Viceroy, who established internal manufactures, and commenced the extension of territory into New Mexico in the years 1590 to 1595; after an absence as Viceroy of Peru he was again Viceroy from 1607 to 1611, during which time the great *Tajo de Nochistongo* was begun, and the Alameda established.

The ninth Viceroy was Don Gaspar de Zúñiga y Acevedo, Conde de Monterey, who ruled from 1595 to 1603. He extended the domain to California and founded the town of Monterey, California, and in Mexico he removed the city of Vera Cruz to its present site. Don Diego Carrillo Mendoza, Marques de Galves, was the fourteenth viceroy, 1621 to 1624, doing much to exterminate the bandits that infested the highways of Mexico. The twenty-second Viceroy, Don Francisco Fernandez de la Cueva, Duque de Alburquerque, in 1653-60, colonized New Mexico, and founded the town of Albuquerque.

The worthy Fray Payo de Rivera Enriquez was the twenty-seventh Viceroy, and also Archbishop of Mexico, from 1673 to 1680. During his reign, the causeway and aqueduct of Guadalupe was built. Don Melchor Portocarrero Lazo de la Vega, Conde de la Monclova, twenty-ninth Viceroy, 1686 to 1688, built, at his own expense, the aqueduct of Chapultepec, colonized the State of Coahuila, and founded the town of Monclova. Don Gaspar de la Cerda Sandoval Silva y Mendoza, Conde de Galve, was the thirtieth Viceroy, from 1688 to 1696, during which the domain was extended to include Texas, and under his direction the town of Pensacola, Fla., was founded, in 1693.

The thirty-second Viceroy was Don José Sarmiento Valladares, Conde de Moctezuma, which title of Conde came through his wife, a lineal descendant of Moctezuma III. Don Juan de Acuña, Marques de Casafuerte, was the thirty-seventh of the line of Viceroys. During his reign, from 1722 to 1734, the first newspaper, Gaceta de Mexico, was published. Don Pedro Cebrian y Agustin, Conde de Fuenclara, was the fortieth Viceroy, from 1742 to 1746, during which years the State of Tamaulipas was colonized.

Don Joaquin de Monserratte, Marques de Cruillas, forty-fourth Viceroy, established the first regular army in Mexico between 1760 and 1766, and caused the houses in the City of Mexico to be numbered. Don Carlos Francisco de Croix, Marques de Croix, was forty-fifth Viceroy, from 1766 to 1771. He expelled the Jesuits from Mexico and extended the Alameda to its present dimensions.

The forty-sixth Viceroy was Don Antonio Maria de Bucareli y Ursúa, from 1771 to 1779. Mining and minting was greatly increased during his reign, and nearly

$130,000,000 was sent to Spain. He died in Mexico, and is buried in the little church on the hill of Guadalupe.

Don Juan Vicente de Güemes Pacheco de Padilla, Conde de Revillagigedo, was the fifty-second Viceroy, and the great reformer of the period 1789-94. He paved and sewered the city, executed bandits, and sent out exploring expeditions, one of which penetrated Alaska. He attended the erection of public works in person, and was on the alert day and night, so that nothing escaped him. It is said that one night he tripped on an uneven piece of pavement, and had the workmen called from their beds, and told them to have it fixed before morning. On another occasion he found a street that was barricaded by some native huts. He sent for an officer and ordered the street opened, so he could pass through on his way to mass next morning. To this day the street is called Calle Revillagigedo.

Don Miguel de la Grua Salamanca, Marques de Branciforte, was the fifty-third Viceroy. During his reign, 1794-98, Florida was ceded to France—that portion east of the Perdido River.

Don José de Iturrigaray, the fifty-sixth Viceroy, 1803-8, for his favors to the native element during the interregnum between Ferdinand VII. and Joseph Bonaparte, was arrested, imprisoned on the island of San Juan de Ulúa, and sent back to Spain. The fifty-seventh Viceroy was Don Pedro de Garibay. He executed the Licenciado Verdad, the first martyr of Mexican Independence.

Garibay was succeeded by the then Archbishop of Mexico, Francisco Javier de Lizana, as fifty-eighth Viceroy.

The Revolution—The Viceroys from 1809 were beset in all directions by the revolutionary spirit that was afire throughout the country. The first conspiracy was discovered in Michoacan and promptly stamped out. In 1810 the first decisive steps of the Revolution were taken by the joint action of the patriot priest, Hidalgo, in the town of Dolores, in the State of Guanajuato, and Allende, Aldama, together with the officers of the Queen's regiment (then garrisoned at San Miguel), and greatly assisted by Doña Josefa Ortiz of Querétaro, who, under pretense of a literary society, was holding patriotic meetings at her house. These plans were discovered and the patriots compelled to act before they were quite ready. On the morning of the 16th of September, Sunday, the comrades came to the house of Hidalgo, in Dolores, and told him of the discovery of the plot. The padre said they must act at once; at early mass he told the people that the yoke was no longer

IN THE PLAZA OF AGUAS CALIENTES.

Spanish but French, and the time for its throwing off had come. His people responded, the *grito de Dolores* cried for help, and he set out with Allende and his companions at the head of a band of 300 men armed only with clubs and knives. As they passed the Santuário de Atotonilco, Hidalgo took from the altar the banner of Guadalupe, and it became the standard of Independence. At San Miguel, the regiment of Allende joined the insurgents, and the march to Guanajuato was commenced. The people of the country flocked to his aid, and he came to the town with a heavy force; the Alhondiga de Granaditas was taken, and the city occupied by the patriots.

The march thence was toward Morelia, then called Valladolid, and thence towards the capital, his forces being constantly augmented, and at Las Cruces, almost within sight of the city, October 30, 1810, met the Royal forces and drove them back, but for some reason Hidalgo himself decided to retreat, and retired towards the interior, encountering the Royalists again November 7th, near Aculco, where he was defeated and driven back, but reached Guadalajara in safety, and organized a government there. Hidalgo met the Spaniards again January 16, 1811, on the bridge of Calderon and had his little army dispersed.

The defeated patriots made their way northward with the hope of reaching the United States in safety, but were betrayed into the hands of the Spaniards, and were captured in the little town of Acatita de Bajan, on the 21st of May, 1811, and conveyed to Chihuahua, where they were executed, Hidalgo on the 31st of July, Allende, Aldama and Jimenez on the 26th.

The death of these leaders had only a stimulating effect on the cause of Independence. The entire country was aroused and a desultory war carried on in every district for more than four years, until the execution of Morelos at the orders of the Inquisition, December 22, 1815, at Valladolid, now called Morelia, in honor of the patriot. As fast as they were captured the patriots were shot, but others came to take their places, and in some cases came over from the Royalist forces, as in the case of Yturbide, who captured and shot Matamoras at Valladolid, February 3, 1814, and seven years later himself promulgated the cause of Independence; the famous Plan of Iguala, which was the establishment of the Roman Catholic church to the exclusion of all others; the absolute Independence of Mexico as a moderate monarchy, with a Spanish prince on the throne; the union and equality of Mexicans and Spaniards. These three clauses were called "the three guarantees," represented in the national colors: green, union of the Mexicans and Spaniards; white, religious purity; red, independence.

Yturbide's army, known as the "Army of the Three Guarantees," finally accomplished the Independence of Mexico.

The cities of Valladolid, Querétaro and Puebla were captured, the latter on August 2, 1821, and at once commenced the siege of the capital. The last Viceroy, Juan O'Donoju, had just arrived at Vera Cruz. He found that he could not reach the City of Mexico and set about arranging a personal interview with Yturbide, which occurred at Córdoba, on August 23, 1821, and an agreement, known as the Treaty of Córdoba, was drawn on the lines of the Plan of Iguala, with amendment that O'Donoju should be one of the regents to govern Mexico until a king could be selected. This arrangement practically ended Spanish rule in Mexico. Yturbide returned to his army, and on September 21, 1821, entered the City of Mexico in triumph. The territory within the boundaries of Mexico at that time included Guatemala, all of the present Republic of Mexico, and that part of the United States from the Red and Arkansas Rivers to the Pacific Coast, extending north to the British possessions,—one of the greatest empires of the earth.

Agustin de Yturbide was born in Valladolid, now Morelia, September 27, 1783, joined the army at the early age of fifteen, and by his merit as a soldier was rapidly advanced. He was never in favor of the Republic, though he desired the

Independence of Mexico, and probably hoped for his own enthronement, which was accomplished for a brief season.

On the 24th of February, 1822, the first Congress of Mexico assembled in the capital. Their election had been provided for by a committee of regency based on the Plan of Iguala and the Treaty of Córdoba. Almost immediately there were two important factions among the people. They resolved themselves into two political parties, one composed of the army and the church, that had for its object the placing of Yturbide upon the throne. The other party, composed mostly of prominent people, had an idea of an Empire under a prince of Spain. The Spanish Cortéz had, in the meantime, February 13, 1822, annulled the Treaty of Córdoba. This gave encouragement to the army and clergy party, and Congress was forced to make selection of an Emperor. On May 19, 1822, Yturbide was elected by a vote of 67 to 15, and on the 21st of July of that year, Yturbide and his wife were crowned in the Cathedral, as Emperor and Empress of Mexico. The Emperor was titled Agustin I. The Empire was short lived. Congress, which had been friendly to Yturbide, was dissolved by him and a sort of parliament organized, called a "Junta."

Before the end of the year the Empire came to an end by the proclamation of a Republic on December 6, 1822, at Vera Cruz, by General Antonio Lopez de Santa Ana, and early in January the entire country had gathered under the banner of the Republic, leaving only the City of Mexico as the Empire. Yturbide called Congress together, tendered his resignation, which was not accepted, as the election had not been regarded as legal, and his actions as Emperor were also illegal. He was banished from the country, but granted a pension of $25,000 for his previous services to the country.

He went to England, and from London he wrote to the Government warning them of the machinations of the clergy for the restoration of the Spanish rule in Mexico, and offering his services in defense against them. Congress did not accept the information or his services, and at once a decree was issued, pronouncing Yturbide a traitor, and placing the penalty of death, should he return to Mexico. Yturbide was ignorant of the issuance of this decree and returned to Mexico, landing at Soto la Marina, a little town on the Gulf coast, in the State of Tamaulipas. He was arrested at once and taken before the legislature of Tamaulipas, then in session, condemned to death, and shot July 19, 1824.

The second Congress, really the first of the Republic, assembled in the capital on the 7th of November, 1823, adopting a Constitution very similar to that of the United States, giving to the several states of Mexico similar rights to those of the United States. It created a National Congress, to be composed of a Senate and Chamber of Deputies, placing the executive power in the hands of a President, and the judicial in the Supreme and Circuit Courts. This Constitution was proclaimed on the 4th of October, 1824, and on the 10th of that month the first President of Mexico, General Guadalupe Victoria, took the oath of office. Congress was dissolved on the 24th of December, 1824, and the first Constitutional Congress convened January 1, 1825. In that year Fort Juan de Ulúa, the only place held by the Spanish, was evacuated and the Republic of Mexico was recognized by the United States and England.

From 1828 to 1846 there was a constant series of revolutions, growing out of the disregard of the election between the Centralists and the Federalists. The second election for President occurred in 1828, when General Gomez Pedraza was elected, General Santa Ana dissenting and starting a revolution, which placed General Vicente Guerrero in office.

Congress passed an act on the 20th of March, 1829, banishing all Spaniards from Mexico, which, of course, brought retaliation from Spain. A force was organized in Cuba, which landed at Tampico in July, 1829. This invasion was met by the opposition of all the people in Mexico. Santa Ana organized a force at Vera Cruz and proceeded to Tampico, which was reënforced by General Mier y Teran. A battle occurred on the 9th of September, which, on the 11th, was followed by the surrender of the Spanish invaders. This was the last act of the Spaniards to regain possession of Mexico, and was followed by the recognition of the Republic by Spain, December 28, 1836.

The Liberal Congress, in March, 1833, commenced the enaction of laws against the clergy, tending to the abolishment of monasteries and convents, and to forbid the priests teaching in State or National schools. This law was, however, withdrawn by Santa Ana in 1834.

While these stormy scenes were being enacted in Mexico, that part of the great Empire known as Texas had been settled, to some degree, by Americans, who, in 1835, under the leadership of Sam Houston, declared their Independence.

General Santa Ana was in command of the army sent to quell the revolution, and was met by the Texans in several bloody battles, among which was the massacre of the Alamo. Texas existed as a separate Republic until 1844, being recognized by the United States and the European powers. On the 12th of April, 1844, a treaty was concluded between President Tyler and the Texans, by which Texas was admitted as one of the United States. This treaty was ratified by Congress in March, 1845, which action, of course, did not meet with the approval of the Mexicans. As Texas was an independent power, and had been recognized as such by the Mexican Government, their right to be annexed by the United States was not questioned by any other power.

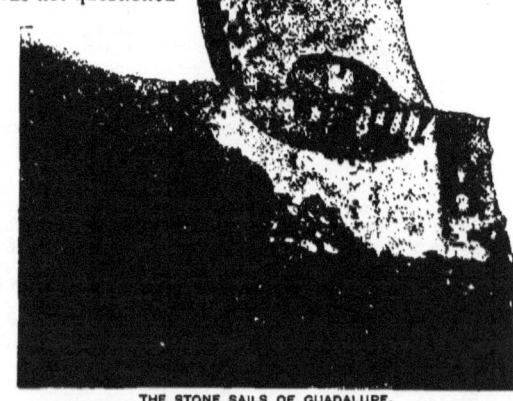

This was the beginning of the Mexican War, and the first battle was fought April 24, 1846, in which sixteen Americans were killed and wounded, and the remaining force captured. In the next battles, which were Palo Alto, on May 8th, and Resaca de la Palma on the next day (both of these places in Texas), the Mexicans were defeated.

General Taylor crossed the Rio Grande at its mouth, on May the 18th, and occupied the Mexican town of Matamoros. The Americans had provided for the prosecution of the war by an appropriation of $10,000,000, and 50,000 volunteers were called for. Before the war commenced an envoy of the United States, Mr. Slidell, had

THE STONE SAILS OF GUADALUPE.

been refused an audience by General Paredes, who had obtained the place of the Presidential office of Mexico, so that all efforts looking to a peaceful settlement were abandoned. General Taylor advanced from the Rio Grande, captured

Monterey September 20, 1846, and on the 23d of February, 1847, fought another battle at Buena Vista, about five miles south of Saltillo.

Generals Doniphan and Price marched through New Mexico, where they had engagements with the Indians, then proceeded in the direction of Chihuahua, which they occupied on the 28th of February, 1847, after the battle of Sacramento. General, then Captain, Fremont, acting under orders from the Government at Washington, started a revolution against Mexico in California, and on the 7th of July, 1846, Commodore Sloat occupied the town of Monterey, California, and the next day Commander Montgomery occupied San Francisco. On the 17th of August, Commodore Stockton issued a proclamation taking possession of California, complete occupation of the State being made by Stockton and Kearney.

The expedition against the Mexican capital was under General Winfield Scott, who landed at Vera Cruz March 9, 1847, and captured the city after five days bombardment, on the 27th of March. On his march toward the capital he met General Santa Ana at Cerro Gordo, and defeated him on the 18th of April. Without further opposition General Scott reached Puebla, and entered the Valley of Mexico on the 9th of August, defeated the Mexicans at Padierna, August 20th, and marched to the field of Churuhusco on the same day.

On the 8th of September occurred the battles, Molino del Rey and Casa Mata, and, on the 12th and 13th, the Americans took possession of Belem and San Cosme, entering the City of Mexico on the 15th of September, 1847. A treaty of peace called the "Treaty of Guadalupe-Hidalgo," was concluded on the 2d of February, 1848, by which Mexico ceded to the United States all the territory north and east of the Rio Grande, for which the United States Government agreed to pay to Mexico the sum of $15,000,000, thus concluding a war, whose settlement, on its face, would seem to be the most liberal in the history of wars, but concluding a war that General Grant pronounced the most unholy and unjust ever waged by a stronger nation against a weaker one.

In 1851, Mariano Arista was elected President. In less than two years, in the midst of a revolution, he resigned the place. The following two years, from 1853 to 1855, General Santa Ana was Dictator. On December the 12th, 1855, Comonfort was elected President, commencing his administration with the enforcement of the laws against the Church.

In 1856 he ordered the sale of all landed estates owned by the Church, the Church received the money, and the ownership of the lands passing to private individuals. In the same year, September 16th, he announced the suppression of the Monks, which was instigated by a conspiracy of the San Franciscans. During his administration a new Constitution was framed and adopted, February 5, 1857, Comonfort remaining as President until the election under the new Constitution, when he was elected to succeed himself. He entered upon his second term, December 1, 1857, and one of his first acts was to overthrow the Constitution that he had sworn to support. He dissolved Congress in December and imprisoned Benito Juarez, who had been elected his successor. All of his plans failed, he left the country in 1858, and did not return until the French Intervention, when he joined the Mexicans against Maximilian. After the departure of Comonfort, Juarez became the Constitutional President, but was compelled to abandon the capital, and at once set out for Guadalajara, where his Government was organized. He proceeded to the Pacific Coast, thence to the United States, returning to Vera Cruz, from which point he administered the Government. During this time another Government was in existence in the City of Mexico, under Felix Zuloaga, whose administration commenced a vigorous prosecution of the War of the Reform, which extended over the entire country. In this Juarez took prominent part by his proclamation of the Laws of the Reform at a time when there seemed the least possible chance of success. This was the bitterest war in the history of Mexico. Juarez proclamation was dated July 12, 1859, and had the effect of a settlement of the causes of the dissentions of fifty years. Juarez entered the City of Mexico, January 11, 1861, and commenced operation of the Laws of the Reform from the capital.

In 1861, July the 17th, the Mexican Congress passed a law suspending payment on the bonds and interest of the Republic held by foreigners. This law gave the European powers an excuse for the intervention. The first intervention in Mexican affairs, however, was during the administration of General Busta-mente, when a claim of $600,000 was made by France for damages suffered by French subjects during the various wars.

One of the items of this claim was made by a French cook for $60,000 worth of pies, alleged to have been stolen from him by the soldiers. This claim of the French was derisively called "La Reclamacion de los Pasteles," the claim of the pies. A French fleet arrived October 27, 1839, and captured the City on the 5th of December, on which day the French were attacked and driven back to their ships by General Santa Ana, who in this battle lost his leg. A treaty was concluded in March, 1839, when the full claim of $600,000 was paid.

The intervention of 1861 was then the second, and the outcome of an agreement called the Treaty of London, entered into October 31, 1861, between France, England and Spain, binding these nations to occupy the coast of Mexico, with the idea to put the Mexicans in a position to establish a government of their own.

The fleet of the allies arrived at Vera Cruz in December, 1861, and January, 1862, bringing commissioners—General Prim, of Spain, M. de Saligny, of France, and Admiral Wyke, of England—who were authorized to treat with the representatives of the Mexican Government. These commissioners issued a proclamation declaring that their presence in Mexico was for the purpose and question of finance only. A conference between the Government and the commissioners, called the Treaty of La Soledad, signed February 19, 1862, allowed the Spanish troops to advance as far as Orizaba, and the French troops to Tehuacan. The English made no advance of troops into the interior; in fact, only 1,000 marines had accompanied the English fleet as a guard of honor. It was stipulated that the troops should be withdrawn as soon as the treaty should be confirmed by the English and French commissioners. The Spanish forces were withdrawn, and the English and Spanish ships left Vera Cruz. The French troops remained, and were reënforced in March to the number of 40,000 men under Marshal Forey, who arrived in Mexico in January, 1863. Their advance towards the capital was repulsed at Puebla on the 5th of May, 1862, by General Zarazoga's troops. Puebla was captured on the 17th of May of that year.

Juarez abandoned the capital and the French soldiers entered the City of Mexico June 9, 1863. On the 10th of July, 1863, an "Assembly of Notables" was called together in the City of Mexico, and a declaration made by that body to the effect that Mexico should be governed by a hereditary Monarchy, under a Catholic prince, and that the throne should be offered to Maximilian, Archduke of Austria, also a representative of the ruling house of Spain, and brought Mexico, in 1863, practically to the position she occupied in 1821. Maximilian accepted the throne on two conditions; first, that he should be elected by a popular vote in Mexico, second, that the Emperor Napoleon should give him military aid as long as it should be necessary.

Maximilian arrived in the City of Mexico, June 12, 1864, with his wife, Carlotta, daughter of Leopold I., King of the Belgians. They were crowned Emperor and Empress in the Cathedral in the City of Mexico.

Maximilian continued to enforce the Laws of the Reform, and thus increased the opposition of the Clerical party. As President Juarez had, or was believed to have abandoned the country, Maximilian issued a decree declaring all persons in arms against the Government to be bandits, and when captured should be shot. The decree aroused bitterness of opposition throughout the country, following the execution of Generals Arteaga, Salazar, Villagomez and Felix Diaz. The opposition to Maximilian was not confined to Mexico. The United States Government was opposed to the re-establishment of a monarchy on the western continent. Secretary Seward informed the French in a diplomatic way, that as soon as he could be relieved of some little difficulties that he had on his own hands, in his own country, at that time, he would look at the occupation of Mexico by the French army, as a grave reflection on the United States, and that the United States could not tolerate the establishment of an Empire in Mexico based on military support of a foreign country.

Napoleon, on reception of this note, abandoned Maximilian, and ordered the evacuation by the French in November, 1866. Maximilian had not secured the support of either of the parties of Mexico. He had burdened the country with an excessive debt, due possibly to evil councilors, one of which was Marshal Bazaine. The collapse of the Empire was immediate. The appeal of Carlotta to the French Emperor and to the Pope was unavailing. The last of the troops left Mexico in February, 1867. Maximilian decided first to leave the country, but reconsidered his decision and concluded to remain.

President Juarez had left Paso del Norte and was advancing southward; during all this time he had maintained his authority as President of the Republic.

General Miramon was sent out to capture Juarez and was defeated at San Jacinto on the first of February, 1867, and fell back to Querétaro, where he was joined by Maximilian. While these movements were being prosecuted in the North, General Porfirio Diaz captured Puebla on April 2, after a siege of twenty-five days, and defeated Marquez at San Lorenzo on April 11, and at once commenced siege of the City of Mexico. General Escobedo commenced a siege of Querétaro in March and continued it until its capture on the 15th of May. Maximilian was captured on the stony hill called Cerro de Las Campanas, and on the spot where he was captured he was executed, together with his Generals Miramon and Mexia, at seven o'clock on the morning of June 19, 1867. A request from the United States Government that the life of Maximilian be spared was not heeded. Nineteen Generals of Maximilian's army were also condemned to be shot, but were pardoned by President Juarez.

STATUE OF CHARLES IV. CITY OF MEXICO.

The City of Mexico surrendered to General Diaz June 21, and President Juarez entered the capital on July 25, 1867. The Constitution of 1857 was placed in effect throughout Mexico, a new Congress was convened, and Juarez re-elected President October 12, 1871. During this administration the various railway and telegraph lines were projected. They were only slight disturbances that occurred in Mexico after the fall of the Empire. In a subsequent election the opposing candidates were Juarez, Lerdo de Tejada and Porfirio Diaz. Juarez was elected December 1, 1871, and took his seat for the third time, the result of which was a slight revolution, occurring in various parts of the country. These were headed by Porfirio Diaz on his Hacienda of La Noria in Oaxaca. A manifesto was issued proposing a convention and assembly of Notables, to reorganize a government with Diaz as commander-in-chief of the army, until the establishment of such government. The movement was interrupted by the death of Juarez and the succession of the President of the Supreme Court, Lerdo de Tejada. The administration of Lerdo was peaceful, and he was elected President, December 1, 1872, continuing in office for three years, during which time the railroad between Vera Cruz and the City of Mexico, called the Mexican Railway, was opened on January 1, 1873.

Another Revolution occurred in Oaxaca, January 15, 1876, and once more the country was in the midst of a strife. Lerdo was forced to leave the country, and General Diaz entered the City of Mexico November 24, 1876, and was proclaimed President; on the 6th of May, 1877, he was declared Constitutional President, in which office he remained until November 30, 1880, during which time he put down small revolutions, and executed nine Revolutionists on June 24, 1879.

On the 25th of September, 1880, Congress elected General Manuel Gonzales President. During the administration of General Gonzales the celebrated Nickel riots of 1883 occurred, the common people refusing to accept nickel coin in the place of silver, entailing on them considerable loss. The national debt of Mexico was also greatly increased, and his administration was practically a financial failure.

General Diaz was again elected President and took the oath of office December 1, 1884. He found an absolutely empty treasury and a country without credit. It was a condition and not a theory that confronted Diaz—a condition that theories alone could not ameliorate. Urgent and immediate action was the only remedy for the deplorable state of the country. General Diaz was the man of action of the day, who delayed not for the state of urgency in anything. To perceive a need, with him, was to act at once, and promote the prosperity and peace of his country. The railroads and the telegraphs had only been proposed; the commerce of the country was in a state of lethargy. Diaz' quick, restless, active disposition called it to life, and his liberal, wise and efficient administration of the Government made it possible to complete the railroads and telegraphs, and it promoted the internal improvements in every direction, so that his own acts have placed President Diaz among the foremost statesmen of Mexico and of the world.

A patriotic Mexican writer says: "With the restless, inconstant character of our race, the long tenure of office by one man is one of the greatest dangers for the peace of the nation. Yet, notwithstanding, General Diaz has succeeded in avoiding shipwreck on this shoal, making himself all but indispensable to the completion of the reconstructive and conciliatory work of which he is the true and only author. The work of pacification accomplished by General Diaz has consisted in the strengthening of the central power, and the discreet use of his personal prestige and influence for the purpose of securing in all the states of the Union the adhesion of governors attached to him personally, and resolved to second him at any cost in the task of assuring to the country the supreme benefit of peace, as the most imperious necessity of the Mexican people. The patriotic conviction of the urgency, for a nation bleeding and weakened as ours has been, of a convalescent political regime to enable us to recuperate our shattered strength, has facilitated the insensible and voluntary creation of a system of governmental discipline wherein the federated units, like the wheels of an immense machine, receive without shock the impulse of force, action and movement which is conveyed to them from the great central motor."

Practical Matters.

Railway Tickets are regulated by a code of rules similar to those in effect in the United States. They are first, second and third class, at prices in accordance with accommodations furnished. Through unlimited tickets or limited and excursion tickets are good to stop-over within their limit; all others must be used through to destination.

Baggage and Customs Regulations—On arrival at the border cities, travelers should have their baggage ready for examination by the Mexican officials, and on the return by the Americans. The duty is quickly and courteously performed, without trouble or annoyance to the well-intending traveler. Hand baggage should be taken to the baggage room of the station, where the trunks are also taken to be opened by the owners. No fees are required or expected, and it is bad taste to offer them. Nothing except wearing apparel, watches and jewels worn on the person, fire-arms, tools of trade, a broken package of cigars or cigarettes, and such other articles, are on the free list. *When the examination has been completed let the passenger request that his trunk be wired and sealed, and it will go through to destination without further*

A TRAINED NURSE. *examination.* This is important, as baggage is subject to customs examination at any State line, or for municipal duties anywhere in Mexico. On the return the American officers are equally polite and courteous, and their examination a mere form, but under the law nothing is free except wearing apparel, hoop-poles, skeletons, sauer kraut, bologna and joss sticks. The ninety-nine cigar fallacy is long ago exploded, and idols, antiquities, rag figures and presents for friends at home, are all dutiable, though they are often passed free in small quantities.

The baggage regulations on the railways are the same as in the United States to holders of tickets purchased in this country, 150 pounds free on each full ticket, and 75 pounds on half tickets. On local or through tickets within the Republic thirty-three pounds is the limit of baggage carried free. On those leading to the

United States or other foreign countries the full 150 pounds is allowed. Agents of transfer companies board incoming trains as they approach the larger cities and check baggage to hotels or residences, call for baggage to be checked to all points in the Republic and the border cities. *Cargadores,* public porters with numbered badges indicating a license, may be trusted with baggage to and from trains.

Money—The money of Mexico is the same as that of the United States, *i. e.,* dollars and cents, called in Spanish *pesos y centavos;* that is the legal way of counting it, as enacted by a law taking effect in 1890, but the people still use the old system to some extent, though they understand both. A *tlaco* is a cent and a half, a *cuartillo* is three cents; these are of copper. The silver coins are *medio,* 6¼ cents, *real,* 12½ cents, quarter and half dollars, and dollars, though these are never so called; they are *dos reales* (pronounced *do reales*), and *cuatro reales,* and seventy-five cents is *seis reales.* Regardless of the law to the contrary, prices are quoted in *reales,* up to one dollar, then in most cases it is *pesos y reales,* thus: a dollar and a half is *un peso y cuatro reales,* one dollar and four *reales.*

The fifty-cent piece is sometimes called a *toston,* and 25 cents a *peseta,* though rarely. The Mexicans make change to a nicety and are credited with splitting *tlacos,* literally, and with a hatchet.

Gold is little used—an *onza de oro* is worth \$16; a *media onza de oro.* \$8; *pistola,* \$4; *escudo de oro,* \$2; *escudito de oro,* \$1.

The paper money in circulation is in notes of the National Bank of Mexico, the State banks and the Bank of London, Mexico and South America all passing at par, except some of the State banks beyond the limits of the State where issued, then only at a slight discount.

Silver is to be depended on at all times, and, although bulky and heavy, it is the best. The native possessed of a sufficiency carries it in a hand bag with a shoulder strap.

It is not necessary to buy Mexican money before reaching the border; in fact it is better not to do so, as better rates of exchange can be obtained there and in Mexico. The ticket agents at Juarez City, opposite El Paso; City of Porfirio Diaz, opposite Eagle Pass, and New Laredo, opposite Laredo, can always furnish sufficient funds to reach the interior where American paper is always worth a premium.

The gold and silver is not so acceptable; New York exchange also commands par or premium.

ON GUARD.

Measures and Distances—A *vara* is 33½ inches and corresponds to the yard in the dry goods stores. A *metre* is a yard and a tenth, and a *pié* is about 11 inches, corresponding to the foot, and is so translated into English; a *pulgada* is about an inch. A kilometre is about five-eighths of a mile, and a *legua*, in English a league, is about 2.6 miles, the mile (*milla*) not being used except on rare occasions.

Climate—Because it is in the far south; because it lies almost wholly within the tropics and near the equator, Mexico is supposed to be a warm country; the contrary is the case. The climate is the most equable in the world; the only difference between summer and winter is, that in the summer it rains almost every day, while in winter there is scarcely a shower during the whole season.

It is the extremely high altitudes of nearly all the cities and towns of Mexico, except those near the coast, that give them the delightful and healthful climate they possess. The rays of a tropic sun are tempered by cooling breezes blowing over snow-clad mountains. The time for a tour of Mexico may be at the tourist's convenience. Traveling is pleasant at all seasons. The only places to be avoided in summer are those in the *tierra caliente*, Vera Cruz, Tampico and other cities near the sea coast, and except at these places it is healthful at all times.

Clothing—The proper clothing is that used in this country for spring and autumn wear; light overcoats and wraps are needed only after nightfall or at points of extremely high altitudes.

Cabs and Carriages—If we could strike an average between the coach of state of the Emperor Maximilian, as shown in the National Museum, and the "yellow-flag" cab of the streets, the City of Mexico would have the finest cabs in the world; as it is, she has more different kinds than any other city. They are good, bad and indifferent, carrying little tin flags, about two by four inches, when not engaged. These flags indicate the class and rates of fare. The blue-flag rates are one dollar fifty per hour for one or more passengers, or seventy-five cents per passenger from hotel to station or short ride of few squares. The red flag indicates one dollar per hour and fifty cents per passenger. The yellow flag's tariff is fifty cents per hour and the horses usually earn it, the time of transit being usually so long that it would be cheaper to get a blue-flag hack at once. A medio or a real may be added to these rates as a fee to the driver, and another to the small boy who may have been on the box with the driver and who may have opened the door for you. But this is as you please. If an attempt to overcharge is made, a request for the "*numero*" usually effects his departure in short order. After dark, and on Sundays and Feast days, these rates are increased about fifty per cent.

If the cab is needed for less than an hour it is best to ask how much for the ride; if for longer than an hour, say *por hora* and get in. Compare your time with the driver and dismiss him promptly at the end of the ride. The hackman of Mexico differs not from his brethren in all the other parts of the world, and further advice to the traveler would be a waste of words.

Horse Cars—The horse car of Mexico, nine times out of ten, is a mule car, the mule figuring as the almost universal motive power, standing still at times, looking without life, but when the word is given he goes with a rush, galloping to the other end of the line with all his might, as if in a hurry to get to stand still again. The driver simply holds the reins and lets the mule go, his, the man's, duty being principally to wind the brake, blow a tin horn at street intersections, and to frighten, though he always fails, the droves of donkeys—though this is not the fault of the horn, which is not unlike the campaign horn, or the Christmas horn of the American small boy, as highly hideous in its hootings—but without effect on the burros, which regard them not, and listen even lightly to the hissing whistles and the *andele! andele!!* of their own drivers. But the horse cars have the right of way, and hurry on through the droves, often jostling their heavy loads. There are first and second-class cars going in pairs within a block of each other, the best car first. The first-class cars are painted buff, and the others green. The fares are from five to twenty-five cents, according to the distance traveled. The second-class fares are cheaper. The conductor sells tickets and a collector boards the car at certain points and takes them up, thus doing away with the bell punch. Special cars may be hired for parties; these bear the legend "Especial" over the lamp, and the public do not attempt to use them. There are also freight cars, box cars and flat cars, and cars for sheep and goats. And there is in Mexico, as nowhere else, a funeral car, with a raised dais and catafalque beneath a four-post canopy capped with a cross. The funeral car is painted black or white. These cars, with a number of "Especiales," with closely drawn curtains, make up a funeral train for those not able to hire a hearse and carriages. The name tramway is in use, and is translated to Spanish as *tran-via.* The system in the City of Mexico is a fine one, nearly all the lines starting from the main plaza and returning there.

Hotels and Restaurants—More has been said against the hotels and restaurants of Mexico than they ever deserved. The only trouble the American has in the Mexican hotel results from his own misfortune, not to say his fault, in not being able to speak the language to make his wants known, but no man who can say *hamone e waivos* or *bif tek e café* need go hungry in Mexico. All comers will find clean beds; they may be somewhat hard sometimes, and not as wide as the home bed, but scrupulously clean, as the rooms are also.

On arrival the guest is shown to a room; if accepted then, he may register, and his name is written on a blackboard with his room number. It is needless to use up a hotel register if the room don't suit, and what is the use of having a clerk to tell where the guests' rooms are, when the caller may look on the black-board and see for himself. Once assigned to a room, the guest is left severely alone, the manager's sole duty, after the assignment, being to keep books and collect the bills; and yet everything moves smoothly, and all wants are supplied when made known. A Mexican of mature age presides over the key-rack, and when you have called for the key once, you won't have to again; the master of the keys recognizes you as you approach, has your key ready, with any cards or letters left for you, and with a cheery *buenas noches, Señor,* bids you good-night. The hall boy—and there is one on every floor—is a sort of Pooh-bah in his way. He is bootblack and porter, messenger and chambermaid, and agent for remote and unknown laundries; he removes soiled linen, and *en mañana* has them back again, clean and snowy white, with no one on earth except himself knowing where in Mexico he takes them or whence he brings them. More than this, the hall boy runs a sort of free school for the dissemination of the Spanish language to the ignorant guests; this he does *con mucho gusto*, and is pleased to tell you the name of anything, if he can catch on to your pronunciation of the question, *como se llama eso?* Almost all hotels are on the European plan. Rooms may be obtained at from one to five dollars per day, according to size and location; if two or more persons occupy the same room, a reduction is made. It is well to know the price of the room before engaging it, then there can be no discussion at departure. Rooms may be engaged by mail or wire (the message may be sent in English), and they will be kept and charged for from the time indicated in the letter or telegram. Lights, candles and lamps are provided for rooms, but guests are expected to furnish their own matches and soap. In nearly all the best hotels there are good baths. The baths of Mexico are to be commended, and are appreciated as a comfort and a luxury not expected.

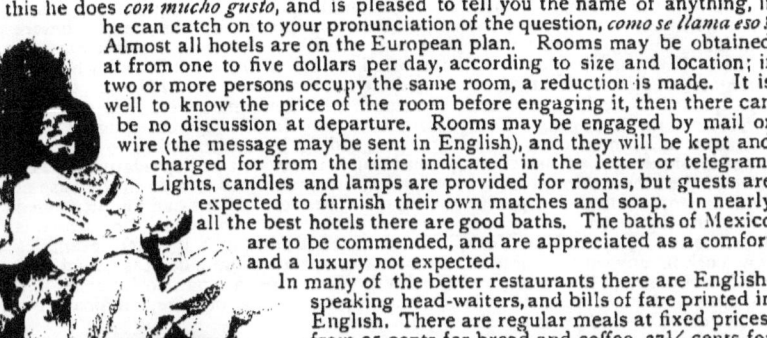

In many of the better restaurants there are English-speaking head-waiters, and bills of fare printed in English. There are regular meals at fixed prices, from 25 cents for bread and coffee, 37½ cents for eggs and coffee, to 50, 62½, 75 and $1.00 for dinner or supper. Where meals are served *a la carte* the prices are affixed to each article. Arrangements may be made for board by the day or week, at rates for two or three meals per day, as desired. It is best for persons not speaking the language to take regular meals, *table d'hôte*, and the meal can be served without trouble and served well. Whatever may be said of the restaurants in Mexico, it should be added that the good ones are managed by natives, and the bad ones by foreigners, as a general thing, and, with few exceptions, the restaurant advertised as English or American is to be avoided.

BEGGAR ON THE STAIRS OF GUADALUPE.

The hours for meals are somewhat different in Mexico from what they are in other countries, but the "meals-at-all-hours" rule applies to all the first-class places. In the early morning the custom of Mexico—and it is a good one—is to take coffee and bread, and, if you please, fruits; the best kind of fruits are to be had everywhere. About noon is the breakfast hour; the meal commences with soup and follows a menu very much like an American noon-day dinner, ending with dessert, and coffee, of course. The other full meal of the day takes place at from five to eight o'clock in the evening, and is called dinner or supper, as the fancy dictates, and resembles the earlier bill of fare of the noon-day in every particular, commencing with soup and ending with coffee.

The *chili con carne*, chile with meat, of Mexico, when nicely prepared, is as palatable as it is hot. The meats are fresh, with only the fault of being generally overdone; the poultry is fine; fresh vegetables are to be had every day in the year, as well as the fruits of every clime—apples and peaches from the temperate zone, and pineapples and oranges from the hot country. The bread is always good, the coffee stronger than in other countries; little butter is used, and is made and served fresh without salt.

The drinks peculiar to Mexico are many and varied. Pulque is the national beverage, drank in public places by the poorer people, but in almost every family of all the classes. Pulque is the juice of the maguey, taken from the heart of the plant, and after the fermentation of twenty-four hours is ready for use; pulque more than a day old is useless. Tequila and mescal are a distillation from the different varieties of the maguey, the heart of the plant being roasted and then put through the process of distillation. A small quantity of tequila is a drink, taken with a grain of salt; literally the salt is placed on the tongue before drinking. The wines are for the most part good, the sherry and claret particularly so. The champagnes are all imported, as are also brandies and whiskies, which are used in moderation. Beer and ale are manufactured in Mexico, though large quantities are imported and the taste for the Teutonic beverage is growing.

Stores and Shopping—Every store and shop in Mexico has a name, and that name is painted over the door; sign reading is as interesting to the newcomer in Mexico as to the country cousin on his first visit to city relatives. The name of the store is not always appropriate, but sometimes it is, as in the case of the drug store called in Spanish the "gate of heaven." This can be questioned only in the last word; a drug store may not be the gate to heaven. One saloon is known as the "Port of New York," though there is nothing in it which resembles New York in any way. Another is more appropriately named; it is called "El triunfo del diablo," the triumph of the devil. The stores are named for cities and countries and have fanciful titles. Other signs, ending in "*ria*," indicate the wares for sale: *Zapateria*, shoes; *relojeria*, watches; *joyeria*, jewelry; *sastreria*, tailor; *bonneteria*, millinery; and *plataria*, silverware. The goods are usually in a line of shelves running parallel with the street and very near the doors, so they can be seen by the passers-by. The clerks stand in a line behind the counter like a file of soldiers. Smoking is permitted everywhere, and the clerk on duty enjoys his cigarette at pleasure.

The prices quoted are nearly always higher than it is expected to obtain, as it is presumed that all customers will want to "jew" the figure down, and the sharp driver at a bargain usually succeeds. The moral of which is, never give the first price quoted. This rule applies to the street vender, in the flower market, the markets, and the shops as well, but the larger and finer stores do not practice this generally.

There are many very fine stores in the City of Mexico and the larger cities that will compare favorably with those of the cities in other countries, and there are many novel features to make a visit interesting, whether you buy or not. The shopper will find the round of the shops even more fascinating than among the bargain counters of New York or Chicago. There are novelties to look over that are not anywhere else. Of course there are silks and satins and all that, and there are *rebosos* of cotton, linen and silk, and *tapalos* and mantillas and *zerapes* that are not to be found in New York or Chicago, and opals and bargains in antiquities not found anywhere in the world, to make shopping in Mexico interesting.

Cigars and Tobacco—He never chews, but the Mexican smokes at all times and under all circumstances. Before breakfast and after breakfast, before and after, and during his dinner, and between the courses he rolls and smokes his cigarette, as he

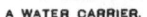

A WATER CARRIER.

does when he goes to bed and when he gets up. Only when he sleeps he does not smoke. The men do this, but the ladies do not smoke as they have the credit of doing, though a gentleman always offers his cigarettes when he takes one himself. Elderly ladies enjoy a cigarette, and occasionally a *ranchero* (a farmer) and his wife may be seen to smoke an the cars, and many women of the middle or lower classes smoke incessantly, but in polite society it is not the custom among the women to smoke.

In the restaurants and hotels smoking is permitted in the dining room, and is indulged in. On the cars the Pullman is the only place where smoking is prohibited. At all other places it is permitted; at the theatre, but not during the performance, at the circus and bull fight it is the thing to do. At the bull fight cigars, instead of bouquets, are thrown to the *toreadores*.

The cheap and middle grades of Mexican cigars are better than the domestic

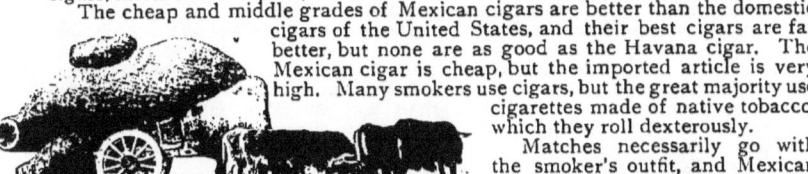

A FULL CARGO.

cigars of the United States, and their best cigars are far better, but none are as good as the Havana cigar. The Mexican cigar is cheap, but the imported article is very high. Many smokers use cigars, but the great majority use cigarettes made of native tobacco, which they roll dexterously.

Matches necessarily go with the smoker's outfit, and Mexican matches are the best in the world; they are double-enders, light at both ends. A stroke of economy goes with every match—the striking of the other end. If you are asked for a light the unused end is always returned. It is good as a picture to see the courtesy and politeness exhibited in giving and taking a light--the wave of the hand in thanks and the return of the match—and another one to see three or four cigarettes held over the blaze of a single match. The community of interest in that little fire, protected from the blowing out by one man's hand, is wonderful, and the sociability of the scene pleasing to a degree. Some other man of some other race might have blessed the man who invented sleep, but I think every Mexican blesses the man who invented smoke.

Police and Military—The police are not as hard to find in Mexico as in some other countries, and there are soldiers everywhere, not as a menace, but as a protection. Time was when bandit tales had their scenes laid in Mexico and footpad stories told of her cities, but that is ancient history; the *rurales* of the country districts, the police and military in the towns and cities, have been regulators that regulated, till now all is peace and protection.

The police of the cities are a well-trained, disciplined body of men, and always within call. In the City of Mexico, and in the larger cities, a policeman stands at street intersections; his lantern is placed in the middle of the street, and the long row of flickering lights up and down, in either direction, tells of the watchmen of the night, who watch while we sleep.

A national feast day will show what Mexican soldiery is; a fine, well-trained body of men, whose pride and patriotism is to be applauded. Of the infantry, artillery, or cavalry, the rurales are the pride and the pink of the army.

The rurales are the country police, mounted on the finest horses, and uniformed in the most picturesque manner, with saddles and trappings richly decorated, The men are fine specimens of humanity, stout and well built, wearing the broad *sombrero* of the country, a short leathern jacket and trousers braided and bedecked, all with silver braid and gold. They are armed to the teeth with latest improved arms, and well they know how to use them, for they were born to their use as their fathers before them.

Doctors and Medicines—The physicians of Mexico rank high among the doctors of the world. A great many of them speak English, French and Spanish.

There are physicians from Germany, France and England and the United States, and very many of them prominent in their profession. The country is healthy, but at the same time the infomation as to physicians and medicines is essential, and one need not be in Mexico without the best medical attendance.

Cargadores—This gentry combines the usefulness of the district telegraph boy and street porter. They are strong, heavy built men that carry the greatest weights, from a trunk to a piano; they meet all trains and are in and about the hotels ready to take the place of an expressman, and will convey baggage or do errands of any kind. The men are trusty and reliable, are licensed by the City Council, and carry on their breasts a brass plate with the number of their license. The tariff varies according to the service to be performed.

Church Visiting—The Mexican venerates the very walls of his church; he does not pass in front of it without removing his hat, and it behooves the visitor to respect what the native venerates. It is not advisable, nor is it necessary to follow the native customs, but no man will forget himself and wear his hat in the church, or treat with levity what the others may do. The attendants in the churches are usually very courteous and willing to show whatever may be there of interest. There is not always a fee for this service, but an offering for the poor of the parish is always acceptable. It is a good custom that will commend you to these people to make a contribution, however small. In the towns and villages throughout this country the best information may be obtained from the priest, and you secure his good will by calling on him for it. The people seeing you on good terms with the padre regard you as a person of importance, and will join in their attentions. Without exception the priests are most courteous and obliging, and will often put themselves out for your convenience.

Post Office—The rate on the letters from Mexico to the United States and Canada is 5 cents for each half ounce or fraction thereof; to all points in Mexico the rate is 10 cents; to all other countries in the postal union 10 cents; the registry fee is 10 cents; newspapers, 1 cent for each two ounces or fraction thereof; other printed matter, 1 cent per ounce and three-fourths, or fraction thereof, to the United States and Canada, and 2 cents to European countries.

The limit of weight of printed matter is 4.4 lbs. In the larger cities there is a regular system of delivery by carriers, and a letter with its proper address will be delivered promptly.

There is a printed list in the Post Office, posted in the lobby, announcing letters on hand not delivered; these lists are posted daily. Letters from the United States to Mexico are 2 cents per ounce or fraction thereof; newspapers the same as to domestic points.

Express Service—The Wells Fargo Company operate over the Mexican Central and Sonora Railways; the Mexican National operates its own express line. All other railroads have an express department that connects with the other express companies.

Telegraph—The Mexican Government owns and controls a system of telegraph wires reaching to all parts of the country. The various railroad companies also operate commercial wires along their lines, having connection with the

Western Union and Postal Telegraph Companies at the border. The Cable Company has wires from Vera Cruz to the City of Mexico, and sends messages to the United States via Galveston.

Baths—In the smallest villages and towns, and in all of the larger cities are unusually good baths. They are not always to be found in the hotels, but in some central location, or convenient place near a street-car line. As a rule the baths are good and clean. The soap furnished is just the size necessary for a single bath. The attendant furnishes this, together with towels, comb, brush and a small bottle of oil, presumably for the hair, and a wisp of the fibre called ixtle, all of which is included in the price, which varies from 12½ to 25 cents.

Servants—The servants in the hotels and restaurants are polite and attentive, which politeness and attention is always greatly enhanced by a fee, and which is always expected. They are not accustomed to large fees, and a medio or real is about the average; this custom applies also to the hackmen, who always expect this in addition to their regular fare.

Dulces—The dulces of Mexico are very toothsome. These sweets come from Celaya, Querétaro and Morelía. These places are most famous for these delicacies.

Streets—Within the last few years the government of the City of Mexico passed an ordinance renaming the streets and avenues, and renumbering the houses, but the old names of the streets are still in use, and the old numbers designate the houses. The custom of naming each square is still observed, and where a name is extended to more than one square the name is prefixed by a number, as in the principal thoroughfare—San Francisco—there is a 1st and 2d San Francisco. The word *puente* as applied to a street, as Puente de Alvarado, means that there was once a bridge in the causeway of this street. The Spanish names are: *Calle*, (ki-ye) street; *avenida*, (av-e-nee-da) avenue; *paseo*, (pas-*say*-o) boulevard; *callejon*, (ki-ye-*hon*) alley or narrow street; *calzada*, (cal-*za*-da) cause -way; *rinconada*, (rin-con-*ah*-da) corner; *plaza*, square; *plazuela*, (plaz-u-*ai*-la) little plaza; *garita*, (gar-*e*-ta) gate; *numero*, (*noo*-mer-o) number, and *casa*, (kas-sa) house. The sacred names, as applied to streets, are derived from a church of the street, and partakes of no more sacrilege than in such cases in other countries, as for example, Trinity Place from Trinity Church, St. Paul, etc.

Customs and Costumes—I had heard of the courtesy and hospitality of the Spaniard, and remembered, when I entered a Spanish home, being welcomed and told "this house is yours," and when I had admired some object, I was informed that it was mine; when I came to Mexico I found the descendants of old Spain had lost no whit of cordiality, and the welcome at place of business, or the home, was warm and spontaneous to a degree. Every house was mine, all that was in it my own, and everybody at my orders.

The dress of the Mexican is a picturesque one, of which the wide *sombrero* is the feature, often richly trimmed in gold or silver lace, with a crest or monogram on the crown. This elaborate head-gear often costs fifty to sixty dollars. A short jacket coming to or a little below the waist is also trimmed in gold and silver; the tight-fitting trousers, wide at the sharp-pointed shoe, have two to three rows of gilt buttons. The complete costume always includes a *zerape* of many colors; a *zerape* is a blanket or shawl worn over the shoulders, thrown in knightly fashion, with the fringed and tasseled end over the left shoulder. Men of all classes wear the *zerape*. Overcoats are almost unknown, except among the better classes. The principal and favorite part of a costume is the sombrero. A Mexican may go barefooted, and wear cotton trousers, but he'll have a thirty-dollar hat if he can get it. The man on horseback in Mexico is a symphony in gold lace and buttons, and the trappings of his horse and saddle are most elaborate.

There are dudes in Mexico. They call a dude "*un lagartijo*." He wears the most gold lace and buttons, the tightest trousers and the widest hat. In other respects he differs not from the dude of other countries, and further space need not be wasted here.

For ladies of high degree, the Spanish *mantilla* of black or white lace still does a fascinating duty in place of the hat or bonnet, and the Spanish costume from shoulder to high-heeled pointed slipper. The middle classes wear a black *tápalo*, a shawl which is both wrap and head-gear. The lower classes and Indian maidens wear in the same way a scarf of cotton, usually blue or brown; this is the *reboso*. Mexican women are almost without exception of fine form, healthy and robust. There are thousands of pretty faces, of richest color, long lashes, soft and downy ear-locks, black as jet, and with long, inky black hair. Under the tapalo or reboso is many a Venus; the corset is unknown, and nature forms to perfection.

Ladies embrace each other at meeting, and kiss on the cheek. Men embrace their friends, and pat each other on the back. In passing on the street, instead of saying " How'dy," they say "*Adios*—Good-by." Other salutations are: Before noon it is *buenos dias;* after noon, *buenos tardes;* after dark, *buenas noches.*

Politeness and courtesy are characteristic of Mexico, and it is seen constantly everywhere; a Mexican will not enter a door

A COFFEE MILL.

or pass up a staircase ahead of his companion without an insisting "*Pasé señor,*" urgently put, till it is seen that one must go first, and then age or rank, or guest takes precedence.

Following the customs of their ancestors, the young people of Mexico have not that freedom of association as in America. A young lady may not indulge in the society of her young man except in the presence of others; in fact, he may not even call upon her, as in this free and enlightened country. He must win her by *haciendo del oso*—playing the bear. This does not mean that the young man indulges in any idiosyncrasies of the bear, when he (the bear) catches a victim. At a certain hour in the day the devoted lover comes under the lady's window, and when she comes to the casement he may stand and look at her, exchange glances, smiles and nods, go away and come back again to-morrow and do it all over again. If he is faithful and keeps this up for two or three years, he may finally be allowed to call and see her in the presence of another member of the family. If all goes smoothly they "marry and live happy to the end of their days," as in the fairy story.

They are a music-loving people, whose souls are moved by a concord of sweet sounds, and if the love of music is the test, few Mexicans are fit for treason, strata-

THE FIRE DEPARTMENT ON PARADE.

gems and spoils. No *jacal* is too humble but what its adobe walls listen to the tinkle of the guitar, and no village so small but its band of native musicians will play in the little alameda in the evenings. In the larger towns and great cities there is music in some plaza or park every day by the military bands—an example set by the Government in giving the people music, that might be emulated by the United States greatly to its credit.

There be fiddlers in Mexico and some violinists. The fiddlers sometimes come under the car window of a passing train, and in hopes of a *centavo* thrown, give samples of native music. There are some who carp at these crude musicians, but they are those who do not appreciate fiddling as an art, or the difficulties thereof. Themistocles said he "could not fiddle, but he could make a small town a great city," proving that the attainment of proficiency in fiddling is attended by hard work. When the weird sounds come into your window let the *centavitas* go, for whatever work the player may not have done, he has learned the fiddle.

There is music everywhere, there's music in the air, a music peculiar to the country and the people, a music of song, of stringed and wind instruments that plays at morning, noon and night. There are songs of praise and songs of mirth, and love songs.

There are songs of home. The people have their "Home, sweet home" in the notes of La Golondrina. Since music, heavenly maid, was young, she hath not ceased to soothe the heart of savage and civilized man, and her songs of home have been sweetest and dearest to his ear. That song of "Home, sweet home" is one that touches the American heart, as the home song melts the Mexican and brings memories of his, whether it be of adobe or of stone. Whether the soft melodies are picked from the strings of a guitar, or señorita sweetly sings the touching notes, or organized orchestra fills the ambient air with its tuneful tones,

A FIRE DRILL.

all there is of sentiment even in the stoutest, sternest heart, wells up in tenderness when the home song's music greets the ear, brighter, glistening eyes and quicker heart throbs tell that the melody strikes the soul.

Official Permits—Permits or passes are required to visit the various public institutions, such as the Palace of Chapultepec, the National Palace, etc. They are obtained from the Governor of the Palace, who is very courteous and obliging. When visiting an hacienda or for the ascent of Popocatepetl, permits should be obtained from the owners, most of whom reside in the city.

Laundry—The laundry as it exists in this country has not been established in Mexico. The bell boy on your floor of the hotel is agent for numerous and sundry *lavanderas*, washerwomen of more or less proficiency, but in the main do very satisfactory work. The bell boy will attend to all details, and the linen delivered to him will be safely returned. Lists should be retained and checked with the returned articles, and any missing pieces will be looked up; rarely is anything lost through these people, and their work is, for the most part, promptly and carefully done. Prices are about the same as in cities of the some size in other countries.

TACUBAYA PASTIMES.

Amusements.

Teatro Principal—As the Church was interested, and a prime mover in nearly everything else in Mexico, so it was in the organization of amusements in that country. The Brothers of the Order of San Hipólito built the first theatre, and in a little wooden building gave the first actual performance in Mexico, with a company of players employed for the purpose. The first performance was given January 19, 1722; the programme included " The Ruin and Burning of Jerusalem," and an afterpiece called " Here was Troy." The Burning of Jerusalem resulted in the burning of the theatre. The natives looked upon the burning as a visitation of Heaven for the unholy means taken to obtain money for the use of the Brotherhood, but the Brothers did not look at it in that light, and proceeded to build another theatre, completing it in 1725. The entrance of this theatre may still be seen about the center of the portales, on Coliseo Viejo Street. The present building is that of the Teatro Principal, and was completed on Christmas Day, 1753. The opening performance was a comedy entitled "Better it is than it was." This theatre formerly belonged to the Hospital Real, later to the College San Gregorio, until 1846, when it passed into private hands. The old theatre is one of interest in Mexico. The heavy stone wall between the boxes and stalls is a contrast with the light wood-work of our theatres. It is very massive, and looks more like a jail than a theatre.

Teatro Nacional—The National Theatre is the most fashionable theatre in the City of Mexico; it is comparatively new, having been opened in 1844. It has a seating capacity of over three thousand. This theatre has a very handsome foyer, and a portico with heavy Corinthian columns. The best dramatic and operatic companies always play at the National; it is always the place of public function, commencements of schools and colleges of a high class, such as Chapultepec.

The **Arbeu Theatre** is near the Street of San Félipe Neri, and was opened in 1875. The Hidalgo is in the Street of Corchero; these are the theatres of the middle class, not fashionable, but altogether respectable.

Salon de Conceirtos is a concert hall of the Conservatory of Music, where high class concerts are given by such associations as the Philharmonic Society. It has an audience hall with full theatre attachments, and is one of the handsomest in the city.

Circo-Teatro Orrin, as its name would indicate, is the circus theatre of the Orrin Brothers, located on the Plazuela Villamil. Its handsome iron building was put up at a cost of nearly $100,000. The interior has a dress-circle, parquet, a stage and a ring. During the performances both the stage and the ring are used, but when only the stage is used, the ring is removed and the parquet extended over it, with regular theatre chairs. The ring is sometimes transformed into a lake, with steamboats, sailboats and canoes, managed by a company of diminutive Mexicans. During the performance it may be transformed into the Palace of Cinderella, which will appear in the place of the ring, and in full view of the audience. The novelties introduced by the Orrin Brothers are refreshingly new, and on more than one occasion have been copied by the managers of the United States. In the summer time when the circus company is on the road, light opera performances are given.

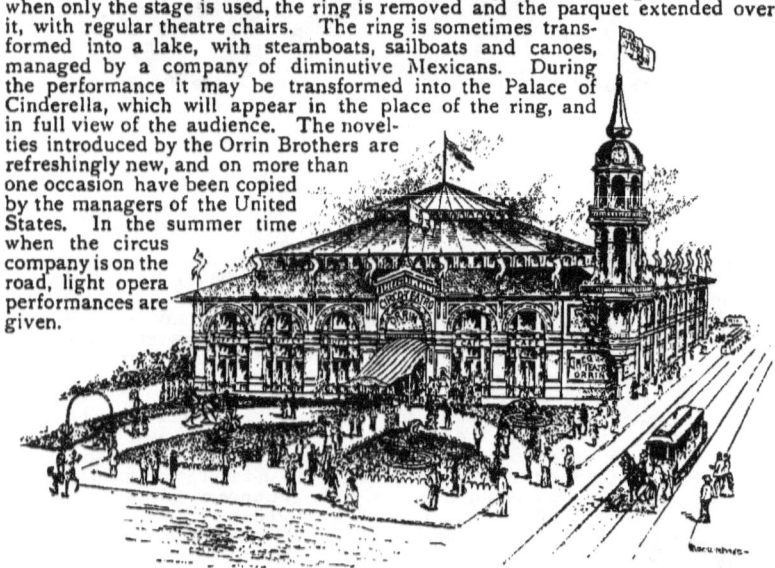

CIRCO-TEATRO ORRIN, CITY OF MEXICO.

The Orrin Brothers are noted for their liberality and charity, giving frequent benefits for the support of charitable institutions, both for native and those of the foreign colonies. On the gala nights of each week the theatre is handsomely decorated with flowers, and on great feast days each private box is decorated profusely with flowers. The occupants are presented with corsage bouquets and boutonnieres, and the aisles leading to them are completely carpeted with roses.

Bull Fights—Laws forbidding bull fights within the limits of the Federal District have been passed from time to time, and have as often been repealed. The laws may or may not be in force now, but the interdiction of bull fights does not apply in other parts of Mexico. The sport is indulged in, in almost every large city in Mexico. The fights are given on Sundays and feast days. The *Plaza de Toros* is in shape very much like the cyclorama buildings of America, only much larger and without a roof; inside is a monster amphitheatre, seating thousands of people. Encircling the arena is a high fence or barrier with a foot-rail about eighteen inches from the ground, on the inside, on which the performers step and leap over the fence when too closely pursued by the bull, landing in an open space between the audience and the ring. The opening of the performance is very brilliant and exciting. The audiences are nearly always large, sometimes numbering fifteen to twenty thousand, all eager for the fray. Gay colors are everywhere, bands are playing the liveliest airs, and all is excitement. The feeling of an American under the circumstances is one of amazement and anxious expectation. There is a grand flourish of trumpets, a gaily caparisoned horseman dashes in, gallops to the President's box, and a key is thrown to him; it is the key of the door leading to the pens where the animals are kept. The horseman catches the key—woe be to him if he don't—and gallops back to the entrance and disappears; if the key is not caught the man is hissed

ENTRANCE OF THE BULL.

out of the ring. Another flourish of trumpets and loud huzzas from thousands of throats announce the coming of the company.

It is, indeed, a brilliant spectacle, the *matador, capeadores* and *banderilleros* on foot and *picadores* on horseback, all clad in the gayest, gaudiest costumes, in all colors and gold embroideries. They march to the President's box. The President is a municipal or state officer, and has full direction of the proceedings. He is saluted by the company and the fight is about to commence. Now the wildest excitement prevails, and

THE PICADOR.

the scene is a perfect picture of pandemonium. All eyes are turned toward the low strong doors under the band stand; they are thrown open, and from a darkened pen the bull bounds into the ring. As he passes under the rail a steel barb, with ribbons attached, showing the breeder's colors, is fastened in his shoulder. He gallops to the middle of the ring, stops and looks about with fear and astonishment. He is a grand-looking beast. Surprise and fear give way to rage; he paws the earth and snorts in his frenzy, and discovering the red cloak of the *espada* starts towards him on the run. The man goes over the fence, but not too quickly, for he has

PLACING THE BANDERILLAS.

hardly disappeared before the bull's horns are thrust through the boards. The animal turns and spies a horse, and woe be unto the horse; his day has come. The *picador* with his lance is totally unable to keep the bull from goring the horse, and it is killed on the spot. The horses are not valuable ones, being old veterans retired from service, feasted and fattened to friskiness for this occasion. They are blindfolded and ridden in to certain death. Another man is chased out of the ring and another horse severely wounded. A signal from the President and a bugle call directs the horses to be removed.

ESPADA CALLING THE BULL.

Now comes the really interesting feature of the performance, the thrusting of the *banderillas*. The bull is alone with his tormentors; it is a contest between skill and brute strength. A banderilla is a stick about two feet and a half long; on the end is a very sharp barbed point. The stick is covered its entire length with colored paper ribbons. The banderillero is the man who places them in the bull's shoulders. He must stand in front of the animal, without

HE COMES.

flag or cloak, must stand still and wait the attack. The bull, maddened at his audacity, starts at him at full speed. The man steps out of his way gracefully, and skillfully thrusts the banderillas in the bull's shoulders as he passes by. As soon as the animal can check his headlong speed he turns, now furious with rage, only to find another banderillero with two more banderillas. These and two more are thrust into his shoulders, all hanging there. Bellowing now, he is wild. Another signal from the President instructs that the bull has had enough and must be killed. This is where the *matador*, the *primer espada*, distinguishes himself. His skillful killing of the bull by a single thrust of the sword is what determines the brilliancy of the star. The matador must face the bull, sword in hand, and await the attack. It is assassination to strike while he is at rest, and calls for hisses and missiles from the audience.

The blood-red cloth or *muleta* is flaunted in front of the bull. The maddened animal closes his eyes and makes one more dash for life and falls in death. The sword of the matador is thrust between the shoulders to the hilt and has pierced the animal's heart.

Wild bursts of applause fill the air; hats, canes, cigars by the bushel are thrown into the ring by the delighted spectators; men shout and sing, and ladies wave their handkerchiefs and mantillas. The matador bows his acknowledgements, throws the hats and canes back to their owners, who seem grateful that he should honor

CLOSE QUARTERS

them thus. The band plays, the gates are opened, and three gaudily decorated mules harnessed abreast are driven in. A rope is thrown over the dead bull's

BUT HE PASSES BY.

horns and he is dragged out. The wait between the acts is not more than a minute; the bugle calls, the low doors open and another bull gallops in, and thus till six are killed at each performance. The skill and agility of the performers is something wonderful and consists of holding the red cloth in such a way that the bull rushes for the cloth instead of him who holds it. The bull shuts his eyes and does not see the man as he quickly steps to one side and escapes, but often he must save his life by flight and a leap over the barrier around the ring.

The *Plaza de Toros* is the bull ring. The *funcion* is the performance. The best seats are on the shady side, those in the sun being sold at cheap prices. Seats in the shade $2 to $3; boxes from $12 to $20, according to the company playing.

The star fighter is the matador or espada. He it is who finally kills the bull with the sword. The banderillero is the man who thrusts the banderillas in the animal's shoulders, and the banderilla is a dart with a barbed point ornamented with colored ribbons. The little plait of hair or queue worn on the back of the head by a bull-fighter indicates that he has passed the degree of banderillero. If he commits any offense against the code of ethics or repeatedly fails in the act of placing the banderillas, his queue is cut off in public and he is forever disgraced. The picador is the man on horseback, but he don't stay there long after the entrance of the bull; yet while he does he goads with a pike or pole with a steel point. The *capeadores* are the men who handle the capes or cloaks which are flaunted in the bull's face to worry. The muleta is the red cloth used by the espada at the killing, and the *cachetero* is he who puts the finishing dagger stroke between the horns; and when he has done so six times (if there are only six bulls) the show is over.

The history of bull-fighting in Mexico is but another chapter added to that of Spain, simply changing the names of the stars of the profession. The people of Mexico inherit the bloody fascination of the sport, and what has been written of the exciting *funcions* in the *plaza de toros* of Spain will describe as well the

THE DEATH.

46

TAKING AWAY OF THE BULL.

fights in the arenas of Puebla, Toluca, Tlalnepantla, the City of Mexico, or any other of the Republic. Star matadors from Spain and Cuba have visited Mexico, notably Mazzantini and others at different times, but they have not dimmed the glory of the home constellation, for Mexico believes in patronizing home industry when it comes to bull-fighting, and Mazzantini's reception was not cordial nor his engagement prosperous, so the field is left to the home talent.

There are famous names on the roll of tauromachy of Mexico, such names as Corona, Hernandez, Gonzales, Gaviño, and a host of others, but none have reached that pinnacle attained by the idol of the day, the great and only Ponciano Diaz—a man commanding the admiration of the entire people, a man of whom a native paper says: "Should some day a man be required to fill the archiepiscopal see at Mexico, and the bull-fight going people be called to elect a man for the place, Ponciano would be the man. Should a presidential election be left to the will of the masses enthusiastically patronizing the popular sport, Ponciano would be the president. Should it ever come to the point of abolishing the republican system of government in Mexico and create a monarchy instead, we would see thousands of the young matador's admirers propose the name of Ponciano the First for the Mexican throne. That's the kind of a man Ponciano Diaz is." It does not follow that the bull-fighter is a "tough." Mazzantini was a graduate of a college at Rome and an A. M., and Ponciano Diaz a modest, well-appearing man of intelligence and good breeding, brave but not a bully, correct but not foppish, and altogether not spoiled by his professional successes.

Ponciano is a semi-god to the masses; he is the impersonation of all that is great to the people. Do you doubt? Then you have not seen a delirious mob unhitch the mules from their hero's carriage the day he went to see the first bull-fight by Mazzantini at Puebla, and hundreds of them haul the coach as a triumphal chariot through the streets, until they reached the hotel with their idol, shouting as they ran. Then you have not witnessed the ovations that he receives wherever he goes, and on the street the young and old, boys and girls and little children, point out—*There goes Ponciano!* If a man can reach the pinnacle of popularity, Ponciano is that man It is with the masses that the taste for the sport seems to be ineffaceable; the upper ten as a class do not, as a rule, frequent the bull-ring, though there are many and very brilliant exceptions, and I have seen the most elegant carriage on the Paseo whose occupants were little children dressed in the full costume of the toreador. And the Mexican small boy plays at bull-fighting, as the American does at base ball or as the more sporty one puts on the gloves with his fellows and does what he can to knock them out. Is it, then, any wonder the custom prevails, when the children are taught to admire it?

PLAYING AT BULL FIGHTING.

The City of Mexico.

The story of Mexico has its chiefest charm in the story of its chiefest city, whether the chapters are of the early days of the Toltec times, of the Conquest of Cortéz or the days of Diaz; whether their scenes are laid in Tenochtitlan or the City of Mexico; and as the Spanish conqueror fought his way up the rugged hills from the sea, with all energies bent for the wonderful city, so the traveler of to-day passes by the other cities till he comes to the greatest one.

No authentic chronology has named the date of the founding of Tenochtitlan, though all traditions agree as to the place; that its temples were in the midst of the lakes that spread out in the broad Vale of Anahuac, and that the temple of temples was near the spot of the great Cathedral of to-day. Clavigero, not always a reliable authority, but a faithful and laborious worker, deduces the following data:

The Toltecs arrived in Anahuac	A. D.	648
They abandoned the country	"	1051
The Chicimecs arrived	"	1170
The Acolhuans arrived	"	1200
The Mexicans reached Tula	"	1196
They founded Mexico	"	1325

And if these be true, Tenochtitlan was a city of two centuries before Cortéz threw down the teocali and its temples. The ancient city took the name from its miraculous origin. For a long time after their coming, the Mexicans led a migratory life, till, after a series of wanderings, they halted on the southern and western border of the principal lake, in the year 1325, on the spot where they beheld, on the stem of a prickly pear, a royal eagle of extraordinary size and beauty, with a serpent in his talons and his broad wings opened to the rising sun. They hailed the auspicious omen, announced by an oracle as indicating the site of their future city, and laid its foundations by sinking piles into the shallows, for the low marshes were half buried in the water. On these they erected frail dwellings of reeds and rushes, and sought a precarious living from the fish and

THE PLAZA MAYOR, CITY OF MEXICO, SHOWING THE PALACE, INDEPENDENCE DAY, SEPTEMBER 16.

fowl of the lakes. The name Tenochtitlan is from *tunal*, a cactus, *on a stone*, though the popular name of Mexico is derived from Mexitl, their god of war.

The early settlers did not prosper. They were torn by internal dissentions, but after a hundred years of feuds, wars and discord, the Aztecs, the Tezcucans and Tlacopans, allied their States for offensive and defensive wars, with an equal share of the spoils between the other two, after the little State of Tlacopan had been awarded one-fifth; but from either superior prowess or civilization, the survival of the fittest was with the Aztecs, and the other nations disappeared or merged under the dominions of the first Montezuma a hundred years later. When yet another century had passed, Cortéz came, and from Texcoco's shores sounded the knell of the Montezuma dynasty, threw down the temples of Tenochtitlan, and on their zócalos founded the

THE AUDIENCE AT THE TRAIN.

Church of God. From the time his ships hovered off the coast of Vera Cruz, the Spanish commander received repeated embassies from Montezuma, warning him not to approach his capital—warnings that went unheeded, and though not unopposed the intrepid adventurer, with only a handful of followers, marched through the land, built his *bergantines* at Tlaxcala, and set them afloat at Texcoco. On the 8th of November, 1519, Cortez marched across the narrow tongue that is between the waters of Texcoco and Chalco, and the day is memorable as the one in which the European first set foot in the capital of the Western world, and the story of it is as a romance whose very fascinations may be doubted. It was a peaceful entry that day, but the peace of it was not enduring; there were three years of wars and hostility, during which the ancient city of Tenochtitlan was utterly destroyed. Not until the year 1522 was the foundation of the Spanish city established in the building of a naval arsenal for the guarding of the *berguntines* near the site of the present Church of San Lazaro. From a modern standpoint, the city did not grow rapidly; it was more than two hundred years before it had a hundred thousand inhabitants. The original city was only about one-quarter the size of the present one; the center was the great *teocali* on the present Plaza Mayor; the limits reached about the Alameda, on one side, and the canal on the other.

The founder of the modern City of Mexico was the Viceroy Don Juan Vicente Güemes Pacheco, Conde de Revillagigedo, who accomplished many reforms that tended to beautify it and make it a place of health in its cleanliness. Unlike Spanish cities in general, the streets are wide, and for the most part, in the central district, are well paved, and the modern city is one of metropolitan appointments. The principal streets are lighted by electricity, gas and oil. The water supply is abundant, brought in by aqueducts and pipes; besides there are more than 600 artesian wells. The drainage, which was commenced by the Viceroy Pacheco, has been perfected under the administration of President Diaz. The great tunnel that is to drain the lakes, or at least cause a steady flow of water from the city, has been bored through the eastern hills, and it only remains to connect the sewers and the important work is done. The police system is excellent. The streets are patrolled by trained men. At each street intersection an officer stands night and day, and at night must have his lantern in the middle of the street, trimmed and burning, so that one may always know just where to find a policeman in the City of Mexico.

The City Government is on the same principle as in the cities of the United States. The city council have their offices and hold their sessions in the Ayuntamiento, on the south side of the Plaza Mayor, where the seat of municipal government has remained since 1532; the present building dates from 1720.

The Markets, always interesting in Mexico, are not particularly so in the capital. The Volador, just south of the Palace, is the market; for many years the land was rented from the heirs of Cortéz, but it was finally purchased by the City in 1837. The other markets are Merced, Jesus and Santa Catarina.

The Flower Market adjoins the Cathedral on the west side, not a very extensive one, but most interesting. A little pavilion of glass and iron, in the shadow of the Cathedral towers, is filled every morning with the choicest flowers, brought there from all over the valley and sold by the Indians; to strangers the prices are always higher, but no stranger ever bought as many flowers for so little money anywhere else in the world. Twenty-five cents will buy all you can carry, and when one starts out with a purchase of even that size, small boys will tag along importuning to carry the burden.

The Portales are the columned archways under which certain sidewalks 'pass. Around each column of the better class of portales are show cases filled with small wares, and in the poorer places second-hand goods are spread out on mats laid on the ground. The finest portales are on the Plaza Mayor, on the west side, and in front of the Ayuntamiento; others are the streets of Viejo Coliseo, Refugio, Tlapaleros, and in the old Plaza de Santo Domingo. The vendors always price their goods at about four times what they are willing to take, and, indeed, it is not always safe to offer one-fourth unless you really want to buy. Sundays and feast days are great days on the portales.

The National Palace, on the Plaza Mayor, is built upon ground that was once the property of Cortéz, who seems to have had an eye for valuable real estate, and a penchant for corner lots in town; however, before it became his property, " Montezuma's new house " was built on this spot. Later, Cortéz built a palace here that remained in the possession of his heirs until 1562, when it was

51

bought by the Crown for the residence of the Viceroys. The Palace of to-day occupies an entire square, fronting nearly 700 feet on the Plaza Mayor. It is occupied by the President's offices, the Department of State, Treasury, War, Archives and other minor branches of the Federal Government. The long white walls afford no idea of the interior magnificence of the halls and salons. The Hall of the Ambassadors is a magnificent room, running nearly half the length of the front. It contains portraits of many of the presidents, statesmen and soldiers of Mexico, notably those of Hidalgo, Morelos, Allende Matamoras, Juarez and

ON LA VIGA CANAL.

Diaz, and our own Washington. Of the other pictures, that of the "Battle of the 5th of May," and an allegorical work, "The Constitution," are the most worthy. The Senate holds its session in the Palace, but the House of Deputies occupies the old Yturbide Theatre, which was remodeled for congressional uses.

The Mint, or Casa de Moneda, is one of three mints established by the King of Spain in 1535; the other two were in Santa Fé and Bolivia. The machinery is of the modern improved patterns. The stamps were made in the United States.

The coinage of Mexican money is let out by contract. Since the establishment of the mints, nearly $100,000,000 gold and $3,000,000,000 silver have been coined. During Maximilian's reign, only $3,000,000 were coined, most of which was recoined into the dollars of the Republic.

The National Library occupies the old Church of San Agustin, one of the many magnificent buildings of Mexico. It has gardens on two sides, separated from the streets by a high iron railing, the posts of which bear the busts of Mexican celebrities in literature and art. The Toltec races, the Spaniards and the later day Mexicans are all represented. In the great hall of the library, a splendid room, are heroic statues of the greater lights of learning, from Confucius to Humboldt.

The library contains nearly 200,000 volumes, comprising all branches of literature, among which are some very ancient and valuable works. The library is open daily, except feast days, from 10 A. M. to 5 P. M.

The National School of Fine Arts, commonly called the Academy of San Carlos, is of comparatively modern foundation. The school was opened in 1779, the royal decree issued in 1783, and formally opened on the 4th of November, 1785. Painting in Mexico began as early as 1523, and sixty years later the art boasted some great students, native and Spanish, the greatest among whom were, perhaps, Tresguerras, painter, sculptor and architect, of Celaya, and Arteaga, Vasquez and Echave, of Spain, and the great woman artist, called La Sumaya, who painted the San Sabastian over the altar de Perdon in the Cathedral. Among the Indians were Cabrera of Oaxaca and Instolinque.

The great mass of pictures are of religious subjects; among the most notable are the "Meeting of Mary and Elizabeth," "Adoration of the Magi," "Christ in the Garden," "The Holy Sepulchre," "Women of Samaria," "The Crucifixion," "Virgin of the Apocalypse," "Martyrdom of St. Laurena," "Virgin de la Purísima."

There is a "San Juan de Dios," by Murillo, a replica of another of his in La Caridad de Sevilla. The other pictures, by the same artist, are "San Juan of the Desert," and "San Rafael." The examples of Rubens are his "Christ Tormented," and a portrait of the painter himself. There is also a San Sabastian by Van Dyke. The picture of the Dominican nun is said to be a portrait of Maria Ana of Austria, wife of Phillip IV. The building is open from 12 to 3 P. M., daily, and on Sundays and feast days from 9 A. M. to 3 P. M.

The National Museum is one of the most interesting in the world, possessing, as it does, so many relics of the unwritten history of the mystic races of a mysterious age.

The ground floor contains the great heavy monoliths that have been gathered here from all parts of the country. The Calendar Stone, for many years imbedded in the western tower of the Cathedral, was brought here in 1886. It is sometimes called the Stone of the Sun.

The idol Huitzilopochtli was the war god of the ancient Mexicans. It is a combination of two figures, one of which is Teoyaomiqui, supposed to represent male and female.

The Sacrificial Stone was unearthed in the Plaza Mayor, 1791. It is circular, a basin in the center with a channel to the rim, which was supposed to have carried off the blood of victims.

El Indio Triste, "the sad Indian," was dug up in one of the streets of the City of Mexico, now called the Calle del Indio Triste, in the year 1828.

The group of serpents was a part of the wall of serpents of the city Tenochtitlan. The stones were found under one of the columns of the Cathedral in 1572, were buried again and resurrected in 1881. The Coiled Serpent is also a feathered serpent coiled in pyramidal shape, called in other countries by other names; in

Mexico it is Quetzalcoatl, the god of morality, who is regarded by some writers as the Saint Thomas of these people.

Chac-Mol, the "god of fire," is one of the most notable of the idols in the museum, a recumbent figure, holding with both hands a basin on the stomach. It was brought from Yucatan. Three other similar figures have been found in other parts of the country.

The museum contains very many interesting relics of the later people of Mexico, in the time of the Montezumas. There are examples of Aztec picture-writings, representing the wanderings of the tribes, among which is a shield of Montezuma II.

The banner of Hidalgo, bearing the image of the Virgin of Guadalupe, which the patriot priest took from the Santuario de Atontinilco, his gun, handkerchief,

A PUBLIC LAUNDRY.

chain and cane, are in the museum, as are also the red standard of the Conquest and a portrait of the Conqueror; also the arms, armor, helmet and breast plate of Alvarado. There are portraits of the Viceroys, the silver and state coach of Maximilian, together with articles innumerable connected with the history of Mexico.

The Cathedral of the City of Mexico, the most ambitious church building in the Western world, is built upon the site of the great temple of the Aztecs, destroyed by Cortéz shortly after his occupancy of the city. The first church, a small one, in 1523, was enlarged a few years later. The corner stone of the present Cathedral was laid in 1573; foundation and walls completed in 1615; under roof in 1623, and the first mass said three years later, but the final dedication was not made until 1667. The work was delayed between 1629 and 1635 by the overflow of this part of the City. The towers were completed in 1791, they alone costing $190,000, the entire work amounting to over $2,000,000. The great bell, called Santa Maria de Guadalupe, in the west tower, is 19 feet high and cost $10,000. The massive walls are built of cut stone and the roof is of arched work in brick and stone. The length of the building is 387 feet, the width 177 feet, with an interior heighth of 179 feet. The towers are 204 feet high, very handsome, and crowned with bell-shaped domes. The architect of the Cathedral was Alonzo Perez Castañeda.

The interior is a marvel of carving and gilding, fluted columns, vaulted roofs, and altars gorgeously adorned. There are twenty fluted columns supporting the vaulted roof, which is in the shape of a Latin cross, and in the center of which is the very beautiful dome.

The choir is in the center aisle, the immense organ .reaching high up under the arches. In front of it is a space inclosed by a railing made of a composite of gold, silver and copper.

Under the altar of Los Reyes, the finest in the Cathedral, are buried the heads of Hidalgo, Allende, Aldama and Jimenez, brought here after the Independence of Mexico had been recognized. This Altar of the Kings was built by the artist of a similar altar in the Cathedral of Seville. Over the Altar of Pardon (Del Perdon) is a fine painting of San Sebastian, by the great woman artist, La Sumaya.

There are several chapels on each side. The Chapel of San Felipe de Jesus contains some relics of that Saint and the font in which he was baptized. Here rest the bones of Yturbide the First, called the Liberator. La Capilla de las Reliquias contains portraits of martyrs by Herrera. The Chapel of San Pedro holds the remains of Fray Juan de Zumárraga, the first Bishop of Mexico, and also those of the Mexican "Man with an Iron Mask," Gregorio Lopez, believed to have been a son of Phillip II.

The Sacristy walls are completely covered with pictures, great paintings, the work of Juan Correa and Cristóbal de Villalpando; in the Meeting Room are the portraits of all the Archbishops of Mexico. In the Chapter Room are three of the finest pictures, one, a Virgin of Bethlehem, by Murillo; another Virgin, by Cortona, and a representation of John of Austria, imploring the Virgin at the Battle of Lepanto, by a native artist. The Bishopric of Mexico was created by Pope Clement XII. in 1527, with Fray Juan de Zumárraga as first Bishop. The Archbishopric was created by Pope Paul II., January 31, 1545, when Bishop Zum-árraga was made Archbishop.

La Capilla de las Animas is just in the rear of the main building. It was dedicated to prayers for the release of souls from Purgatory, one priest, the good Don Cayetano Gil de la Concha, having said mass 45,324 times.

The first parish church on the site now occupied by the Sagrario was officiated in by the chaplain of Cortéz, Juan Diaz, until the year 1523. In 1524, four other parish churches were established: San Juan Bautista, named Moyotla; San Pablo, called Teopan; San Sebastian, called Atzacualco, and Nuestra Señora de la Asuncion, called Tlaquechiuhcan. Three of these are still parish churches, San Juan Bautista now being known as de la Penitencia. There are now fourteen parish churches, of which the following data relates: The Sagrario Metropolitano, a part of the Cathedral building, adjoining it on the east, founded in 1521, and dedicated to Santiago. The original building was destroyed by fire, and the present one completed in 1768. It is the handsomely carved façade just east of the front of the Cathedral. The decorations, interior and exterior, are superb, and the pictures are by the best artists. The little Capilla de la Soledad is between the Sagrario and the Cathedral.

San Pablo was founded in 1569, and San Sebastian in 1524. Santa Maria la Redonda contains a miraculous image that was commenced by a certain pious Indian, who was called away from his work, and on his return found it completed. In this church, also, was kept for many years the "feathered serpent," now in the Museum.

Santa Vera Cruz was founded immediately after the Conquest. It contains a crucifix concealed in a shrine behind seven veils, which gives another name to the church, "El Señor de los Siete Velos," "the Lord of Seven Veils." To visit this church every Friday of the year obtains a plenary indulgence.

Santa Cruz Acatlan was once a convent, and contains some fine pictures. Santa Cruz y Soledad was founded in 1534 as an Indian Mission. It contains a large image of Nuestra Señora del Rufugio. Santo Tomas de la Palma was founded in 1550.

IN A FRUIT MARKET.

San Antonio was founded in 1593, and contains a miraculous image of San Antonio de Padua. It was from the tower of this church that Lieutenant Grant trained his gun on the village of San Cosme. Here also is the tomb of the Viceroy de Acuña, Marquis de Casa fuerte. The church contains a miraculous image of Nuestra Señora de la Consolacion, within the tabernacle of the main altar; the picture is more than two hundred years old.

Regina Coeli is the parish of the Salto del Agua, and was built in 1553. The interior is richly decorated with wood carvings and in bright colors and gold, and is one of the prettiest churches in Mexico.

Santa Maria Mártir contained some curious altars before the confiscation of church property. This was one of the richest parishes in the city.

Santa Ana was built in 1754, and contains the font in which Juan Diego, the Indian to whom the Virgin of Gaudalupe appeared, was baptized.

San Miguel was built in 1690. In this church is held annually, on the 18th of October, a solemn service to the patron Saint of the Butchers. The door is beautifully carved.

San José dates from 1524, and was the first parish church of the Indians. The present building was finished about the year 1800, and was much injured by the earthquake of July 19, 1858.

Religious Orders of Mexico—For three centuries after the Conquest, Mexico was practically under the rule of the church, and the various religious orders flourished in all their glory.

The Jesuits were suppressed June 25, 1767, and finally expelled from the country in 1856. Other minor orders were suppressed by the Spanish Cortéz in 1820, and the few remaining orders were extinguished in 1859 by an order from President Juarez. At midnight on February 13, 1861, at the tolling of the bell of the Church of Corpus Christi, was the first act, and the nuns were removed from the various convents and concentrated in a number of small convents. On February 26, 1863, a law was passed suppressing female religious orders, except that of the Sisters of Charity, and the convents were required to be vacated within eight days. On December 14, 1874, the Order of the Sisters of Charity was suppressed. This law left Mexico without a monk or a nun, and so it remains to this day.

The enforcement of the Laws of the Reform was made with more energy than charity, but it is consistent with the Mexican, when once he has made up his mind to do a thing, to do it, and a great many acts of vandalism were committed. Pictures were torn down, and in some cases the soldiers rode their horses into the churches, lassoed the Saints and dragged them from their pedestals. But, on the other hand, when some of the atrocities committed by the bigoted fanatics of the religious orders are considered, the acts of the soldiers of the Reform seem amply justified.

The order of San Francisco, in its history, is closely identified with that of Mexico, and the establishment of it was identical with that of the Conquest. In the Church of San Francisco Cortéz attended mass, and within its walls was sung the first Te Deum of Mexican Independence, and it was, indeed, a Law of Reform that could convert such a church into a Protestant Cathedral; so that to-day the only thing that remains of the great Church of San Francisco is the memory of it and its walls.

The twelve founders of the order of San Francisco in Mexico were called the "Twelve Apostles of Mexico." They came from San Gabriel, in Spain, under the leadership of Fray Martin de Valencia, who has been called the "Father of Mexican Churches," and who "with his own hands reduced no less than 170,000 Pagan idols to dust."

The twelve Apostles landed at Vera Cruz on the 23d of May, 1524, and from the coast they walked to the Valley of Mexico. At Texcoco they were joined by Fray Pedro de Gante, who walked with them to Mexico. The

WANDERING MINSTRELS.

Apostles arrived in the City of Mexico on the 23d of June, having occupied just one month in their weary tramp.

The work of the Franciscans was rapidly extended and provinces established throughout New Spain. The first house of the Franciscans was on the site of the present church at Santa Teresa la Antigua. Afterwards they were established on the lands which had formerly been the zoölogical garden of the kings of Tenochtitlan. Their first church was built from huge stones taken from the

A PULQUE SHOP.

great teocali. The grounds were in the center of the city bounded by the present streets of Zuleta, San Juan de Letran, Coliseo, and the first San Francisco. The garden is now the garden of the Hotel Jardin, and the hotel itself was the residence of the chiefs of the order. The stable east of the garden was the refectory of the monastery, in which was a room where 500 of the brothers could sit down together at meat. The present Church of San Francisco was dedicated in 1716, and while greatly injured during the war of the reform, it is still one of the most interesting churches in Mexico, and one of the most elegantly decorated. The silver tabernacle of the altar alone cost $24,000. Originally the group was called the Seven Churches of San Francisco: El Senor de Burgos; the Chapel of Dolores; the Tercer Orden, aud Nuestra Señora de Aranzazú, facing on San Francisco Street; San José de los Naturales, on Gante Street, and the main churches. The Church of Nuestra Señora de Aranzazú, on San-Francisco Street, excepting that part of the group on Gante Street now occupied by the Protestants, is the only one of the churches remaining, and this has been made a new church by the recent addition to the front of the old building.

The portion of the Church of Tercer Orden may be seen between the walls of the houses on First San Francisco Street. The chapel was destroyed in 1862. The Church of San José de los Naturales was destroyed in 1862, and the building was removed for the opening of Gante Street.

On the 14th of September, 1856, information reached President Comonfort that a conspiracy had been formed among the brotherhood of San Francisco to overthrow his government and to re-establish the clerical party, and that the revolution was to take place on the 16th of September. On the morning of the 15th, which is Independence Day in Mexico, the president sent his troops to the monastery, and arrested the entire community of monks. On the 16th he issued a decree for the opening of the new street to be called Independencia, which should be directed through the monastery. On the 18th he issued another decree suppressing the monastery, which was rescinded February 19, 1857. On the 27th of December, 1860, Juarez ignored the latter decree and put in effect the original one of July 12, 1859. The monastery was closed; the jewels, decorations and paintings removed from the church to the Academy of Fine Arts; the altar was destroyed and the bell taken from the tower; the building of houses commenced, and in the following spring the street was cut through the old monastery grounds. The street was called Gante, in honor of one of the prominent members of the order of San Francisco.

Santiago Tlalteleco, the domed church, was established in the year 1543, and in 1537, a college for the instruction of the Indians was established. After being closed several times, the college finally came to an end in 1811. The life-size equestrian statue of Santiago was removed to the Church of Santa Maria, and the font in which Juan Diego was baptized was placed in the Church of Santa Ana.

Santo Domingo—The Dominicans arrived in Mexico on the 23d of June, 1526. Their first building was on the site of the present College of Medicine. In 1530 they removed to the monastery near the present Church of Santo Domingo, and the first church was completed in 1575; the present church was dedicated in August, 1736. It is one of the best in the city and contains some very handsome pictures, and an elegantly carved altar, with magnificent decorations. Another church of the Dominicans was Porta Coeli, founded in 1603, in connection with a college, which was suppressed in 1860.

The Inquisition, for which the Dominicans, through their leader, Saint Dominick, were directly responsible, came to Mexico in 1527, and in 1529 the first council of the Inquisition was held in the City of Mexico.

The President of the Audencia was Bishop Fuenleal; the other members were the Bishops of Mexico, the chiefs of Dominican and Franciscan orders, members of the City Council and two private citizens. The Audencia announced its deliberation as follows: "It is most necessary that the holy offices of the Inquisition shall be extended to this land, because of the commerce with strangers here carried on, and because of the many Corsairs abounding on our coast, which strangers may bring their evil customs among both natives and Castillians, who by the grace of God should be kept free from heresy."

August 16, 1570, Don Pedro Moya de Contreras was appointed Inquisitor General for New Spain. The royal order exempted Indians from the jurisdiction of the tribunal. On the site of the present College of Medicine was the first headquarters of the Inquisition; in later years the present building was finished, and in 1736 was occupied by that tribunal.

The *brasero*, or burning place, was on the grounds now occupied by Alameda, on which was erected a platform with stakes, to which was fastened the condemned to be burned; being raised above the ground, the burning could be easily seen by the people. When the burning was completed, the ashes were thrown into the marsh near the Church of San Diego. The first burning, by order of the Inquisition in Mexico, was in 1574, at which time were burned "twenty-one pestilent Lutherans." After this very many persons were executed in this place, though many of them were mercifully strangled before being burned.

April 10th, 1649, fifteen persons were burned, though only one, Thomas Treviño, a Spaniard, was burned alive, his offence being that of having "cursed the holy office and the Pope;" the others were burned after being strangled. The end of the Inquisition began in 1812, was re-established in 1814 for only a short time, then finally suppressed, by the revival of the original order of 1812, on May 31, 1820.

Among other acts of the Inquisition was the execution of the patriot Morelos, who was declared "an unconfessed heretic, an abettor of heresy, and a disturber of Ecclesiastical hierarchy; profaner of the Holy Sacraments; a traitor to God, to the King, and to the Pope." The sentence of the Inquisition was that the condemned do penance in a penant's dress. He was shot December 22d, 1815, in persuance to this decision of the Inquisition. A great many cruel acts of this bloody body of merciless priests have never been placed on record, and their cowardly acts will never be known until all secrets are revealed.

The life of the Inquisition was a reign of terror wherever its courts existed. Few but the bravest had the temerity to make even a defence. It is related that

f a Mexican cavalry regiment was summoned to appear before
o were assembled in their diabolical and nefarious court, in the
: the College of Medicine. He obeyed the summons, but did
ordered out the regiment and marched to the door of the build-
iquisition was seated; drawing them up in line, he spoke to his
i that he had been summoned before the court; that if he did
ity minutes they should enter the building and come to him.
ed within twenty minutes. The cowardly Inquisitors had not
to detain him a single minute. They held highly their own
s were regarded so cheaply.

f San Agustin was established in Mexico in 1533. The cor-
in 1541, and at the completion of the church, which was of
rtion, the cost exceeded a quarter of a million dollars.

ENT'S DESK, CHAPULTEPEC.

The first church was
destroyed by fire in 1676,
and the new church
dedicated in 1692. In
this church is now estab-
lished the National
Library.

San Hipólito is one
of the most interesting
churches in Mexico. It
is located on the spot
where the great slaugh-
ter of the Spaniards oc-
curred on the memorable
Noche Triste, "the dis-
mal night."   The first
church was of adobe,
afterwards replaced by
a more pretentious
building, commenced in
1599, dedicated in 1739;
it is called also the
Church of the Martyrs,
from the great number
of soldiers who lost their
lives on this spot. On
the wall surrounding the
church is a tablet bear-

'ith a representation of an eagle carrying an Indian in its
:ription in Spanish: " So great was the slaughter of Spaniards
iis place, on the night of July 1, 1520, named for this reason
that after, in the following year, re-entering the city triumph-
ors resolved to build here a chapel, to be called the Chapel of
'hich should be dedicated to San Hipólito, because the capture
d on that Saint's day." For many years afterward the 13th of
ted as a feast, called "The Procession of the Banner," in which all
s of the state, city and church took part, and in which was carried
r of Cortéz, which is now preserved in the National Museum.
ra de Loreto—The Jesuits of this order, founded by Ignatius
Mexico in 1572, and erected their first church in 1576; they im-
nemselves in conflict with the Dominicans, and were finally

suppressed in 1856. The present church was begun in 1809 and completed in 1816; it contains some very notable paintings. The church was closed from 1832 to 1850 on account of the sinking of the walls, resulting from the inundation of the valley, but on examination it was found that the settling of the walls did not render it dangerous. They were never repaired, and it is known at this time as the Church of the Leaning Tower.

Nuestra Señora de la Merced—The Order of Our Lady of Mercy was one of the first to be established in Mexico, one of its members having come with Cortéz. The first church and convent was founded in 1601. There seems to have been some difficulty in obtaining the land desired for the building of the church, a street occupying the desired spot. The brothers of the order made application for the use of the street, but were refused. They paid no attention to the refusal, and one night built two walls across the ends of the street and closed it up. The first stone of the church was laid March 20, 1634, and dedicated twenty years later. In 1860 the church was partially destroyed, and the grounds of the convent are now occupied by the Merced Market.

San Diego—The foundation of the Church of San Diego was commenced in 1591, but the church was not completed until 1621, on the spot just west of the Alameda. The church is elegantly decorated, and has some very handsome pictures.

The Chapel of Los Dolores is one of the prettiest chapels of all the churches of Mexico.

Belen de los Padres—This church was founded in 1678, and completed and dedicated in 1735.

Nuestra Señora del Carmen—The first Carmelite church of Mexico was established in Mexico in 1605.

Nuestra Señora de Monserrate—The church of this name was built in 1590. The brothers of the order introduced into Mexico many of the fruits and vegetable products of Europe. There are a number of fine pictures in the church.

San Juan de Dios—The first chapel was built in 1582, and the present church dedicated May 16, 1629.

Betlemitas—The corner stone of this church was laid June 2, 1681; the church was dedicated September 29, 1687. The order of the Betlemitas was suppressed in 1820; the monastery was used as the Military School, and the church transferred into a Public Library.

Colegio de las Niñas was founded in 1548 as a school for poor girls of the better class.

San Fernando—The corner stone of this church was laid in 1735. It is one of the largest in the city, but was badly damaged by the earthquake of June 19, 1858. It contains some very handsome pictures.

San Lazaro—The Hospital of San Lazaro was the outcome of an attempt by Cortéz to establish a hospital for lepers, and was founded in 1572. The church was built in 1721, with a cost of over $100,000, with an organ that cost $10,000.

San Antonio Abad—The brothers of this order established a church in 1628, with a hospital for contagious diseases, located in the southern part of the city, a locality which is still known by that name, as are several streets and gates.

La Profesa—This church is more properly known as San José el Real, dedicated August 28, 1720. The property of this company was in the very center of the city and very valuable. The first church was destroyed by the earthquake of April 4, 1768. The present church is one of the most elegant in the city. The interior is finely decorated in white and gold; the main altar is magnificent in drapings of crimson velvet, embroidered with gold. It is in this day one of the most fashionable churches in the city. The location is at the corner of

Third San Francisco and the Calle Profesa, the garden of the church fronting on San Francisco Street.

San Camilo was established in 1755. The church is handsomely decorated in white and gold, and exists now under the name of the Church of the Seminario Conciliar.

La Balvanera—This convent and church was founded in 1573; the corner stone was laid in 1667, and the church dedicated four years later.

Santa Clara—The Church of Santa Clara was completed on the 22d of October, 1661. This and the convent was destroyed by fire in 1755. The present church dates from 1756. The church remains open, but the convent is occupied as a stable.

Nuestra Señora de la Concepcion—This order was founded in Mexico in 1541. The present church was built at a cost of nearly $300,000. The tower is one of the highest in the city; over the altar is an image of the Virgin Purisima Concepcion. Back of the organ there was a continuous dropping of water, the source of which could not be found. After a diligent search of the roof, the

A PALACE PATIO.

source of the water was not discovered until after a vision to one of the nuns, to the effect that the dropping of the water marked the years of the convent's existence, and that when the water ceased to fall would be the end of the convent. In the days of the convents of Mexico this was one of the most fashionable, the nuns coming from the first families in Mexico. When the property was confiscated by the government it was valued at nearly $2,000,000.

Jesus Maria—This was originally the convent to be recruited from the descendants of the conquerors; the first nuns entered the convent February 10, 1580. About the year 1582 there came to this convent a nun who was the daughter of Phillip II. of Spain, and the niece of the then Archbishop of Mexico and the first Inquisitor General of Mexico. This made the convent one of royalty, and it was maintained under direction from the Crown. The corner stone was laid March 9, 1597, and the church completed in 1621.

San Gerónimo—This convent was founded in 1586. It is notable from the fact that Juana Inez de la Cruz, the great poetess and writer, became a nun and lived here many years, dying in the convent April 17, 1695.

Santa Catalina de Sena—The corner stone was laid August 16, 1615, and dedicated March 7, 1623.

San Juan de la Penitencia was founded in 1524 in a part of the city called Moyotla. In the church there is a wooden figure of the Child Jesus that a legend says saved the church at the time of a great earthquake. The uplifted arm of the figure stopped the falling of the walls, after which miracle the figure was regarded with great veneration. The corner stone of the church was laid February 6, 1695, and dedicated on January 24, 1711.

Nuestra Señora de la Encarnacion—The convent of this order is one of the best preserved in the country, at the same time one of the finest, and during the convent days was one of the richest establishments, the church alone costing over $100,000, and the ceremonies of dedication over $3,000. In this convent were deposited many of the pictures taken from other convents. After the confiscation by the government, it became a law school. The value of the property taken by the government was over $1,000,000. The main altar of the church is a mass of gold and carvings.

San Bernardo—The corner stone was laid in 1685; the church dedicated June 18, 1690.

Corpus Christi—This church was originally a convent, into which only girls of noble families and high caste Indians were received. The corner stone was laid September 12, 1720, and dedicated July 10, 1724. In taking the veil the novices were dressed in Indian costumes of the richest design.

Santa Brigida, the most fashionable church in Mexico, was completed December 21, 1744. Upon the confiscation of church property, Santa Brígida was bought by a rich Mexican family and held in trust for church purposes.

Santa Inez—The church was dedicated July 20, 1770. The fine entrance is richly carved in wood. The convent was closed during the Laws of the Reform, but the church was opened again in 1883.

San Lorenzo was founded in 1598. The present church was dedicated July 15, 1650. The convent is now used as a School of Arts.

San Jose de Gracia—The church was built about the year 1610, and rebuilt in 1658, the dedication taking place November 24, 1661.

Santa Teresa la Antigua—The corner stone was laid October 8, 1678, and the dedication took place September 10, 1684. The crucifix of this church was brought from Spain in 1545. After a lapse of time the crucifix became injured and was thrown into the fire to be burned; the fire failing to have any effect on it, it was buried and later resurrected, and it was found that its freshness had been wonderfully renewed. The crucifix was first placed in a little mining town called Cardonai, in the State of Hidalgo. During the repairs of the church, made necessary by an earthquake, the crucifix was placed in the Cathedral and brought again to this church May 9, 1858.

Santa Teresa la Nueva—The corner stone of this church was laid September 21, 1701; dedicated in 1715.

Enseñanza Antigua—The church was dedicated November 23, 1754. It is now partly occupied by the Palace of Justice and partly for a school for the blind. The new church of the same name was intended exclusively for the education of Indian girls.

The College of the Sisters of Mercy, located on the Plaza de Villamil, was built at the cost of nearly $200,000, and was intended exclusively for Indian girls of great beauty. It was called the Colegio de las Bonitas (the college of the pretty girls), and was finally used for the convent of the Sisters of Charity. The church called La Caridad is elegantly built, with magnificent interior decorations in white and gold; dedicated May 8, 1854, at which General Santa Ana acted as padrino, or godfather. The Sisters of Charity were the last of the nuns to leave Mexico, departing in January and February, 1875.

Jesus Nazareno—This church was founded by Conqueror Hernando Cortéz about the year 1524, but the church was not completed until 1575, and dedicated nearly a hundred years later, in 1665. In this church is the image of Nuestra Señora de la Bala. In the chancel of the church, under a handsome marble monument, at one time reposed the bones of Cortéz. It was the will of Cortéz that, should he die in Spain, his bones, after ten years, should be brought to Mexico and deposited in a convent which he proposed to build at Coyoacan, but the convent was never built. Cortéz died December 2, 1547, in the town of Castilleja de la Questa, and the body buried in great state in the chapel of the Duke of Medina Sidonia. At the appointed time the bones were brought to Mexico, and first placed in the Church of San Francisco, at Texcoco, where they remained until 1629. On the 30th of January of that year his grandson, and last of the male

SECTION OF OLD AQUEDUCT CITY OF MEXICO.

line, Don Pedro Cortéz, died and was buried, and with him the bones of his grandfather, in the Church of San Francisco in the City of Mexico, on the 24th of February, 1630. On the 2nd of July, 1794, the bones of Cortéz were again removed to the marble tomb in the Church of Jesus Nazareno. In the time of the revolt against Spain, the hatred of the Spaniards was so intense that it was thought best to remove the remains of Cortéz to some place not so well known, and on the night of September 15, 1823, they were hidden in another part of the church, and afterwards secretly removed to Italy, where they are now in the vaults of the Duke of Monteleone.

Nuestra Señora de los Angeles—There is a tradition concerning the founding of this church, that says that an Indian chief named Isayoque found a beautiful picture of a Virgin floating upon the water of the inundation of 1580, and he built a shrine or adobe immediately upon the spot where he found the picture and where the sanctuary now stands. The original picture was not kept in the chapel, but an exact copy of it was made on the walls of the shrine. In the year 1595 a more elegant chapel was built over the other on which the picture was painted. There were many angels upon the picture, so that the church became known as "Our Lady of the Angels." It was completed in the year 1808. The picture is kept in a glass case, so that it is impossible to tell on what substance it is painted, as, also, only the face and hands can be seen, the other portions of the picture being concealed in a dress made for it by a very pious tailor. In the church is also a life-sized picture of Santiago.

Salto del Agua—The corner stone was laid March 19, 1750, and became a parish church in 1772. The name is derived from the fact that it is near the fountain at the end on the aqueduct of Chapultepec.

La Santisima Trinidad was founded about the year 1658. The present church was begun in 1755, and dedicated in January, 1783. The building has a very handsome façade and two very fine towers.

Schools and Colleges—In the City of Mexico there are many public schools supported by the city government, for which there is a special appropriation of $150,000. The number of schools in the district is over 300, attended by over 20,000 pupils, which include the private and parochial. The schools are mainly housed in buildings that were convents or churches.

A Conservatory of Music was established by a Royal Order of the Emperor, Charles V., September 25, 1551, and the institution opened January 25, 1553. The present building was erected in 1787, and the Conservatory of Music was established here in 1877. In the interior are some beautiful cloisters surrounding the patio, in which is a pretty garden. There is a fine and elegantly-decorated concert hall, and a handsome stairway, over which is a painting by Vallejo. The Conservatory has a fine library and collection of music.

School of Medicine—The decree authorizing a School of Medicine was made March 16, 1768. The building was formerly occupied by the Inquisition. It has a fine audience hall, committee rooms, cabinets of chemistry, natural science and library.

School of Mines—The department of mines was founded May 4, 1777, and the permission for the school was granted by the Royal Order in 1783. The building was completed April 3, 1813, at a cost of nearly $2,000,000. The building is one of the finest, in point of size and architecture, in the city. It has fine patios, galleries and stairways, and a splendid audience hall. The chapel has a fine altar in bronze. There is a good library, astronomical and meteorological instruments, observatory, cabinets of splendid specimens of geology and mineralogy. When General Grant was in Mexico, he was entertained and lived in this building.

Preparatory School—The school was authorized in 1588. The present building was completed in 1749, at a cost of nearly one half million dollars, and is a very handsome one, containing patios, surrounded by portales, and has all the apparatus for the study of chemistry, philosophy and natural history.

The School of Agriculture was founded in 1854, and is located in an hacienda near the suburb of Tacuba.

Lancasterian Society—Schools were opened in 1822.

Benevolent Society—Schools were founded in 1842.

Catholic Society—Schools are about twenty-five in number.

Commercial College is located in the building near that of the School of Mines.

The Law School is established in an old convent of the Encarnacion.

The Catholic Theological Seminary was established in 1691, and occupies the old Monastery of San Camilo.

Hospital de Jesus Nazareno—This hospital was founded by Cortéz in the year 1590, and is maintained by an endowment made in the will of the Conqueror.

Hospital de San Hipólito—The present building was erected in the year 1773, and was used as a military hospital during the revolutions, and latterly as a medical college.

Hospital del Divino Salvador was opened in 1700.

Hospital de San Andrés was established as a pesthouse during the plague of smallpox in the year 1779. It is now operated by the Municipal Government, and includes a department for the treatment of diseases of the eye.

Hospital Morelos stands on the spot of its predecessor, erected in 1582, for the care of mixed races, Indians and mulattoes.

Hospital Municipal Juarez—The first patients received in this hospital were the wounded men from the battle with the Americans at Padierna, August 19, 1847, and was used as a military hospital during the American War.

Hospital Concepcion Beistigui was founded March 21, 1886, in the old convent of Regina Coeli, and is one of the best hospitals in the City.

Casa de Maternidad was erected April 10, 1865, under the imperial decree of Maximilian and under the presidency of Empress Carlotta, who, after her return to Europe, sent a fine set of surgical instruments and a large amount of money for the support of the hospital.

Foreign Hospitals—The American, French and Spanish Colo-

ALL FOUR.

nies each have a hospital in different parts of the city, located in private dwellings, or houses that were private dwellings.

La Cuna is a Foundling Asylum. The word La Cuna literally means the cradle. It was established January 11, 1766. It had an endowment fund of about $250,000, but is now supported by the city. The children are taught useful arts as well as the primary branches of education.

Hospicio de Pobres is literally a poorhouse. It was opened March 19, 1774, and has a subsidy from the government of $1,000 per month.

Monte de Piedad is a national pawnshop, an institution that is really a charity. As an effect to prevent the extortion of pawnbrokers, such an institution is found in most every city and town in Mexico, and might be of benefit to the people if adopted in this country.

The Monte de Piedad was opened in the City of Mexico February 25, 1776, and was finally removed to the present building opposite the Cathedral. Originally no interest was charged on loans, it being left to the borrowers to make a gift to charity on the return of his pledge. Of course this privilege was abused, and regular rate of interest was fixed, but even in the present arrangement they are most liberal. When an article of value is brought to the national pawnshop, a loan something like its true worth is made. After a certain length of time, if the pledges are not redeemed, they are exposed for sale at a price, of course, higher than the amount of the loan. In a month this price is marked down, and in another month marked still lower. The borrower is privileged to redeem the pledge at any time before its sale, and if the article is sold for more than amount of loan, the excess less the interest, and original amount of loan is paid to the borrower. The business of the institution amounts to over $1,000,000, distributed amongst 60,000 borrowers. This it one of the most interesting places to tourists, and often relics or interesting pieces of bric-a-brac may be found there.

A PULQUE VENDOR.

Colegio de la Paz—This institution was established by the charity of some rich merchants, who desired to establish a school or asylum for poor children. The corner stone of the building was laid in 1734, and was dedicated to San Ignacio Loyola. The school shows to-day a cost of nearly $2,000,000. The direction of the institution is managed by the government, and is one of the most extensive institutions in the city.

The Plaza de la Constitucion is the main Plaza; on the north side is the Cathedral; on the east the National Palace; on the south the Casa Municipal or Ayuntamiénto, and on the west side a perfect bazaar of handsome shops under a fine portal. The Plaza Mayor is also referred to as the zócalo, a word meaning "foundation," derived from the foundation laid about fifty years ago for a monument to Mexican Independence, that was never built. The zócalo proper now supports a music pavilion, where military bands play for the poorer classes on Sundays, feast days and certain evenings of week days. When this great city was Tenochtitlan, and a capital of the Toltecs and the Aztecs, the

Plaza was occupied by the temple and its gardens. Just after the Conquest the square was occupied by numerous and sundry small buildings and shops, and was a sort of market. These, by a Royal Order dated January 18, 1611, were ordered removed, but it was nearly fifty years before the order was obeyed. On the 16th of November, 1658, a fire broke out in these buildings and greatly assisted in carrying out the King's order; the hucksters who escaped the fire were ordered to go at once to the present Volador market site. After a while the shops came back, but were all destroyed in the great riots of June 8, 1692, caused by the famine of that year, when for vengeance for the murder of one of their number the Indians assaulted the palaces of the Archbishop and the Viceroy, built fires at the doors and fed the flames with the demolished shops of the Plaza. The fire was lost sight of in the terrors of the riot, and the loss was over $3,000,000.

April 19, 1703, a handsome stone building erected by the Ayuntamiénto was completed, with accommodations for merchants, that was called the *Parian* or bâzaar, and with this example before them the shops came back. An old picture shows them and the gallows in front of the Viceroyal palace, with the frame for criminals' heads. This was the state of affairs until the coming of the Viceroy Conde de Revillagigedo in 1789, who removed the shops, gallows and criminals' heads and effected a great many reforms in the way of cleaning up and drainage, and made the Plaza the beautiful place it is. The *Parian* was the center of the retail trade of the city then, but in the present time largely extends to other streets. During the revolution of 1828 the stores were looted and the stolen goods publicly sold in the Plazuela of Santo Domingo. The *Parian* was demolished in 1843, and the trade went to San Francisco and Plateros Streets.

A wooden, gilded statue of Charles IV. was placed in the Plaza November 9, 1803, and subsequently removed. As it is the center of the city, the Plaza Mayor is the heart of it; here the people come from all the other towns round about, and here they come to start home again. All the car lines to all parts of the city and to the suburbs, arrive at and depart from the Plaza Mayor.

The **Plaza Seminario** is simply a part of the Plaza Mayor on the north side, adjoining the Cathedral. It contains a monument to Enrique Martinez, the engineer who conducted the cutting of the great Nochistongo Canal. The monument shows inter-

A FRIENDLY GAME.

esting data of the rise and fall of the waters at different periods. The bronze figure on the monument is emblematic of the City of Mexico.

La Alameda—Every Mexican town has its Alameda, a park of recreation; the name is derived from alamos, poplars, the trees first planted in the Alameda of the City of Mexico. Previous to 1592 the place of the Alameda was occupied by the Tianquis de San Hipólito, an Indian market, and a part of it was called the Plaza del Queréndaro, from the stone platform that was erected here for the burning of criminals and the victims of the Inquisition. The Viceroy Marques de Croix, hail to his memory, ordered this *queréndaro* or murder removed, at the risk of his own life at the hands of the murderers who erected it for the heresy in daring to undo their villainous work; but the *queréndaro* was removed and the Alameda established, and became the pretty park and resort of the fashionables. In its early days the Alameda was inclosed by a high wooden fence and later by a stone wall and the iron gates that had been around the statue of Charles IV. in the Plaza Mayor. A moat was dug around the outside of the wall. The fences and walls were removed in 1885 and the moat filled up; roses were planted, fountains established, the beautiful music pagodas built and the Ala-

A 5 O'CLOCK TORTILLA.

meda became the charming resort and place of promenades. There is music Sundays and feast days from 11 A. M. to 1 P. M. The fashionable folk come to listen, to see and be seen. Here is held, also, the Feast of the Flowers and the fiestas on the national days that the Mexicans celebrate.

Paseo de La Viga runs along the banks of the Viga Canal, and was intended to be the fashionable drive, but it is as interesting as it is not fashionable, for fashion has taken itself entirely to the Paseo de la Reforma. The drive along La Viga or a voyage by gondola is especially interesting during the Feast of

Flowers about Easter time, when the banks of the canal, the boats and the houses are almost buried in flowers. About half way down the Paseo is a bust of Guatimotzin, the last of the Aztec kings.

Paseo de Bucareli starts from the glorieta of Charles IV. and runs southward to the Garita de Belen. Midway of the Paseo is a handsome fountain and Statue of Victory erected in 1829, in honor of Guerrero.

Calazadas are causeways. There were three of them that in ancient days extended from the city to the main land. The southern causeway was called Acachinanco, that diverged at San Antonio Abad in two causeways, one leading to Coyoacan and the other to Ixtapalapan; the latter was used by Cortéz in his approach to the city, and his first meeting with Montezuma, which occurred at the corner of Calle Paja and Calle Jesus. The western causeway led to Tacuba, or,

CORTEZ HOUSE, COYOACAN.

as the old town was called, Tlacópan, and was the shortest one to the main land, and for this reason was kept open by Cortéz for the purpose of possible retreat, after his sad experiences of the Noche Triste, which occurred on this calzada. The calzada to the northward led to Tepeyac, now called Tepeyácac, and was improved and enlarged by the celebrated Fray Juan de Torquemada, of the then monastery of Tlalteloco.

The causeway to Guadalupe was commenced in 1675 and finished in 1676, at which time it had a large glorieta midway, but now fallen into decay. There are fifteen beautiful shrines of stone, elegantly sculptured, set at regular intervals, and dedicated to the fifteen parts of the rosary. In front of these shrines the walking pilgrims stopped to pray. The shrines, glorieta and arched bridges are disappearing and the calzada has come to the baser uses of the railway. The Mexican Railway line runs along the causeway on the route to Vera Cruz.

Aqueducts were, until very recently, the means of conveyance of the city's water supply. The water is now conveyed in pipes, and the picturesque aqueducts are disappearing. The great aqueduct that brought the water from the mountains of Leones near the Desierto, over stone arches, commenced at Las Cruces, about four miles out, passed by Chapultepec, and by the Alameda where the people climbed upon the arches to get a view of the burning of the victims of the Inquisition. This aqueduct was built under the direction of the Viceroy Marques de Montes Claros in 1603–7. There are nearly a thousand arches of stone and brick, laid on a foundation of stone, with a coping and water channel also of stone. The aqueduct from the springs of Chapultepec is the one that ends in the beautiful fountain called the Salto del Agua, one of the most inter-

AT SANTA ANITA, ON LA VIQA CANAL.

esting relics of the Spanish age in Mexico. It was built under the administration of the Viceroy Don Antonio Maria de Bucareli, and completed in March, 1779. An inscription over one of the arches in Spanish, says: "The course of this aqueduct is identical with that of the aqueduct built by the Aztecs during the reign of Chimalpopoca, who was granted the use of water of Chapultepec by the King of Atzcapotzalco, to whom the Aztecs were subject until the reign of Itzcohuatl, when they gained their independence." The aqueduct is rapidly disappearing, the material being used for the macadamizing of the suburban roads, and the water is now conveyed in iron pipes.

Monuments—The monuments and statues of Mexico are unique and apart from other monuments and statues in other parts of the world. The most notable and the oldest of Mexico's monuments, and the largest single piece of bronze in the world, is the great equestrian statue of Charles 1V., at the junction of the Avenida Juarez and the Paseo de la Reforma.

It was originally intended to place this statue in the Plaza Mayor, and pending the casting of the bronze, a wooden model, gilded, was placed there on the pedestal prepared for the present statue. The casting was made in the gardens of San Gregorio.

OLD BRIDGE, COYOACAN.

Two days were required to fuse the mass of more than thirty tons of bronze, and the work was completed at 6 o'clock, on the morning of August 4, 1802, when the first piece of bronze statuary in America came from the mould without a flaw.

The statue was placed upon its pedestal in the Plaza Mayor and unveiled with impressive ceremonies December 9, 1804, where it remained until 1822, at which time the feeling against Spain was so bitter that it was covered by a huge wooden globe in blue; but this did not protect it from patriotic insult, and it was taken down in 1824 and removed to the patio of the University, where it remained until 1852; the ardor of the feeling of the Mexicans against the Spaniards having cooled, it was placed where it now stands in 1852. It is a solid, single piece of bronze, 15 feet 9 inches high, weighing thirty tons or more. The king is dressed in royal robes, with a wreath of laurel on his brow, holding in his right hand the sceptre of Spain. The horse is in the act of walking, the left fore foot and the right hind foot being raised. The statue is of magnificent proportions and drawn in perfect lines. The sculptor was Don Manuel Tolsa; the casting was made by Don Salvador de la Vega.

The statue of Columbus, in a glorieta of the Paseo de la Reforma, was one of the first monuments to the discoverer erected on the continent he discovered, and one of the handsomest ever raised. The base is ornamented on its four sides by basso-relievos; the arms of Columbus in laurel wreaths; the rebuilding of the monastery of La Rabida; the discovery of San Salvador; a fragment of Columbus' letter to Raphadi Sauris, and the dedication of the donor, Señor Escandon. On the four corners are life-size figures,

A FAMILY GATHERING.

in bronze, of Padre Marchena of La Rabida; Padre Fray Diego Dehesa, confessor of King Ferdinand; Fray Pedro de Gante, and Fraye Bartolomé de las Casas. Above these is the graceful statue of Columbus drawing the veil aside that has concealed the New World.

In another glorieta is a statue that is the special admiration of the Indians,— the statue of Cuauhtemotzin or Guatimotzin,—the admiration of which is not confined to the natives. It is of exquisite workmanship and beautiful in conception and execution. The plumed and feathered warrior stands upright, with steadfast look ahead, and in the act of taking an arrow from his quiver. The basso-relievos show the scenes of the torture and other incidents in the life of the Aztec monarch.

The monument to Juarez is on the Panteon de San Fernando. The recumbent figure of the Indian president rests beneath a Grecian temple of purest white marble. Half supporting the body is the figure of Mexico mourning for her dead. The beautiful work is by the Islas Hermanos, who have accomplished a perfect result from a graceful and perfect design.

The statue of Morelos is of white marble and enjoys the distinction of having been unveiled by Maximilian on the one hundredth anniversary of the hero's birth. There is also a statue of Guerrero in bronze.

Houses of Note—Near the Hotel Humboldt is a house once owned by the Condes de Santiago, one of the oldest families of Mexico, and one of the wealthiest. The doors are richly carved, with the family arms as a center piece; there is a magnificent patio, and in the rear a small park from which the street Parque del Conde derives its name.

The Palace of Yturbide is now the hotel of that name. It was erected by the Marquesa de San Mateo Valparaiso more than a hundred years ago. The house was occupied by the Emperor Yturbide during his brief reign. Near the Garita de San Cosme is the "house of the masks." Don José de Mendoza, Conde del Valle de Orizaba is responsible for the entirely unique idea of covering the walls of his

OLD FOUNTAIN, CITY OF MEXICO

house with stone masks. He died before the house was finished however.

The house of Humboldt is at No. 3 Calle de San Agustin, where the great traveler resided during his stay in Mexico. A tablet in the walls records that fact and the date of his birth.

The house of Marshall Bazaine is in the street called Puente de Alvarado.

The House of Tiles at the corner of the Plazuela de Guardiola was built by the Conde del Valle de Orizába. There is a proverb of the Spaniards that applies to the spendthrift, to the effect that "he will never build a house of tiles," and it is said that the proverb had been applied to the Conde, and that he built this house to refute the imputation.

Fronting the Plazuela is the magnificent house of the family Escandon.

Near the center of the Puente de Alvarado there is a space between the houses, shut off from the street by a wall and an iron rail that tradition says is the spot of Alvarado's leap on the eventful Noche Triste.

The Streets of the City of Mexico are peculiar in their nomenclature. The names were chosen from every conceivable source, from the Divinity to Diaz, including the Savior and his apostles, as well as the heroes of Mexico and Spain. There is a Calle Espiritu Santo and a Calle Jesus, a Calle Hidalgo and a Calle Juarez, and one Calle Niño Perdido, Street of the Lost Child. The names change at each corner, or if the name continues more than one square, numbers are prefixed. Thus the principal street, the Broadway of Mexico, is called San Francisco; where it begins at the Alameda it is called Puente de San Francisco; in the next block it is 1st San Francisco, and in the next 2d San Francisco, and so with many others. This is what is called the old system, but is still in use, although by city ordinance the streets are now numbered north and south, as are the avenues that cross them at right angles. Difficult as the old one was, it will be a long time before the new system comes into general use, and no explicit directions can be given. A map may be of some use, but a hackman is the surer method of finding any particular street. Still one is not liable to lose the way; the streets run at right angles, and one soon becomes familiar with the landmarks. Many of the objects of interest are within a few minutes' walk of the principal hotels. For the distant places the street cars are preferable to carriages.

Panteones—The cemeteries of Mexico are always interesting. That of San Fernando is the finest in the country. Here lie the remains of Juarez, Guerrero, Miramon, Zarnagoza, Comonfort and other prominent men of Mexico.

The Cemetery of Dolores, beyond Chapultepec, is a beautiful place indeed.

The French, English and American colonies have their cemeteries. In the latter are buried nearly five hundred American soldiers of the war of '47.

In the cemetery on the hill of Guadalupe General Santa Ana lies buried. Other cemeteries are San Pablo Piedad, Campo Florido, Salinas and Los Angeles.

Funeral cars of all classes are operated on the street-car lines leading to the panteones and cemeteries.

Newspapers.—The *Two Republics*, printed in English, is issued every morning. The *Anglo-American* is a weekly. The *Mexican Financier*, a weekly devoted to financial and commercial interests, is printed in both English and Spanish, parallel columns. All the American dailies of the larger cities are on sale at the various news stands, and also the latest weeklies and magazines.

The Sonora News Company has agents on all first-class trains of the trunk lines in Mexico, with the latest periodicals and literature of the day.

Among the daily papers printed in the Spanish language are *El Universal*, *El Tiempo*, *El Nacional*, *El Partido Liberal*, *El Diario Official* and others, giving foreign and domestic news; these and the English papers mentioned are published in the City of Mexico. The other larger cities of the Republic all have their newspaper publications.

PLAZA DE TOROS, CITY OF MEXICO.

Around the Capital.

Chapultepec—Popular tradition has it that on the Hill of the Grasshopper was the summer palace of the Montezumas. A causeway led from the city of Tenochtitlan across the marshes and the lake and aqueduct was built upon it. After the Conquest the Spanish Viceroys built a palace on the hill. It remains to this day. It was the palace of Maximilian, and is the summer home of the President of Mexico. The present palace was commenced in 1783 by the Viceroy Don Matias de Galvez and completed by his son, Don Bernardo, in 1785. It has been undergoing completion ever since by the various kings, emperors and presidents, each one adding to its size and cost.

The interior decorations are beautiful and unique to a degree, with Pompeiian color and decoration in the tiled galleries. A smoking-room has hangings of embossed leather. A desk and dresser in another is inlaid pearl and onyx. A fine stairway has a ceiling decorated with coats of arms from 1474 to 1887. A drawing-room has the walls hung in the most delicately tinted satin, has tapestries and the richest ebony furniture. Bedrooms with the daintiest boudoirs are furnished in regal elegance. In an ante-room are two oaken chairs that belonged to Cortéz. The palace is on the very crest of the hill, approached by only one winding road. This Hill of the Grasshopper rises out of a forest of giant *ahuehuetls;* its rocky sides are carved here and there with figures and heiroglyphics that are declared to be dates and names of Aztec history. On one side a cave is shown that is the opening to an underground passage that ends immediately under the palace, and connects with a well or shaft that opens in the garden at the top; this was a means of secret passage in the olden times. The cave is seen from the drive on the ascent, and the well is shown in the garden of the palace. On the eastern side of the hill is shown the tree of Montezuma, where

A MODERN TOLTEC.

that unhappy monarch also experienced a *noche triste*, where he wept as Cortéz wept, and for defeat. The views from the wide galleries of the palace are grandly magnificent. On one side are the volcanoes, on another the fields of Churubusco and Molino del Rey. From the front is the grand view of the city, lakes and the plain, with towns and villages everywhere, and the mountains on the other side. In the foreground are the great cypresses of the park, the rocks and steep hillsides, and the old aqueduct of the city's water supply.

The grand old trees rise in sombre majesty like a race of giants among pigmies, and the dim aisles beneath their lower branches are made still more beautiful by the almost intangible softness of draperies of gray moss festooned and swaying from limb to limb. Through this wood, shadowy as twilight even at midday, the carriage road winds and mounts to the summit. Standing on the terrace, whence rises the grand old castle, one looks across the Valley of Mexico. Surely, of all beautiful views in this beautiful country, the most wondrous is this!

With the remembrance of scenes in other lands which have been inspiration and delight, with the memory of the Yosemite in its blended aspect of mystery and majesty still foremost in thought, this lovely landscape loses nothing. Even the glamour which ever surrounds the past fades before the reality. From this beautiful spot one looks across a valley fair as a dream of paradise, with soft green fields and waving hedges and avenues of lofty trees outlining gray country roads that fade into the azure distance. A faint line of pale blue mountains, purple sometimes with deep shadow, rest like brooding and watchful spirits around the dim horizon; and farthest of all, beautiful with that sublime sense of remoteness and awfulness which belongs only to them, the solemn presence of Popocatepetl and Ixtaccihuatl rises like radiant clouds against the serene heavens above. Everything before known of mountain scenery becomes secondary in the imagination compared with these wonderful heights! The great serenity of the Plain, the softly changing greens which cover its entire extent, and the undulating, exquisite line of hills, like the frame of some rich jewel, is something unspeakable when contrasted with the grand solitary state of these twin monarchs who dominate them all. If no more of loveliness than this view can give were added to one's inner life, the journey to Mexico would be fully requited.

The park and hill were the scene of a conflict between the Americans and Mexicans on the morning of September 13, 1847. The palace was bravely defended by the Cadets of the National Military Academy, which is a part of the palace. Many of the brave boys fell under the merciless fire of the enemy. A handsome monument in the park, at the foot of the hill, was erected to their memory. The horse cars for Tacubaya pass near the park gate. It is best to visit Chapultepec by carriage and go early in the afternoon, returning to the Paseo in time for the drive when all the fashionables are there, from four to seven o'clock. To be admitted to the castle of Chapultepec it is necessary to have a permit from the Governor of the National Palace.

Molino del Rey, the field of the battle between the Americans and the Mexicans on the 8th of September, 1847, is reached by a branch horse-car line, connecting with the Tacubaya cars just beyond Chapultepec. The battle has been declared by General Grant to be one of the unnecessary fights of this unholy and unjust war.

Tacubaya is not inaptly termed the Monte Carlo of Mexico. The "wheel of fortune," or misfortune, rolls under the white umbrellas in every street, where the poor men, women and children play their earnings away. In the gardens the higher classes play at the same game with higher stakes. From this society the stranger is not ostracized; he is always taken in.

After the great inundation of 1629-34, it was proposed to remove the city to the more advantageous higher ground of Tacubaya, but for many reasons it was abandoned. The Alameda and the Plaza of Cartagena are very pretty little parks. In the western part of the town are the quaint old mills of Santo Domingo, and near by the *arbol benito*, "the blessed tree," which, a legend says, was blessed by a priest who had rested in the shade, and bade it be ever green, whereupon a spring gushed forth from its roots. The tree and spring are both in evidence. The very beautiful gardens of Tacubaya are private property, but may be visited on permission.

Horse cars run from the Plaza Mayor to Tacubaya, passing the gate of the park of Chapultepec. Another line of horse cars starts from the Plaza, and just out of the city are attached to a steam train.

Mixcoac, a mile south of Tacubaya, is the place of the beautiful gardens of La Castañeda, a place of public resort and very much in favor on Sundays and feast days. The old adobe walls enclose some beautiful gardens, where flowers are grown for the market in the city. Mixcoac is reached by horse cars from Tacubaya or via the Tlalpam steam line, changing to the cross country horse cars at San Mateo.

San Angel is another of the little garden cities of the valley on the cross-country line between Tacubaya and San Mateo. San Angel derives its name from the old Church of San Angelo Mártir, built in 1615-17, and dedicated to that saint. There is a deserted monastery and church, with beautiful domes of tiles, once occupied by the Carmelites, who dedicated it to Nuestra Señora del Carmen, in which there is much to interest the lover of the antique. San Angel is beautifully located on the sloping hills, overlooking the valley and surrounding villages, a very healthful place, and much resorted to in the summer months.

Coyoacan was the home of Cortéz and the seat of his government after the Conquest, and from here he directed the building of the City of Mexico; hence, Coyoacan is the older town. The house of Cortéz is now occupied as the city hall. Over the doorway is his coat of arms. Near by is another house of Cortéz, in the garden of which he drowned his wife. The Church of San Juan Bautista was founded in 1530; the date of its completion, 1583, is graven on the façade. In the church yard is a stone cross, placed there by Cortéz. Coyoacan is reached by horse cars from Tacubaya, or by the Tlalpam steam road to San Mateo, where change is made to the cross-country line.

ON THE BARRANCA ROAD.

Churubusco is near the station of San Mateo, on the Tlalpam Railway, about a half mile distant. It is only a straggling village, but in ancient times was an important city, Huitzilopochco, in which was a temple to the god Huitzilopochtli, from which the name of Churubusco is said to be derived, but by what process of derivation the chronicler sayeth not. The place had a bad name as the abode of

BY THE WAYSIDE.

demons and evil spirits that made night hideous with their howling and diabolical noises, but these were vanquished by the establishment of the Christian church. The Church of Santa Maria de los Angeles was completed in 1678 and dedicated May 2d of that year. The church is beautifully decorated with tiles. There are some wonderful carvings in wood on the old organ and the busts of the saints. In the patio of the monastery is a spring of clear water bubbling up through a stone basin.

In the little plaza is a monument in memory of the battle with the Americans, August 20, 1847, under Generals Smith, Worth and Twiggs. General Pedro Maria Anaya was the brave commander of the Mexicans. After the battle he was asked by General Twiggs where he could find the ammunition. The gallant Mexican replied: " Had I any ammunition you would not be here."

Tlalpam is a beautiful little city at the southern border of the Valley of Mexico, reached by the steam trains of the Valley Railroad; the cars are drawn by mules from the Plaza in front of the Cathedral to the outskirts of the city and there made up into a train with a locomotive. It is a quaint old town of gardens and orchards, and relics of the bygone times. In former times a great gambling féte was held here at Whitsuntide, but on account of its excesses the féte was finally suppressed. In the southern part of the town are the ruined walls of an oratorio, richly carved, against which a thrifty native has built a lowly home, the adobe walls and thatched roof in strange contrast with the departed magnificence of the oratorio decorations. One of the most delightful and interesting day's outings that can be made from the capital is a trip to the towns of the south of the valley. It will take a day to do it and the start should be early. Take the Tacubaya line of horse cars, change at Tacubaya to the cross-country line, stop over one car at Mixcoac to visit the Tivoli de la Castañeda. Stop an hour at San Angel, two at Coyoacan, two at Churubusco and another two at Tlalpam, returning to the city via the Valley Railroad. There are no restaurants, but in all the towns the tiendas keep canned goods, bread and eggs, and the trip may be made a picnic.

Noche Triste—The famous tree is in the suburb of Popotla. Beneath the tree Cortéz sat down and wept on the night of his terrible defeat, July 1, 1520. The tree is of the kind of those in the park of Chapultepec, called *ahuehuetl*. Some years ago, some fanatic built a fire about its trunk and seriously burned it. Since that time an iron rail has been placed around it. Relic hunters are warned off by the arrest, some years ago, of a party of American vandals, who were very properly fined for their nefarious practices, in this case of breaking off twigs from the tree.

Tacuba is the place of the residence of the Archbishop of Mexico. In olden times it was a city and capital of the primitive monarchs Totoquiyauhtzin I, Chimalpopoca, Totoquiyauhtzin II and Tetlepauquetzaltzin, who was hanged by Cortéz in 1525. Near the Archbishop's residence is a very handsome church, enclosed within a wall of inverted arches, where solemn services are held during holy week.

Atzcapotzalco was the capital of the cruel king Maxtla, a monarch of the Aztecs until the rightful heir, Netzahualcoyotl, overcame the usurper and regained the throne. The almost unpronounceable name means "the ant hill," on account of the very numerous population. The church and monastery were erected by the Dominicans in 1565. The present church was completed in 1702. On the tower is a huge ant, graven in the stone. The church is a large one, with a high tower and two fine domes. Back of the town is the village of Zancopinca, where there is a little lake and a ruined aqueduct. The lake has a legend that in its waters, in a palace of crystal, a bad fairy lives, called the Malintzi. She lures passersby to the waters by the music of her singing; whoever hears her voice and stops to listen, and does not run away, disappears forever. If he lingers, a languor creeps over him, fills him with ecstacy, and he is irresistibly drawn into the depths by the Malintzi's beauty also, and disappears forever. The Indians say that this lake is the hiding place of the treasure of Guatimotzin, that even the cruel torture he suffered at the hands of Cortéz did not make him reveal. Another legend relates of a spring that was under the roots of five great *ahuehuetls*, near the monastery, a spring whose water never flowed from it, and to drink of it meant to disappear forever. The holy fathers counteracted the evil effects of the spring by preaching against it, with the additional and perhaps more effective covering it up with stones which the multitude cast into it, and then placed over it an altar to the Virgin; but he who will listen with his ear to the ground may still hear the murmuring of the waters and the singing of the bad fairy beneath the ground.

The cars for Atzcapatzalco start from the Plaza Mayor. It is not necessary to ask for the car; the name is painted on the side.

La Piedad is just beyond the Garita de Belen. It consists of a church and an abandoned monastery, founded in 1652, and contains a much venerated picture of the Virgin with the dead Christ. The tradition is that the picture was commenced in Rome, but when the monk, who was to take the picture to Mexico, was

ready to start, only the outline of the figures was drawn. It was concluded to take it anyhow. On the way over a violent storm came up, and the mariners vowed to the Virgin, if she would bring them safe to land, they would build a temple to her in Mexico in which the picture should be enshrined. The prayer was heard and the vow fulfilled—and behold, when the picture was opened, it was found to be finished in the most beautiful colors. It was placed above the main altar, dedicated February 2, 1652, and is there to this day. Horse cars start from the Plaza Mayor.

La Viga Canal—The floating gardens, *chinampas*, on the Viga Canal, are reached by horse cars from the Plaza Mayor, near the Cathedral, to Embarcadero, and thence by canoe for a few hours or for a day. The boats are a sort of Mexican edition of a Venetian gondola, broad and flat-bottomed, with seats underneath a canopy of bright colors. The boats are propelled by a pole in the hands of a dusky gondolier. The excursion is altogether a novel one, particularly on Sundays and feast days, and should not be overlooked. Unless you are thoroughly Mexican it is best to make a picnic of it and take your provender along, but there will come alongside a longer and narrower canoe hewn from the trunk of a single tree. In one end of this quaint craft stands a swarthy Mexican with a single oar of long handle, in the other a comely woman and often a pretty girl, who will offer, for a *tlaco* or a *cuartilla*, the native sandwich, a *tortilla con carne* or a *tortilla con dulce*. I offer no advice as to this purchase, but the tortillas of La Viga, as I found them, were clean and toothsome.

This excursion is the most novel of all. The boatmen meet the horse cars at the terminus and bid against each other for patronage. There is no regular tariff, twenty-five cents, *dos reales*, each passenger being sufficient to Santa Anita and return. The longer excursions to the lakes and towns beyond, of course, cost more. Santa Anita is a sort of native Coney Island and is a great resort, but the charm is in the ride thither, passing the low-arched bridges, and the market boats laden with fruits and flowers, which must stop at the La Viga gate and pay a duty to the city, levied on all imports from the country. There are great, long flat-bottomed passenger packets, also propelled by poles, going to and from the towns across on the other shores of Xochimilco and Chalco, crowded with men, women and children and dogs starting or returning from a voyage of a day and a night.

Any day will do for the La Viga voyage, but Sunday, or, better still, on a feast day, there will be flowers afloat and ashore, and music, music everywhere, of all sorts, from the tinkle of a guitar to blare of a brass band; gayly dressed men and more gayly dressed women, singing and dancing on the boats or under the trees of the Paseo de La Viga which runs along the canal.

The floating gardens really were entitled to the name when Cortéz came, and the *chinampas* were described among the other features of exceeding beauty that met the astonished eyes of the Spaniards, but now are only bits of land with little canals, instead of walks, through the beds and plots. These canals are too narrow for the boats from the city. To see the *chinampas*, the gardens that float, walk through the streets of the village a few yards and take a small boat for a voyage through acres and acres of flowers.

On the banks of La Viga once lived El Señor Don Juan Corona, of most happy memory, revered for deeds of daring, and loved for his charity. He was not a soldier or a Sunday school superintendent. In life Don Juan was a bull-fighter, and much renowned in his day, but his career is not to be written here.

Ask your gondolier to stop at the hacienda of Don Juan Corona. Enter beneath an hospitable roof and find a house intensely Mexican, shaded by trees and almost hidden by climbing vines and flowers. Every room is a museum in itself, filled with relics of every age and time of Mexico's history; curious objects collected from all over the country, in dozens and scores. There is a cigar case once owned by the patriot priest, Hidalgo, also a pistol and sword carried by him; some pieces from the table service of the Emperor Maximilian; several idols found in the pyramids of San Juan Teotihuacan; weapons, feathers and war-dresses used by the Aztecs; one of the guns with which Maximilian was shot; the bed used by General Santa Ana, while President of Mexico; a rifle used by General Miramon in the siege of Querétaro; a magnificent collection of *chicaras*, chocolate cups, painted by the Indians of the State of Michoacan; very curious ancient bull-fighter dresses, among which is the one used by the Spanish matador, Bernardo Gaviño, when he was killed in the ring at Texcoco.

The collection of this bric-a-brac was Don Juan's hobby; but another and more philanthropic pleasure of his was the care of the children of the poor of La Viga, and from his savings he established a school for them. He was called the father of the destitute. The school will be shown in one of the rooms of the hacienda. As a visitor enters, the bright little beneficiaries of Corona's bounty rise in salutation and welcome. The school has not the ample means it had in the life of the good Don Juan, and any offering is not only acceptable but is a tribute to the memory of a good man.

The Paseo, or, to be explicit, the Paseo de la Reforma, is *the* drive of the city. Carriages are necessary to the proper seeing of the Paseo and to save a walk up the steep hill at Chapultepec. It is about two and one-half miles long, reaches from the City to Chapultepec, and is a magnificent boulevard, where the *bon ton* are pleased to drive every afternoon from four o'clock till dark, when the magnificent procession of fine equipages files down San Francisco Street and disperses. The carriageway is broad and shaded by great trees, two rows on each side, between which is a wide promenade. At regular intervals the Paseo widens into a *glorieta*, a circle 400 feet in diameter, where there are stone benches. In three of these circles are to be placed statues of the nation's heroes; that of Charles IV., said to be the largest bronze in the world, is at the entrance, and Columbus and Guatimotzin further along; Juarez and others are to be placed in the other *glorietas*. On each side of the drive, near the curbs, are smaller statues of Mexican heroes, presented by the various states. At the further end of the Paseo rises the hill and castle of Chapultepec, surrounded by a forest of cypress which is not surpassed for magnificence on this continent.

The Desierto, some sixteen miles southwest of the city, reached only on horses or burros, was, in olden times, an abode of a company of Carmelite monks, which the ancient chronicler called a stately cloister set upon a hill, among rocks in which the monks fashioned out holes and caves, where they lived and prayed, and where they kept their implements of self-torture—rods of iron, hair-cloth girdles with sharp wire points, which they wore on their bare flesh, and such other pleasant articles of diversion. But with all the name of *el Desierto*, it is by no means a desert. There were gardens and orchards, and rare flowers, and among the rocks springs of clear flowing water. It is a beautiful spot, indeed, and the ruins, the caves and holes in the rocks intensely interesting.

San Juan Teotihuacan is the place of the Pyramids of the Sun and Moon, and the ruins of a prehistoric city. The Pyramid of the Sun is 216 feet, 8 inches high, with a base of 761 by 721 feet, 7 inches. At the top it is 59 feet, north and south, and 105 feet, east and west. The "Moon" is 150 feet, 11 inches high, with a base of 511 by 426 feet, 5 inches. At the top it is 19 feet, 8 inches square. An entrance to this pyramid, discovered some years ago, leads to a chamber whose walls are of cut stone, in direct lines of the compass. The other pyramid has no entrance as yet discovered.

South of the Pyramid of the Sun is the *ciudadela*, the citadel, 262 feet wide by 32 high. In the center of the enclosed square is a small pyramid, and on the outer works fourteen smaller pyramids placed at regular intervals. Between the "Sun" and "Moon" is a causeway called the *Calle de los Muertos* (the street of the dead). These works are supposed to be the work of a race older than the Toltecs or the Acolhuans. The pyramids are reached in an hour's ride by the Mexican Railway from Buena Vista station. They may be seen from the cars, looking from the windows on the north side.

Tlanepantla is a town of bull fights, but an interesting, primitive place, at the end of a horse-car line that commences at the Plaza Mayor. The old church was commenced in 1583, and dedicated four years later.

Tajo de Nochistongo, one of the greatest works ever attempted, was designed by an engineer, Enrique Martinez, to drain the waters of Lake Zumpango, the highest of the lakes of the valley, and prevent its overflow to the other lakes and the inundation of the city. The work was begun November 28, 1607, and in less than a year a tunnel, four miles long, eleven feet wide and thirteen feet high, was completed by the work of 15,000 Indians, who were utilized by the sinking of a number of shafts. The tunnel walls were of adobe with a stone facing.

On June 20, 1629, the rainy season being unusually copious, the uncompleted tunnel was ordered closed for fear of the result of too great a volume of water that might destroy the work. In a single night the waters rose and covered the city to a depth of three feet. The great flood lasted from 1629 to 1634. It was at this time that a royal order was given, changing the location of the city to the higher ground of Tacubaya, but a very dry season coming on, the order was not carried out. Martinez was imprisoned as the cause of the calamity, but finally released and ordered to execute the work he had commenced. The tunnel was reopened, but it was constantly caving in, and It was finally concluded to open the tunnel into a canal, which was done. The width is from 300 to 600 feet, depth 150 to 200 feet, and the length 67,537 feet. But after all this cost of time, money and life, the Tajo failed of its purpose; it is a drainage canal that does not drain. The tracks of the main line of the Mexican Central Railway pass through the Tajo de Nochistongo, and the great work may be seen from the windows on the west side.

Guadalupe—There is a positive similarity between the Aztec and Toltec legends and mythology and that of the Christian religion. The Aztecs had a Mother of Gods which they called Tonantzin, and which was worshiped at the identical spot where the Virgin of Guadalupe appeared to the Indian, Juan Diego.

This pious Indian lived at the town of Tolpetlac, and on the morning of December 9, 1531, as he was on his way to hear mass in the Church of Santiago Tlaltelolco, and near the hill of Tepeyacac, he heard the music of singing voices, and looking up beheld a lady who spoke to him, and bade him tell the Bishop that he should build a church on the spot where she stood; when she had disappeared he hastened to the Bishop with the message that he had received. The Bishop was Don Juan Zumárraga, who listened to his story, but with unbelief. The Indian returned to the hill and found the lady there again. She listened to what he said of the Bishop's answer, and told him to come again to that spot on the following Sunday, at which time she appeared to him for the third time, and repeated her behest that a temple should be built in her name. The Indian again repeated his story to the Bishop, who was still incredulous, and told him to bring some token that might indicate the truth of his story. When the Indian departed, the Bishop sent two of his servants to follow him, but Juan Diego managed to evade the watchers, and when he had come to the hill, behold, the lady was there. She told him to come again the next day and that he should have the token the Bishop required. On the return of Juan Diego to his home he found his uncle very ill with a fever, and for some days was busied with his attendance on the sick man, who grew worse, and early on the morning of December 12th, Juan went to call a confessor. He did not go by the usual path, but by a nearer one, in the hope that he might not be delayed just at this time by the appearance of the lady, but as he passed the hill he saw her coming down and she called to him. He told her of his uncle's illness, and of his errand. She replied that already his uncle was well. Then she told him to gather some flowers. To gather flowers in such a place seemed impossible, but at her feet he found them growing in the barren rocks. Joyfully he gathered them in his tilma. The lady bade him show the flowers to no one except the Bishop, as they were to be the sign required, and as she vanished, behold, a spring of water gushed from the spot where she stood. He hastened away to the Bishop's house, and waited at the door until he

VISIONS OF JUAN DIEGO, FROM OLD PAINTINGS AT GUADALUPE.

appeared, and when he came, the Indian emptied the flowers at his feet, and behold, an image of the Virgin, in beautiful colors, appeared upon the tilma. The Bishop took the miraculous tilma and placed it in his oratory. Juan Diego returned to his home, and found that his uncle had been cured of his illness in the very hour that the Virgin declared that he was well.

The temple was built upon the spot where the Virgin had first appeared, and where the roses had sprung from the barren rock. In this temple, on the 7th of February, 1532, was placed the tilma of Juan Diego, and the good Indian and his uncle became the servants of the Virgin in attendance there.

The little chapel at the foot of the hill, and the spring that is there, mark the spot of one of the visions of Juan Diego, and for many years the tilma hung above the altar. Afterwards it was removed to the larger church near the Plaza, where it remains until the completion of the great Church of Guadalupe, on which already nearly $2,000,000 has been spent. This is to be the final resting place of the image of the tilma.

The wonderful part of the story is, that the tilma retains the colors, bright and fresh, while other pictures near it are faded and worn. Eminent artists and authors have examined the tilma and decided that the picture is not painted; that they have no knowledge of how the colors are put on. The tilma is the cloak of the Indians, made of a coarse textile fabric taken from the fibre of the cactus. The image of the Virgin of Guadalupe differs from the other images of the Virgin, in that it has a halo around the entire figure instead of around the head alone.

December 12th is the great feast of Guadalupe, and from all parts of the country the Indians come to the fiesta. It is the day on which Juan Diego carried the flowers in his tilma and placed them at the Bishop's feet. When Hidalgo pronounced the *Grito* of Independence, he took the banner, with the image of the Virgin of Guadalupe, from the little Church of Atotonilco, near San Miguel de Allende, and it became the banner of Independence. It fired the Indian heart and Guadalupe became the war-cry that led them on to victory.

When you go to Guadalupe, whether on the day of fiesta, or at a more propitious time to see all the wonders there, walk through the little park to the southeast corner, then through a little street to the Capilla del Pocito (the chapel of the well), where there is a flowing spring of clear fresh water that gushes forth from the rocks where the Virgin stood.

To the left stone stairs lead to the chapel at the top of the hill. About half way up are the stone sails of Guadalupe. The legend goes, that a ship's crew were sore distressed in a great storm, and vowed to the Virgin that if she would bring them safe to shore they would carry their ship's foremast with its sails and set them up on the hill of Guadalupe. The sails are there, encased in stone, as an evidence of the protecting power of the Virgin.

On the top of the hill is the Capilla del Cerrito. This chapel of the little hill marks the spot where Juan Diego gathered the flowers that sprung from the hard stone where the Virgin stood, and carried them as a token of his story to the Bishop.

Down on the other side of the hill is a curious little grotto built in the side of the rocks, ornamented with mosaics of broken china, glass, shells and bits of bric-a-brac, the work of the Indians.

Guadalupe was made a city by an Act of Congress, February 12, 1828. It has a population of about 5,000 people. Here was signed the Treaty of Peace between the United States and Mexico, February 2, 1848, called the Treaty of Guadalupe-Hidalgo.

The Church of Nuestra Señora de Guadalupe is at the foot of the hill, on the spot of the fourth apparition of the Virgin to Juan Diego. Adjoining the church, on the east, is the old Convent of Santa Coleta, closed by the Laws of the

Reform and the nuns banished. In the patio are the cells of the rooms, each about six feet square, with a stone bench for a bed.

Street cars run from the Plaza Mayor, in front of the Cathedral, along the line of the ancient causeway. On the left are seen the shrines erected by the Spaniards, and where the processions and pilgrims stopped to pray.

Los Remedios—Westward of the Plain of Mexico is the hill of Totoltepec and on its top the shrine of Our Lady of Succor, called the Church of Los Remedios, whose legend is quaint and curious. A holy image of the Virgin was brought to Mexico by Juan Rodriguez de Villafuerte, a soldier of the Conquest. During the first occupation of Tenochtitlan the image had a place and a shrine on the great *teocali*. When the defeat of the Noche Triste came the image was carried out of the city by Villafuerte, who, being sorely wounded and unable to carry it further, hid it under a maguey on the hill Totoltepec, near the temple of Otoncapulco, and left it there.

Twenty years later an Indian chief, Cequauhtzin, whose Christian name was Juan de Aguila Tobar, was hunting on the hill and saw a vision of the Virgin, who told him to search under the maguey for her image. He found it, and took it to his home, but it returned again to its place under the maguey. He carried it again to his house, and set tempting food before it in a dish made of gourd, but with all this the image fled and was found again on the hill. For the third time the Indian took the image to his house, and this time put it in a strong box, secured with locks, on which the chief slept; but still the image disappeared to its place under the maguey. Then the Indian went to the holy fathers of San Gabriel, in Tacuba,

and told them of the strange happenings. The fathers at once perceived a miracle, indicating a wish of the Virgin that a temple should be built on the hill of Totoltepec in her honor, which was done. The present church was commenced in 1574, completed in 1575, and dedicated in 1629, for the second time. Adjoining the church is a large building, erected for the clergy and the high dignitaries of church and state, on the occasion of the fiesta of September 1st of each year, when they came to bring the Holy Image in state to the city for invocation for needed aids. The surrounding walls were to enclose a place for the Indians to sleep when they came to the fiesta. The jewels and ornaments were of great value, costing over

XICACA, GODDESS OF WATER.

$1,000,000, and her shrine most magnificent. The silver railings and the silver maguey have all disappeared. A slab of onyx, with an inscription, marks the spot where the image was found. In an inner room the original image is kept. It is about ten inches high, and has a tiny Jesus in its arms. It is darkly tarnished

HOME IN THE RUINS OF THE ORATORIO, TLALPAM.

with age, but some of the jewels and ornaments remain. The gourd in which the Indian offered food is also preserved in the same shrine.

An abandoned aqueduct extends from the church to the higher hills; it was built in 1620. It is doubtful if any water ever flowed through its conduit, though an authority and a half legible inscription says that there was water in 1724.

Nuestra Señora de Los Remedios was the patroness of the City of Mexico, and when she was conveyed to the Cathedral in times of need, the highest officials of church and state followed humbly in her train and participated in the solemn ceremonies. She divided honors in the times of war with Our Lady of Guadalupe, and after the battle of Las Cruces, when Hidalgo seemed about to capture the capital, her aid was invoked. She was made Generala of the armies of Spain, and while the war cry of the Revolutionists was "Guadalupe," the Royalists shouted "Los Remedios."

After Independence was secured it was intended to banish the image of Los Remedios from the country, but the order was not executed, and the fiestas of September 1st are continued, as they have been for three hundred years.

A visit to Los Remedios requires a full day, by morning train of the Mexican National Railroad to Naucalpan, thence by burros up the hill of Totoltepec, returning by the afternoon train. The views of the valley from the church are simply magnificent.

LAW SCHOOL OF GUADALAJARA.

The Cities and Towns of Mexico.

There were cities in Mexico before the man who discovered the country was born, aye, cities with hundreds of thousands within their gates, a thousand years before the city was built that boasts the discover's birth, and towns were there on the plains, and on the lake shore, and on a hundred hills, looking down to the valleys below, where villages nestled in their shadows. These have passed away, and only their ruined temples, here and there, have left their pillars and graven walls, uncovered by the sands of fleeting centuries, in unrefuted evidence of a glorious magnificence and pre-historic civilization.

And there were cities and towns in Mexico when the greatest of these in the United States of the North were but straggling villages. Their streets were paved with stone, while the grass grew in ours, the shadows of high walls shaded the passers by, instead of the trees that made the shady side of our thoroughfares, and the first that is written here was a city nearly a hundred years before the Mayflower unloaded its cargo on Plymouth Rock.

These remain till this day, and the traveler of the newer cities of the North may come and walk in the same paved pathways, pass under the same darkening archways, may bow down at the altars that were reared when the stones of the Pilgrims' churches were unquarried, and he may live under a roof that may have sheltered a courtly cavalier of old Spain, come here attendant at a vice-regal court. The streets of the then, are the streets of the now, and the oldest inhabitant knows not, except from history, when his house was built.

I have not chosen to put one before the other here; I have written of them in the order of their curious names, alphabetically as to the letters of their spelling, leaving the pronunciation all to you, and to the native who tells you how.

Acámbaro
Ak-kam-baro On the 19th of September, 1526, Nicolás Montañes de San Luis, an Otomite ally of the Spaniards, who was also Cacique of Xilotepec, declared Acámbaro a city, and the next day, with all the pomp and circumstance of state, he marched his soldiers up and down the plain where the streets were to be, and coming to the place where the plaza now is, a mass was said in a temporary chapel, on the spot where now stands the parish church, and the Church of San Francisco was named that day. After the religious ceremonies,

the first city election was held, that is, Don Nicolás appointed the officers, and Acámbaro became a full-fledged city, more than three hundred and sixty years ago.

It was no mushroom growth in the advancement of the town. The date of its birth is recorded, but not so the date of its completion, and if we may judge from its narrow streets, the tumble-down houses and neglected plaza, its finishing must have been a century or so ago, and the chiefest charm is in its antiqueness. It is the same old Tarascan town that Nicolás Montañes intended it should be, and the

ENTRANCE OLD SPANISH BRIDGE, ACÁMBARO.

coming of the railroad has not disturbed its siesta. The trains come and go, and the people ask not whence they come or where they go, neither do they care.

The Tarascans gave the town its name as meaning "the place of the maguey," though little of it grows in the surrounding fertile plains, the lands being tilled in more valuable products. Located on the King's highway to the Pacific Coast, it was a trading place of note many years ago, and it was then that the great stone bridge over the Lerma was built, and later, in 1810, Hidalgo concentrated his troops at Acámbaro, with the intention of marching to the Capital. When the railway builders came they found the place in the way of their lines, and it became —— a place to change cars, that's all. A day at Acámbaro may not be, by any means, the least delightful. A minute's walk from the handsome stone station and the tracks, will take you backward another century, and (if you hear not the whistle or the engine bell), to another country strange and quaint. There is no way to ride, and there is no need to; you must walk and you will prefer to, through Amargura Street, passing the fourteen *capillitas chiquitas*, the stations of the cross, to the church of Soledad, at the top of a little hill, coming back another way to the plaza, where you may rest under the great trees.

Near by is the church of San Francisco with its deserted convent, one of the oldest in all Mexico and one that has never been closed for repairs, though there is a new and unfinished chapel that was commenced in 1850 as a thank offering for the escape of the town from cholera, intended to be dedicated by Fray Macedonio Romero to Nuestra Señora del Refugios, but it was never finished. These and the Church of Guadalupe are all to be seen.

Near the railway track, about a quarter of a mile from the station, is the great stone bridge across the Lerma that was built, long ago, in the old Spanish days; the massive arches and columned entry-ways make an antique picture that is in consonance with the sleepy old town. The water supply is conducted from the hills in an aqueduct, built by a Franciscan brother, Antonio Bermul, in 1527. In all the years of its existence Acámbaro has attained but 10,000 inhabitants, and there is nothing modern in the place except the railway station, which is also the hotel where travelers may find rooms and meals in a more modern style than at the one on the plaza. Located in the State of Guanajuato, Acámbaro is on the main line of the Mexican National Railroad, 178 miles from the City of Mexico, and at the junction of the western division of that road running to Morelia and Patzcuaro. The altitude is 6,084 feet above sea level.

Aguas Calientes
Ah-wns Cal-i-en-tees

The name of this city may not be difficult of remembrance. It may have impressed itself upon your mind, if you were a traveler in Mexico in the early days of railroads there, when some friend, better posted on the language, had coached you how to ask for something you did not get—for the hot water that never came. Aguas Calientes is a veritable city of hot water, and the citizens are in it the most of the time, as may be seen, even from the windows of the passing train.

The hot springs, that have made the city famous, are about a mile from the station, on the east side, and at the springs the first baths were established, curiously named after John the Baptist and the Apostles, with their names written over the doors, with the figures indicating the temperature of each particular Apostle. The ditch, which is the waste-way from the springs, runs alongside the avenue, shaded by immense trees, crossing the track at the station; here are the scenes that have been talked of, and written of, where the people come for their baths, and for their laundry, at one and the same time. At first thought, the idea does not seem effulgent with dazzling features—but the one of economy, both as to time and clothes, and the attendant laundry expenses, should not be overlooked. One need have but one suit, that can be washed and dried while you wait, the intervening time occupied by your own bath, with the added experience of every man his own washerwoman being fully realized.

The scene along this hot-water canal, and at the pools, is an interesting one—not always on the bills, as the theatre people say. Looking up from the station platform there is a long line of busy beings striving at a compliance with nature's first law. They are in all stages of beginning, continuing or completing the ablution or the laundry, with, as a writer says, no other protection than the blue sky of heaven and the Republic of Mexico; babies tied to a string paddle in the

warm waters, while their mothers tend strictly to the business in hand. The picture is brightened by the many-colored garments hung out to dry on the bushes that hereabouts do duty as clothes lines. A wide avenue with great over-hanging trees affords a shady drive, or horse-car ride, from the main plaza and the railway station to the baths at the head waters, or for a fine walk if you are equal to one of a mile. There are other baths in the city, near the station and near the plaza. These, with the delightful climate of Aguas Calientes, render the stop an attractive one.

Like the old-fashioned towns of Tennessee, these in Mexico have a public square, here called the plaza. The one at Aguas Calientes is most beautiful with its trees and flowers, winding walks, the towering monument over all; in the centre is the band-stand, where sweet music entertains the people in the evenings, and, on the four sides, fine buildings make this plaza a very attractive one. The monument seems unfinished, but it is, or was. Originally it was surmounted by a statue of Ferdinand VII., erected to commemorate the founding of the city, October 22, 1575. The Mexicans were wont to throw things down in times of war, even if they set them up again when the war was over. The statue was

AT AGUAS CALIENTES.

thrown down, but never replaced, and the monument is utilized to perpetuate other data in the city's history. There are a dozen other plazas, including the very beautiful Jardin de San Marcos and the Tivoli de Hidalgo, reached by the horse cars in a very short ride. Near the main plaza are the markets, always interesting in Mexico, and here especially so.

At any season the visit to Aguas Calientes may be made, but during *la fiesta de San Marcos* is the best time to see the city in all its glory. The feast com-mences April 23, and extends till May 10, when St. Mark takes possession of the town, and all business is given over to merriment and turkeys, this season being as disastrous to the latter as a November Thursday in "los Estados Unidos."

The public buildings are very fine, indeed. The Palacio de Gobierno, State House and Casa Municipal are on the main plaza, and adjoining it the Teatro Morelos. The Parian market is one square north of the plaza. On the Jardin de San Marcos is the Salon de Exposition and Scientific Institute. The parish church has some very fine pictures, painted by Andreas Lopez, in 1797, depicting the life of San Juan Nepomuceno. In the other churches are some really fine pictures, notably, an Adoration of the Magi, by José de Alzíbar, in 1775, and another canvas of his is in the Church of San Juan de Dios. Perhaps the best paintings of the

Stations of the Cross, in Mexico, are at the Church of the Encino, also by Andreas Lopez. In the Church of San Francisco are some good pictures, one representing scenes from the life of St. Francis, by Juan Correa, painted in 1681, another is the Vision of St. Anthony of Padua. Under the church are the bones and bodies of mummied monks. Aguas Calientes is an important city of 36,000 people, located on the main line of the Mexican Central Railway, 364 miles from the City of Mexico, at the junction of the Tampico Division, where the railway company has extensive shops and an employés' hospital. The altitude is 6,261 feet.

Amecameca
Ah-*may-ca-may-ca*

One may go out from the City of Mexico to the foot of the great volcanoes before breakfast, but not as the newly arrived tourist at Denver did, when he thought, from the marvelously clear atmosphere, that he would walk out to Pike's Peak. You may take an early train from San Lázaro station in the city, and arrive at Amecameca in less than two hours.

Amecameca lies on the plain just at the foot of Popocatepetl and Ixtaccihuatl, and for the near views and the ascent one must go to Ameca—the name has recently been shorn of one "meca." The train rounds a curve and comes to a stop just at the foot of the sacred mountain. A wooded hill lies on the right of the track, and just below the station is a stone-paved causeway, marked at intervals by the stations of the cross; it leads to the shrine on the top of the Sacro Monte. This causeway was built for the processions that, during the fiestas of Holy Week, pass between the shrine and the parish church. Once upon a time, very many years ago, there lived on this mountain a good, kind old man. He lived in a cave, and he was so gentle and kind that the birds came and sang to him, and the little animals of the forest played about his door, and followed close on his footsteps. He was Fray Martin de Valencia, one of the "Twelve Apostles" of Mexico, sent by Pope Adrian VI. as a missionary to the Indians, with the title of Vicar of New

ROAD UP SACRO MONTE, AMECAMECA.

Spain. The Fray was greatly beloved by the people, and when he died and was buried at Tlalmanalco, it is said that the Indians secretly removed and buried him in the cave where he had lived so happily. The cave is now a part of the shrine, in which is kept a very curious image of the Christ of the Holy Sepulchre. It is made of some very light material, probably the pith of the alder, or some like porous substance, that, although it is life-size, it weighs only about two or three pounds. The legend goes, that some men were conveying, on the backs of mules, some images intended for another part of the country, and that one of the mules strayed from the train, made his way up the side of the mountain, stopped in the entrance of the cave, and waited there for the Fray to return. This was taken to be as a token that the image was to abide there; it was placed in the cave and has remained there till this day—except, that on Ash Wednesday of each year it is taken, with great pomp and ceremony, from the shrine, and conveyed to the parish church, where it remains till Good Friday, and then returned to its abiding place.

This is the great fiesta of the year at Amecameca. The pilgrims come from all parts of the country to see what we call the Passion Play, just previous to the return of the image to the shrine. The enaction of the Crucifixion, by Indian actors, is curiously interesting, and when, after nightfall on Good Friday, the image starts on its return, a great multitude with torches follow up the stone steps of the causeway, some of the more devout crawling on their knees up the rough hillside, a scene wondrously weird and altogether indescribable; you look upon it with awe, and it is well that this is so, as any indication of contempt or amusement might be resented.

On the crest of the hill of Sacro Monte is the shrine of Guadalupe, where there are some fairly good pictures of the saints and of the Virgin of the Castle, by Villalobos. In the hard clay of the mountain are seen crude representations of the cross, and on the trees and bushes are little pieces of the dress of the pilgrims, hairs from their heads, or some other token of their devotion left there for *buena fortuna*. From the crest of the hill at Guadalupe is the finest view of the volcanoes, the plain and city. The parish church of Nuestra Señora de la Asuncion and San Sebastian is on the plaza and near the railway station, founded by the Dominicans, in 1547. It is quite an extensive building, with a mutilated figure of San Sebastian over the entrance, said mutilation resulting from the earthquake of 1884, which also destroyed the tower of San Juan and furnished material for the building of the Casa Municipal, on the Plaza Mayor.

Adjoining the church is an abandoned chapel, and between them an open court filled with old sepulchres, as is the church yard. Over the door of this Capilla de la Santa Escuela is a glazed tile, with an inscription to Yturbide, the liberator, asking the prayers of the people for the repose of his soul. In the eastern part of the town is the little chapel of the Rosario, with some excellently carved doors, altars and images of Santa Ana and San José.

To ascend the volcanoes of Popocatepetl you must come to Amecameca. The ascent is attended with more fatigue than danger. It takes three days to accomplish it; the first is going from Amecameca to the *rancho* of the owners of the mountain; the second from the *rancho* to the crater and return; and the third by the return to the plain. Permission must be obtained from the owner in the City of Mexico, guides at Amecameca, good warm clothing and a plentiful supply for the inner man must be taken along. The ascent is slow, as the guides must go ahead with ropes, but the descent takes less time; you sit down on a mat of rushes and w-h-s-h-t! you are back at the *rancho*—at least that's the way the sulphur miners in the crater go and return from work.

You may have the grandest view of the world, and a toboggan slide which, if it ends in your favor, you will never forget, and if it ends adversely for you, your friends will remember it, and you will have the highest and whitest monument on earth for them to point to; you would gain a monument which might not be accorded you if you had not made the ascent, but really there is more of discomfort than danger.

Amecameca is on the Interoceanic Railway, twenty-five miles from the City of Mexico, and has a population of 12,000 people.

The elevation is 6,261 feet above the sea.

There are no horse cars or carriages and none are needed; all that is here to be seen may be reached on foot, with no tiring distances.

HAPEL ON THE SACRED MOUNTAIN, AMECAMECA.

Catorce
Kah-tor-see

Nearly every town in Mexico has a name that may be translated to mean something. *Catorce* means, in the Spanish language, *fourteen*. It is a mining town; the mines were discovered by a band of bandits, fourteen in number, and for want of a better name it was called the Real de Catorce. Silver was discovered here about the year 1780, and the district at once took rank among the most important in Mexico. Ore of fabulous richness was found, and the records show that for more than thirty years, commencing with 1790, the value of the output amounted to over three million dollars annually. Here are hundreds of mines and miles of shafting and tunneling. The drainage tunnel of one mine alone, the San Agustin, extends into the mountain for more than a mile and a half, and was excavated at a cost of a million and a half dollars. For its entire length a tramway has been constructed which is operated by mule power. Catorce should be one of the very interesting places in Mexico to the tourist. Here are found the customs of Mexico in their purity, unaffected by the

CATORCE.

influence of the stranger. Difficult of access, the town can only be reached by horseback, or on foot. The ride up the mountains to the town is something, once accomplished, always to be remembered, partly from its element of personal peril, but more because of the beauty of the landscape encountered at every turn. Glancing down as you near your journey's end, you catch the gleam of the white walls of the town of Los Catorce outlined against the green of the mountain side. Thousands of feet below shimmer the waters of a mountain stream. The shifting coloring of the mountains, as light and shade chase each other over their ragged expanse, the browns and greens of the valley far below, and the hills in the hazy distance, are exceedingly beautiful. The Real de Catorce is built on the side of a ravine near the top of the range, and has a varying population of from 8,000 to 20,000, as the mines are paying poorly or well. Here are found all varieties of silver ore, from carbonate to refractory ore, assaying $15,000 to the ton. Catorce has a fine church, richly decorated, and a pretty plaza, the only level spot in the place. To use a railroad phrase, it is a combination of a cut and a fill, so that to tumble into it on one side or out on the other would be extremely disastrous. The streets are neatly paved, and run up and down hill, many of them at an angle of forty-five degrees.

The story of the wheels or, rather, the no-wheels, is a true one, literally, with the single exception in the conveying (was about to say "carting," but conveying is better), a carriage on burros to the city by a rich mine owner, but was abandoned; the wheels would roll one way easily enough, but it was difficult to get back to the starting point, and the innovation of wheels at Catorce was not accomplished.

Catorce may be reached by horses or burro-back from the station of the same name, on the Mexican National Railroad, 471 miles from the City of Mexico, or from Vanegas by a branch road that runs within two miles of the city.

Celaya It was more than three hundred years ago that the fame of the
See-*li-ya* beautiful Laja Valley came to the ears of the Spanish king, and through his Viceroy, Don Martin Enriquez de Alamanza, a company of sixteen married men and their wives, and seventeen young bachelors, was sent north to spy out the land and to build a town in the valley. Just why this particular combination of married men and bachelors was chosen, probably only Don Martin

AT THE HACIENDA.

ever knew, and the chronicler sayeth not. By these the city of Celaya was founded, October 12th, 1570, under the name of *Zelaya*, which, in the Biscayan tongue, means "level land," but it was not until nearly a hundred years later, October 20th, 1655, that Philip IV. decreed it a city, and not till three years later that the citizens heard of their metropolitan good fortune.

Since its founding Celaya has not figured greatly in the country's history. Built in a peaceful valley, its ways have been the ways of peace, and, although located on the main highways of the country, the city has escaped the rigors, and I doubt very much if its people heard much more than the rumors of wars. If you come from the north or the south, the east or the west, you may see the towers of Celaya from afar off, across the broad plains, as you may see a ship coming from sea; as the sails are seen first, the rounded domes come to view above the trees, the towers of the Church of Our Lady of Carmen or of San Agustin. One of the most beautiful in this land of churches, is the Church of Our Lady of Carmen in Celaya. It is in form a Latin cross, 220 feet long and fifty-five feet wide, by sixty-nine feet high. Not an old church, as churches go in Mexico, this one was commenced in 1803, and completed in 1807. The magnificent adornment, the frescoes and the superb paintings were by Eduardo Tresguerras, a native of Celaya, and an artist of renown, combining a superior knowledge of painting, sculpture and architecture in all his work. One of his famous paintings is of Our Lady of Carmen, in the chapel of the Last Judgment, where are, also, some portraits of himself as a young and old man. Another notable picture is the Triumph of Mary, by Nicolas Rodriguez Juarez. This picture is much older than the others, having been painted in 1695; it was rescued from the fire which destroyed the old Church of Carmen.

The Church of San Francisco, in the midst of a group of churches and chapels, was founded in 1570. Only the façade and dome of the original building remain; the other parts were erected in 1715, and the altars, the exquisite work of Tresguerras, were added in the early part of this century. The parish church and Tercer Orden are of the Franciscan group, both built in the early part of the seventeenth century. In the little chapel of Nuestra Señora de los Dolores is the tomb of this great artist architect, built, also, by his hand. The Church of San Agustin, a short distance from the San Franciscan group, was built in 1603–10; the tower is by Tresguerras. This wonderful man, whose handiwork is in every Celayan church, with such lines of exquisite art, was born in Celaya, May 13, 1765, and died there August 3, 1833. He left, in his own work, such monuments as might never have been erected to his fragrant memory.

Celaya, in the midst of a most fertile agricultural district, is also a manufacturing city of carpets and woolens, calicoes, rebosos, soaps and *dulces*; the *dulces* of Celaya are famous the country over. *Dulces* are sweet-meats, made from fruits and from milk; what bon-bons are to the French and candies are to the American sweeth-tooth, the *dulces* are to the Mexican, and Celaya is where they make them to the queen's taste, so to speak. The sale of *dulces* is not confined to the dulceria. The populace meet you at the train with boxes of *dulces*, as those of the surrounding country bring strawberries and opals to the passing trains, and lie in wait for the unsuspecting traveler—literally lie in wait, for no matter what the hour of arrival may be, the venders are there. They lie in their beds on the roadside and wait for the trains. They may not be officially notified of a change of schedule or of a delayed train, but that doesn't make any difference; they know it has to come some time and having nothing else to do, they just wait. Naturally disgusted by these waits, the prices when the train stops are bullish, but the bears get the best of it before it leaves, and when the conductor cries "vamanos!" you can buy the entire visible supply for a quarter.

The theatre, the portales, the baths and the markets are to be visited, and, altogether, Celaya is one of the places where the lover of the beautiful will wish to linger. The city, in the State of Guanajuato, is located, commercially, to great advantage, at the crossing of the Mexican Central and Mexican National Railways, 182 miles from the City of Mexico, at an altitude of 5,816 feet above the sea, and has a population of 22,000. Horse cars run from both stations to the main plaza in the center of city, and they are far more comfortable than the hacks that rumble over the stony streets.

Chihuahua
Che-wow-wn

When we come down from the Grand River of the North at El Paso, and have traveled a lonely night across the chaparral-covered plains, the appetite of novelty has been whetted by the little bit of Mexico, gleaned in the glances from the windows, as the train passed through Juarez City, and the first morning in Mexico is waked up to with the delights of anticipation that are rarely disappointing in this land of eternal sunshine. And, unless you are a very early riser, Chihuahua will present the first picture of a panorama that must compare with any, no matter in what lands your travels may have been.

. Chihuahua is an old city, as most Mexican cities are; it was founded in 1539, by Diego de Ybarra. The ancient name was Taraumara, later San Felipe el Real, and then Chihuahua, meaning a "place where things are made," and not, particularly, a place of small dogs, as popularly supposed in the average tourist idea, though the pronunciation of the latter syllables might indicate that, rather than the actual meaning of the name.

The pronouncing of Mexican names seems an insurmountable difficulty at first, but the newest traveler soon grows familiar with them, and rolls them off as glibly as a native, and in a little while begins to tell how he used to pronounce Chihuahua and Jimenez—just as they are spelled—but now can say Che-wow-wa, in a tone of voice that would make a small dog, with a soft spot in its head, prick up its ears, as at a sound from home.

The fame of the Chihuahua dogs has gone abroad throughout the land, and the native has bulled the market accordingly; the demand largely exceeds the supply. The dogs are noted, primarily, for their diminutive size, sharpness of nose and length of toe nails; but if they possess any further attribute, the fact has not been reported. It has been suggested that the soft place on the head of the genuine article has been left for an after injection of brains. I speak thus, firstly, of dogs, because it is probable that the first man to greet you, when you get off the train at Chihuahua, will have one under his arm.

The train, as it comes from the north, or the south, comes from behind high, intervening hills, so there is no view of the city until it stops at the station. The city is on the west side of the track, and, as the train passes over the barranca, between the shops and the station, there is a good view of the town, with the high towers of the Church of San Francisco standing out against the western sky.

Few Mexican towns are located conveniently near the railway stations, and Chihuahua is not an exception; street cars there are, and hacks, for all parts of the city. The car line from the station passes the Mint, State Capitol, Hidalgo Statue, the plaza, Church of San Francisco, the market, the hotels and on through the old paseo to the Santuario de Guadalupe; the fare, six cents, takes you to nearly all the places of interest. A carriage must be taken for the new paseo and alameda, and the fine views from the hill in the south part of the city, for which the prices vary according to the style of turnout, from one to two dollars an hour, with a twenty-five cent fare for short distance rides, as from the station to the plaza.

Being near the border, Chihuahua is a much Americanized town, and there are many fine buildings, of a semi-Mexican-American style of architecture, on the principal streets, around the plaza and along the new paseo and alameda. The State Palace is a handsome new edifice, on the street leading from the station; in the rear is a plazuela, with a fine monument and statue of Hidalgo on the spot where he was executed, July 31, 1811, and his compatriots, Allende, Aldama and Jimenez, on June 26, of the same year.

Just opposite the palace, in an old building, formerly the Hospital Real, is the Mint; in one of the rooms of the square tower, over the entrance, the patriots were confined previous to their execution. The manufac-

MONUMENT OF HIDALGO, CHIHUAHUA.

ture of money in the mint is not as crude as the old house seems to be; the dollars drop from the stamps, sixty every minute, while the wheels turn. The silver for the most part comes from the mine of Santa Eulalia, near the city, one of the richest in the country, and one of the oldest. A tribute, levied by the clergy, in the early days, of twenty-five cents on each pound of silver, produced $800,000 for the building of the parish chuch.

The Church of San Francisco, erroneously called the cathedral, is the parish church that cost so much money and time to build. It was commenced in 1717, and not completed till 1789. It is said that an inclined plane of earth was raised against the walls during their building, on which the material was carried up, and by the time the towers were finished the plane extended beyond the plaza. The church faces the plaza and occupies such a position that the towers can be seen from all parts of the city. The façade is elaborately ornamented; there are thirteen statues of San Francisco and the twelve apostles, and under the arches of the dome are basso-relievos of the fathers of the church. A broken bell is shown in one of the towers, as having been pierced by a cannon ball fired by the French during the bombardment of the city in 1866. The Church of the Compañia was founded by the Jesuits, under Don Manuel de Santa Cruz, in 1717. Another church is that of San Felipe Neri, also the Santuario de Nuestra Señora de Guadalupe, at the extreme west side of the city, just beyond the terminus of the horse-car line, at the end of the old paseo, where there is a remarkable image of San Ygnacio Loyola.

Just beyond the sanctuary of Guadalupe, beyond the top of the hill, is the old aqueduct of the city's water supply, a continuous line of stone arches, about four miles long, built a hundred years ago, but in a fine state of preservation. Near here are, also, the principal baths of the city. The old paseo, or alameda, is much neglected, but the new one is too modern to be particularly interesting, except for the fine views of the city and the surrounding mountains ; El Coronel was so called from the execution of a revolutionary colonel at that point.

Chihuahua was for years the market for all northern Mexico, the trading trains traveling between that city and Santa Fé. Col. Doniphan, of the United States army, occupied the city in 1847, and afterwards made the famous march to the south and joined Gen. Taylor.

Chihuahua, the capital of the State of Chihuahua, is on the Mexican Central Railway, 999 miles from the City of Mexico, and has an elevation of 4,633 feet. The population is 20,000.

Córdoba
Cord-ova
To go to Córdoba means to go to the tropics; indeed, the little city is just on the border of the *tierra caliente*, as the Mexicans call the hot country, in the foot-hills of the mountain ranges, with an elevation that offers a comparative immunity from the malarial fevers of the lowlands. In fact the location of the town was made with the idea of a place of refuge from the plains below, when it was founded, April 18, 1618, under an order from the then viceroy, Don Diego Fernandez de Córdoba, who knew the fertility of the valley of the Rio Seco, and chose the hill of Xitango as the site of the city to be called by his name.

The tropical scenes have become familiar on the ride hither; the train stops at a station, under palm trees, and the horse-car ride, uptown, is through coffee groves and bananas, with gardens everywhere, with every fruit that ripens under the tropic sun, oranges, lemons, guavas, pineapples, chirimoyas and granaditas. After this ride through the woods and the gardens, you come to the narrow streets, where the low houses, roofed with red tiles, have long projecting eaves that shade the narrower sidewalks—picturesque to a degree. The plaza and the market may be something like the other towns, but there is the tropic charm that the others do not possess. Within a square of the market there is one of the most beautiful gardens in the world. It is a tangled mass of fruits and flowers overhanging winding walks, with fountains, here and there, and pagodas for resting places.

The churches are San Antonio, founded in 1686, and San Hipólito, in 1793; the latter was also a convent and hospital. On the plaza is shown a house where Maximilian stopped over night on his way to the capital, and another where was

STREET AND CHURCH, CORDOBA.

signed, by Yturbide and the Viceroy O'Donoju, the treaty acknowledging the Independence of Mexico.

Sunday is a great day in Córdoba, when the country folk come to town from Amatlan, and other villages roundabout, not in silk attire, but in the gaudiest cotton, in all the colors of the rainbow and in the plumage of the birds of their primeval forests; the trimmings are on the whitest of white cotton—beads of coral, laces of their own handiwork and ornaments of silver, till they are a sight to see.

Córdoba, in the State of Vera Cruz, has about 7,000 people, is located on the Mexican Railway, 198 miles from the City of Mexico, at an elevation of 2,713 feet above the Gulf at Vera Cruz.

Cuautla Long before the train arrives at Cuautla, the place where the city
Kwout-la lies may be pointed out, but for its surrounding, and almost over-covering of green trees, it can not be seen, save the white spot of tower gleaming in the sunshine. Down where the sugar cane grows, on the southern slope of the hills that are beyond the volcanoes, is the very pretty little town, in the midst of fertile fields and luxuriant gardens of fruits and flowers, a very picture of tropical beauty. In the approach to the town the train backs in on a Y and comes to a stop in the quaintest railway station that ever was. To what base uses may we come! This railway station was once a convent and church; the tower and bells are still there, and it may be that the confessional is the ticket office and the altar a desk for way-bills; the nave is a storage-room for freights, and where was

the convent-yard now resounds with the locomotive's whistle.   Just outside this church-station is the prettiest plaza imaginable, with playing fountains of clear water under the trees that shade the streets and the park, where there is a music-stand, seats and promenades for the people, and on the opposite side a very good hotel indeed, not good alone for Mexico, but good for a town of Cuautla's size anywhere, with a garden of fruits that will justify any description.

The streets of Cuautla run at right angles, with their low adobe houses, but presently they merge into shady lanes, hedged with cactus, behind which are thatched huts of reeds and rushes almost hidden by the bananas and the orange and lemon trees and trailing vines and bowers.   These are Cuautla's chief charms, and amply repay the rambles of a day's visit.   Everywhere is running water, through the streets and roads, in the gardens and parks, along the railroad track and through the fields.   These native engineers have taken the river from its bed, made its waters run where they willed, till the land blossoms as the rose.

A horseback, or a ride by burros, may be made to the sulphur baths, just east of the town, and to the old stone bridge over the Rio Xuchitengo, or to the hacienda of Coahuixtla, either of which is well worth the ride—the baths of fine medicinal qualities, the antiquity of the massive bridge, or the charming novelty of hacienda life in the lowlands.

Cuautla was a city when Cortez came and fell into his possession. The date of the Spanish city is from 1605. After the war for Independence the city

AT CUAUTLA.

received the surname of Morelos, and is now called Cuautla-Morelos, in honor of General Morelos, who so heroically defended it against the Royalist forces under General Calleja, who laid siege February 19, 1812, and so completely drew his lines about the place that it was impossible to get in or out.   There was more or less fighting for nearly three months, till Morelos was forced to evacuate, which he did effectually, but not until he was starved out. It is said that, during the siege, food was so scarce that cats were sold for six dollars, and rats and lizards for one and two dollars.

The parish Church of Santiago was founded in 1605, and the Church of San Diego furnishes the Interoceanic with the oldest railway station in the world, dating from the seventeenth century. There are chapels, shrines and churches in the town, of various dates and names, but they are not so numerous in the lowlands as they are up in the hill country.

The sugar industry may be further investigated by a stop at the great Hacienda de Santa Ynez, on the line of the railway, three miles west of Cuautla. The manager is an affable and courteous gentleman, and most hospitable withal. Cuautla is in the State of Morelos, on the Interoceanic Railway, 85 miles from the City of Mexico, at an elevation of 3,556 feet above the level of the sea. The population is 12,000.

Cuernavaca
Kwer-na-vaca

At this writing Cuernavaca is not a railroad town, but before this edition is exhausted the old-time city may have its echoes wakened by the roll of the wheels and ring of the bell of the engine. However, there is that, at that favorite home of Cortéz and of Maximilian, that is worth all the going there, either by *diligencia*, from the terminus of the Mexico, Cuernavaca & Pacific Railway until that road is completed to the town, or by

PALACE OF CORTEZ, CUERNAVACA.

horses from Yautepec, on the Interoceanic Railway, in four hours. The scenery is wonderfully grand; the ascent from the valley of Mexico is with a winding, twisting track from the plains to the mountain, and the view looking back over the cities of the plain, the lakes, the volcanoes and lesser mountains makes a picture that is not easily described. The climb continues till an altitude of 10,000 feet is attained at La Guarda, then a little further on, at La Cruz del Marques, the descent commences and continues on to Cuernavaca. The grand views of mountain and valley scenery are in endless variety and without cessation throughout the journey.

The old Indian name, Quauhnahuac, has a more impressive meaning, "where the eagle stops," than the Spanish word Cuernavaca, "cow-horn." But it has the advantage in pronunciation, probably, at least after you once know how to call either one of them. The high headland, between the deep barrancas, would seem to give origin to the ancient name, anyhow it does give to the town a most picturesque and delightful location. The mountain streams have been changed in their courses, and through reservoirs, sent through the streets and gardens, till the town is one vast garden in itself, the overhanging trees almost hide the houses.

The Calle Nacional is the principal street, and the Plaza Mayor, of course, the plaza of the town. The State Capitol is in a building that was once the palace of Cortéz, and here, in this place, the conqueror rested before his advance on the City of Mexico, and here the great adventurer spent some of the last years of his life, and when you have seen it you will not wonder at his choice.

There were millionaires in those days, who were only poor boys, just as in these days and this country, and Cuernavaca points with pride to the house where José de la Borda lived. The native will tell you of his millions made in mining; the amount, from forty to fifty millions, taken from mines at Tlalpujahua, Tasco and Zacatecas. You will be shown the garden of fruits and flowers, with terraced slopes, cascades and fountains that cost a million, and it may have cost more, for it is very beautiful, indeed. And the native will tell you of the big church at Tasco, where Don José placed another million.

The Church of San Francisco was also a convent, in the old days, when convents were permitted in Mexico, and was founded in 1529. It is more a group of churches and chapels, with connecting roofs and walls ; the tower contains a clock that was once in the cathedral of Segovia, presented to Cortéz by Charles V. of Spain. Asuncion is the parish church ; the others are San Pedro, Tercer Orden and Guadalupe, the latter built by de la Borda; Guadalupe is in the suburbs of the city.

The whole country roundabout is full of interest, and it will take some days and horses to do the region as it should be. There are the waterfalls in the Tlaltenango, Amanalco and San Antonio ravines. In the village of San Antonio, reached over a good road, are some potteries and a lake of great beauty ; here also is another house of Cortéz, near it a rock with some pre-historic carvings. On a neighboring hill is a lizard in stone, nearly nine feet long, and about three miles farther to the south is the hill Quauhtetl—"the stone eagle," an eagle in stone that measures three feet from tip to tip. It is eighteen miles to the ruins of Xochicalco, which are intensely interesting and in every way worth the ride. One of the buildings, that may have been a temple, measures seventy-five feet long by sixty-eight feet wide, built of cut stone. Forty-five miles from Cuernavaca are the wonderful caves of Cacahuamilpa, some of the most famous in Mexico. Some of the sugar plantations have old-time buildings, erected two centuries or more ago, notably on the Hacienda de Temisco; another hacienda is that of Atlacomulco, where all the fruits of the tropics may be seen in the fields and gardens.

Cuernavaca is the capital of the State of Morelos, and is reached by trains of the Mexico, Cuernavaca & Pacific R. R., fifty miles from the City of Mexico; elevation, 4,960; population, 13,000.

Durango It may be called an Iron City, to follow the simile of the Silver
Doo-rang-o City as applied to some of the others of Mexico, though Durango has of silver enough to entitle her to some claim in that direction also; her best boast is in the baser metal. Within the corporate limits of the city of Durango there is iron enough to supply the world for three hundred years, and yet, before the railroad was completed to the city, manufactured with wooden machinery and water power, the products of the wonderful iron mountain of Durango sold for thirty-five cents a pound, and if the mountain could be sold at that rate it would exhaust the treasures of the universe to pay for it ; it is almost solid iron, the ore averaging from 75 to 90 per cent. of pure metal. The iron mountain is just north of the railway station, and only about half a mile distant. A cavalier in Cortéz army, Señor Mercado, was induced to come here by the report of a mountain of silver, but only found iron. The mountain is called Cerro Mercado in his honor.

Durango is a city, spread out on a plain, with its streets, for the most part, running at right angles, with low, but subtantial buildings on either side, with patios filled with flowers and fountains. Here and there are pretty plazas and plazuelas, with other fountains, and green trees galore. The Plaza Mayor is a garden, surrounded on its four sides by fine buildings of two to three floors, the State House being one of them, and one of the finest in Mexico ; the others are stores and cafés. In the center is the artistic pagoda that compares so favorably with the prosaic "band-stand" of the United States. These of Mexico are always architecturally artistic, and always pretty, while ours are painfully and politically plain. The Mexican has built his with an eye to harmony with the music that is to be beneath its bended roof. The American has built his with an eye to the hominy that is to be bought with the net results of his contract. The walks are paved, and hedged about by flowering shrubs, native in name and to the land they grow in, though there are also roses and lilies. In this plaza the people most do congregate in the evenings, to promenade and to hear the music of the band. And here, again, the Mexican scores another against us, the music being furnished by the Government, the bands are under pay of the people and they must play for the people; there are stated days of the week for music, and at least twice of every week in the year the bands play. Here, in our country, we must pay for a seat to hear the Marine Band, or go to some dress parade of some regiment or battalion before we can hear the music we have paid for, or if the band is induced outside the barracks it is for an extra stipend that the players are not entitled to.

Near the northwest corner of Plaza Mayor is a pretty little plazuela, that is in the courtyard of a church and ancient convent, a most picturesque little nook where only the electric light is younger than a century or two. Two or three squares west is the beautiful alameda and the paseo, with their great big trees and the picturesque bridge across the little *rio*. At the end of the paseo, toward the north, is the public wash place, where there are scores of *lavanderas* to be

A LONE WORSHIPER, CHURCH INTERIOR, DURANGO.

seen washing clothes in a curiously arranged laundry of stone basins, through which there is running water. All of the pretty places are not in the city. Near it, within two or three leagues, are some of the most delightful *jardins* in the world; these are not public gardens, however, but the property of private citizens, and admission is only by permission.

Two squares east of the main plaza is the very interesting market, and all in this district are the stores that in their stocks and seeming activity are a surprise, but it is to be remembered that Durango was a great city for three hundred years before the railroad came, and was a market of supply for a very large territory of interior country. There is little to see of the city residences, except a glimpse of the patios through the grated archways in the high surrounding walls, but there is sufficient in this to tell of their exceeding beauty of interior, whatever the uninviting exterior may be. It is thus of the hotels, also. A look into these of Durango is satisfying as to the comforts within; the tables, with snowy covers, are either in the shaded patios or beneath the arched and pillared portales.

Three hundred and fifty years ago, the spot where Durango now is, was a ranch, and where now is the corner of Calles Principal and Teresas, was a large tree, under which an altar was built, and the first mass was said. Afterwards a little church was built at the corner of Calle Constitucion and Calle Mayor; this has been rebuilt, but many of the original timbers remain. The ranchero who owned the lands gave lots to settlers to increase the defense against the Indians. Later a mine was discovered on his lands, his wealth increased fabulously, and a precentage of the output was levied for the building of the Cathedral. Afterwards he built the house now used as the Governor's Palace, and the adjoining theatre, all of stone, and the second theatre built in Mexico. He sent as a present to the King of Spain $2,000,000, asking permission to build galleries and portales of silver around his home. This was refused as a privilege pertaining to royalty only. He put up porches of wood, but on the occasion of a christening in his family he paved the street from his house to the church with silver bricks. The descendants of this Crœsus live in Durango to-day, but they do not use silver as a pavement.

AN ODD CORNER IN DURANGO.

The Cathedral was commenced in the year 1695, by Bishop Garcia de Legaspi, and the first public service was held in 1715, at which time was completed the thirteen arches and one tower. The second tower and the other departments annexed to the temple, as they exist to-day, were not completed until 1844, under the direction of Señor Zubiria. The entire work is of the Tuscan order of architecture. In the crypt are deposited the remains of eleven of the twenty-four bishops of Durango. During the latter part of the last century a terrible fire destroyed all the archives and antiquities, and the political revolts of 1854 to 1860 finished all the books and modern documents. The Church of San Francisco is the oldest of all the Durango churches, the first foundations having been laid, on this spot, in 1556; and in that year was established the first Spanish settlement, under Fray Diego de la Cadena. This first temple was solemnly blessed in 1563, on the reception of the mandates from the Viceroy, Don Luis de Velasco, at the hands of Captain Alonso Pacheco. The Church of San Agustin was founded in 1626, by the first Bishop of Durango, Fray Gonzalo de Hermosillo, a *religioso* of the order of San Agustin. In this church is a very notable image of Jesus, the Nazarene, that was brought from Spain in 1673, to which tradition attributes an infinity of miracles. Santa Ana is a very modern foundation for Mexico; it was commenced in 1777 and completed during the episcopacy of Don Francisco Javier Olivares in 1809. El Colegio was erected by the Jesuits in 1684 as a part of the college they directed until 1720, the year in which was founded a seminary in the same building. This church opened to the public in 1776, when the Parroquia was transferred here from the cathedral. El Santuario de Guadalupe was built in 1714 by the 12th Bishop of Durango, Don Pedro Tapiz; the interior was renewed in 1885. Analco, one of the primitive churches, was founded by the first Spanish settlers, in 1560, in the only place inhabited by the Indians who lived in this valley. The ruins of this church were reconstructed, in 1862, by Don Gerónimo Silva. San Juan de Dios was founded as a hospital, in 1770. On a high hill overlooking the city, and which may be seen for miles before you reach the city, and from every part of it when you arrive there, is the old church of Los Remedios, a very ancient foundation, said by some to antedate the Cathedral. Every pilgrim who will visit this church on the 8th of September of each year subtracts seven years from his stay in purgatory.

THE START FOR THE BARRANCA, GUADALAJARA.

There is nothing new under the sun in Durango, except the very modern railway station, prettily built, of stone, for use both as a passenger station and residence of the agent. It is surrounded by a pretty lawn, shaded by young trees, a piece of another country, it seems, transported here, and strangely in contrast with the very antique surroundings. There is a general freight depot, but each of the large dealers and mine owners has a freight house of his own, with side tracks, etc. Horse cars run from the station to the plaza and the hotels, and throughout the city. Very good carriages may be hired for places not reached by the cars. Durango is the capital of the State of the same name, located on the main line of Mexican International Railroad, 155 miles from Torreon, the junction with the Mexican Central Railway, 706 miles from the City of Mexico. The population is 35,000; altitude, 6,316 feet.

Guadalajara Early in the sixteenth century an expedition, under the cruel
Wahd-tha-la-*har*-a and treacherous Nuño de Beltran Guzman, started to the northwest, and proceeded as far as the boundaries of the present State of Jalisco; and, in the year 1530, the band under Juan de Oñate founded a city under the name of Villa del Espiritu Santo de Guadalajara, not, however, on the site of the present city, and the one chosen soon proved to be undesirable. Another, in the Tlalcotlan Valley, was selected, and the settlement moved there. This location was as bad as the first, and, in the absence of Guzman, who, on account of his atrocities, had been recalled to Spain, a third selection was made, this time by the people themselves, in the beautiful valley called by the Indians Atemaxac, and there was founded, in 1541, the present city of Guadalajara, which has become the cleanest, brightest, and most delightful city in all the regions round-about. There

is always a desire on the part of the traveler to proceed to the Capital, to the City of Mexico, and whatever may retard his going there at once seems to him to defer a pleasure. That may be, but once in the Capital, and having done its more metropolitan attractions, it is easier to see the charms of other cities, and if a well-worn and time-honored policy of "save the best for the last," were to be carried out, the Capital would be nearer the first, and Guadalajara very near indeed to the end of the string. It is one of the most charming, most fascinating places in the world, in every way. It is beautifully located; the climate is superb, every day being one of springtime; the streets are clean as a floor that is swept; the parks and plazas are ever green with pretty trees, and brightened with lovely flowers, that bloom in December as in June. Guadalajara may well be written down as Mexico's famous city. Every street and plaza has some novel attraction, its suburbs some novelty not found elsewhere, and in the near neighborhood such views of lake, cascade and cañon beauties as are not surpassed in the world.

SAN JOSE, GUADALAJARA.

The one single objection to the city is, that it has been repaired, renovated and repainted—and this latter, covering up the wrinkles of age with fresh color, is to be deprecated, on any pretext—but, in reality, none of this detracts from the pleasure of a visit. Long before the train arrives at the station, the towers of the Cathedral can be seen, and the outlines of the city discerned. The view is from the windows on the right-hand side of the cars. Guadalajara lies in the midst of a plain—on three sides rising in terraces to the mountains that almost surround it, and on the west side is the jumping-off place to the *tierra caliente* where the mountains seem to cease, and the plain and sky come together.

The train does not stop on the outskirts, as at most places in Mexico, but comes to a station in the city, near the garden of San Francisco, and very near the principal plaza. The streets run at right angles, intersecting the parks and plazas, of which there are a score or more, with fourteen portales that cover the sidewalks for many squares, fourteen bridges, five theatres, that of Degollado being the largest on the continent, except, perhaps, the Metropolitan Opera House, in New York, or the Auditorium, of Chicago. There are five tiers of seats, stalls and boxes, and the decorations are very handsome indeed. The Degollado was opened in 1866, by the famous Mexican cantatrice, Peralta. The other theatres are the Apollo, Principal and the Circo de Progreso. There are twenty-five baths, twenty-three restaurants, and twenty-eight hotels, and when it is remembered that this city did not have a railroad till 1888, these statistics have more import.

The public buildings, the Cathedral, Governor's Palace, the Mint, Degollado Theatre, and the State Capitol of Jalisco are magnificent specimens of Mexican architecture not expected in this far-away place. The Paseo is a beautiful drive on both sides of the Rio San Juan de Dios, which runs northward in the eastern part of the city; the drive extends from the Alameda to the southern boundary.

Besides the Alameda the principal parks are the Plaza de Armas, Jardin Botanico, Parque Alcade, and the Calzada de San Pedro, beautifully adorned with tropical trees and ever-blooming flowers.

As to churches, the Cathedral is a magnificent structure. The original foundation was laid in 1548, in a hut thatched with straw. The present building was commenced in 1561, the corner stone was laid ten years later, on July 31st, by Bishop Ayola, and the building was completed in 1618; the towers were thrown down by the earthquake of 1818. The clock between the towers was also injured by the earthquake. The interior is rich in decorations and paintings; one, the Assumption, by Murillo, is especially fine, and there are others too numerous to attempt description. The two towers are wholly unlike any others in Mexico, but more like the steeples of the churches of this country. In one of them is the "*Campanita del Correo*," literally, the little bell of the courier, or post, which rang only in announcement of some event of importance. Another bell, called San Clemente, was, in former times, rung during a thunder storm, to ward off the lightning. An adjunct to the Cathedral is the Sagrario, a comparatively new structure, commenced in 1808 and completed in 1843.

The other churches are San Francisco, San Agustin, San Felipe, La Compañía, Guadalupe, Mexicaltzingo, Jesus Maria, Capuchinas, Santa Teresa, Santa Maria, La Merced, Santa Monica, El Carmen, San Jose de Analco, San Sebastian de Analco, La Parroqua de Jesus, San Juan de Dios, Aranzázu, La Soledad, San Diego, Belen, La Concepcion, La Trinidad y la Parroqua del Pilar, with others in course of construction.

One of the most famous institutions of Guadalajara is the Hospicio, and one of the most notable in the world. It is a handsome building of white stone, covering an entire square, and containing twenty-three patios, or courts, with fountains and flowers. It is not a hospital, as popularly supposed, but a home for the poor of all ages, from the baby in the cradle to old men and women bent with their infirmities. The institution is admirably managed, under authority of the State of Jalisco. Children are taught all that may be learned in schools, and as they grow older they learn some useful occupation in the arts and sciences, and the product of their labor is offered for sale, in support of the Hospicio, among which are some of the most exquisite embroideries and laces, made by the girls. Music, painting and calisthenics are a part of the tuition, while the more practical matters of life involve serious attention. No permit of entrance is required. You will be met at the gate by one of the Sisters in charge, and placed under the guidance of an attendant, who will show you one of the most interesting places you may find in all your travels.

The towers seen from the right-hand windows of the cars, on the approach to Guadalajara, are at San Pedro, a suburb of Guadalajara. The village is about two leagues east of the city, reached by horse cars that start from near the northeast corner of the main plaza, and run over a very picturesque road, the Calzada de San Pedro, shaded by large trees and ends in a very pretty plaza. The wealthier class of Gaudalajara have their summer residences at San Pedro, and some of their houses are very beautiful indeed. The famous Gaudalajara ware, that is known the world over, is from the potteries of San Pedro, and at San Pedro only is it absolutely certain to be able to get the genuine. It is sold at greatly reduced prices from those asked in the curiosity stores in the city, where there is no certainty of genuineness. If you will walk two squares east on the street that leads from the southeast corner of the plaza of San Pedro, turn down to the right half a square, you will come to a low adobe house on the left side of the street. The latch string is on the outside, and a warm welcome within its doors from Juan Panduro, the Indian sculptor, who will show and sell samples of his exquisite handiwork, or, rather, their handiwork, for there are two artists — father and son; and if you desire a bust or statuette of yourself of life-like likeness, it may be modeled while you wait, afterwards baked and sent to your hotel, or the artists will call at the hotel and do the modeling in your room.

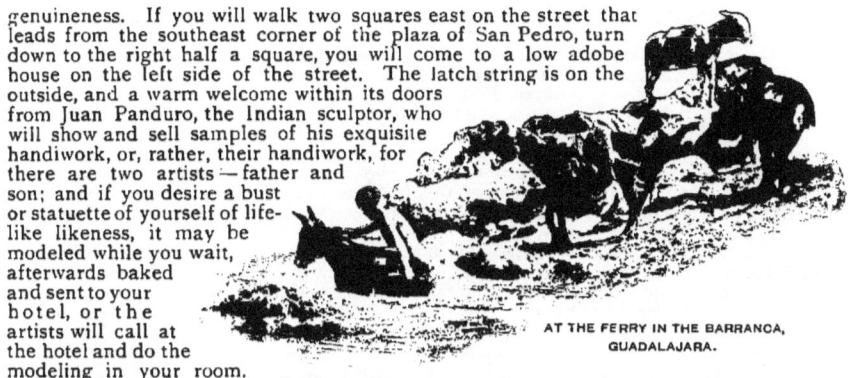

AT THE FERRY IN THE BARRANCA, GUADALAJARA.

There are four horse-car lines leading to as many suburbs, each an interesting ride. If there is time to do them all they are worth it.

But to the barranca is not so easy a journey, yet not one that even the fatigue of a burro ride will bring any regrets. It is two hours through the streets and across the plain and another hour for the descent; this latter hour is worth a hundred anywhere else for the very novelty of it. It is a narrow winding path down the mountain side, a path just wide enough for the trains of burros to pass as they go up and down. They come to the mouth of the cañon without any hint of it till you are on the brink of a yawning chasm that looks ten thousand feet deep, but it is not quite so much as that; it is only two thousand feet, and the road makes the descent in little more than a mile, though its crooks and turns make it about three miles; these crooks and turns are so short that a train of twenty burros will in some places have four turns in it, so that the riders see each other immediately above and below.

The scenery is grandly magnificent and wholly indescribable, so wildly picturesque, not as seen from a car window; here you are in the very midst of great castled rocks, frowning precipices and unfathomable abysses, passing first the scraggy mountain oaks till, in the lower road, the path is through a forest of bananas and shaded by their broad leaves. At the bottom of the barranca is the Lerma River, here called the Rio de Santiago, and on either side the towering mountains lift up in perpendicular cliffs, in the grandest pictures of sublime magnificence. A little ferry, with narrow boats pulled from side to side by a rope, transfers passengers and the freight brought by the burros, while the poor little beasts that never get a ride anywhere must swim here. The return takes a little longer time, as the ascent is more difficult, but the riding is more comfortable going up hill, and the journey back to the city is about four hours. All in all the trip is a thousand times worth the fatigue of it.

Near Guadalajara are the beautiful Falls of Juanacatlan, a cascade with a clear leap of over seventy-one feet—a veritable Niagara, of somewhat abbreviated dimensions, but, truly, the wonder of this country. Like the greater Niagara of the North, the waters have been harnessed to turn the wheels of a mill and the dynamos for the lights of Guadalajara. To reach the Falls of Juanacatlan, stop at the station of El Castillo, either as you come or go.

Guadalajara is the capital of the State of Jalisco, and is on the western division of the Mexican Central Railway, 381 miles from the City of Mexico. The altitude is 5,872 feet, and the population 100,000.

Guanajuato
Wan-a-wa-to. The nomenclature of the cities and towns of Mexico requires a curious spelling that is often at variance with the pronunciation, but when once you know how to call the names they are as musical as at first they seem hard to say. The derivation of these names is for the most part from the Tarascan or the Otomite tongue, or of Toltec or Aztec origin, in latter days given a Spanish spelling which, properly enunciated, bears some resemblance to the original.

The Tarascan Indians named this place *Quanashuato*, signifying the hill of the frogs, and the Spaniards changed either spelling or pronouncing very little when they spelled it Guanajuato and pronounced it *Wan-a-wa-to*, with just a suspicion of a "g" before the "*wan*." As to the wherefore of the "hill of the frogs" does not appear in the legend, unless the hill was named in honor of one of their gods, one of which, in the shape of a huge frog cut in stone, was found here.

To reach Guanajuato the traveler must go to Silao on the Mexican Central Railway, where there is a branch road leading twelve miles eastward to Marfil; thence by horse cars up the *barranca*, nearly three miles, to the center of the city, over the most interesting road, for its length, in Mexico. From Marfil to the Jardin de la Union and the Presa de la Olla the route is along the highway that leads up the gulch, as an American miner would call it, through, under and over the immense silver production works. A good plan is to retain seats on the horse cars as far as Jardin de la Union, and then change to another, going on up the hill to the Presa de la Olla. Perched on the steep hillsides that rise almost perpendicularly are the low flat houses in such out-of-reach places that it is a wonder how anything but a goat could ever get there; there are hundreds of these houses on both of the mountains, some of them so far up that they look like dry-goods boxes that might have been carried there by a cyclone and lodged on some crag or jutting rock, and the fact that they are all inhabited is proof that the Mexican is a good climber whatever else he may not be. This highway along which the street cars run is crowded with people, burros and dogs, going up and coming down, in all shapes and sizes, laden or unladen as the errand may or may not have been performed.

The houses of that antique mold that suggests Egypt or the Holy Land are larger and better, till at the Jardin de la Union are some really fine buildings, a grand theatre, some fine churches and the Palacio Gobierno. The road does not end here, but continues on up the barranca to what I may call the top of the city, where are some of the most romantic little homes in a most picturesque residence district. A stream which comes down from the upper hills falls from one reservoir to the other, forming little lakelets that are crossed by bridges to the houses on the other side. The walls of the reservoirs and the bridges are covered with vines and flowers, and the houses are completely embowered with them. I remember one of these charming nests—I can't call it anything else— as dainty a piece as was ever a subject for a canvas. There is scarcely room between the rocks and the stream for the house, and it is built on arches that stand in the water. Overhanging trees and vines from the cliffs above make a bower of beauty that casts a grateful shade over the balconies and Moorish arches below, so that the sunlight comes to that house softened by swaying leaves and the air perfumed by ever-blooming flowers.

The Pompeiian colors of the walls and arches added other hues and tints to the brighter ones of the flowers. Some pea-fowls sat sleepily on a wall, a cock with spreading plumes strutted proudly up and down, and in the lake the ducks floated lazily. From an upper casement window where the awning cloth was thrown outside the casement rail, as is the fashion, two dark-haired beauties robed in white, the long braids making inky stripes that must have reached almost to their feet, looked out. Dost like the picture? There were two of them—one in reality, the other in bright reflection in the clear crystal waters of the lakelet.

It is an up-hill walk from the Jardin de la Union to the little alameda at the Presa de la Olla, where the band plays evenings, Sundays and feast days, yet worth it all ; but if you are not equal to it, ride up on the cars and walk down for

THE CATACOMBS OF GUANAJUATO.

the sights by the way and the grand view of the city and the surrounding country. The Mint is one of the finest and largest in the country and coins more money than any other. The process of melting the bars of silver, stamping and milling, is the same as in our mints; but there is the white-haired old Indian, whose locks seem silvered by the metal he has ladled from the furnace to the molds in thirty long years of continual service, and there are the two Indians seated on low stools literally surrounded by the silver coins, handling every piece, and by passing them through their fingers and over the palms of their hands detecting the slightest scratch or minute defect. A long practice has made them perfect, and they never make a mistake in picking up twenty coins at a grasp, no more, no less, and never failing to throw out an imperfect piece. Such a keen sense of touch is truly wonderful, and it is stated as a fact that their work is so perfect that no further examination is made, but the coins rejected by them are returned to the furnace to be melted over again. The mint is curiously built, but a strong, substantial building, that might have been a treasure house in Babylon of old, even to the hanging garden that adorns the roof with growing flowers.

The centre of the field of operations in doing Guanajuato should be at the Jardin de la Union. Near are the churches, the theatres, the hotels, the Mint and State buildings, the Alhóndiga de Granaditas, erected in 1785 as a Chamber of Commerce, now used as a prison. It was captured by Hidalgo in the early part of the war for Independence, and after he and the other patriots were captured and executed at Chihuahua, their heads were brought here and hung on hooks on the walls of this building. Hidalgo is still shown — I mean the hook is still shown. The Mexicans repented them of the execution of the patriot priest, and the hanging of his head on these walls, and erected the bronze statue that stands at the entrance. The Theatre is a fine building built of the beautiful green stone found at the head of the ravine.

There is wealth of paintings in the churches of Guanajuato as there is a wealth of silver in its mines. The churches are fine, especially that of the Compañia, commenced in 1747, and finished in 1765, the shelf cut out of the rock for its foundations alone costing nearly $100,000. The tower contains a chime of bells, and you may have heard before you came, or known, after you heard the bells of Mexico, that they are not usually hung in chimes. The dome somewhat resembles that of the Capitol at Washington, and is the one seen high above all the others in all views of Guanajuato. The old Church of San Sebastián is on the line of street cars leading to the Presa de la Olla; in the churchyard are scores of crumbling tombs with curious inscriptions. The Church of San Diego contains the picture of the Last Supper of San Francisco. The other churches are San Francisco, Loreto and Guadalupe. In the former is the much-venerated image of Our Lady of Guanajuato, presented by Philip II. of Spain.

High up on a hill, in the western part of the city, is a *panteon* that may be called a replica of the catacombs of the Old World. In the vaults are artistically arranged the bodies and bones of lates lamented, whose departure from this vale of tears covers more than one century. The visit to the panteon is not the most cheerful one, but the curious-minded will be entertained. The panteon proper is a cemetery in which there are few graves. The bodies are placed in tombs, arranged in tiers in the thick walls. A stipulated sum is paid for the first five years with the privilege of renewal. If at the end of that time the mourners' grief has cooled, and further payment is not made, the body is taken from the hole in the wall. If nothing but bones remain they are thrown into the heap at the end of the arched corridor under the panteon. If the body is preserved in the dry air of the climate it is stood up against the wall to grin, and bear company to the other mummies that have stood there through the ages. About half way between the station at Marfil and the Jardin de la Union is a little park on the right as you go up ; stop here, and walk up the hill on the north side of the street to the panteon, or call most any Mexican that may be standing by, tell him you want burros; he will have them there in a jiffy, and you may ride up.

The city of Guanajuato is totally unlike any other in Mexico, and the visit there is one that will be remembered ; but the legends and fairy tales would form a volume if they were all written down, from the turning of the hose on the hogs to wash the silver from their bristles, gathered in their wallows in the pools, to the miracles priests performed. I remember mine, and all the sights seen from the galop of the street-car mules up the hill from Marfil, till I bought the *helados* from an Indian boy as I took my seat in the train for Silao. I will explain that an *helado*, or as the venders cry the name, "*e-low*," is a sort of ice cream, frozen in a tin tube about an inch in diameter and four inches long, and it was not the least of the pleasant surprises I found at Guanajuato.

Guanajuato, the capital of the State of the same name, is 250 miles from the City of Mexico, and 15 miles by branch road from the main line of the Mexican Central Railway at Silao; the altitude is 6,837 feet, and the population 90,000.

A PULQUE PILFER.

Irapuato Irapuato means strawberries; not that this is the translation of
Ir-ra-*pwat-o* the word, but when the name of that station is called and the train stops there, all the passengers go out and buy strawberries. No matter if it is December or January, the cry of "fresas!" is heard on all sides—and great luscious berries, the finest and sweetest in the world, are offered at midsummer prices, and the bottom of the basket does not exhibit that rising tendency so common to the strawberry box of the United States. Irapuato is also celebrated as the place to change cars for Guadalajara.

The city is on the west side of the track; only the church towers may be seen from the station above the green trees which surround them. Here is a pretty little city worthy of a stop-over check for one train at least, or if en route for Guadalajara there is often time for a horse-car ride up town. The town is irregularly laid out, if indeed it was ever laid out, the narrow streets turning here and there, converging to numerous little plazas, and to the Alameda in the center of the city, where there is a combination of cleanliness and beauty of artistic gardening. There is also a queer combination in the two old-fashioned well-sweeps that might have come from "down south," and the beautiful music stand that exists only in Mexico. The wells and well-sweeps are for irrigation purposes for the exquisite flower beds that adorn the park, the borders of which are in fantastic shapes, laid with pebbles and boulders in different colors. The trees and shrubs are also similarly decorated and protected about the roots.

The music stand, the necessary adjunct of every Mexican town, is at Irapuato a thing of beauty and a joy to its people, when the band plays in the evenings and on the feast days and Sundays. It is in the center of the park, under the trees and surrounded with flowers—so there's fragrance with the melody.

There are churches and churches, and pictures and pictures, in name from Guadalupe to San Fransisco and each seeming different from the last one, so there

THE MARKET PLACE, IRAPUATO.

must be a look into each arched door and a stroll through nave and sacristy and climbs to belfry tower as everywhere else, and withal there is nothing disappointing in Irapuato, from the strawberries to the little fonda on the plaza.

Irapuato is on the Mexican Central Railway, 212 miles from the national capital; it has an altitude of 5,054 feet, and a population of 26,000 people.

Jalapa *"Ave Maria purisima, que venga el sol,"* be your prayer when you
Ha-lap-pa come to Jalapa, as the Jalapeño invokes the Virgin to let the sun shine through the mists that almost constantly hang over the place—not that it rains, but a fine filmy mist prevails, in contrast to the bright sunshine of all other Mexico. But when the sun shines, than Jalapa there is not a brighter spot

on earth, nor one more quaintly curious, nor yet any other more charmingly fascinating. Whether your coming be down from the mountains or up from the sea, you may look from your window in the car with an anticipation not akin to the thoughts as you came to the others of these old-time towns. Either way the approach has been through tropic forests, and the stop at the station is in the midst of one.

There is an incongruity in the modern newness of the railroad surroundings, the electric lights and the horse cars. A glance beyond these is looking backward into another century. In the ride up town, the nineteenth is between the rails of the track and the sidewalk is back in the sixteenth, where the red-tiled roofs project over the walk-way, and casemated windows are strongly iron-barred to keep bandits and lovers out, and sweethearts and wives within. These iron bars may have been a necessity in the old bandit days, but not for that purpose now, although it may be they are retained 'gainst the lovers, for the women are reputed for their beauty, till it has become a proverb among the Mexicans, "*las Jalapeñas son halagüeñas*," "bewitching, alluring are the women of Jalapa," and whether this is the principal reason why Jalapa is considered as "a part of Paradise let down to earth" does not appear. However that may be, the American who has

IN JALAPA.

never been there, and knows only the product, the jalap of the old family doctor, is apt to consider it anything else but Paradise, and perhaps has wondered if any good could come from the town; but when he has seen "*las Jalapeñas*" he may even forget the jalap's dose.

In the days when the journey thither involved a horse-car ride of seventy miles and two days' time going and returning, the attractions were sufficient to allure hundreds of tourists, and now that it is on a main line between the City of Mexico and Vera Cruz, and reached within a few hours from either city, their numbers will increase.

There is a fashion to speak of Mexico as "old Mexico"—eminently proper but unnecessary. There is nothing new there but the railways; but whatever ancientness that may impress elsewhere, there is something older about Jalapa; really it

A STREET OF JALAPA.

seems to have the age on all the other towns in the country. It was a place of importance when Cortez came. The houses on both sides of the narrow streets are of a cumbersome style of architecture, with here and there traces of the Moorish or Castilian. The long windows, heavily barred with iron, reach nearly to the ground, and if there is a second story, there is a bit of projection forming a casement or balcony, and over the railing the brightly colored curtain in yellow and red keeps out the too intense rays of a tropic sun, and may also keep out the too intent gaze of some son upon the face and form of the señorita that may be behind it. And this makes a memory of some old Castilian story of maiden and mandolin, of *caballero* and casement, of music and moonlight—for here are the very walls ('tis well they have not ears) and there the window and the balcony where some Romeo may have climbed, and some Juliet leaned her cheek upon her hand. Jalapa lies on the eastern hillsides of Meniltepec, and the streets running on steep inclines, or across the slopes, are cleaned by every passing shower, so that cleanliness, as well as beauty and antiquity are attributes of this delightful city—an example of nature's, emulated by the natives within their homes and gardens.

The grandeur of the scenery round about is unsurpassed. Just back of the city is a great mountain with a great chalk-like rock, which from its shape—like a chest—is called the *cofre*, the *Cofre de Perote*, and farther away to the southwest is the snow-capped peak of Orizaba, another of Mexico's extinct volcanoes, towering high above the surrounding mountains. To the east the hills get lower and lower, till far away the dim outline of blue defines the coming together of sky and sea.

Excursions to Coatepec may be made by horse car, or by the old highway through tropical forests and coffee groves, on foot or burro-back. The quaintly pretty little town and grand view of the Coatepec Valley is worth all the journey there. Another very interesting trip may be made to Jilotepec, about six miles away down in the valley, to be made on horseback or by burros. The burros are rather to be chosen, for the very novelty of it, and for safety as well—one does not have so far to fall.

The Palacio Gobierno is the building of the city, though by no means the most interesting. Its location is on the Plaza Mayor. There is a very pretty little theatre, most unique in its appointments, hardly to be expected in this so long out-of-the-way place. The Institute of the Ordnance Survey is located at Jalapa, and has produced some fine maps and topographical drawings.

The present Cathedral was formerly the church of the Conception, founded in the sixteenth century. The other churches are San Francisco, founded in 1555, San Juan de Dios, San Hipólito, 1641, San José, 1770, and the Calvario, 1805, dating their foundations from the sixteenth to the nineteenth centuries.

While there is much of interest in their altars, shrines and paintings, the charms of Jalapa are without the walls of these or any other buildings, unless it be those where live the Jalapeñas.

Jalapa means a "place of water and sand." It was an Indian town when Cortez came, and being on the main road from the coast to the capital was a place of importance. From 1720 to 1777 an annual fair was held for the sale of goods brought from Cadiz to Spain. Jalapa is the capital of the State of Vera Cruz. The city is located on the main line of the Interoceanic Railway, 257 miles from the City of Mexico. The altitude is 4,372 feet, and the population 15,000.

LAGOS.

Lagos
Lah-gose

A city three hundred years old in Mexico is not uncommon, and some of them had gotten their growth when their charters were granted; that is about the age of the city that was formerly called Santa Maria de los Lagos. In modern times it has lost much of its trade and some of its name. It was formerly the point of connection with diligencias for Guadalajara and San Luis Potosi, but the completion of the railways to both of these cities took even this business away. However, it is not commercial importance that attracts to the average Mexican town, and Lagos has what all the others have, and a visit will not be disappointing. It is a pretty town, on the west side of the track, yet hardly to be seen, it is so overshadowed by trees. There are many interesting features in its churches, markets, streets and plazas, and there is a boast of good provender and good wine at the hotels

Lagos is in the State of Jalisco, on the Line of the Mexican Central Railway, 296 miles from the city. The altitude is 6,134 feet; the population is 40,000. Horse cars run from the station to the center of the city.

JUDAS ON SALE— PHOTO AT LEON.

Leon
Lay-own

On a broad and fertile plain watered by the Rio Turbío is the greatest manufacturing city of all Mexico, though the fact is not discoverable from the cars. There are no many-storied buildings with tall chimneys indicating such industries, but they are here at Leon. Every citizen lives in his own house. and his home is his workshop. There is scarcely an article of use or ornament but what is made at Leon. The beautiful saddles, bridles and horse accoutrements so much affected by the Mexican; shoes and all other leathern goods, zerapes and rebosos answering the purpose of coats and shawls for men and women, cotton and woolen goods, iron ware and cutlery, are all manufactured at Leon, and every one of the little low, square-built houses is a busy shop of some kind or other.

There is no indication, from the station, of a city of such size and importance, nor from the street cars as they wind through the cactus-hedged lanes for a mile or more, and come to the long, narrow streets, crossing others at right angles that seem of the same interminable length with their never-ending rows of houses as far as the eye can reach. This car line reaches to the main plaza, a very pretty one, with the market at one corner, and the Casa Municipal on one side, and on the other three, the portales, with clean, well-kept shops and stores, offering the products of the town. The plaza is shaded with trees, and there are flowers and fountains and the inevitable music stand. Horse cars lead out to an old causeway, now resorted to as a *paseo* for promenades and drives to the pretty gardens in the suburbs. A little further out, on the road to the north, are some hot springs and baths.

The establishment of the church in Leon received a set-back at the start, in the murder of the cura, Espinoso, by the Chichmec Indians in 1586, but the church survived, and those buildings now in existence are very interesting, both for their great age and peculiar decoration. The one with the great dome and two high towers was formerly the Church of Nuestra Señora de la Luz, commenced in 1746 (now, since 1886, the Cathedral), and is over 200 feet long but only forty-five wide. Here is an original painting of Our Lady of Light, the Patroness of Leon, presented, as attested by the Jesuit signatures on the back, by José Maria Genovesi, in 1740. In the Church of Nuestra Señora de los Angeles are some very curious carvings by a native artist, one Muñoz of most happy memory. The other churches are La Soledad, San Felipe and San Juan, the former being the oldest.

Some idea of the size of Leon may be formed from the knowledge that there are 507 streets, 7,820 houses, 236 manzanas, and ten plazas. There was a Spanish town on this site in the year 1552, referred to in the royal archives as the town of Leon, from which time the city dates its age, though the formal order for its foundation was not issued by Viceroy Almanza until 1575, and this order not royally confirmed until 1712. It was not made a city until after the war of 1810, when it was so declared by the State of Guanajuato, in which State it is.

Leon is on the Mexican Central Railway, 259 miles from the City of Mexico; the population is 100,000, and the altitude 5,863 feet.

Lerdo Near the Nazas River, and in the midst of a very fertile cotton
Luerdo region, this is one of the newest towns in Mexico, and its boast is in an equable climate, cotton mills and oil manufactories rather than antiquities.

There is a pretty garden in the principal plaza with seats under the trees. There are four churches, a market and the Plaza de Toros to be visited.

The soil of the Lerdo plain is very fertile, and the climate is particularly adapted to the culture of cotton; it is claimed that two and three crops may be made without replanting, and as to corn and wheat they just grow all the time. It is only three miles south from Lerdo to Torreon, the junction point of the International and the Mexican Central Railroads. The city is on the west side of the road and about three miles distant, reached by horse cars that run across the plain, through an avenue shaded by green trees.

Lerdo is on the Mexican Central Railway, 684 miles from the capital; altitude, 3,844 feet; population, 11,000.

FROM THE STATION TO THE TOWN—LERDO.

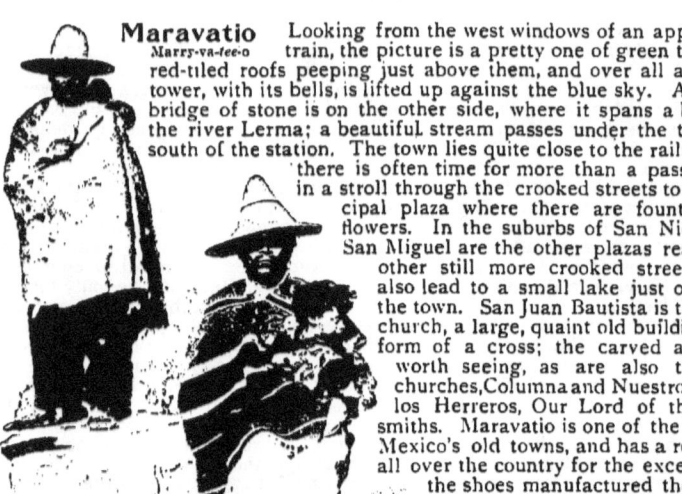

Maravatio
Marrs-va-lee-o

Looking from the west windows of an approaching train, the picture is a pretty one of green trees, with red-tiled roofs peeping just above them, and over all a Moorish tower, with its bells, is lifted up against the blue sky. An arched bridge of stone is on the other side, where it spans a branch of the river Lerma; a beautiful stream passes under the track just south of the station. The town lies quite close to the railroad, and there is often time for more than a passing view in a stroll through the crooked streets to the principal plaza where there are fountains and flowers. In the suburbs of San Nicolás and San Miguel are the other plazas reached by other still more crooked streets, which also lead to a small lake just outside of the town. San Juan Bautista is the parish church, a large, quaint old building in the form of a cross; the carved altars are worth seeing, as are also the other churches, Columna and Nuestro Señor de los Herreros, Our Lord of the Blacksmiths. Maravatio is one of the oldest of Mexico's old towns, and has a reputation all over the country for the excellence of the shoes manufactured there. The original town was called Maravatio el Alto, located 15 miles southwest, and was founded in 1535; the present town was founded in 1541.

One of the old houses near the parish church bears date of 1573. Maravatio is on the Mexican National Railroad, 138 miles from the city; population, 6,000; altitude, 6,750 feet.

RESTING

Monclova
Mon-clo-va.

has a history, and seems to be content with it. When Texas and Coahuila were one State, Monclova was the capital; now it is the capital of neither, Texas having one of her own, and that of Coahuila having been removed to Saltillo. Monclova is in the center of a rich mining district; the most important are the mines Cuatro Cienegas and Sierra Mojada. Monclova is a very old town, and as such is a very interesting one. It was named for the Viceroy Melchor Portocarrero Lazo de la Vega, Conde de la Monclova, but for obvious reasons has not retained the entire name, which is to be applauded if for no other reason than for the benefit of the trainman who calls the stations along the line, since he has such inferior success with the shorter ones. Monclova is on the Mexican International Railroad, 942 miles from the City of Mexico. It is in the State of Coahuila; altitude, 1,936 feet; population, 5,000.

Monterey
Mon-te-ray

The Spaniards had penetrated far into the interior and to the northward, before the middle of the sixteenth century, and in 1560 had reached near the now American border. In that year they founded the town of Santa Lucia, that was afterwards called Monterey in honor of the then viceroy, Don Capar de Zuñiga, Conde de Monterey, the permanent settlement being made in September of 1596 by Fray Diego de Leon. If he had sought the country over he could not have found a more lovely site for a city than in this valley of level lands. It is completely surrounded by high hills, curiously shaped, and the prettiest in Mexico. So curiously shaped are their dark blue outlines, clear cut against the sky, that the one, Cerro de la Silla, 4149 feet above the plain, is a perfect saddle of the military type known as the McClellan, and, at the peak, is shaped exactly like the saddles seen in Mexico, requiring no stretch of the imagination, as in the case of the old Man of the Mountain and Anthony's Nose, the saddle mountain being recognized at a glance. The Cerro de las Mitras, 3618 feet high, is the mountain of the mitres. It does not so assert itself, but the mitres are just as compelling as the saddle, and that piece of the bishop's vestments is as discernible to the average vivid vision. They are the bluest of blue mountains standing out against the very bluest sky, and the marvelously clear atmosphere is responsible for it all.

These mountains surround a lovely valley watered by clear running streams and carpeted by the green of fertile fields that are brightened further by flowering gardens, with great trees to shade the lanes and streets. In the midst of this is Monterey, as quaintly novel as the valley is very beautiful.

Here, through the city, there runs a living stream of cold, clear water that has its source in the great spring, the Ojo de Agua. Along its banks the people come to bathe under the shade of the overhanging foliage. On a bridge, La Purísima, where one of the principal streets crosses this stream, the Mexicans made a valiant stand against the advancing Americans in '46, and while, as the legend says, the Virgin of Guadalupe hovered over the banners of Mexico, they held the pass as the Spartans at Thermopylæ.

In the western part of the city are the *casas del campo*, a semi-suburban district where the houses are in beautiful gardens of fruits and flowers, with streams of running water and fountains under beautiful trees. These are reached by horse cars, as are all of the points of interest in and around Monterey. Special cars may be hired at reasonable rates, and they are much to be preferred to the carriages that rattle in an uncertain way over the stony streets; especially are the horse cars to be preferred for the rides to the Bishop's Palace and to Topo Chico. The Bishop's Palace is a very picturesque old ruin on a high hill northwest of the city, seen from almost every part of it and from the cars. The Palace was commenced in 1782 and completed in 1790, by Bishop Verger, for a summer residence. It is now fallen into disuse, and occupied solely by two sentries, whose lonely watches are changed once a month. These two are but a memory of the gallant army that defended the hill against the assaulting Americans, under General Worth, on the 21st of September, 1849, when the capture of the hill meant the surrender of the city. It is a pleasant ride across the plain to the Hot Springs of Topo Chico. The wonderful hot waters issue from the side of a hill about three miles to the north. The ride through the fields is a pleasant one, and at the end of it there are pavilions, baths and a good hotel. The legend of Montezuma's daughter, her journey to Topo Chico and miraculous cure by the all-healing waters, lives in the centuries after her—how she came from the far-away Hill of the Grasshopper, a weak and puny maiden, but when she came again to Chapultepec it was with renewed life and vigor, to the rejoicing of all. The court of the plumed and feathered king became, at once, agents for the Topo Chico.

The waters are only to be bathed in to insure their own recommendation, and they so resemble the great Hot Springs of Arkansas that they are only to be as well known to make them equally popular.

The other excursions by horse car and carriage from Monterey are to Santa Catarina and the chapels of Guadalupe and Lourdes, and eight miles further to El Potrero, the road leading through a beautiful cañon to a valley of meadows surrounded by mountains. About nineteen miles south of the city, reached by rail, are two wonderful caves near the little village of Pesquería.

The only really old church of Monterey is that of San Francisco, dating from 1560. The present church was built in 1730, though there are some of the old ruins adjoining it, near the Plaza Mayor, where there is a picturesque old convent with a garden. The Cathedral is a massive structure after the style of the average church of Mexico; it was commenced in 1792, finished in 1833, and consecrated on the 4th of July of that year. It was used as a powder magazine during the American war, and its walls and towers give evidence in their scars of the vicissitudes of war.

The main plaza is a very pretty one indeed; it is, in fact, two plazas, with the Casa Municipal between them. At the east end is the Cathedral, and just south of it is the Episcopal Palace. Near by is the State House and Theatre. The Alameda and Campo Santa are in the northwest of the city.

Monterey is a much Americanized city, with its great smelters, factories and breweries, but it is Mexican withal, and is a most delightful first-view town across the border. Monterey is at the crossing of the Mexican National and Monterey & Mexican Gulf Railroads, and is the capital of the State of Nuevo Leon. The population is 30,000; altitude 2,010 feet above sea-level, and is distant from the City of Mexico 667 miles. Horse cars run from both railway stations to the Plaza Mayor.

AT MORELIA.

Morelia
Mo-ray-lia

Than Morelia there is no more lovely city in all Mexico, and its people are content with it, to remain within its walls, going not abroad except where business calls, and that only when it is most urgent; when you have seen them in their homes there will be no wonder at their contentment. In the olden days when the Viceroys of Spain or their emissaries were going about in Mexico founding cities, they, with one accord, seemed to have had an eye for the beautiful in the selection of a site, and particularly did Mendoza have when in 1541 he founded the city of Valladolid, (now called Morelia in honor of the patriot Morelos,) when, as the ancient chronicler says, the Viceroy found a site having the seven qualities of Plato, and founded a small but very noble city, now grown to a large and nobler size, whose towers are seen from afar with their belfries and crosses over the intervening hills. There is a "saddle" mountain at Morelia and others as curiously shaped on all sides, sloping down to smaller undulating hills and valleys in the midst of which the city is. Coming from the east the track runs along the river bank, where a large proportion of the populace do congregate for the launder of their clothes and themselves. It is a pretty river with great overhanging trees on either shore, making dark shadows over the waters, and a cooling shade protecting from rays of a southern sun. The river is on the north of the track, and the scene from the windows on that side is novel and interesting for a mile or more before the station is reached.

Horse cars run from the station to the pretty plaza, to the very excellent hotels of Morelia and beyond to the suburbs, where there are the most charming and cosiest flower-embowered homes in the world. It is a pleasant horse-car ride, but it is best to leave the car just where it starts down the hill by the old aqueduct and passes under its arches—then walk through the Calzada de Guadalupe, a wide stone-paved paseo that leads to the Parque de San Pedro. On each side is a massive stone balustrade, and at intervals convenient resting places on the benches, also of stone. There are two rows of tall trees with intertwining branches above, lending a constant shade over the causeway and over the houses on both sides. If you have never seen the Mexican home that you may have read of, and which you may have thought was described extravagantly, you may see it here, If haply some arched doorway is swung ajar you may have a glimpse of fairy-land that you would never dream could exist behind such a cold gray wall. The *patio* is filled with flowers; some vines have climbed to the upper galleries and almost hidden them with a bank of blossoms, blending in a perfect harmony of color from a deep carnation to a delicate pink, relieved by tints of blue and purple, with here and there some white and gold flowers. From a bed of flowers in the center, sparkling waters, as if from their petals instead of from hidden jets, fly in crystal globules to the overhanging leaves of a feathery palm. You may not see the birds, there are so many flowers to hide them, but the twittering, the whistling and singing in a hundred notes tell that they are there. Such are the homes of the Calzada de Guadalupe that leads from the city to the Parque de San Pedro, a park of great beauty, shadowed by a forest of great trees, a favorite resort of the

AQUEDUCT AT MORELIA.

people. Through the park runs the old aqueduct built by the good Fray Antonio de San Miguel Iglesias, in the year of the famine, 1785, as a means to provide food for the people. Under one of the high arches is a tablet commemorating the bishop's charity.

The Cathedral, one of the finest in all Mexico, and the Palacio de Gobierno stand facing each other in the city's center, fronting the plazas. The main plaza is called the Plaza of the Martyrs, commemorative of the execution here of a company of patriots in 1830, and here also Matamoros was executed ten years later. The plaza east of the Cathedral is that of La Paz where the market is, and where may be bought the dulces for which the town is noted, and also the curious pottery of Uruápam ; the other plaza is that of San Francisco, in front of the church of the same name. In the Plaza de los Mártires the band plays, under a beautiful pagoda in the midst of a garden of trees and flowers ; here the people most do congregate, and here may Morelia's folks be seen at their best, (in the evenings when there's music, as there is two or three times a week,)—men of high and low degree, women who wear the mantilla and her more lowly sister of the reboso, both showing the beauty of the city's people.

The Hotel Oseguera is a part of the building that was erected for the bishop's palace, but as its cost created talk among the people, it was abandoned to more profane uses and became a hotel, and one of the best and most unique in the land. The Hotel Michoacan has also a convent legend. The Ocampo Theatre is the chief place of amusement, excepting always the Plaza de Toros, built after the fashion of the bull-rings of old Spain, entirely of stone, very substantial and of immense seating capacity.

Of the churches, of course the Cathedral is the most prominent, in fact there are few finer edifices anywhere than the Cathedral at Morelia ; its towers, the great organ, the silver altar rails, vestments and vessels, images and candelabra, all of fine silver, have not an equal—though what is there now is only a remnant, nearly half a million dollars' worth having been confiscated by the government in 1858, for the refusal to pay a levy of $100,000, and one wonders how it all could have been used and where to put it. There are some interesting pictures and handsome carvings and the silver font in which Iturbide and Morelos were baptized. The Cathedral was founded at Tzintzuntzan in 1538, was removed to Patzcuaro in 1540, and finally to Morelia in 1579, to the little church of La Cruz. The present building was begun in 1640 and completed in 1706.

The Church of San Francisco was founded in 1531, but not completed until seventy years later; it is said that an underground passage leads from the church to the fields beyond the city. The Church of Nuestra Señora Socorro dates from 1550, and contains a much venerated image of that Virgin. In the Santuario de Guadalupe are shown the chains around the atrium that were once used to shackle the prisoners of the State. The other churches are Carmen, 1596, with some fine pictures by Juan and Nicolás Juarez and Calvera. The Compañia is of Jesuit foundation, a very handsome group of buildings, dating from 1582. The churches of Santa Catalina de Lena, Las Teresas and Capuchinas were originally convents. La Merced and San José are smaller churches. The College of St. Nicholas is the oldest college in America, having been founded in 1540, by Bishop Quiroga, a portrait of whom is preserved in the building. Among the pupils of later years were Morelos and Yturbide. The college was closed during the wars from which the country suffered, but remains to-day the oldest and one of the most flourishing institutions in the country. Morelia has also a very fine seminary for young ladies, however, of modern establishment.

The surrounding country is very picturesque and ten miles west are the famous hot springs of Cuincho, famed for their cures. Morelia is very famous in the country's history and suffered greatly in its wars, and many have been the dire and dark scenes enacted that made bloody marks on her escutcheon; but the fair city of to-day rejoices in honoring her heroes and dwells in contentment and peaceful hospitality. Morelia is the capital of the State of Michoacan; it is located on the western division of the Mexican National Railroad, 225 miles from the capital of the Republic. The altitude is 6,226 feet, and the population 35,000. Horse cars run from the station to the plaza and suburbs.

Oaxaca
O-ah-*haak*-ah

It was in the year of Montezuma's downfall that the conqueror, Cortez, sent bands of men, here and there, to spy out the land he had invaded. He had deposed the Aztec princes, and the Emperor was in chains, a humiliated slave to the Spanish King. There was a lull in the wars, and the projects of peace claimed attention. The open road of the sea at Vera Cruz left no protection for the Spanish ships. A surveying party proceeded down the coast, guided by a chart that Montezuma had shown them, and found a harbor at the mouth of the great river Coatzacoalcos, that offered safe and suitable accommodations. A spot was selected for a fortified post, and a detachment of a hundred and fifty men, under Velasquez de Leon, was sent to form the colony.

PARISH CHURCH, OAXACA.

The route of Velasquez was direct to the southeast, through the cañons, down through the Valley of Oaxaca, where Cortez obtained a grant of a large tract of land, and laid out plantations for the crown. The estate was soon so prosperous that its value was more than twenty thousand ounces of gold. The report gives detailed descriptions of large and beautiful edifices, and some of them the most elaborate specimens of Indian architecture in the Province of Oaxaca. The princely domain comprehended more than twenty large towns and villages, and 23,000 vassals. Of these twenty large towns and villages, Mitla was one, and another was Oaxaca.

On his return to Spain, Cortez was, by a decree of Charles V, dated July 6, 1529, created Marquis of the Valley of Oaxaca, a title by which he was known in those days even more than by his own name. To speak of "the Marquis," meant

Cortez. The decree granting the estates of the valley was signed in the month of July, of that year.

The route that the little band of Velasquez marched over was down through cañons where now runs the Mexican Southern Railroad, the mouth of the great river Coatzacoalcos, the eastern terminus of the Tehuantepec Railroad.

Oaxaca was a city, then, before the Spaniards came, and the date of its original foundation is as obscure as that of the Ruins of Mitla, though its Spanish occupation and building commenced very early in the sixteenth century; therefore it is one of the oldest foundations in the land, and one of the prettiest of all its cities. The approach of the railroad is down through a lovely valley. The towers may be seen, above the trees, while the train is yet some miles away, and when it stops it is under the shadow of a high hill that stands up on the east side, and between it and the green fields on the other side of the track, stands the station.

Tram-cars lead from the station to the Plaza Mayor, passing first a little plaza shaded by great trees, in the midst of which is a fountain of running water; then through the narrow streets, passing the old Church of La Soledad, and stopping at the plaza.

The main plaza, or rather plazas, for there are two of them, are very beautiful, shaded by immense trees, and filled with flowers; the two join at the northeast corner, at the jutting of the Cathedral pavement. The main plaza is styled the Plaza de Armas, and in its center is a monument to Juarez, who was a native of Oaxaca, as is also General President Porfirio Diaz; the other park is called de Leon.

One of the finest buildings is the Government Palace, facing the Plaza de Armas, and it is, indeed, a palace, with its arched portales extending the entire length of the square. The churches of Santo Domingo and La Soledad have been monasteries and fortresses as well, and more than once have had cannon within their walls, that thundered forth in liberty's cause. There is a scientific institute, a seminary, an historical museum, and a library, by way of public institutions. The houses of commerce and trade would do honor to a larger city, and one with older railroad facilities. There are superb baths, with elegant appointments, with tiled floors, full-length mirrors, and mantel shelves of onyx. The market, within a square of the plaza, is intensely interesting, somewhat like the others of Mexico's markets, and yet unlike them, in the tropic dress of the people. Every fruit in the world is offered, and flowers at ten cents a bushel; the most exquisite roses, in February, as many as you can carry, for a *real*, that would cost a mint of money at home.

Oaxaca boasts of good hotels, and there may be good living while you stay in the beautiful city, for its beauties will entice you to linger, and the hospitalities of its people make you welcome always.

ON THE ROAD TO MITLA.

The Ruins of Mitla

The archives of the Acropolis of Athens are written, and the tale of Thebes has been told in ancient history; but that history runs not far enough back in the ages to tell of the builders of the temples of Mitla, Palenque and Uxmal, whence they came, or where departed. The parchments that bore the builders' tracings have mouldered to ashes in the century of centuries, and the hieroglyphics worn to polished stone in the drifting sands of a passed eternity, till the tale must forever remain untold. Yet stand, as mute monuments, the chiseled columns, that call back the cultured civilization of the mighty men of Mitla, and Palenque's people, in whose temples we walk, wondering at their magnitude and magnificence; calculating, hopelessly, upon the task that modern men would tire under, and wondering and wondering how these walls were laid, how their mosaics where graven, how these monoliths were raised, and where their quarries were; how they were brought hence, how these massive columns where raised, and how the corner stone was put in its place. Afterwards we turn away in disappointing ignorance of it all, and hopelessly, for there is no history, nor yet a legend, to fathom the mystery of it.

The journey to Mitla is an easy one. It is by rail to Oaxaca; thence, over a wide road, hard beaten by much travel, through a valley almost treeless, save where the verdure is along the banks of a little *rio*, or clustered here and there about an hacienda or straggling village, or on the sides of the mountains which hedge this valley in, and help to make the journey a pleasant one, with pretty pictures of scenic beauty.

Diligencias or carriages may be obtained at Oaxaca, and they will roll over the broad road as easily and smoothly as on a street. The start should be made at a convenient hour in the morning, not later than nine o'clock. This will bring you to Mitla at four in the afternoon, and the return may be started at ten the next morning, thus giving the afternoon and morning sun on the weird pictures

128

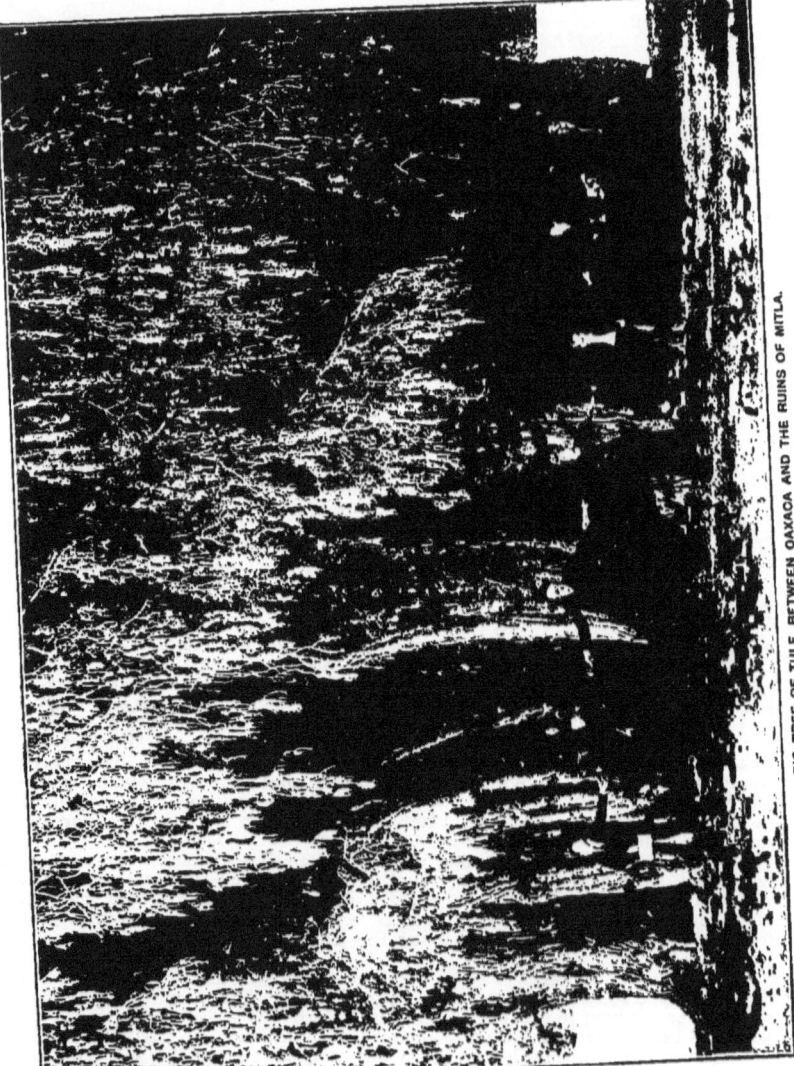

BIG TREE OF TULE, BETWEEN OAXACA AND THE RUINS OF MITLA.

of the ruins. Lunches may be taken from Oaxaca, but this is not absolutely necessary; the *fonda* at Tlacolula, the little more than half way town, is surprisingly good, where good coffee, excellent bread, and all the fruits may be obtained, and at the hacienda of the *muy amable*, Señor Don Felix Quéro, at Mitla, there are good beds, and an excellent dinner is served, by a genial host, who will welcome in cordiality and speed the parting guest with good wishes, till you will, with the memories of the wonders, the pleasant journey and the good living, bless the day you came to Mitla.

SOUTH TEMPLE.

The only rough part of the road is over the stony pavements of Oaxaca; after that, it is up hill and down dale, but easy rolling all the way, with plenty to interest in every mile, from the city gates and the old stone bridge just without its boundaries, down to the big trees of Tule. You have told your driver that if he *drives* there is something in it for his own account, and he will drive—but there must be a stop at Tule. The village is in a grove of trees, and a turn out to the right is through an avenue of tropical verdure that all but shuts out the sunlight. It is scarcely half a mile from the main road to the big trees. The populace will turn out to greet you, in a kindly way, and, from the purest curiosty, follow you about.

The big tree of Tule is in the church yard of Santa Maria del Tule. A great, grandfather of trees, that must have been still a great tree long before the Spaniards came, or even while the builders were at the temples of Mitla. It is 154 feet and 2 inches around the trunk, six feet from the ground, and, as a native says, "it takes two looks to see the top." To give a better idea of its immense size: if twenty-eight people with outstretched arms, touching each other's fingertips, stood around the trunk, they could barely complete the circuit.

HALL OF THE MONOLITHS.

On the east side of this giant of the forest is a wooden tablet, with an inscription signed by Humboldt, the great German traveler, and probably placed there by him, or by his order. It has been there so long that the bark has grown over it, almost completely embodying it in the tree, and partially obscuring the inscription, so that the beginning and ending of the lines cannot be read. In the native tongue the tree is an ahuehuete, a species of cypress. Back on the main road

again, and the little mules go in a gallop across the valley, then over the barren foot-hill of the mountain, with still a broad even road, though at a slower gate till the turn at the top, than you may go as fast as you please. There is a pretty view from this hill, back to one valley of green fields, and forward to another. Looking toward the valley to the south there is seen what seems to be a vast pyramid, in the midst of it, perfect in shape, but on closer view it is found to be covered with small trees, but it may be a pyramid for all that. We are in a land of mysterious wonders, and there may be yet undiscovered relics of the forgotten ages. You will see the white towers of the little villages of the valley, and the driver will point out the spot where lies the larger town of Tlacolula. You

FROM THE EAST TEMPLE.

can take an hour for luncheon and coffee at the Hotel Cerqueda at Tlacolula, and, while it is being prepared, you may walk across the market place and come to the Plaza of the Casa Municipal, one of the prettiest plazas in all Mexico; then come back through the church yard, and through the quaint old church of the parish. If you are not indeed hard to please, you will not regret the luncheon at Tlacolula — still I have not advised to start on the journey without a basket.

The mules have rested, the drivers been refreshed, and it is a whip and a hurrah through the streets of the east side of the town, with a thousand dogs coming out to bark at your flying wheels; down through the cactus-hedged lanes, and on into the fields again, with the greater part of the journey behind you, and a down-grade road to Mitla. On the right is the valley; on the left the mountains have come closer, till there are huge boulders, of thousands of tons, that may have rolled down from them and lodged on the smaller hills, close to the roadside; not one or a dozen, but hundreds of them,

INTERIOR, NORTH TEMPLE.

probably shaken from their places by some violent quaking of the earth. There are a few miles of this, then, across a wide, rocky bed of a large river, in the rainy season, though only a rivulet now, and up the hill on the other side, and you are at Mitla—at the hospitable door of Don Felix Quéro, to whom it is well, as well as courteous, to bring a letter, and one also to the Jefe Politico of Tlacolula, from the Jefe of Oaxaca, or the owner of the diligencias, or from the agent

CORRIDOR OF MOSAICS.

of the Southern R.R., although neither is absolutely necessary. An exchange of courtesies with Don Felix, rooms arranged for, the order for dinner given, and you are ready for the ruins.

If the journey has been well done, without delay, you should reach the ruins while the sun is yet high. If the journey is a hurried one, you may have the sun with its afternoon shadows, and the opposite in the morning, before you start on the return. It is only five minutes walk from the hacienda to the Ruins, through a straggling village of thatched huts, through narrow streets hedged with giant cacti, across a little *rio*, up a rocky hill, and you stand within the graven walls of a temple that may be older than Solomon's.

I have called them temples, and temples they may have been, raised to the honor of the gods their builders worshiped, though there is little similarity to the teocalis found in the city of Tenochtitlan and the other cities of Anahuac on the plains to the north. These low walls differ radically in their construction and decoration from the high pyramidal temples of the Toltecs, though the absence of arches and curved lines in the walls of the temples of Mitla would indicate that the builders were of the same school, as the Toltecs had no arches in their architecture and avoided curves and circular decoration.

If not a temple, then it may have been a fortress, a most impregnable one, and unless the instruments of war were more formidable than those of later generations, or even those of the present day, the thick walls would have resisted the most persistent assaults. The fortress idea further obtains from the fact that there are no windows or other openings in the walls, and the only entrances open into the inner square or plaza; for these reasons the fortress idea is in favor, but the people of the earlier ages did not need such works of defense.

NORTH TEMPLE.

The palace of a king or mighty chieftain may have been within these walls— the Hall of the Monoliths, a banquet hall, the Corridor of Mosaics, a royal bed chamber, and the central court might have been the throne room and audience hall, but I adhere a first impression and say, here was once a great temple. This may have been one temple, or four. There are four walled courts facing about an open patio, lying exactly at the four points of the compass, with their walls on lines true to the needle. Of the southern court, only three of its walls are standing. The east wall is in the best condition, next the north, while the south is almost crumbled away. The east court has only one of its walls standing, two columns that are not thrown down. Others, and the heavy cornice stones and cap pieces, lie at the base of the wall.

The north court is in the finest state of preservation, and gives ample evidence of the magnificent handiwork of the men of a buried and forgotten race, whose civilization is attested in the intricate carvings here; in the shaping of these stones; in the lifting them from their quarries, and setting them in their places, as with a

CORNER OF CHURCHYARD,
MITLA.

mason's tact, that all the earth's tremblings have not shaken, nor the warring elements effaced their gravings. The north court is built on the same plan with the others; its walls are in a most complete state. The entrances of all the courts open into the open patio in the center, with no openings at all in the outer walls. There are no windows anywhere.

The heavy cap piece of the entrance to the north court is supported in the center by a huge column of hewn stone. Under it leads a passage underground, that may extend to the other courts, as there is a subterranean gallery running the entire length of the court, east and west, with a short extension due north, and these may have existed, also, in the other courts of this great temple. As this court is the best preserved, it is also the most extensive part of the ruins. Above the ground, extending the entire length, and immediately above the underground gallery, is a grand corridor, called the Hall of the Monoliths. Here are six massive columns, nearly seven feet in circumference and twelve feet high, ranging down the center of the hall. An underground passage leads to a second larger room, whose walls also face the compass points. This room is surrounded by four smaller ones, the one on the west side being in an almost complete state. The walls are laid in the most intricate mosaics, of small pieces and of the most beautiful and unique designs, fitted and put together without mortar or cement.

The ancient races of this land had no arches in their architecture, as is evidenced by everything that is left of their meager history, and here, over their square-cut doorways, are magnificent monoliths, twelve to eighteen feet long, four to six feet in width, and three to five feet in thickness.

Down the hill, towards the village, in the yard of one of the residences, discovered within the year, is what the Indian guide calls "the sepulcher," now

ALTAR AT TLACOLULA, NEAR THE RUINS OF MITLA.

used as a corn bin. It is about eight feet long and six feet wide, and below the level of the ground. The architecture and cutting of the stone is exactly the same as in the larger ruins on the hill.

Of these ruins no more may be written, truthfully, than I have here. Descriptions may be elaborated, and yet not do them justice. History is painfully silent as to their origin. They were as they are to-day when the Spaniards came, and Cogolludo, who saw them in the middle of the seventeenth century, speaks of them with admiration, as works of "accomplished artists," of whom history has preserved no tradition. His visit to these ruins was written of in 1688.

We are left to wonder what race of men carved these walls and laid their intricate fittings. Where did they quarry these huge stones, and how were they hewn to their perfect shapes? How did they transport them hence, and how lift them to their places, since men enough could not get around one to lift it? What edged tools could cut their flinty substance, since only chisels and axes of soft, untempered copper have been found? All is deeply, darkly secret against all research. We come to them, and go away, knowing as little as before we came, and pass on with a silent salute to the artisans of so enlightened a race, whose work has made the arrogance of the nineteenth century silent in its wonder and admiration.

These ruins have withstood the ravages of time, perhaps a thousand centuries, but here cometh, in this day and generation, a destroyer who can destroy in a year what may not be built in a hundred; may do what time and the elements have not done in a thousand. The relic hunter comes to take away what the sands have not covered up Let him who reads these lines beware. Let him look upon these walls, but not lay his hand upon them to take their smallest pebble. And if any man shall show you a stone, and say that it came from the walls of the Ruins of Mitla, say to him that he is a thief; for that he is, indeed, and in truth.

IN ORIZABA.

Orizaba was a town long before Cortéz came, and had a Spanish popu-
Oriz-uh-ba   lation in 1533, when it had one of the unpronounceable names of
the Chichmec Indians, who saw "joy in the waters" of the numberless cascades hereabouts and called the place "Ahauializapan;" but the Spaniards, not being able to call it that, without dental danger, from time to time cut out some of the letters and reduced the name to Orizaba.

With its charming location in a lovely valley, it is just on the first terrace above the *tierra caliente*, where the high hills are close up to the city's borders to throw their shadows across the red-tiled roofs, trees and gardens, and domes and towers, and to cool the waters of its clear running streams and fountains, and with just a glimpse of the snow-capped volcano gleaming in the tropic sun, Orizaba is beautiful and very charming.

Horse cars run from the station to the hotels, to the Alameda and the plazas, through the city, and extend westward through the very pretty gardens to Yngenio, the little lake, the church and the mills at Nogales. The rides and drives may be made to the cascades that abound in these hills; the first in the Rincon Grande, the next and larger Tuxpango, and two others near El Barrio Nuevo and at Santa Ana, very attractive excursions, occupying only a few hours; and, besides *las cataratas muy bonitas*, there are flowers and ferns and orchids to be gathered by the wayside.

There are hills to be climbed for the very fine views and to visit historic spots and legendary location. The cross on the summit of the Cerro de Borrego, seen from the cars, marks the spot where some French soldiers were slain, and the narrow path up the side was their line of march, where a party of Zouaves surprised and defeated the Mexican forces on the night of July 13, 1862.

Long centuries ago the healthful climate of Orizaba was a resort for the fever refugees from the coast districts, and remains a favorite in these modern days, where they come from Vera Cruz and the Gulf coast cities to pass the summer days under the shadow of the hills and in the grateful shade of the trees beside the clear, cool waters of La Joya Valley. The place was a favorite resort of Maximilian.

In the pretty little Alameda is a monument to Ygnacio de la Llave, one of the notable men of the town. The streets and plazas are marvelously clean and the white-walled houses gleam brightly in the sun.

The first parish church, called El Calvario, and later Santa Teresa, was built in 1564. The present parish church, San Miguel, is a remarkably handsome building of stone, completed in 1720, after nearly fifty years of building, and the tower was not completed till twelve years later. The north chapel is called the Corazon de Jesus, and the southern, the Chapel of the Rosary. The church contains a magnificently inlaid chest of ebony and ivory for the keeping of the sacerdotal robes and vestments. The Church of San José de Gracia is another fine group of chapel, church and convent, but of very modern build, having been completed in 1810. The pictures and frescos are by a native artist, Barranca—an artist not without fame in these parts, and whose son has proved himself a worthy heir to his father's brush. Pictures by both are to be seen in all the churches of Orizaba. About the year 1600 the Church of San Juan de Dios was founded. It was permanently injured by an earthquake, in 1696, and a new church was commenced; in 1714, it was completed, but the final completion and dedication was not until 1763. It was originally a hospital, built by the charitable townsfolk, for the fever refugees from the lowlands; the worthy charity originated by Don Juan Ramon, Don Pedro Mexia, and Don Sebastian Maldonado, exists to this day, but not as the original hospital. That is long since in ruins. The healthfulness of Orizaba is perfect, and a more charming little city is not to be found anywhere. Orizaba is in the State of Vera Cruz, on the line of the Mexican Railway, 181 miles from the City of Mexico, and, although only eighty-two miles from the sea, is 4832 feet above it. The population is 16,000; horse cars from the station and to all parks and points of interest.

Pachuca
Pa-chcw-ka

Pachuca is a windy city. The winds blow down from the mountains, and up from the valleys, and it seems, sometimes, as if they came from both at once, blowing hot and cold, so that it is not essentially a resort town, except, it may be, for miners, for here are some of the richest mines in all this country. There are nearly three hundred mines in and about the city and suburbs, and in the near-by districts of Regla and the Real del Monte. The mines are said to have been discovered by a poor shepherd, nearly four hundred years ago. They have been worked constantly ever since, yielding fabulous sums every year, till it is impossible to say what the total has been, one mine alone, Trinidad of old, having yielded nearly $50,000,000 in ten years; and the others, Rosario, Candado and Xacal have made many fortunes. The old "patio process," or amalgamating process, was first used at Pachuca. The principal modern mines are Rosario, Santa Gertrudis, Cayetano and the Dolores, but no accurate estimate can be put on the amount of treasure that has been taken out of their depths.

The streets are narrow and necessarily very crooked, as they wind up and down the steep hillsides, and are, withal, very picturesque. Among the notable buildings is the Caja, a fine structure, with great towers above, built in 1670, by the Marquis de Mancera, Don Sebastian de Toledo, as a treasure-house for the

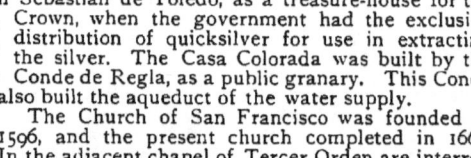

Crown, when the government had the exclusive distribution of quicksilver for use in extracting the silver. The Casa Colorada was built by the Conde de Regla, as a public granary. This Conde also built the aqueduct of the water supply.

The Church of San Francisco was founded in 1596, and the present church completed in 1660. In the adjacent chapel of Tercer Orden are interred the bones of the good Fray Cristóbal de la Cruz. What is now the school of mines and mining, was once a college of the missionaries.

The great feast of San Francisco extends from September 30 to October 8, when the city is given over to bull-fighting, cock-fights and a general good time, after the fashion of the people. Further up in the mountains is the very curious Real del Monte, reached from Pachuca, over a very fine road. The town is in the very heart of the mountains, picturesque to a degree in its combination of English houses, with peaked roofs and chimneys, for it is cold here sometimes, and the flat-topped houses of Mexico. The great house of the town is the Maestranza, containing the offices, storehouses and machine-shops of the Cayetano mine.

In the year 1739, Don Pedro José Romero de Terreros, a great miner of his day, and an operator of Querétaro, was en route for his home in Spain. He came to Pachuca; the richness of the prospect was too much for him; he stopped here and spent his fortune, but remained by his venture till he had made another and larger fortune.

The output, from 1762 to 1781, being over $12,000,000, and in 1818 the total reached the enormous figure of $30,000,000. An English company came into possession in 1824, with shares at a par value of £100, that in a year were sold at £16,000, but at the end was a complete failure. The mines are now operated with satisfactory results.

Pachucha is reached by a branch of the Mexican Central Railway from Tula; is on the main line of the Hidalgo Railroad; on branches of both the Interoceanic and Mexican Railways, distant from the city 84 miles. The altitude is 8,000 feet above the sea. The population is 20,000.

Patzcuaro
Patz-quaro
If ever you should come to Patzcuaro and see its quaint and curious streets, narrow and crooked, with shrines and saints set in the walls at every zig-zag corner; with its tree-covered plaza, where, on the market night, the fishwomen sit beside little oil-wood fires and the native comes to buy the fish, and the copper and earthen pots to cook them in. If you should ever come to Patzcuaro, make the climb to *Los Balcones* and look out over the valley, with its scores of towns, and the lake, with its islands rising out of the clear

THE START FOR TZINTZUNTZAN.

waters in cone-like peaks, you will say that the ancient Tarascan kings were correct when they called the city "Patzcuaro," as they did when they were aweary of the pomp and circumstance of state, and would hie away to Patzcuaro. I say hie away, because they took the high ground of medical ethics, and Patzcuaro, that an exalted and a pure air are the best recuperatives for overworked and exhausted kings, so they left Tzintzuntzan and hied to Patzcuaro in their royal canoes, their ships of state. It was a place of delights, on those hills to the southward of the lake, and the city that grew under royal patronage was called Patzcuaro, which, in the Tarascan tongue, means "place of pleasure."

Between the station and the town is about a league, over a winding road, hard beaten with much travel up and down the long steep hill. The mode of transportation is the *diligencia* of the old Mexican type, and its creaking leathers only quicken the anticipation, but not the pace of the mules. The wayfarers met or overtaken, and one meets more than are overtaken, are on foot or on the backs of burros, taking the product of the field or the yield of the lake from the valley to the markets of the town, or returning with the proceeds and purchases, so that the speed—speed is not exactly the word here—of the coach is not objected to; and the view gradually grows by inches as it were, till the ride is one of the pleasures of Patzcuaro.

When one comes to the top of the hill there is not time to enjoy the panorama spread out in the valley where the lake is, and then there is so much right at the wheels that is new and novel to claim attention. The mules, finding the pulling easier than on the incline of the hill, trot along at a brisker rate and are soon at the hotel—not a pleasing prospect from the façade, but the patio with its flowers and the gallery all around are reassuring; the rooms are not so inviting, but the clean newly-made-up beds are satisfying, so that it does not matter if there are no carpets and only a tiled floor, one is only to stay there when one can go nowhere else, and while one does stay there, it is to sleep—to sleep, perhaps to dream of castles in Spain, and wake to find a no less pleasing reality in a beautiful land, whose civilization is older and whose ruins and legends as interesting.

The plaza of Patzcuaro is a pretty one, and in the center of it is a beautiful pagoda, where the band plays in the evening. Over the flowers and fountains, which bloom and play from January to January, are the grandest of grand old trees that may have sheltered the Tarascan potentates when they came to this place of pleasure, and the same perennial verdure is there in the leaves.

A market night in Patzcuaro is such as could be nowhere else in the world. Scores and scores of little fires light the scene. By each fire sits a woman, a man or a boy, with their wares around them; the fruits, vegetables and fish are in little stacks on mats on the ground. Everything is sold at so much per stack in a Mexican market, and if you don't like the size of it, you can go where the stacks are larger, or the prices smaller; some sell fish, others fruit of every kind that ripens under a tropic sun; the stock in trade of another is peppers and potatoes, tomatoes and tamales; another offers earthen vessels and some of copper, for household uses, and there are flowers in abundance at almost every stand—or, more properly, at every sitting, as the venders all sit on the ground surrounded by their stock in trade.

The *portales*—columned archways—extend over the sidewalk on the four sides of the plaza in front of the stores where they sell *zerapes* and *rebosos*, which answer the purpose of overcoats for the men, and shawls and headgear for the women.

A delightful morning walk is through some narrow, crooked streets where, in the niches in the walls along, are the fourteen stations of the Cross in the street that leads to the Hill and Church of Calvary.

Los Balcones is a stone parapet or balcony in front of the Church of El Calvario, where there are several stone benches on the edge of a precipice, a thousand feet above the plain where the lake is. When the sun is just peeping over the eastern peaks of the distant Sierras, tingeing the sky from blue to gold and putting on a mellow light, it is the very prettiest picture. The valley and the lake spread out, with the forty-three towns of the plain, and the islands rising from the blue waters of the lake like the peaked and castled ones in Como, in Italy, makes a picture of surpassing beauty and fascination.

The plaza, in the morning, is not so weirdly picturesque as when the oil-wood fire-light blazed flickeringly, but as fascinating. The old churches, with their crude, quaint pictures and their relics and offerings are to be looked over, and another visit to Los Balcones is to be made to see the setting of the sun that was

ON LAKE PATZCUARO.
THE VOYAGE TO TZINTZUNTZAN.

so bright in its rising. After an early breakfast of the most luscious fruits and the delicious coffee from the plantations of Uruápam near by, and some fish fresh from the lake, it is time to start for Tzintzuntzan. Canoes should be arranged for and they will be waiting—curious canoes, long and wide, with high projecting prow and stern, hewn from great trees, each one a solid piece. The oarsmen are Indians, with ladle-looking paddles with long handles, which are industriously plied, and you are soon on your way up the lake.

The slow progress could not be monotonous on Lake Patzcuaro; there is that to see here that could not be seen anywhere else. The islands look like the peaks of submerged mountains with just the tops above the water. On the steep sides are some quaint little houses, and rising above the trees, almost at the top, gleams the white tower of a church, whose little bell sends forth a sonorous peal over the water. The picture is a pretty one, and has its double, as distinctly outlined as the original, in the marvelously clear water, and every single canoe is two, coming together at the keel, as the reflection makes it look. The fishermen are busy everywhere; their canoes dot the lake for miles around. They are long flat-bottomed boats, with a piece of cotton cloth stretched on hoops for a shelter, not unlike the cover of a country wagon. The fishermen stand in the bow with a long pole, which has a net on the end. This is dipped in the water at random, and with more or less success. The canoes hug the eastern shore, and it is not a long row—not more than three hours—to Tzintzuntzan, where the famous Titian is. Tzintzuntzan was once a great city, and the capital of the Tarascan kings; now, only a straggling village with a group of ruined churches.

Your carefully studied salutation in Spanish, a handful of cigars and a bottle of wine, will make the padre and you the best of friends.

He will know, even before you ask him, that you want to see the picture, and will open the high arched door of carved wood which leads to a *patio* or open court.

A little surpliced Indian boy brings a lighted candle. The padre leads the way, and a wondering little procession follows through a dark corridor that leads up to another massive door, barred and chained and padlocked.

You are back in ancient feudal days, in some old castle opened to you. The clanking chains and rusty, creaking hinges are on your prison doors; but the boy holds the tallow dip high, and shows the padre's kindly face. You are only at Tzintzuntzan, in search of a Titian.

The door opens into an inner room as dark as night. The padre unfastens a grated window, and a flood of golden sunlight comes through, and falls full upon the picture.

Such coloring, such composition, such feeling, could only come from a master-hand. Whose? Tradition says Titian, and presented by Philip II. of Spain. Eminent men, authors and artists agree. The padre closes the window and the door, locks and chains them again; the boy holds up his flickering torch, and you go out, leaving the padre and his treasures as a dream too unreal to be true. An effort has been made to buy the painting, and $50,000 was offered by the Bishop of Mexico, but the faithful, devoted Indians refuse, and the price that bought the "Angelus" would be no temptation. Yet the "Entombment" is some hundreds of years older, is the work of an old master, and is big enough (the figures are all life size) to make a hundred of the "Angelus;" and yet its price would not buy it, the Indians refusing absolutely to allow the picture to be taken away.

In the Casa Municipal of the village is a painting of the Calzontzin Sinzicha receiving Christianity. Some attempts at excavating were made in 1855, but the Indians were superstitious and quietly filled up the trenches as fast as they were dug.

The See of Michoacan was removed from Tzintzuntzan to Patzcuaro, and the building of a great Cathedral was commenced, under a bull of Pope Julian III., published July 8, 1550. But only a part of the church was finished, since the See was removed again to Morelia, and it is now used as the parish church. It will hold 3,000 people. The bones of the good Bishop Quiroga, in wrappings of silk, are preserved in the church, on the left of the main entrance. Here also is an image of Nuestra Señora de la Salud, dedicated by Bishop Quiroga. Connected with this church there was, in ancient days, a very rich nunnery. There is an altar over the spring which supplies the city with the water which gushed forth

CHURCH AT TZINTZUNTZAN, CONTAINING THE ENTOMBMENT, BY TITIAN.

from the rock struck by the staff of Bishop Quiroga. The staff is also shown in the Cathedral at Morelia. The Church of San Agustin was established in 1576, San Juan de Dios in 1650. The other churches are San Francisco and Guadalupe. About a mile eastward of Patzcuaro is the chapel of Humilladero, erected on the spot where the Indians received the Spaniards with overtures of peace, which were hardly reciprocated by them.

Of the islands of Lake Patzcuaro there are three, Xanicho, Xarácuaro and Pacanda, that are populated by a community of fishermen. Xanicho is the largest, with a population of 1,200, and a quaint little church, Geronimo, and a school for boys and girls.

Near Tzintzuntzan is the little town of Iguatzio, where there is a pyramid, from which idols, ornaments and arms have been taken, and under which are subterranean passages, with supports of timber, which tradition says communicated with those of Tzintzuntzan, discovered in 1855. These and the paved road were in existence when the Spaniards came.

The cruel acts of Niño de Guzman greatly retarded the peaceful work of the emissaries of Cortéz, Guzman's cruelties culminating in the burning of the Calzontzin Sinzicha to extort the secret of supposed treasure. After the recall of Guzman to Spain came Vasco de Quiroga, a lawyer, afterwards the good bishop, who did much to repair the cruel doings, and through him came about the good works of peace, and the frightened people returned to their homes and were taught to make copper ware and to work in other metals, as well as the other arts of peace. The good effect of his teachings are felt in this region to this day, and his name is much venerated. He died at Uruápam in 1565, March 14, at the age of 96 years.

The city of Michoacan, which included Tzintzuntzan and Patzcuaro, was founded February 28, 1534, by a Royal Order of Charles V., but the seat of the See was finally to be at Morelia, where it now is.

Patzcuaro is on the western division of the Mexican National Railroad, in the State of Michoacan, 274 miles from the City of Mexico. The altitude is 6,787 feet; population, 15,000.

Puebla
Poo-eb-lah

It is called the City of the Angels, but Puebla is a city of tiles. Tiles are used everywhere, from the domes of the many churches of the valley to their walls and floors; glazed tiles of many colors adorn the exterior and interior walls of residences, and in varied hues on the towers they glisten in the sun. One house in the Calle de Mercaderes has its façade entirely of tiles; and in the Church of Nuestra Señora de la Luz, and the old convent of Santa Rosa, are some very beautiful mosaics of tiles. Looking down from the surrounding hills, or in the approach across the plain, the tiled towers present a picturesque effect.

The history of Puebla is romantic, and full of legends. The original name of the city was Puebla de los Angeles, from the vision that led to its founding on this site, or rather, two visions. One legend goes on to tell of the marshalling, in mighty hosts, of the angels above the place where the city now stands. The other story is, that the good Fray Julian Garces, desirous of founding a halting-place between the coast and the capital, set about to find a site for his city, and one night, as he rested from his labors, he dreamed a dream, and in it saw a beautiful plain, on the slope of the great volcanoes, with two little hills about a league between; there were springs in the plain, and two rivers of abundant waters, with living trees and flowers. While he looked upon this, two angels appeared, with rod and chain, and measured streets and squares. After this remarkable dream, the Bishop awoke and immediately set out. Guided by the same power that showed the vision, says the chronicler, he soon came to the plain of his dream, saying "Here hath the Lord, through his angels, shown me the site

142

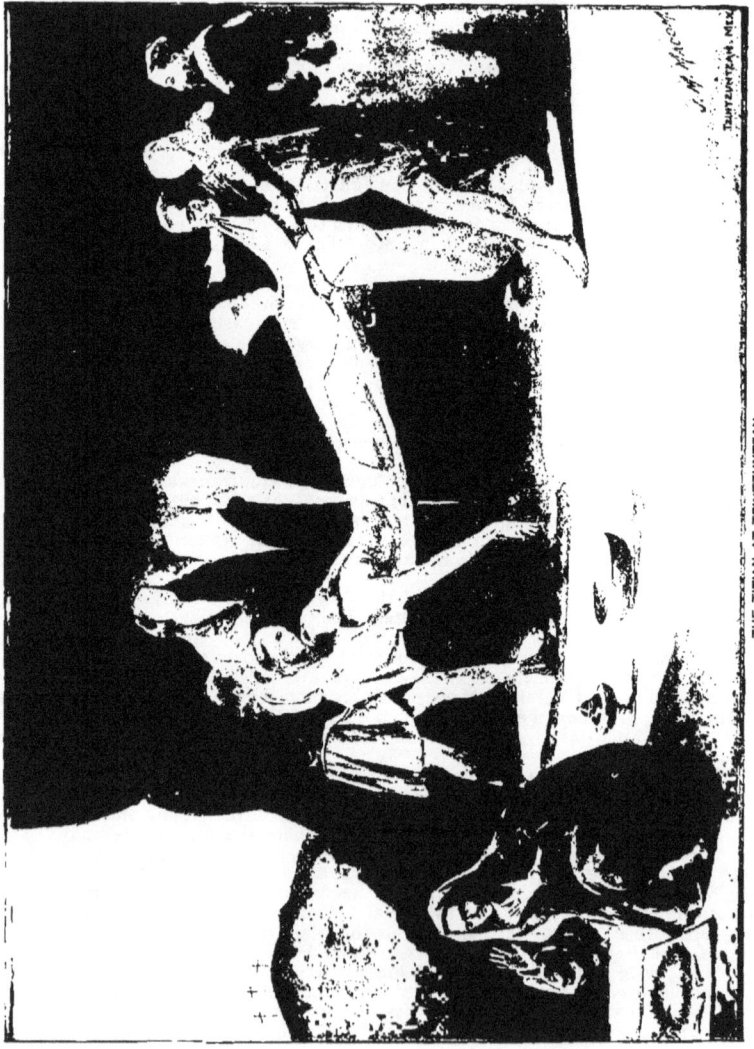

THE TITIAN AT TZINTZUNTZAN.

of the city, and to His glory it shall be made." And thus came the name Puebla de los Angeles. But more substantial history relates that some fifty families of Spaniards, from Tlaxcala, came to this valley, and, on the 16th of April, 1532, commenced the building of houses of the city that for more than three hundred and fifty years has borne the name derived from the vision, till it was officially changed to Puebla Zaragoza, in honor of the hero of the battle of the 5th of May, 1862.

Puebla has seen much of the vicissitudes of war, and, next to the capital, has suffered most. It was captured by Yturbide, August 2, 1821; occupied by General Scott, May 25, 1847; was the scene of Zaragoza's victory, May 5, 1862; recaptured by the French on the 17th of the same month, and in turn taken from them four years later, April 2, 1867, by General Porfirio Diaz.

Northeast of the city, within the suburbs, is the hill and fort of Guadalupe, named for the church that was there in the earlier days. Here was the battle ground of the 5th of May, 1862, when General Zaragoza, with 2000 men, repulsed the 6000 French soldiers, under de Lorencez, and, in 1867, April 2, General Porfirio Diaz recaptured the forts and made prisoners the entire French garrison of Puebla. The ruins of the church were used for fortifications, and, with the stone, the fort was built, though the church was not completely de-molished. The crypt was used as a magazine, and the other parts put to baser uses. On a slightly lower hill, called Loreto, about half a mile north, is the fort of Cinco de Mayo, and within its walls the little chapel of Loreto. The view from the hill of Guadalupe is one of extreme beauty.

The city is spread out on the plain in the foreground. To the eastward the great volcanoes of Popocatepetl and Ixtaccihuatl; to the north is the mighty Malintzi, and to the east old Orizaba; the lesser hills are Tecolote on the left, and the Cerro del Conde; to the right Amaluca, near by the hill and fort of Loreto; to the left, the Cerro San Juan, with its arched hacienda, and beyond it the Pyramid of Cholula. There are churches, churches, everywhere, and in all directions, with their walls and domes of all the colors: San Agustin is white; San José, red; Santo Domingo, white; Concepcion, brown; Santa Teresa, yellow; San Cristóbal, red; Carmen, yellow; San Angel de Analco, red; Compañia, blue; Soledad, white; San Francisco, grey; while towering

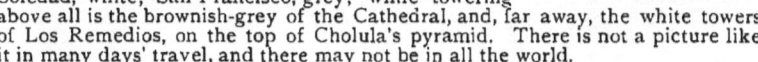

AT PUEBLA.

above all is the brownish-grey of the Cathedral, and, far away, the white towers of Los Remedios, on the top of Cholula's pyramid. There is not a picture like it in many days' travel, and there may not be in all the world.

It is not a long walk to this hill of Guadalupe, a trifle tiresome, but very pleasant, if you take your time. The way is through the Plazuela de San Francisco, out by the old Plaza de Toros, across the stone bridge over the Atoyac, through the little paseo, and by the group of churches of Calvario San Juan del Rio and Piadosas, and over the old causeway where marched the processions in olden times; this is the way to Guadalupe.

The streets of Puebla are wide, as streets go in Mexico, and are wonderfully clean, sloping from curb to center, where, in some of them, are running streams, while others are flooded for sanitary purposes. The parks and plazas are pretty, indeed, with their trees, and flowers and fountains. The markets are more metropolitan than Mexican, though many curious articles are offered in the stalls. Mats and baskets of colored straw, the crude crockery of Puebla manu-facture, clay figures and Indian carvings of onyx. The buildings are more pretentious than in the average city of this country, though built in purely

Mexican style. They are two and three stories high. There are two theatres and two bull-rings, and the bull-fights of Puebla are notable for their excellence, if that word may be used in connection with the sport.

The public buildings are not so ambitious as might be expected in so fine a city. The legislative sessions are in the old Alhóndiga, on the Plaza Mayor, and the Courts are in the old Colegio de San Pantaleon; but the penitentiary is one of the finest in the land. There is a State College, with libraries of nearly 40,000 volumes; a Normal School, and other educational institutions, and an Academy of Fine Arts; also, several hospitals.

The Cathedral of Puebla rivals the great Cathedral of the City of Mexico, and, except in point of size, is regarded by many as the finer church. Bishop Zumárraga laid the corner stone of the first church, in 1532, and of the first Cathedral in 1536, but the present building was not begun until a hundred years later; it was consecrated April 18, 1649. The location is on a stone terrace, to the south of the Plaza Mayor. The church is surrounded by an iron railing, placed in 1886-87. This, with a monument, is in memory of Pius IX. Between the two tall towers of the west front is the main doorway, with the date above, 1664, marking the completion

FUNERAL PROCESSION. of this portion of the building. The building is 323 feet long and 101 feet wide, with a height on the inside of more than eighty feet, the whole surmounted by a splendid dome. The old tower, which alone cost $100,000, contains eighteen bells, the largest of which weighs nearly 20,000 pounds. The great choir, built of stone, is in the center of the nave, enclosed in wrought-iron gratings, made in 1697. The carvings of the organ are superb, in native woods, as are the doors of the entrance-ways. The intricate marquety work is a revelation. On the door that leads to the Bishop's seat is an inlaid picture of St. Peter, and in the shrine above is preserved a thorn from the crown of Christ.

The great altar was commenced in 1789, and completed in 1819, at a cost of $110,000. It is constructed of every conceivable marble of Mexico, and the exquisite onyx of Puebla, the work of a native artist, Manuel Tolsa. Beneath the altar is the tomb of the Bishops, this also laid in beautiful slabs of onyx.

The chapels are the Capilla de los Reyes, with a shrine and image of Nuestra Señora de la Difensa, to whom is attributed many miracles; the Capilla de San José contains a fine figure of that saint, and an ivory crucifix, a present to Bishop Vasquez by Gregory XVI.; the Bishop's tomb is in front of the chapel. The Capilla de los Relicários has an altar of richly carved wood, and a silver urn, containing the ashes of San Sebastian de Aparicio, also the busts of other saints, with relics of their bones carried, under glass, on their breasts. Here are scores of boxes, containing relics innumerable.

In the sacristy are many pictures, set in golden, carved frames; the tables have slabs of richest onyx, and the vestment chests are handsomely carved.

Among the portraits in the Cathedral are those of the various Bishops of Puebla, of Gregory XVIII., Charles V., Fray Julian Garcés, first Bishop of Puebla, Leo X; in the sacristy are some rich tapestries of Flanders, presented by Charles V. Among the other pictures are the Fourteen Stations of the Cross, the Holy Sacrament, the Assumption, the Apparition of Nuestra Señora de la Merced to San Raymundo de Peñafort, a Virgin and Child, by Ibarra, a Dolores de Acazingo, the Triumph of Mary, and a Last Supper, with many others.

The parish church adjoins the Cathedral, where there are other fine pictures, and a beautiful baptismal font of onyx.

The Church of San Francisco is next to the Cathedral in point of interest and beauty. Founded in 1532, on the hill above the Atoyac, the present church was begun in 1667. The very high tower is built of a bluish-grey stone, beautifully carved, and laid in panels of tiles. The old convent of this church is now used as a military hospital. The flat arched roof, the story says, was not trusted by the architect; he feared to remove the supporting timbers, and left it to the priests to do. They were afraid to send laborers to take them out, and it was concluded to burn them out. It was done; the arch remained intact, and is to-day, after more than two hundred years. In this church is a little image, carved in wood, of Nuestra Señora de los Remedios, called La Conquistadora. It is only about eight inches high, with a little child in its arms. This was presented by Cortéz to Axotecatl Cocomitzin, the Tlaxcalan chief, in token of his friendship for the ally.

Here also is the chapel of San Sebastian de Aparicio, who first introduced wheeled carts and oxen into Mexico, and who drove an ox-cart between Vera Cruz and the city, and later, in 1542, on the roads north to Zacatecas. The Fray's bones were formerly kept in this chapel, until they were removed to the Cathedral where they now are. There is a most interesting old panteon in connection with the church. La Compañia was founded April 15, 1587; the present church completed in 1690. There are two towers and a tiled dome. San Cristóbal was founded more than three hundred years ago. The pulpit is of onyx. This is one of the few Mexican churches with seats, with the unusual feature, also, of having separate seats for men and women.

Of the other churches, San Antonio contains a relic of the skin of one of the saints; Nuestra Señora de la Luz is particularly noted for its beautiful tile work; Santa Clara possesses a thorn from the crown of Christ; San José is the saint who protects Puebla from the lightning, an image of whom is in his church, carved from a tree destroyed by lightning; La Soledad is one of the finest of the forty-six churches of Puebla, but to write their history, or even record their legends, would make many volumes.

The Pyramid of Cholula
<small>Cho-loo-la</small>

The date of the building of the Pyramid of Cholula is unknown. Even before the Aztecs came to the plain of Cholula, the great pyramid was there in the midst,

CHURCH DOME, PYRAMID OF CHOLULA.

and the people told them the legend of it, that it was built by a race of giants descended from the two survivors of a great deluge that overspread the land, and whose intent it was to raise its heights to heaven, but they incurred the displeasure of the gods, who sent forth fires and destroyed them. This indeed is the story that is coincident with the Chaldean and Hebrew accounts of the Deluge and the Tower of Babel, of which there is so much in the traditions of these people that is similar to the tales of the Bible. On the summit stood the sumptuous temple of the mystic deity, Quetzalcoatl, the "god of the air," whose image was there, under its pinnacled towers, as the chronicler says, with ebon features, wearing a mitre on his head, waving with plumes of fire; a resplendent collar of gold was about the neck; pendants of mosaic turquoise in his ears; a jeweled scepter in one hand, and a curiously painted shield, emblem of his reign over the winds, in the other. Cholula was, in those ancient days, what Rome is to-day. Pilgrims came from hundreds of miles—as do the Mohammedans to Mecca—to bow down before the temple of Quetzacoatl, in the holy city of Anahuac. Cortéz declared that he counted four hundred towers in the city of Cholula, yet no temple had more than two, and some only one. High above the rest rose the great temple on the pyramid, with its never-dying fires spreading their radiance over the capital, proclaiming the return of the deity to resume his rule over the land. Such was the pyramid and city as the Spaniards saw it at their coming, and the people they found there could tell little else of its history than is written here. The temple was thrown down as promptly as was the custom of the conquerors, and a Christian church placed in its stead, that stands to this day.

The pyramid has the appearance of a natural hill, as its sides are overgrown with trees and bushes, which is but an evidence of its great antiquity, as the interior is composed of alternate layers of sun-dried brick, clay and limestone. The height is 177 feet above the plain. The four sides face the cardinal points, and are laid in terraces that now are overgrown with shrubs and flowers. The base lines are more than a thousand feet on each side, or twice as long as the great Cheops; or, to give a better idea of its size, is to say that it covers twenty acres of the plain. A paved road leads up the steep west side, with steps of hewn stone, to the arch and cross of the entrance-way to the Church of Nuestra Señora de los Remedios, on the very top. From the balconies the view of the valley and surrounding mountains, the many churches, with their glazed tile towers, and the towns and villages of the plain, is superb.

ALTAR OF THE CHURCH OF THE PYRAMID OF CHOLULA.

The town of Cholula has dwindled, from the great capital of a mighty nation, to less than 5000 people. The market place, "Tianquiz," is still called by its ancient name. Near the plaza is the ruins of an abandoned monastery of San Francisco, founded in 1529. The church on this spot, called San Gabriel, was founded in 1604; it has a very handsome altar of expensive adornment. Near by and adjoining the walls, is the Royal Chapel and Tercer Orden, whose roof of domes is supported by sixty-four round columns. This church was built in 1608, for overflow meetings. There are twenty-seven other churches in Cholula, and from the pyramid the towers of thirty more can be counted.

The ride on the horse cars across the Atoyac Valley, from Puebla to Cholula, is a delightful one, passing out of the city of Puebla through the arch of the Garita de Mexico. The track runs along the highway, between it and an arched aqueduct. The hacienda of San Juan is the arched stone building on the crest of a hill to the left. The way is across a stone bridge, with arched entrances, over the Atoyac River, passing churches and haciendas in numbers, on both sides, with something to interest in every one of the eight miles.

Querétaro
Kay-ret-aro

Querétaro occupies a prominent place in Mexico's history. It was an Otomite town before the Spaniards came, and was made a city as early as 1655, by a decree of Philip IV., of Spain. Nearly every Mexican town has its legend; that of Querétaro is, that an Otomite chief, Fernando de Tapia by name, undertook to Christianize the town by fighting, which seems to have been the earlier method. He came from Xilotepec and Tula, to challenge the people of Querétaro to what might be called a "fair fist and skull" fight, the citizens to be baptized or not as they were beaten or victorious. But it was not to be a fair fight, after all, for while the performance was proceeding, a dark cloud came up, and the blessed Santiago was seen in the heavens with a fiery cross. This ended the "mill," the people of Querétaro were baptized, and in commemoration of the miracle, set up a stone cross, on a site now occupied by the church of Santa Cruz, which is shown to prove the aforesaid.

As in the case of many Mexican towns, this one derives its name from an Indian word meaning a game of ball, or from "querénda," a rocky peak.

Querétaro was the place of the ratification of the treaty of peace between the United States and Mexico, in 1848, and figured, more or less, in the later wars and revolutions, till the town is full of warlike reminiscence. Maximilian's last stand was made here, and his surrender on the 19th of May, 1867.

The story of "poor Carlotta" is one of the saddest, and had its saddest feature at Querétaro, where her beloved, but unfortunate, husband met his death. Maximilian was executed on the Cerro de las Campanas, just in the northern limits of the city, June 19, 1867, and with him the Generals, Miramon and Mejia. The place of execution is marked by three little crosses of stone. The two generals fell at the first volley, but it required a second firing before the Emperor was dead. He had requested that he might be shot in the body, that his mother might look on his face. He had been led to believe that "poor Carlotta" was dead, a story of consolation, in pity given. The body was taken to an old convent of the Capuchins, but subsequently to Austria and buried at Miramar. A martyr cruelly betrayed by the French Emperor, and seemingly deserted by all the world except a devoted wife, who pleaded for succor in vain to the Pope of Rome. The Government of the United States protested against the execution, although an imperial power on this continent is inimical to its doctrines, but the protest was unheeded. The Princess Salm-Salm, remembered in our own war times, rode 160 miles to San Luis Potosí, and on her knees begged President Juarez to spare the captive, but all unavailing, and Maximilian died a martyr to a political principle.

The court-martial was convened in the Yturbide Theatre, June 14, 1867, at 10.00 a. m., and at 10.00 p. m. on the 15th the sentence of death was pronounced, and at once approved by General Escobedo, who ordered the execution to take place the next day, but a telegram from Juarez, at San Luis Potosí, postponed the execution till the 19th. The theatre remains now as then. In the State Capitol are shown the table on which the death warrant was signed, the wooden stools on which the prisoners sat during the trial, and the coffin of Maximilian. The convent of the Capuchins is now a dwelling, but its owner will show the room in which the prisoners were confined. In the pretty little plaza was a favorite promenade of the Emperor Maximilian during the siege which ended so disastrously for him. The fact that the Emperor took his evening walks in the plaza became known to the besieging army, and their cannon were aimed so as to drop the shot in the right place. Maximilian escaped, but the fountain, near which he sat one day, was struck by a cannon ball and the stone sent flying in all directions.

The cathedral, formerly the Church of San Francisco, built in 1698, has some very beautiful decorations in sculpture, carvings and paintings. Near by is the Chapel of San Loreto. Santa Clara, founded by a rich Indian, the Cacique Diego de Tapia, son of the introductor of Christianity in the town, San Felipe, Santo

Domingo, San Antonio, San Agustin, Carmen, Merced, Santa Teresa, Santa Rosa, and Santa Cruz, containing the stone cross that was set up and worshiped by the Indians, on their conversion on the day of Santiago, nearly 400 years ago, are among the many churches, whose towers are seen from the cars. At the village of San Francisco is the church, or rather shrine, of Nuestra Señora del Pueblito, containing a curious image of the Virgin, which at intervals weeps and sometimes assumes a countenance anything but pleasant, much to the disquiet of the Indians, and who, for the time being, are put on their good behavior, at least till the clouds roll by.

The city of Querétaro lies to the eastward of the track, and a good view of the city may be seen from passing trains. Just after leaving the city, going south, the track passes under the aqueduct of the city's water supply, which is nearly five miles long. The tallest arch is nearly a hundred feet high. The water comes from the mountains, passing through a tunnel, over the aqueduct, and is distributed through the city by fountains. One of the prettiest is in the main plaza, amid a very bower of palms and tropical trees; and, by the way, you that

CORNER OF THE MARKET PLACE, QUERÉTARO.

have been looking for palm trees all along may see the first at Querétaro. The climate is very delightful. Year in and year out it is one succession of early summer days.

Querétaro is the place of opals. The mines are in all the region round about. The opal and Querétaro are synonymous only from the fact that both are found in the same locality, and not that the town is considered an unlucky one. In fact, the citizens are singularly prosperous, and visitors are lucky to an average, until they buy an opal; and then the only ill luck that follows is in paying too high, or buying a stone that has a flaw.

Some of the citizens meet all trains with a supply of opals, and with more or less luck in their disposition, as the passenger is more or less inexperienced. Others of the inhabitants also make connections with the fast express trains of the Central, with a view of catching a passenger with a stop-over ticket, and show him or her, or both, the town.

Querétaro is the capital of the State of Querétaro, and is one of the most important cities of Central Mexico, being a distributing point and a manufacturing centre. The principal industries are the manufacture of cotton goods, leather and leather wares, and sugar. The Hercules cotton factory is one of the largest in the country; it employs several hundred operatives, taken from the native population. The mill uses both steam and water power; there is a 200 horse-power engine and an immense water-wheel nearly fifty feet in diameter. The mill has a beautiful location, just in the eastern suburb of the city, surrounded by tropical gardens of fruits and flowers, and is one of the objects of interest in a visit to Querétaro.

Horse cars run from the station to the plaza, and beyond to the Hercules mills and the suburbs. The population is 50,000; altitude 5963 feet; distance from the City of Mexico, 153 miles.

Saltillo
Sal-*teel*-yo

That picturesque garment, the *zerape*, so much affected by the Mexican, and which does overcoat duty for a large contingent not possessed of the wherewith to buy a *sobre todo* of more modern fashion, has its chief point of manufacture at Saltillo; at least those that have artistic coloring, and whose textile is the most delicately woven, with the softest finish, are native to that city, and to possess one from the hand looms of that city was to own the very best. The zerape of to-day is machine woven, and though some are made by hand, they are not the things of beauty they were in times past, and one of ancient date is really a joy forever. An old Mexican explained to me the difference in colors then and now, and the cause of the change. He said that in the old days the designs of decorative colors were taken from the plumage of the birds and from the flowers of the land, so there were softer tints where natural beauty blended them, than in these modern days, when the untutored eye is caught by the flaring colors of cheap tints and gaudy combinations of the more civilized but less tasteful foreigner, who unwittingly, in the wares he sold the natives, changed the whole school of coloring in the native mind. This applies, not only to the zerapes of Saltillo, but to the pottery of Patzcuaro and Guadalajara.

Saltillo is the capital of the State of Coahuila, which once included all of Texas. The city was founded in 1586, but was not incorporated until 1827. The location is just on the rise of the plateau, and the climate is a delightful one, with only a very few days of cold weather in all the year. All the fruits of the temperate zone, and many of the tropics, are grown. Apples and oranges, pears and bananas, are found in the same gardens that are on either side of the street through which the railroad runs. The horse car has not made its appearance at Saltillo yet. The short distance from the station to the very pretty plaza may be made on foot, or carriages will be found waiting the arrival of trains. The driver will make a contract, *por hora*, at very low figures, and if there is a lack of elegance in equipage, yet it takes you to the lovely little alameda, to the baths of San Lorenzo or Alta Mira, and to the churches, which we will call San Francisco or Carmen, and brings you safely to the hotel.

The battlefield of Buena Vista is about five miles south of Saltillo, hardly worth the while of an excursion, as it may be seen from the windows of the cars. The field is on the east side of the track. This, and the fort on the hill, a relic of the French occupation, is all there is to connect Saltillo with the country's history.

Saltillo is on the Mexican National Railroad, 606 miles from the capital. The altitude is 5342 feet; population, 12,000.

Salvatierra Down in the Lerma Valley is one of the prettiest towns in
Salva-*te-er-ra* Mexico, and, withal, one of the oldest and most thriving—going on in age to its second century, and possessing extensive cotton and woolen mills. Long ago Salvatierra was a trading point, and its location in the midst of a fertile plain has made it a place of importance.

The tower on the north of the track, seen from the car windows, is that of the Church of Nuestra Señora de las Luces, the parish church, and a very fine one, with handsome decorations and paintings. There are other churches well worth a visit. The Plaza, the Alameda and the markets are all interesting, but the most picturesque is the bridge of stone arches which spans the Rio Lerma, as old, almost, as the city is. It is a picture in itself, with its quaint traffic crossing to and fro, going to town and country with the product of the field and farm, or the results of *tienda* trades in town. The town was founded in 1643, and named for the then viceroy. The lands were donated by Don Andres Alderete and his wife for the city, for which they received an annuity from the crown of 2000 pesos. The location of Salvatierra was in the path of marching armies; the city suffered more or less during the various wars, but recovered rapidly, and now the progress of peace is evidenced in all her streets. Salvatierra is in the State of Guanajuato, on the Mexican National Railroad, 197 miles from the City. The altitude is 5714 feet; population, 11,000.

DROP CURTAIN SHOWING THEATRE, SAN LUIS POTOSÍ.

San Luis Potosí
San Lu-ese Po-to-*see*

There is San Luis and a St. Louis in every country, but there is only one San Luis Potosí—only one San Luis of the Treasure —that in Mexico, the capital of the State of that name, and one of the most satisfactory cities in all that country. In the midst of a spreading plain of great fertility, the gardens and groves extend into fields that stretch away to the circling hills, that are rich in mineral deposits of the precious metals, notably those of the rich San Pedro mines, where the annual silver output runs up into the millions. Long before the advent of the Spaniard the mines were known to the natives, and were revealed by a pious Indian, with the hope of advancing the cause of Christianity. A venerable monk called the place by its present name, from its resemblance to the Potosi mines in Peru. Since then the production has been in untold millions down to the present day, when the annual coinage of the mint is more than $3,000,000.

San Luis was not made a city till about 1666, although a settlement was made there 100 years earlier, so the city has not been one of a mushroom growth; and the advent of the railroad has not been the cause of its prosperity, because this city has been, for a hundred years or more, a great trading center for the eastern, as Guadalajara has been for the western slope. Until the completion of the railways, the means of transportation to the sea was by pack mules across the

FOUNTAIN AT SAN LUIS POTOSÍ.

plains and over the mountains. But now San Luis Potosí has greater facilities and becomes a railroad center, the Mexican National Railroad, leading north and south, and the Central westward to the main line and east to the Gulf of Mexico, at Tampico. The stations of both roads are near the city's center, adjoining one of the principal plazas—a feature not common in Mexico, nearly all the stations being more or less distant, but, as at San Luis Potosí also, with horse-car connections to the hotels and plazas.

San Luis is noted for the cleanliness of its streets, and the bright fresh look of its houses, which is looked after by the City Fathers. An ordinance prevents the citizens from becoming negligent as to the appearance of their dwellings, and they must be kept in order at all times. It is pleasant to walk through these streets, and through the plazas and plazuelas, of which there are many, with their trees and flowers, fountains and pagodas, where there is music in the evenings, and where the people do congregate. And there's many an open doorway that shows the pretty *patios*, with their miniature gardens filled with flowers, fountains and singing birds, and these go to tell that the brightness and freshness of a San Luis Potosí house is not all on the outside. The markets and market places, near by the hotels, are to be included in the walks about town, and are intensely interesting, as all Mexican markets are. The State Capitol, the Library and Museum, with nearly 100,000 volumes, El Instituto (the State College), the Alhóndiga and the Lonja Mercantil, are the prominent places of the city to be visited, and are all buildings above the average in every way. Horse-car rides may be made to Guadalupe and Tequis-quiápan, the Baths of La Soledad, to Axcala and Santiago, the cars starting from the main plaza; the fares are from five to twenty-five cents, according to the distance traveled. In the rainy season, as an additional attraction, the horse cars carry signs conveying the information that there is water in the river. Good carriages may be had at the railway stations, or on the plaza, at from fifty cents to a dollar per hour. The churches are more than usually interesting, and are, for the most part, fine examples of the prevailing styles of architecture—are rich in native decorative art, in carvings, paintings and pictures. The Cathedral, formerly the parish church, is on the Plaza Mayor, a really fine building, with ambitious towers built of stone; the pillars and altars are also of cut stone. The See of San Luis Potosí was not promulgated till 1854, though the first church was founded in 1583. The two tall towers of red stone seen from the west windows of the cars, just south of the city, are those of the Church of Guadalupe, standing high above the plain and the surrounding trees, and can be seen for miles up and down the road, an imposing landmark, that shows where the city is, long before it can be seen.

In the façade of the church is a fine clock, presented by the King of Spain, in return for the gift of the largest single piece of silver ore ever taken from a mine. The church is well worth a visit, which may best be made by a carriage drive out the Paseo, passing the markets, the fountains, with their scores of quaintly costumed water-carriers, with queer wheelbarrows, carrying from one to three earthen jugs, the barracks and the penitentiary—a somewhat dusty road, but an interesting drive, with much to see.

In the Church of El Carmen are some especially fine paintings, illustrative of the saints—both native and foreign—if saints may be so designated. The other churches are Merced, San Agustin and San Francisco; one never tires of the churches of Mexico, and cannot tire of these.

They are a thrifty people of San Luis Potosí, and the stores and shops attest the fact. Every one has a "this-is-my-busy-day" look; the dealers are intent on business, and the customers, in crowds, drive sharp bargains. The gold and silver embroidery of the native is a pretty souvenir to buy; it is in the shape of slippers and pieces for ornament, that may be bought at varying prices, according as the work is more or less elaborate. Pottery, feather and palm work may also be found. As I have said, San Luis Potosí is a railroad center. There is a frequent train service, and the stop may be long or short, going south to the City, north to the United States, east to Tampico or west to Aguas Calientes.

San Luis Potosí is reached by the Mexican National and Mexican Central Railways. The distance from the City of Mexico is 362 miles. The altitude is 5786 feet; population 85,000.

MEXICAN NATIONAL STATION, SAN LUIS POTOSÍ.

San Miguel de Allende
San Me-*gïl* de Al-*yen*-de

A picturesquely pretty city, that is set upon a hill and cannot be hid, is San Miguel de Allende, where its rugged streets, and gardens terraced on the steep sides of the enchanted Cerro de Moctezuma, look down over the valley of Laja and to the blue hills far beyond. The ride of a mile from the railway, in the old-time coaches, is an interesting one, leading over a hill and intervening valley, where an ancient bridge of crumbling arches crosses a stream of clear, sparkling water, and enters the quaint old town that lies spread out on the hillside above; then, with a zigzag course, it is a climb to a plaza that one has no hint or suspicion of, it is such a pretty one, till the coach pulls up in front of the hotel that faces it, and whose casement windows look out over the prettiest of evergreen trees. The hotel is a surprise as well, and was once the palatial home of a wealthy and pious man, Señor Don Manuel Tomas de la Canal, and his wife, who donated the very beautiful chapel of the Casa de Loreto, a chapel that is a very poem of color and carving. If architecture be frozen music, then this gem is a dulcet melody, where there is a delicious warmth in its very congealing. But to go back to the hotel again, the image of the Virgin of Loreto over the door was placed there through the reverence of the family, Canal, when it was their home.

The very beautiful Gothic church on the plaza, the only one of its kind in Mexico, was the work of a native architect, who knew not the process of "blue prints," and drew his plans with a stick in the sand; these were the only guides for the builders to work by. The original church was completed nearly a hundred years ago, and the interior, with the exception of a renovation in 1842-3, remains the same, only the façade and the beautiful Gothic towers being new; this is the parish church. The others are San Rafael, adjoining the Parróquia, in which there are some strange statuary and paintings, and attached to this church is the Casa de Loreto, one of the most beautiful things in Mexico in carvings, gildings and glazed tiles, presented by Señor Canal in 1635. The names of the other churches worth visiting are the Concepcion, San Francisco, Nuestra Señora de la Soledad and the Chapel of Calvario, at the top of a steep hill, which the wickedest sinners approach on their knees, stopping at the fourteen stations of the cross, on the hillside, to pray. San Miguel has an important place in the history of the country. The patriot, Ygnacio Allende, was born here, to which fact is due the addition of Allende to the name of the town. About a dozen miles distant, to the north, is the village and Santuario de Jesus Nazareno de Atotonilco, founded in 1748, famous as the place whence Hidalgo took the banner of the Virgin of Guadalupe that became the standard of Independence, and, with Allende, carried it to San Miguel, where the Queen's regiment joined the insurgent forces, which became a victorious patriot army. The visit to San Miguel is not complete without an excursion to Atotonilco.

In the southern part of the city and high up on the hill are some very beautiful gardens, laid in pretty terraces of flowers, watered by a hundred little cascades of clear water, that come down from the springs still higher up on the *cerro*, where the baths are--delightful baths, where the water comes pouring from under the rocks and into the baths, fresh and pure, accommodatingly warm in winter and cool in summer. To get there one may ride, but the carriage rattles over some very stony streets, and although it is a climb, I would suggest to walk. Leave the plaza, walk one square up the hill, turn to the right one square, then another up and again to the right, till you come to the gardens. These turns to the right break the climb and give you a rest, for the hill is a steep one, but the trip is well worth the going, whether you walk or ride.

As the people of Mexico are all courtesy and hospitality, they are especially so at San Miguel, and are always glad to welcome the stranger within the gates of their beautiful city.

San Miguel is in the State of Guanajuato, on the Mexican National Railroad, 253 miles from the City; altitude, 6231 feet; population, 20,000.

Silao   Silao was founded in the year 1553, by Don Francisco Cervantes Ren-
See-*low*   don, but was not pronounced a city till 1861. It is in the midst of a fertile valley, close to the silver hills of Guanajuato. The completion of the railway, the establishment of shops, and the building of the branch to Guanajuato, enhanced the importance of the place and caused a wakening from the three hundred years' nap, from the settlement to the incorporation of the city.

It is worth the while to wander through the narrow streets. The Plaza Mayor is not far from the station. Santiago, completed in 1728, is the parish church. It has a particularly pretty tower, tall and slender. The Church of El Señor de la Vera Cruz contains a curious figure of the Christ in *papier maché*, antedating the conquest of Spain by the Moors. It was presented to the Indians by the missionaries. The Santuario del Padre Jesus was built in 1798. The only other church of importance is San Nicolás.

Silao is in the State of Guanajuato, on the Mexican Central Railway, 238 miles from the City of Mexico and fifteen miles from Guanajuato, by branch road. The population is 15,000; altitude, 5828 feet.

Tampico
Tam-pee-ko

In the tropical *tierra caliente*, Tampico lies on the Gulf shore, at the mouth of the Rio Panuco, which is a truly noble and great river, in which the navies of the world might ride. Indeed, Tampico is the rival of Vera Cruz, as the chief seaport on the east coast of Mexico, and, with the completed jetties and the deep rivers, the great merchant ships may make fast to the piers, instead of lying outside and "lightering" in. The rivers emptying here are navigable for some miles into the interior, where the scenery is rich in tropic

TAMPICO.

beauty. About ten miles west of Tampico there are the ruins of an ancient city, a relic of the Aztecs, or some other race of the pre-Cortéz days. There is a considerable hill and the remains of embankments and other earthworks, together with a large, rudely sculptured stone. At the summit is a collection of pyramidal and conical mounds, many of them excellently preserved by a sort of shell of rectangular stone slabs set closely together on edge. Some excavations, made several years ago, showed the interior to be composed of earth, commingled with ashes and broken pottery. The ruins extend for several miles, and a populous city must once have occupied the site. It is supposed that the houses of the inhabitants, built of cane and reed, similar to those of to-day, stood on the top of the mounds.

At Tamos, several miles above Tampico, is the first sight of the Panuco, coming from the interior. The stream is navigable to this point for ocean steamers of considerable draught.

Just beyond Tamos, the Tamesi, another large river, is crossed by a long and substantial drawbridge, at its junction with the Panuco. Both streams are navigated by steamboats into the interior, and they are well worth the while of the voyage, the scenery being particularly fine.

At Tampico the station is close to the water, where the view is enlivened by the various craft lying at the wharves and anchored in the stream—steamships, schooners, brigs, river steamers, tugs, lighters, etc.—a respectable fleet altogether, and but an earnest of what will be seen here in the future. Tampico is an attractive looking place, with an architectural appearance quite different from what may be seen elsewhere in Mexico. It seems a combination of New Orleans with a distinctively Spanish style. The buildings mostly have pitched roofs, and wood is more commonly employed in construction than elsewhere in Mexico, though the walls are chiefly of massive masonry. The houses of many colors have wooden verandas along their fronts, at each story, in the style common in the southern states of our country. A large part of the city stands on a bluff, which rises from near the river to a height of perhaps twenty to fifty feet or more, and at the end of two of the streets broad stone steps descend to the water front. On the river front is the most picturesque market, with its tents and scores of white umbrellas. Near it is the Plaza, with an almost darkness of dense shade. The trees are the homes of myriads of twittering, noisy ravens. The river at Tampico is 1800 feet wide, and has an average breadth of 800 feet; for several miles above its mouth, the minimum depth is thirty feet. The rise and fall of the tide is so slight —only about eighteen inches—that there is no inflowing current, and, with the construction of the jetties, there is a constant outgoing scour across the bar. For the greater part of the way the river banks are low and marshy, but on the right shore, two or three miles below the town, there is a line of high, rocky bluffs, that sometime will probably be in demand as a place of summer residence, with their fine view of the sea and sweep of breeze from the Gulf, which, blowing soft and free for most of the time, makes the air agreeably refreshing.

RUINS NEAR TEXCOCO.

To reach Tampico from the interior, change cars on the main line of the Central at Aguas Calientes, and on the National at San Luis Potosí, or proceed, via the Monterey & Mexican Gulf Railroad, from Treveño, on the International, or Monterey on the National road.

Tampico is a regular port of the Ward Line, and other steamer lines from all parts of the world are attracted hither by the fine harbor, made by the completion of the jetties, two long arms of stone walls extending out into the sea, more than a thousand feet, and one of the most important improvements of the age. Tampico is in the State of Tamaulipas; population, 6000.

Texcoco
Tez-co-co

Texcoco was the ancient capital of the great Netzahualcoyotl, and, in 1431, was the rival of Tenochtitlan, now the City of Mexico. At that time Texcoco might have been called the Athens of the western world, as Tenochtitlan was its Rome. Cortéz came from Tlaxcala and Cholula to Texcoco, and brought with him the *bergantines* across the mountains, put them together on the shores of the lake, and prepared to take his army to lay siege to the capital of Montezuma. The Tlaxcalans, already his allies, the Cholulans destroyed by massacre, he found

AT TEXCOCO.

the people of Texcoco in the throes of dissension and civil war, and there was naught in the way of his march to Tenochtitlan. The base of operations was at Texcoco, and here, later, Cortéz made his abode while under a royal exile from the City of Mexico, and here for some years his bones were buried.

In the royal palace of Netzahualcoyotl, at Texcoco, was a courtyard, on the opposite side of which were two halls of justice. In the principal one, called the "Tribunal of God," was a throne of pure gold, inlaid with turquoise and other precious stones. On a stool in front was placed a human skull and crowned with an immense emerald of a pyramidal form, and surmounted by an aigrette of brilliant plumes and precious stones. The skull was laid on a heap of military weapons, shields, quivers, bows and arrows. The walls were hung with tapestry, made of the hair of different wild animals, of rich and various colors, festooned by gold rings and embroidered with figures of birds and flowers. Above the throne was a canopy of variegated plumage, from the center of which shot forth resplendent rays of gold and jewels. The other tribunal, called "the king's," was also surrounded by a gorgeous canopy of feathers, on which emblazoned the royal arms.

Texcoco is a pretty little town, with narrow streets, shaded by orange trees, centering on a plaza, where there is a bust of Netzahualcoyotl. On a corner south of the plaza is a fountain, surmounted by a statue of Hercules, presented by Señor Ruperto Jaspeadó. The old Church of San Francisco, founded by Fray Pedro de Gante, was the tomb of Cortéz.

A CORNER IN TEXCOCO.

There are many ruins and relics of the forgotten ages in and around Texcoco. In the south part are three pyramids, and in the north another. West of the town, about three miles, are the ruins of an ancient wall, near the old Church of Huixotla. About three miles east are the most beautiful gardens of the Molino de Flores (the mill of the flowers). Let the mind be disabused of anything like a flour mill, or a barn-like structure with dusty sides and roof. Heavy gates open through stone walls and admit to what seems the court of a mediæval castle. Tortuous stairways of stone lead to the castle, the summer home of the ancient family, Cervantes, who have owned this bit of another world for some centuries. Beyond the gates, a little farther, are the gardens that might have been a part of Eden. There are grottoes and cascades, and a chapel that is also the tomb of the Cervantes, with sepulchres cut in the solid rock. Near by is the "laughing hill," Tetzcotzinco, the favorite resort of Netzahualcoyotl. There are terraced walks, and stairways winding around the hill. A basin in the rock has been called Montezuma's bath. It was probably a distributing reservoir to the gardens below. There are some wonder-

THE MILL OF THE FLOWERS.

ful examples of native engineering near the "laughing hill," where the hills are connected across the valleys by embankments, in some places fifty feet high, on the top of which was built an aqueduct about two feet wide, with a conduit about a foot in width. In all it was twelve or fifteen miles in length, and much of it yet remains in a perfect state of preservation. Near the Molino de Flores, at Cuatlenchan, was found the idol, Xicaca, goddess of waters, now in the National Museum. Three miles west is the Hacienda de Chapingo, belonging to the estate of the late ex-president, General Gonzales.

Texcoco is in the State of Mexico, on the Interoceanic Railway, twenty miles from the City; population, 10,000; altitude, 7687 feet.

Tlaxcala The very name is synonymous with antiquity and reminiscent of
Tlaz-cal-a   Cortéz and his indomitable band of adventurers. It is one of the most interesting places in all Mexico, both for the beauty of its location and its historic associations.

On leaving the train at the little station of Santa Ana, the visitor will find the two horse cars at the station, first and second class respectively. From Santa Ana to Tlaxcala is about six miles, through beautiful woods or through cultivated fields, the hedges on either side of the road covered with wild flowers, filling the air with perfume. The route is through the quaint little town of San Pablo Apetitlan; thence across the river and past the Church of San Estéban. To the west is a magnificent view of the two mighty volcanoes of Popocatepetl and Ixtaccihuatl, their summits crowned with eternal snows, dazzlingly white and glistening in the sunlight; to the east may be seen the lofty and beautiful "Malintzi,"—the whole forming a picture perhaps unequaled on this continent, or in the world. At last, after a ride of about forty-five minutes, the town of Tlaxcala is reached and the car stops in the queer little plaza.

Tlaxcala is situated in a valley, with hills entirely surrounding it, but we read that at the time of the conquest, when Tlaxcala boasted 300,000 instead of

BULL RING, TLAXCALA.

4,000 inhabitants, as now, the town was built on the hills, the valley being reserved for agricultural purposes, and it is probable that from this fact it takes its name, which means "Land of Bread."

The museum is never "open" to the public, for the reason, presumably, that it is only tourists who care to visit it, but it is a very easy matter to obtain admission. The visitor should call at the Municipal Palace (a building which dates back to the Spanish conquest), situated on the Plaza, and one of the obliging officials will send with you a "mozo" or servant, with the keys of the museum which is situated on the next street. Before leaving, however, he will naturally expect that you will wish to see the Council Room, and if the visitor is not awed on being admitted to this celebrated chamber, he will, at least, be interested in the pictures which adorn its walls. These are copies of the original pictures of the great Tlaxcalan chieftains who allied themselves with Cortéz, namely: Lorenzo Mazihcatzin, Chief of Ocotetulco; Gonzalo Tlahuexolotzin, Chief of Tepeticpac; Bartholomé Zitlalpopoca, Chief of Quiahuiztlan, and Vicente Xicohtencatl, Chief of Tizatlan. The first name of each is the "Christian" name, given to them by the Spaniards 'when they were baptized, which was in the year 1520. The originals of these portraits were lost at sea in 1742. There is nothing more of any particular interest to be seen here, and the next place is the museum. This contains a most interesting collection of idols and of Tlaxcalan pottery, found at various times in the town and surrounding country, but that which the visitor will most wish to see is the "Banner of Cortéz," as it is usually called, but to be more correct, the banner which Cortéz presented to the Tlaxcalans. It is kept in a glass case and is in an excellent state of preservation. In the next case are, also preserved, the silken gowns which the chieftains wore when baptized, and a little to one side are the embroidered vestments of the priests. These are in such a perfect condition

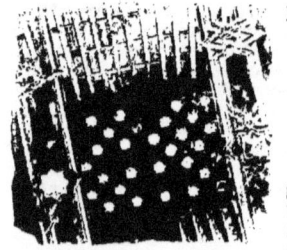

ROOF OF CHURCH, TLAXCALA.

that it is hard to believe they are nearly 400 years old; they are an eloquent memorial to the skill of their makers. Here, too, are more pictures representing the famous four chieftains, as well as old plans and maps of Tlaxcala.

The Church of San Francisco is the oldest in America. Its foundations were commenced in the year 1521, the same year that the conquest of Mexico was completed. Here everything is antique; the very chairs used by the good fathers, at the present day, look as if they might be two hundred years old. After admiring the high altar, turn to the right and enter the chapel of the " Tercer Orden." The first thing which attracts the attention on entering is an enormous font. This is the actual font in which were baptized the four chieftains whose portraits and garments we have already seen. On the other side of the chapel is an old pulpit, the tablet informing us that from it was preached the christian gospel, for the first time "in this new world." The church is situated on the slope of a hill, and is approached by a paved way leading up from the queer old market place, where, if you loiter a while, you will hear as much Indian spoken as Spanish. The men and women sit on the ground beside their wares, laughing and chatting among themselves in the Aztec language. You will find, however, that they talk Spanish perfectly, if you wish to buy any of the luscious fruits or other commodities displayed.

The paved way leading up from the market place to the church passes under an old archway which connects the bell tower with the building which was formerly the convent, but now used by the government as the barracks. Facing the church and the barracks is a paved court-yard, which extends about one hundred and fifty feet to the edge of the hill, the side fronting the cliff being protected by a low wall. Directly under this, about fifty or sixty feet beneath, is the "bull ring," affording the soldiers (or at least the officers) of the barracks an excellent place from which to view the corrida without payment. The "Xicotencatl" Theatre is opposite the San Carlos Hotel, but it looks as if it had not been open for years. It is a walk of about fifteen minutes to the famous Santuario de Ocotlan, built on a hill overlooking Tlaxcala.

This church is built to commemorate the miraculous appearance of the Blessed Virgin of Ocotlan to the Indian Juan Diego, the legend being almost the same as that connected with the yet more famous shrine of Guadalupe, near Mexico City. The church is a very fine building, with two very lofty towers. The interior is splendidly decorated, the high altar especially being a perfect marvel of wood carving.

Before arriving at the church you will probably notice the two curious barrel-shaped structures, about ten feet high, in the middle of the road. These are called "cuitacomatis" and are used for storing corn, preserved safely from rats and mice. It speaks well for the honesty of the little village that the owners do not seem to fear any pilfering by their neighbors, for the "cuitacomatis" are built in the roadway, opposite the homes of their owners, and are only protected at the top by a wooden cover, well thatched to prevent the rain entering.

The view from the churchyard of Ocotlan is most beautiful. From it can be seen the three mountains, Pococatepetl, Ixtaccihuatl and Malintzi. Immediately below is the town of Tlaxcala, and a little beyond is the river, which can be seen for miles, winding its way down the valley of Atoyac. Across the river, which is spanned by a light iron bridge of modern make, a little way from the main channel, the river has cut its way through the rocks, forming a deep cañon, and in one place it has forced its path underneath the rocks, leaving them overhanging, and forming a Natural Bridge.

Tlaxcala is near the station of Santa Ana, on the branch line of the Mexican Railway from Apizaco to Puebla. It is the capital of the State of Tlaxcala. The population is 4000; altitude 7506 feet above the sea.

Toluca
To-*loo*-ca

To go over the hills to Toluca is one of the things to do in Mexico. No matter by what route one may have arrived at the capital, one must go to Toluca. The going there is the chief charm of the three-hour excursion. If you take an afternoon train from the city, you will have the sun behind the Sierra Madres; while the train climbs the eastern slope, creeping along in the darkening shadows, there is still a flood of sunlight over the plain, glistening the towers of

ALAMEDA OF TOLUCA.

the distant city and the lakes beyond, and, above all, whitening still more the snows on Popocatepetl and Ixtaccihuatl—a picture dazzling and grandly, sublimely beautiful. It may be that the sun has dropped behind the further western

HUMBOLDT'S TABLET, BIG TREE OF TULE.

hills ere you turn the crest of these, and there is a softening twilight over the Toluca Valley; but when the return is made on a morning train, the sun is again behind the Madres, this time in the east, making another panorama equally beautiful, with Ocoyacac under the precipice, a thousand feet down, and the River Lerma, stringing in a silver line way across the plain, and lost from sight beyond the hills. On the farther side is Toluca, and, beyond the city, the Nevada de Toluca, the volcano, once called Xinantecatl. Thus, in a little journey of three hours, are two of the world's grandest views, worth a longer journey to see.

Horse cars from the station run through the Calle Independencia, past the statue of Hidalgo, to the plaza and near the hotels.

That Toluca is a marvelously clean city is discovered in the shortest stay; the houses look bright and new, although it is one of the oldest cities in the country, and the buildings are larger and finer than usual. The State buildings—this is the capital of the State of Mexico—erected on the spot where once stood the house of Don Martin Cortéz, son of the conqueror, are the finest in the Republic, and the market, with its pillars of Pompeiian colors is a thing of beauty. It is not far to the hot country, and all the tropical fruits and flowers are to be found. In the *portales* one may find laces, "drawn work," pottery and a thousand things for souvenir purchasers.

The residence of a rich *haciendado* is shown, who, in his time, was a great patron of the bull-ring, and furnished from his hacienda many a *bravo toro*, till they became famous in every ring, and his colors, dangling from a grizzly neck, brought loud huzzas when the animal bounded into the arena. One bull fought his way back to life and liberty. The picadors could not hold him off, and he killed their horses; the banderilleros, if they could place their darts in his shoulders, had them shaken out in his rage, and the matadors were hissed and hissed, because they could not kill him. The old *hacien-dado* looked on with delight, and plead with the president not to allow him to be lassoed and "assasinated," as he said. The wish was granted, and the bull was driven back to the corral, and returned to the hacienda to live some happy years, and when, at a green old age, he died in peace, surrounded by a numerous and belligerent progeny, his body was interred minus the skin, which was stuffed and hung up for ornament in his master's banquet hall.

The view from the hill, just back of the city, is a pretty one, but from the top of the volcano it is a grand one, reaching from the Gulf to the Pacific. The height, as estimated by Humboldt, is 15,156 feet above sea-level. The ascent and return requires two days, though it is not a difficult or perilous one. The top is not more than ten feet wide, and the crater contains a fathomless lake with a whirlpool in the center.

The valley and site of the city of Toluca was within the grant of Charles V. to Cortéz as the Marquis of the Valley, and a settlement was made here in 1530, but not till 1677 was Toluca made a city.

The Church of San Francisco was founded in 1585. The parish church was built in 1585. The Church of Nuestra Señora del Carmen contains the first organ made in America. Near the city, about two miles west, is the Church of Nuestra Señora de Tecajic, containing a miraculous image of the Virgin, on coarse cloth, painted more than two hundred years ago, and held in much veneration by the Indians.

Toluca is the capital of the State of Mexico, on the Mexican National Railroad, forty-five miles from the City; elevation, 8617 feet above the sea; population, 25,000.

Tula
Too-la

It is but two hours from the capital of modern Mexico to the center of the Toltec Empire, where the ruins of the oldest capital of the continent lie half buried in the sands, blown over them in the 1200 years since their building—but two hours from the great houses of the nineteenth century to the *casas grandes* of the seventh. Tula was the capital of the Toltecs, founded about the year 638. After the migration of this people from the north, they halted just beyond the plain of Mexico, and, on the banks of the little river, builded a great city, that became the rival of Tenochtitlan and Texcoco. The place was a "place of reeds," and they called the city Tula, which is also Tollan, and was known by other names, Tlapallan and Huehuetlalpallan, to the ancient dwellers in the land. In these degenerate

AT TULA.

days, the mighty capital is a little railway junction village, a most pretty one withal, with antiquities a thousand years younger than the *casas grandes*, but are older than our oldest walls. The ruins of the ancient temples of the Toltecs are called the *casas grandes*. They are on the Cerro de Tesoro, a hill just beyond the river, reached by a walk of a mile, through a broad way shaded by great trees, over an old stone bridge, of Spanish make, and back, on the other bank of the river, to a point just opposite the town. There, almost buried and walless, are the *casas grandes*. The rooms are laid in terraces, one above the other, in hewn stone and hard cement, and connected with stairways. Some ruined walls, of the style of those around the church in the village, evidently of Spanish make, are near the ruins.

In the plaza of Tula are some of the Toltecan relics, and the baptismal font in the church is of the same origin; many of the houses of the town have Toltec carvings hung up for ornament.

The Church of San José, in partial ruins, was founded in 1553, and completed in 1561. In the primitive days of its building, it was church and fortress combined, and the very thick walls were constructed with that view, as are shown by the battlements on the roof, on the walls, and on the walls of the old church near the *casas grandes*. The church is 190 feet long, 83 feet high, with a tower of 125 feet, all built of stone, roughly cut. The convent, built in 1585, is now used as a cavalry barrack and stables.

RUINS AT TULA.

The pretty little town of Tula—and it is a very delightful one—can be made the object of a day's outing from the City of Mexico, taking the morning train out, and returning in the afternoon. It is on the line of the Mexican Central Railway, in the State of Hidalgo, at the junction of the Pachuca branch, fifty miles from the City, at an altitude of 6658 feet above the sea; population, 3000.

Vera Cruz
Ver-a Crooz

Since the landing of Grijalva, in 1518, Vera Cruz has been the chief seaport of Mexico. Here, also, landed Cortéz, April 21, 1519, on Good Friday. For this, and the reputed richness of the land in gold, the place was named Villa Rica de la Santa Vera Cruz (the rich city of the true cross). There was no harbor for the safe riding of the vessels left behind, and after the conqueror had established himself in the interior, he sent an expedition down the coast and found the harbor of Coatza-coalcos, the present terminus of the Tehuantepec Route, on the Gulf. But this did not affect the importance of Vera Cruz. It was so much nearer the richer districts of the interior, that the city has remained the seaport of Mexico for nearly four hundred years. Ships drop anchor just below the island of San Juan de Ulúa, and the landing is by lighter and small boats, which is not included in the ship's fare. The prices of the landing vary, with the weather, from fifty cents in fair weather, to a dollar on stormy days.

Vera Cruz may be done in a day. A walk about the streets and plazas, and along the Paseo, with its tall, waving palm trees, is all to interest; and to the church of the black Christ, where the image of the Savior is black; there is only one other like it, at Havana, or near that city. There is another thing that will attract the attention of the tourist at Vera Cruz, and that is the Street Cleaning Department. The employés work without salary, and find themselves, and their thorough manner (but not their methods) are to be commended. Their only reward is the enforcement of a city ordinance, which inflicts a five-dollar fine on the indiscreet and reckless citizen who should happen to kill one of them. The natives call these street cleaners, *zopilotes*, but to the American they are just plain, every-day buzzards. I may mention here, that Vera Cruz has an imitator, in this respect, in Charleston, S. C. But, altogether, Vera Cruz is to be visited to make the tour of Mexico complete. The island of San Juan de Ulúa, a prison now, once a fort, was commenced in 1582 and finished

A VERACRUZANA.

about 1750. It has been occupied at different times — by the French, in 1838; by the Americans, in 1847; by the allied French, English and Spanish, in 1865; and was the seat of the Juarez Government, during the War of the Reform. Excursions here, and to La Isla de los Sacrificios, may be made. The hiring of boats, for landing and for excursions, should be made by contract always. A tramway runs down the coast, to Medellin and Alvarado, that may be taken just for the ride and the novelty of it.

The parish church, on the Plaza Mayor, was finished in 1734, and dedicated to Nuestra Señora de la Asuncion. The Church of San Francisco was founded in 1568. The tower is now a lighthouse, and the old convent contains the public library. The church was formerly supported by a levy on all ships coming into the port. The Churches of San Agustin and La Campañia were restored after the great fire of 1619.

On the island of San Juan de Ulúa is a little chapel, dedicated to Nuestra Señora de la Escalera, in which offerings are made for the safety of sailors.

Vera Cruz is reached from the interior by the Mexican and Interoceanic Railways. It is 263 miles from the City of Mexico, in the State of Vera Cruz; population, 20,000.

ZACATECAS.

Yautepec
Ya-ow-te-pec

These little towns, down on the border of the *tierra caliente,* seem farther away from the world, as we know it, and farther behind in the centuries, than the towns of the hills, and when you are in Yautepec, you are in another world and another century. The little town is nestled down in a valley that widens out, to the southward and west, into broad plains, where the sugar cane grows; to the northward, the hills rise, one above the other, and reach to Popocatepetl and Ixtaccihuatl. The cane fields come even to the city limits, and within them the narrow streets crook and turn curiously. The dull gray walls seem cheerless enough, but here and there a half-open gateway reveals the tropical gardens on their other side, and some of the taller trees hang their golden fruit over their tops. You leave the station, and the locomotive that is there, the only evidence that there is any other world but this lazy one you are just entering, as, in the novelty of it, you really forget the other, till the locomotive's whistle calls you back. A cross-topped tower, high over the low houses, will be a guide. Follow the streets that lead to it, and soon come to the plaza, which is also the alameda —a pretty little park with bright flowers and pretty trees, with a fountain under them, where the natives come, with great earthern jars, for the pure sparkling water that flows from it. Sit here on a stone bench; the inhabitants will come out and look at you. In the evening the band plays, and you will have an opportunity to see the "four hundred," as they promenade. There is wealth and beauty in the procession, such as it is not expected to see. At one end of the little park is a long table, covered with corn. "Ah, this is the market place," some one says, "a sort of produce exchange, and these are the samples of corn." When you return after supper you find that he had mistaken the class of traffic. A crowd of men, women and children are around the table. Each has a dingy looking card on the table; the card has three rows of five pictures each. A man at the end of the table holds a bag, from which he draws smaller cards, that have corresponding pictures to those held by the players; he

A TEHUANTEPEC GIRL IN HOLIDAY DRESS.

calls the names of the animals in the pictures, and the person having a similar one places a grain of corn on it, and anyone getting five markers in a row wins the game and the money paid for all the cards, less the percentage of the banker. It is very much like that American game where one man yells something and all the others say something else. Just on the other side of the plaza a rambling stream runs over a rocky bed, almost dry now, but the waters, collected in pools, form a laundry place for Yautepec, presenting a picturesque scene. An old stone bridge, with a single arch, spans the stream for a path that leads to a convent, or priestly residence, whose gardens can be seen from the bridge, in all their tropical luxuriance. In the churchyard are some crumbling old tombs built in the walls of the church, or in the adjoining panteon. At the north end of the village is a pretty little chapel, and near it the plaza de toros.

Yautepec is on the Morelos division of the Interoceanic Railway, in the State of Morelos, ninety-eight miles from the City of Mexico; altitude, 2340 feet; population, 7000.

Zacatecas
Zaca-*tay*-cas

The approach to Zacatecas from the north gives no hint of any city being near. The train climbs the tortuous windings of the track to reach the summit of a hill that is 8000 feet above the level of the sea. A tall tower-like chimney of a smelter that is seen, first on one side, and then on other, is the only evidence of civilization beyond the cars we ride in, and even at the station where the train stops, there is little to indicate the existence of the great city that is in the barranca just beyond the hill, and under the one whose rocky crest is so much like an immense buffalo, that it is called La Bufa. It is after leaving the station, or on the approach from the south, that the passing passenger is treated to one of the finest views in the world, if his seat be on the east side of the car. Away up the immense gulch, the flat-top houses, the domes and towers, seem to have slidden down from both the hills, till it is filled half way up, on either side, and straggling out the mouth of it, down on to the plain where Guadalupe is. And the road between Zacatecas and Guadalupe! where is there any like it? or these two cities—are there any, except in the Holy Land? And the passers up and down that road, and the streets of the city, in the enchantment that distance lends them! do they not bring back the bible lessons of your younger days? There are, also, the veritable Palestinian asses laden for the city, or returning lazily over a road that seems as hard as that which leads to Jordan, and far beyond Guadalupe's towers is—not the Sea of Galilee, but Lake Pevernaldillo. And up the hill, toward the buffalo, is a rocky road, narrow as that which leads to righteousness, hedged with prickly thorns, that leads to the little Church of Los Remedios, founded in 1728, near the summit. Over this road, suffering devotees have crawled to do a cruel penance, at the behest of more cruel masters than ever lived in Palestine. On the hill of La Bufa a battle was fought between the Juarez forces and a revolutionary party, May 2, 1871, resulting in a victory for Juarez.

But the inevitable horse car dispels the Palestinic idea, and it will amply repay you to leave the train and take a seat in one that will take you from the station to the market plaza and to the hotels of Zacatecas. The city is easy of access—one just drops into town. The horse cars leave the station, and, per force of gravity, roll into the city, as they do into the suburb of Guadalupe. The mules work only half the time, but it is an up-hill business when they do work. The cars roll from the station to Zacatecas, or from the city to Guadalupe, but *vice versa*, they must be pulled up by main force. The coming up is as hard as the going down easy. The mules walk leisurely down the hill, without even the labor of carrying the harness, which is piled on the front platform. The city is an interesting one, where some days may be passed in rambles up one hill and down the other. As you saw the city from the train, you could not believe there was room enough, and level enough, for a park, but Zacatecas has two that are filled

with flowers and fountains, and where, of course, the band plays in the evening, Sundays and feast days; in little nooks and shelves in the rocks are numberless plazuelas —beauty spots of ferns and flowers in rocky hillsides. Zacatecas is a busy city, and the streets present quite a metropolitan appearance, some of the buildings reaching three and four stories. The State and Municipal palaces are imposing above the average in Mexico. The churches to visit are Nuestra Señora de la Ascuncion, with its tiled dome and interior of white and gold; it once owned a font of silver that alone cost a fortune. This church was founded in 1612, and is now the cathedral. La Campañia is the church

AFTER THE BULL FIGHT

of the Jesuits, begun in 1746, and contains some very fine pictures. The others are San Francisco, 1567, and San Juan de Dios. It is probable that the oldest Presbyterian church building in the world is at Zacatecas; it was once the Church of San Agustin, now devoted to Protestant uses.

But it is to Guadalupe that the church enthusiast takes his way, very early after his arrival at Zacatecas. It is six miles to Guadalupe. The cars have been drawn by the mules up the hill to the market plaza, from whence they roll back to the market plaza of Guadalupe. Walk through this market, and just beyond it is one of the most interesting churches in this country of churches.

In front of the church is a pretty park of roses, well kept. The grand old church, with its tiled dome, is worthy of all the journey to see. The main altar has life-size figures representing the Crucifixion. Behind there is a canvas painting representing the Hill of Calvary, with the Jews and Roman soldiery in the middle background. These, with the figures in front, produce a very startling effect.

The church is filled with people, kneeling at the various altars and confessionals, at all times. On the right of the church is the old convent, filled with hundreds of curious paintings, illustrating the lives and temptations of the saints—some of them going very much into detail. One fine picture of a giant and cherub, at the head of the stair-

case, is finely executed, and seems to be the work of a master hand. The convent building is now an orphan asylum, where there are over a thousand orphans.

The *Capilla*, or chapel, a more recent addition to the old church, was the gift
of a maiden lady of great wealth, a few years ago, and cost many thousands of
dollars. The floor is inlaid with hard woods of different colors. A superb altar
is rich in gildings, silver and gold, wax figures, silk and satin hangings. The
altar rail is of onyx and solid silver. The walls are finely frescoed, arched
to a dome fifty feet above the floor. This is all new, but is the finest
chapel in Mexico.

The mines may be visited by permit. Some are entered by shaft, others by
tunnel. If you choose the former, the descent is by a bucket let down by horse-

CHURCH OF GUADALUPE, NEAR ZACATECAS.

power windlass. Ladies undertake the trip sometimes, but are not welcomed by
the miners, as they are regarded as unlucky visitors.

Zacatecas was founded in 1548, two years after the discovery of silver, and was
made a city in 1585. It is on the Mexican Central Railway, 439 miles from the
City of Mexico, and is the capital of the State of Zacatecas; population, 75,000;
altitude, 8044 feet.

171

Railway Rides in Mexico.

South Over the Central.'—Whenever there is a schedule that puts the train over the first two hundred miles south of the Rio Grande by night, take it; no matter which route you travel by, there is nothing to see but chaparral and desolate looking hills, and your first impressions would not be of the best. There is just enough novelty in the little towns on the border, that are so oddly new and so old fashioned, to awaken an anticipation for more; it is all the better to sleep over it and dream of what may be to-morrow. I can safely say that these dreams, at least, will not go by contraries. When the first morning in Mexico comes, with a brighter sunshine than you ever saw before, you will be an early riser; perhaps you will roll up the little curtain of your window, before you leave your pillow, and hurry out for a hasty toilet, fearing that you may miss something—and you might, for the scenery begins very early in the morning, and this old, old country is all new to you. The train is rolling along through a narrow valley, level as a billiard board, the veritable high table-lands we have read about, but never saw till now, lying between two close ranges of mountains, shrub-covered and crowned with the most entrancing cloud effects one imagines out of fairy land; the soft, white heaps are tossed above some towering summit or rolled into a blue valley between.

'all it travel, takest for pleasure."
—Shakespeare.

While we are looking skyward there is an entrancing view at our feet; here is a first glimpse of an hacienda. At the farther end of the plain a group of white buildings, a wide corral, fenced in with slight boughs, and a fringe of most exquisite green, along the margin of a fine line of blue water, completes a pretty picture. Out of the corral, on one side, comes an immense herd of cattle, at the other an equally immense herd of goats, black, brown and white. A group of Indian women are filling great red jars at a pool of water, and across the dry water-courses flocks of sheep wander, followed by their shepherds. It is truly another world than that of yesterday.

By and by, between a gap in the deep red mountains, which wall up the narrow valley, there is a wonderful vista full of color, with another glint of another valley, and, far off, the mystical heights of some new range of hills which distance clothes with abundant majesty. The novelty never wears away. But this country is not all of deep valleys and lofty mountains; there are broad, spreading plains as well, yet, in all the land, in its length and breadth, the mountains are always in view.

The railroads seem to come upon these Mexican towns unawares, and there is rarely a hint of them till we are at the station, and they are, with few exceptions, located a mile or more from the line of road. The first stop is at Chihuahua, made at the shops where the restaurant is located, and, until the train starts across the barranca there is nothing to be seen of the city, then the view is from the windows on the west side of the car. It is a good view of the city, with the tall towers of the Church of San Francisco standing high against the sky. While the train stops at the station just after crossing the bridge there is time to enjoy it.

After leaving the station the better view is on the left, where the road to the mines of Santa Eulalia runs through the hills, and pretty soon the buildings and tall chimneys come to view, and just after leaving the station is the *Cerro del Coronel* on the right of the track. The road runs through a semi-lake region, passing through the valley of the Conchos and San Pedro. Near Santa Rosalia there are some hot springs, famous for their curative qualities. Jimenez is a city of some 8000 people, the shipping point for the Parral mining district.

A COFFEE HACIENDA,
MEXICAN CENTRAL RAILWAY.

Stages run from Jimenez to Parral and Allende. Escalon is the junction point of the Mexican Northern Railway, running northeastward to the Sierra Mojada mining district, where is located one of the greatest carbonate camps in the world. Southward now, the road runs along the western border of the great *Bolson de Mapimi,* to interpret, literally, a "pocket" in the mountains. This is the Laguna country, in the rainy season almost covered by water, and in the dry season it collects in ponds or larger lakes. Several rivers, notably the Nazas, flow into this *Bolson,* and unless there is an underground outlet somewhere, the water must escape only by evaporation, but so much is used in irrigation that only a small stream reaches the basin.

East of the line about Conejos is a curious sulphur mountain, easily distinguished by the stripes of the mineral. Here is the rich cotton district of Lerdo,

IN THE BARRANCA, GUADALAJARA.

where the seed requires only to be planted once in three or four years. Lerdo is seen from the windows on the right, and soon after leaving the station the track crosses the Nazas River on a fine steel bridge; look up and down the river and see the dams and storage reservoirs for irrigation purposes. Three miles south of Lerdo the Central crosses the Mexican International Railroad at Torreon, with connections on the east for Eagle Pass and Monterey, and on the west for Durango.

South from Torreon there is a continual up-grade of track, and the mountains are closer than on the borders of the Bolson. Just below the station of Guitierrez the Tropic of Cancer is crossed, and the first place of importance in the Torrid Zone is Fresnillo, once a great city before the overflow of the mines of Proaño. The city is about five miles from the road, and has now only about 20,000 people.

Every hour of the journey, now, is one of increasing interest; still, as it is onward, it is upward, and its windings tortuous among the hills, where the scenery is grand, gloomy and peculiar. The climb is to reach the summit of a hill whose altitude is greater than any on the road, except one, a little over 8,000 feet. The tall tower-like chimneys of a smelter, high above the track, are seen first on one side and then on the other, as the road bends in one horseshoe after another. This is the approach to Zacatecas, one of the greatest mining cities of the world. There is no view of the city in the approach from the north, nor even as the train stands at the station; but, as it moves off, take a seat on the left of the car, or, what is better, go to the rear platform, for one of the finest views of the journey. The moment the wheels begin to roll, sharply down hill now, there is a full view of a city of 75,000 people, for all the world like one of Palestine, with its low, flat topped houses and domed churches, two hundred feet below, spreading up and down the gulch and on the mountain side beyond, reaching down the valley with a straggling suburb, to Guadalupe, six miles away. The track winds around on the sides of the hills, passing directly over some mines and smelters, keeping the city in view all the while. Up and down the road that runs along the valley are curiously costumed people, droves of donkeys laden with silver, carts and cars, goats and cattle on the hillsides, and a hundred things to see not seen anywhere else in the world.

Leaving Zacatecas behind, under the shadow of the great *Cerro de la Bufa*, an immense buffalo, cut in stone by Sculptor Nature, lies on the mountain's crest, keeping guard over this city of silver. Now below, in the valley, is Guadalupe, and far beyond is Lake Pevernaldillo, whose waters seem to meet the sky at the horizon. Those are not monuments over the graves of fallen heroes that you have seen through this mining district; those white tombstone-like objects are landmarks to designate the boundaries of an hacienda or a mining claim. The road enters a more agricultural district below Guadalupe, and

AT CUERNAVACA.

runs through one valley after another down to Aguas Calientes, on the plain. The city is on the west side of the road. No general view of the city may be had, as it is on the same level with the track, and a forest of green trees hides the houses. There is plenty to be seen at the station. The main street of the city crosses the track just below it; the bath-houses are within a stone's throw, and the hot-water ditch, wherein is the public laundry and baths of the Indians, crosses the track just at the end of the platform. From Aguas Calientes, or at Chicalote, nine miles above, the Tampico division connects with the main line of the Mexican Central.

Onward, over the plains to the southward, it is still down grade to the barranca of Encarnacion, which the road crosses on a high iron bridge. Just under it, on the left side, is an irrigation reservoir. The station is just at the south end of the bridge, and a mile or two to the westward is the little town of La Encarnacion, with its towered Church of Candelaria, in view from the car windows, and the white Campo Santo. Now the track winds about over some rocky hills, as far as Las Salas, and then down to the plain again at Lagos, the city seen from the west windows. The scenery is not so wild here, but is very pretty indeed. In the range to the west is the immense El Gigante, high above all the other mountains.

Leon is another of the great cities of this fertile plain, and one of the largest in Mexico. It is on the east side of the road; its streets are hedged with cactus and shaded by trees. Nothing but the towers of the churches can be seen.

At Silao is the branch road for Guanajuato. The city of Silao is on the east side of the road and nearer to it than most of the cities are. The ride of sixteen miles to Guanajuato is a very picturesque one. As the train winds about through the hills there are glimpses of the great mining city, first from one side of the cars, and then from the other.

Irapuato is the junction of the Guadalajara division and the station for strawberries. They are on sale on the arrival of all trains, from June to January, and January to June. The city is on the west side, half a mile from the station. Sala-

INTERIOR CHURCH OF SAN FRANCISCO, CHIHUAHUA.

manca is the next place of importance, and then Celaya, where this road crosses the Mexican National. Both these cities are to be seen from the west windows. In the latter, high above the trees, is the yellow-tiled dome of the beautiful Church of Our Lady of Carmen, and back of the city the plain slopes gradually to a high mountain that is seen miles up and down the road. This beautiful valley is what is called the Bajío region and it seems to have grown in beauty and fertility; hence on, to Querétaro, it is one vast garden between the low ranges of hills on either side. Querétaro is on the east side of the track and just north of the city; also on the east side is the hill where Maximilian and his generals were executed, and south of it the track passes through a pretty suburb, where you may see your first palm tree and the first oranges and lemons in the groves where they grow.

176

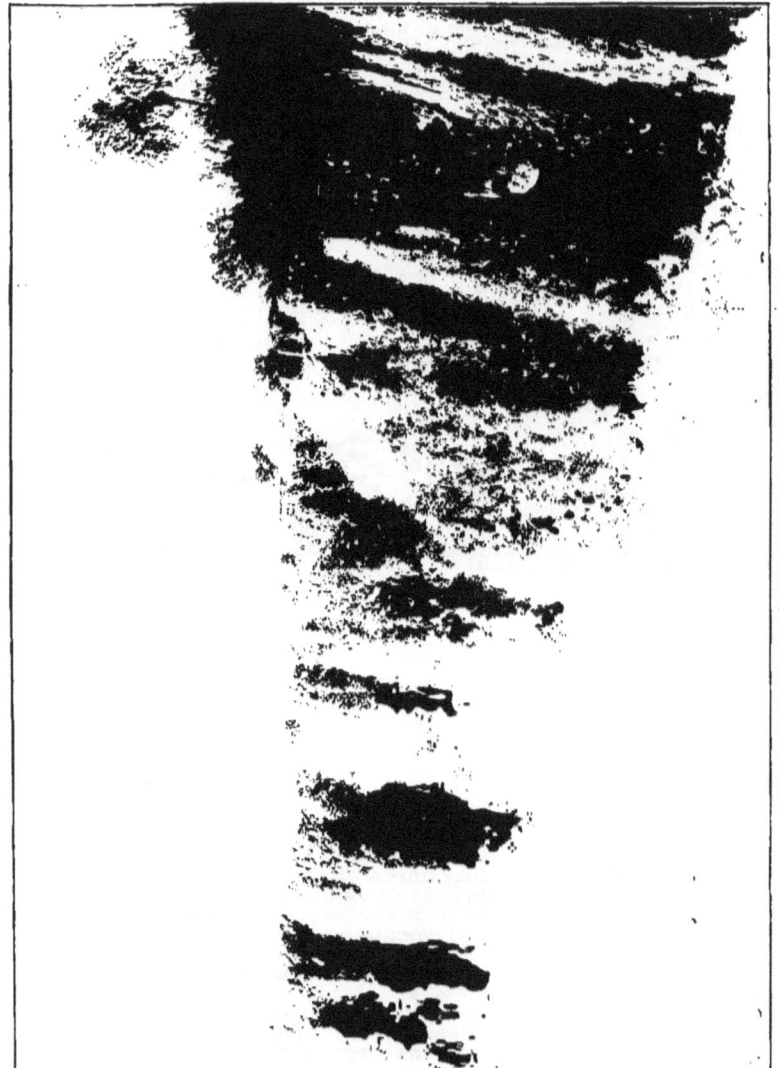

FALLS OF JUANACATLAN, MEXICAN CENTRAL RAILWAY NEAR GUADALAJARA.

Just below these the train passes under the great stone aqueduct that brings the city's water supply from the mountains, five miles away. There are eighty of these arches, the highest of which, near where the track passes under, is ninety-four feet. The view is first on the left and then on the right. The great Hercules cotton mills may also be seen from the right windows.

At San Juan del Rio, the last city on the line, the track reaches an elevation of 6245 feet and commences the climb to the plain of Cazadero; at the little station of Marquez it reaches the highest point on the line, 8132 feet above the level of the sea, then starts on the down grade to the Tula Valley. Tula is the junction of the Pachuca branch. This little city is one of the Toltec towns where there are some old ruins. It is a very picturesque place on the east side of the track.

No matter what may be the time of day, early in the morning, late in the evening, or if there be a moon, no matter what time of night, be ready to see the Tajo de Nochistongo, the great drainage canal, commenced in 1607, with a purpose to drain the lakes of the plain of Mexico and prevent the inundation of the city, but after a cost of millions of dollars and thousands of men, was abandoned. The train passes on the east cut of the canal, so the view must be from the west windows or on the right, going south. When this great work is passed let every window on that side be occupied. At Huehuetoca there is the first view of the snow mountains, the great volcanoes of Ixtaccihuatl and Popocatepetl, and of the plain of Mexico, and within an hour a journey that has been full of pleasure and crowded with novelty ends at Buena Vista station, in the City of Mexico.

Westward to Guadalajara.— The ride over this division of the Mexican Central Railroad, from the main line at Irapuato to Guadalajara, is not exactly like any other ride in Mexico and for this it is interesting. I do not know that the junction point was located at Irapuato as a particular favor to the strawberry Indians, but the necessary time for the transfer of passengers and baggage is very much in their favor, and scarcely a passenger but adds to his outfit. The branch road starts northward but, within half a mile, turns due west and encircles the town on its north side, running along through a tree covered plain. The line is rich in scenic beauty, as all roads in Mexico are, the journey is one of pleasure, no matter what other object it may have, and it is a rich agricultural country as well. The first station of importance is Penjamo, the quaint looking old town lying to the south of the road, and may be seen from the cars. It is a very interesting old place, with its narrow and crooked streets. It has a population of about 8000. La Piedad is the station for the old town of Piedad Cabadas, known in ancient and modern history by other aliases, but now answering to the name given here. It is a city of some 10,000 people, located south of the line, in the valley of the Lerma. Near the station the River Lerma is crossed. Here this longest river in Mexico is crossed for the first time and the road follows its windings, and runs along the south branch for some miles, crossing it again at La Barca, a city of 10,000 inhabitants, on Lake Chapala, where the Lerma empties into it. The river is sometimes called the Rio Grande, and is referred to as the Mississippi of Mexico. It is a curious fact that this river empties into Lake Chapala at La Barca and flows out of it just below Ocotlan, fifteen miles farther on. Lake Chapala is a most beautiful body of water, on which there have been steamboats. The machinery of the first one was brought from California, by sea, to San Blas, and thence packed on burros over the mountains; the boiler lies on the beach, the rusty monument to American pluck and energy. It is not recorded that anybody else has carried steamboats over the moun-

A SHRINE AT CUERNAVACA.

tains on mules. The voyage around the lake is one of seventy miles, and of many delights in the superb scenery, exceptionally beautiful. High and over-hanging cliffs, reflected again in the clear waters, mountains, fertile plains, valleys with fields of fruits and groves of tropical trees. Sometimes, when a high east wind prevails, the waves loosen the vegetation growing in the shallow water of the delta, where the Lerma comes in and sends some floating islands, often an acre in extent, out into the lake. The town of Chapala, on the north shore, is pictur-esquely located under the towering cliffs of the mountain, and has long been a health resort of the natives, on account of the very hot springs that are there, which have a high reputation for their curative properties; the waters, clear as crystal, gush from under the rocks on the mountain side. Continuing the journey by rail, west from La Barca, the track comes to the river again and crosses it, after it has left the lake, near Ocotlan. From the windows on the right there is to be seen a fine old Spanish bridge of many arches, near Poncitlan, and from the left there is another glimpse of the lake. The stream here is more entitled to the name of river than most of the Mexican *rios* are. They are mostly brooks or creeks, are entirely dry, except in the rainy season, when they are roaring, raging torrents; but this is a river that makes a leap of nearly a hundred feet over the rocks at Juana-catlan.

El Castillo is the station for the Falls of Juanacatlan, the Niagara of Mexico, and, though a somewhat smaller edition is not unlike the world's greatest cataract. Horse cars—or rather mule cars—run from the station to the falls. The

PLAZA, CUERNAVACA.

mules go in a gallop, and the trip—one of only about four miles—is accomplished in about twenty minutes; a trip to the fall is one of the things to do. The immense water power, that for centuries has been owned by one of the prominent families of Mexico, was utilized only to turn the wheels of a mill until very recently, when an electric light plant was put in, and from this point the lights of Guadalajara are supplied. Water-falls are not common in Mexico; it is only the rainy season that water falls to any alarming extent. There are cascades and cataracts that are not all in your eye, so to speak, here, there and everywhere, that are not always useful or ornamental for the one requisite of water, but Juanacatlan is a beauty and a joy that goes on forever in the rainy season and out of it.

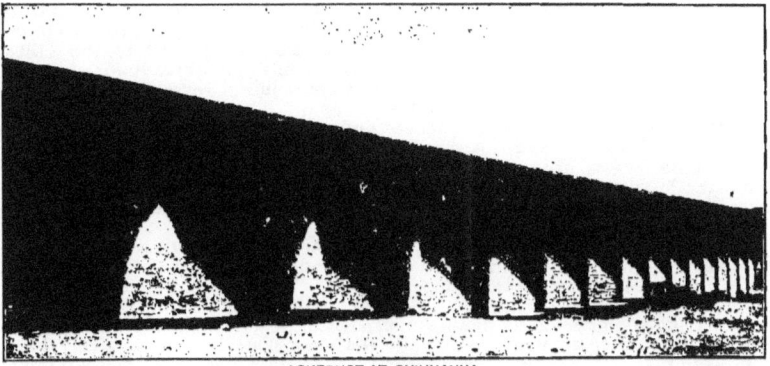

AQUEDUCT AT CHIHUAHUA.

The first glimpse of Guadalajara is to be had from the windows on the right hand, looking forward. The towers begin to peep over the hills, and a little further on those of San Pedro can also be seen north of the track. While you watch these, the train is rolling on up the grade, and in a few minutes is passing the outlying gardens of the very beautiful city of Guadalajara.

Eastward to Tampico.—One writer on Mexico advises one to come to the country by sea and proceed from the lowlands to the highlands, with the idea that this is the best from a scenic point of view—to go upward and let the scene grow upon you. I don't think so, but rather to come from the broad table-lands to an abrupt jumping-off place and look down, even over the tops of other mountains, lower hills and sloping plains, away to the sea, and let the picture fade in its mists. To my mind this is a picture that no pencil can paint nor pen portray. It is often thus in Mexico, and particularly so in this ride eastward to Tampico. The Tampico division of the Mexican Central Railway leaves the main line at Aguas Calientes, at least this is the nominal junction point where trains are made up and where passengers change cars, when that is necessary, but the actual point of junction is at Chicolote, nine miles north, to where trains run on the main line and then switch off to the east-bound track.

The road passes through a fertile irrigated country. The waters taken from the verdure fringed streams of the valleys are made almost to run up hill, it seems, and they do not run much higher anywhere in the world, for these fields of maguey and nopal cactus are nearly 8000 feet above the sea. The maguey of this region is used for the manufacture of mescal. The plant is very much smaller than the pulque-maguey of southern Mexico; it runs to root and it is from the root that the mescal is distilled. The nopal, or, as it is called sometimes, the prickly pear, grows here in the densest thickets. It bears a really palatable fruit that is a staple article of food with the natives, who also use the leaves to feed to cattle, the thorns having first been taken off by slightly singeing in the fire.

The only place of importance between Aguas Calientes and San Luis Potosi is Las Salinas de la Peñya Blanca, a place of 5000 people, near the station of Salinas, where one of the greatest deposits of salt in the world is located; the immense product is shipped to all parts of the country. The hacienda of the Errasu family, the owners of this immense estate, is very like a castle of the olden times, with its moat, draw-bridge, portcullis and all; the walls are as thick as those of a fortress and have their watch-towers and port holes. This was all very necessary in the earlier days of bandits in Mexico. For several years just previous to the completion of the railway, the production of salt was pushed to the fullest capacity, so that there were thousands and thousands of tons ready for shipment when the road was completed, and now there are required several miles of side-tracks to reach the vats and warehouses.

After Salinas the descent commences, and it is more than average down-grade from here to Tampico, and it is simply rolling over one hill after another, down to San Luis Potosi. It is an impressive view of the city, as the train comes down from the highlands, enters the city from the north, through a wide avenue, and stops in the handsome stone station that fronts the alameda, almost in the city's center.

Leaving San Luis Potosi, the road crosses the Mexican National Railroad, on the outskirts of the city, and by the steady and gradual slope of the plain, runs down nearly 1500 feet in forty-seven miles, to Villar. The descent to the coast is by a series of terraces; each terrace has its range of hills on the outward edge, which makes this region peculiarly picturesque. It will be noticed that the east side of these hills is covered with trees, while the west slope is comparatively bare. Here and there these table-lands are cut through by cañons, and down through them tumbles the water, in a thousand cascades, from terrace to terrace, from one table-land to another, on down to the sea.

TAJO DE NOCHISTONGO. MEXICAN CENTRAL RAILWAY.

From Villar to Las Tablas is another drop in the track of about 1500 feet, and then it is a little up-grade to Cardenas. The run has been through the beautiful San Ysidro Valley; the track has twisted and turned about the mountain slopes. The drop has been so gradual as to be hardly noticed, and if you have thought the scenery grand, as it indeed is, do not exhaust your adjectives; they will be needed a little further on, where you can exhaust all that are in all the languages of the world, over these, the grandest views of the world.

From Cardenas to Las Canoas is only fourteen miles, but the drop is about 700 feet, through the very lovely valley where there is verdure bright and green. Las Canoas, being interpreted, means "the canoes," not that there are any canoes hereabouts, nor are any needed, nor is there water enough to float one; there is water enough, but not in any one place, and it is too much on the slant, falling in a hundred cascades. Las Canoas is simply a little canoe of a valley and the prettiest one in the world, because there is no other just exactly like it—"a grassy-bottomed cup, closed in by precipitous mountains, from which strange formations of fantastically disposed rocks reach out into the even ground." One rock near the road, just above the station, seems a gigantic stage setting for the depicting of some scene in old Scotland, though Scotland has no such rocks and hills as these.

GUADALAJARA.

You may see the pretty little cup of a valley while the train stops at the station; it is only a little one, and one look around will cover it, though it induces to dwell upon its very loveliness. Just ahead there, is the beginning of the great Cañon of the Tamsopo. There indeed is the veritable "jumping-off place." There, at that switch, you can see the rails bend downward over the edge of the cañon—a switch with a signal arm so long that it extends across the track; no train or engine can pass it without throwing it down, and the train off the rails. The place is one of such importance that even human watchfulness is not to be trusted, as a car or train once beyond control, and beyond this switch, would be lost, but this is a safety switch that saves. It is always thrown to a side track that runs out on a level place and averts any possibility of an accident; the switch is never opened except while a train is passing, and is closed instantly by the ever attendant watchman.

This is a pretty valley indeed, but there are grander scenes just beyond. Such feats of engineering as you have never dreamed of, no matter what railroad you have traveled over. The beauties and the wonders of it are wholly indescribable and beyond compare. A seat on the left, or north side, of the car is the best; the rear platform, however, is the vantage point if you must travel by train. But if by any possible chance you have an opportunity to roll down the cañon on "the trolleys," do it. It is an experience of a lifetime, which the longest life will not forget. The trolley is what would be called, anywhere else, a hand-car, closely resembling the work-car of a section gang, but provided with a powerful brake, that the simple turning with the fingers will bring in contact with all the wheels in an instant; in fact it is only the experienced hand that prevents the trolley-car from stopping so quickly as to throw the occupants forward. There are seats for five persons on each car, and there are only two trolleys, so the equipment has not

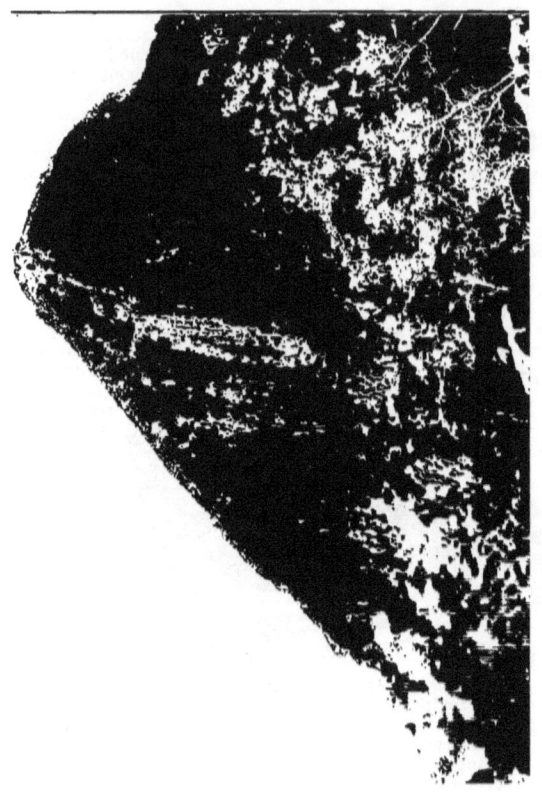

been arranged with a view to a large patronage, but if there were hotels at either end of the cañon, I think their number would have to be largely increased. And I, since I have traveled on the trolleys, would not have missed it, if I had to camp out at both ends of the ride. There is an untrammeled view, forward and backward, up the steep mountain side, thousands of feet, down the deep depths of the cañon, thousands of feet, and across the awful chasm, to the heights and cliffs beyond, with no narrow windows or door to curtail the magnificent grandeur of the view. This is travel by trolley, down the great cañon of Tamasopo, but the average traveler must be content with the Pullman car.

The throttle of the engine is hardly opened to give the wheels a turn at Las Canoas, when it is closed, and not opened again until the mouth of the cañon is reached, seventeen miles away, and no steam is used except for the brakes. One hour and twenty-seven minutes are used to travel these seventeen miles that might be done in ten minutes of real hurry, if there were no curves on the track. The slow time is for safety's sake, and the danger has been brought to a minimum, so that it is not thought of; in fact, there is little thought of anything but the wonderful road and its wonderful scenery.

At the head of the cañon the little river jumps off in a pretty cascade, tumbles over the rocks, foams and frets over the great boulders, for some hundreds of feet, then dives into the ground and is seen no more for several miles. In the rainy season there is such a volume of water that it cannot pass through the underground passage, but runs over what is now the dry bed of the cañon.

The cañon widens and the view grows grandly. Here and there the track is held by great walls of stone, and coming to some jutting crag too sharp, too abrupt to build around, a tunnel is cut through. In one place there are three within a few feet of each other, so that a train of ten cars would be in three tunnels at one time. In our mountains and caves there are pulpits, chairs and slides described as the Devil's, but the Devil's Backbone is here on the Mexican Central, in the Tamasopo Cañon, and there is a hole through it big enough for a railroad train to pass. Passing from the darkness of one of these tunnels into the broad light of brightest day, the marvelous view bursts upon the vision with no warning of its stupendous immensity. Perpendicularly down, more than a thousand feet, is the density of tropical green that is shaded lighter up the mountain side, and in a thousand hues, as the sunlight falls upon them at this angle or that. Over on the other mountain, the bright spots of lighter green are patches of sugar, and here, below our track, is the delicate pink of the rosewood tree; each tree seems as one huge posy, so thick the blossoms are. Far away over the other mountains, far away over the other valleys, the panorama, it seems, stretches to infinity, and while we hear the rushing of the waters, so far below, we think we can see the waters of an aerial river, or the distant seas where earth and air are lost in their intermingling. These mountains are unlike those of the interior, being covered with a tropical verdure, fed by the constantly blowing mists from the sea, while the valleys are luxuriantly rich in the density of the full tropical foliage, and what we see here, we have not seen before in all our travels in Mexico, or other lands we may have traveled in, for there is not its equal in varied beauty or difficulty of engineering accomplishment.

There are six tracks in view, as the road twists and turns down towards the valley, that we seem never to get nearer to, and in one place a track seems just under us, though we must travel six miles before we reach the spot in view. It was here that, on that famous trip of the trolleys, we lost our Mexican attendant, who had gone back as a flagman against a possibly following train, and we left him behind, as we thought, but not if he knew himself, his country and our lunch basket, of which latter he had had a taste. He simply clambered down the rocks and sat down to rest while we rolled off our six miles and caught up with him.

If ever Joseph's brethren had let him down into this pit of St. Joseph—this Hoyo de San José in the Tamasopo Cañon—he would never have gotten out to distinguish himself either in Egypt or anywhere else. It is said to be bottomless.

CHOY CAVE.   MEXICAN CENTRAL RAILWAY.

It is in evidence that various and sundry burros, whose misfortunes forced them over the brink, never returned, and that place whence no burro returns has no stopping place of even the narrowest proportions, and where a burro cannot climb must partake of the perpendicular, or of a polished surface. Indeed, this Hoyo de San José is a wonderful hole-in-the-ground, where rivers of water empty their torrents in the rainy season. There is no outlet, and the pit does not fill up, then is it not bottomless, *quien sabe?* The railroad must describe a figure 8 to get around the pit, and just west of it is established a little station and another safety switch that is always set for the side track. Here now are the full tropics, as you have dreamed of them—great giant trees, with hanging vines from the highest branches. These and the trees are covered with orchids, that flourish in the moisture of the mists from the sea. This almost impenetrable forest is a dense mass of verdure, from the topmost branches to the ferns that grow in their shade. A little farther on, the wild undergrowth has been cleared away. This may not be apparent, at first, as there seems to be, and there is still, an undergrowth of—coffee trees. The road runs through the midst of one of the finest coffee plantations, and if there is time to stop at the little platform on the left of the track, you may walk through it, and down a thousand steps to the Puente de Dios, where a rushing mountain stream leaps in a flying cascade into a beautiful pool, passes out of view, and appears again in other pretty pools below this Bridge of God. If the scenery here is not so wild, so grandly picturesque, it is not the less interesting; passing from the forest and the coffee groves the road comes to an open space and a comparatively level spot where the timber has been cut away. On the right is a village of the timber cutters, a group of thatched huts that, until now, you may not have seen except in pictures, as much a tropical village, both as to architecture and fashion of dress, as you will see.

Here, on the left of the road, is a river fringed with palms and palmettos. The road follows along its banks to Rascon, now a little railroad town where trains are made up, and great heavy double-header engines are kept to take them up the mountain. Just out of Rascon the river is crossed and the grade is downward to Valles, then up a short distance to another cañon, not so great as the one just passed, but with one view at least,

A RESIDENCE OF GUANAJUATO.

it is worth them all to see. It is the Cañon del Abra de Caballeros, and *the* grand view is of El Salto del Abra de Caballeros at the Boca del Abra. The view is from the left or north windows of the cars, or best from the rear platform. The track comes to the head of the cañon and runs along high on the mountain side. The river comes to view only a little below the roadway, but for a mile or more the marvelously colored waters fall in one cascade over another till there is a score or more—some more than a hundred feet in height—all the time in full view from the cars; the roar of the lower falls cannot be heard from the depth so far below.

Here, at the mouth of the cañon, from the high point where the track is, is the most magnificent picture I ever saw. There is a greater fall of water at Niagara, but the high towering peaks are here at El Salto del Abra, and here is a cascade of three hundred feet, and a chain of them more than a mile long. The composition of the landscape is simply superb; there are neither words to describe it and no pencil, however deft, can paint its beauties. The color is of nature's own and in her brihgtest hues. On the other side of the cañon a towering peak is 3,000 feet high, its sides precipitously drop down in gray rocks to the water's edge, washed by the torrent that goes on forever, and the cliffs are whitened by the filmy white foam that rises in mists from this home of the cascades. Back beyond the beginning of the falls, another and a higher mountain raises its head loftily. If you can, persuade your conductor to stop a minute—a minute here is worth an hour anywhere else in the world where a railroad runs—only a minute for the very grandeur of it.

I stood there and gazed rapturously. I asked for another minute, but I was called back to earth from the pinnacle to where I had soared. I took that minute, and my rifle from the car, with the thought to see if it would carry to the cliffs beyond. I fired a shot, and a thousand parrots, startled, flew screaming, circling around above and below us, settling down again in the trees where their dwelling places are.

SPANISH BRIDGE NEAR OCOTLAN. MEXICAN CENTRAL RAILWAY.

While these minutes were flying, the one great picture had so filled the eye that not one look was taken ahead. Here the cañon widens out and we look abroad, over a hundred miles of sloping plain, with undulating hills that lie between us and the sea. Still, however, we are skirting along the sides of high mountains in which there are many caves. One, La Ventana, has a chamber that is nearly 700 feet high. The name comes from an opening or window near the top that may be seen a long way off, in the mountain side. To reach La Ventana requires a walk of several miles, but another, Choy Cave is immediately under the track; in fact, a bridge is built over the skylight of this cavern, and steps have been made down to the entrance two hundred feet below, from which comes a stream of clear, cold water. The chamber of Choy Cave is over 200 feet high and with steps and passage ways along the subterranean river that is nearly a hundred feet deep. Downward the grade is, with plains and the biggest Mexican rivers to see and cross, the rivers Tamesi and Panuco, near Tamos. Near the line are the ruins of an ancient Aztec city that cover some miles of territory, so that it must have been a populous capital. These cities of the ancients of Mexico are not to be seen from the cars, but the more curious and venturesome tourist will find a field to interest him and worth his while to explore, though he must camp out; there is not even a fonda for frijoles or tortillas, and only jacals for shelter.

We came down from these grand mountains to the sea, and when we stopped at Tampico it was night, the car was rolled out on the jetties, and while the breezes of the Gulf fanned us, we listened to the lullaby of the waves, and dreamed of mountains miles and miles in height, that the sea beat against and came down over their tops in a cascade as wide as the ocean.

Eastward Over the Mexican Railway.—The first railway of Mexico was built from Vera Cruz to the City of Mexico, and, long before any of the others were finished, the fame of this one went abroad, and all over the world the wonders of its engineering feats, and the magnificence of its scenery, was told, till people crossed the seas with no other object than to look upon its beauties, and the wondrous work of its building. It is easier of access now, and there are thousands of travelers that start eastward from the capital, or westward from the Gulf, with the same object in view.

Passing out of the fine station of Buena Vista, the track takes a northerly course from the City of Mexico, and runs along the solid roadbed of an ancient causeway, trod by pilgrims to the shrine of Guadalupe for more than three centuries, and on either side of the track stand the shrines where the processions halted, and weary wayfarers worshiped. Along the east side of the track is the more modern road of foot travel, and the line of horse cars, from the city to the shrine. Under the shadow of Guadalupe the track turns somewhat to the east; on the left is the village, the great church, the stone sails, and the chapel on the hill all to be seen from the cars.

There is little choice of seats just here. On the right there are views of the city, the lake and plain, and the great volcanoes. Popocatepetl and Ixtaccihuatl are constantly in view, then Malintzi, and then Orizaba. In two hundred miles there are snow-capped mountains always in sight. On the right is Lake Texcoco, on the left Lake San Cristóbal, and on either side may be seen the great drainage works that are to drain the water from these lakes, and reclaim the lands of the valley.

Near San Juan Teotihuacan are the Pyramids of the Sun and Moon, seen from the windows on the left. Not very formidable pyramids, as seen from the cars, but the "Sun" is 216, and the "Moon" 151 feet high; the former more than half as large as the great Cheops of Egypt. Between the two pyramids is a causeway, called the Street of the Dead, also seen from the cars.

At Otumba is the field of battle between Cortez and the Mexicans, July 8, 1520, during the retreat after the defeat of the Noche Triste.

These scenes left behind, and after passing Ometusco, the junction point for Pachuca, the course is southeastward, across an almost level table-land, to the Plain of Apam, where the pulque grows, the track passing through fields and fields of thousands and thousands of acres of the immense plants that an American would call "century" plants. The Apam pulque is the best, or, perhaps it is better to say, the favorite, with those who drink pulque, and if you have not made the experiment, you will find no better place to try it than at Apam. The dealers meet all trains.

The pulque traffic is a source of great revenue to the railway companies. Regular trains, carrying nothing but pulque, leave the stations in the region from one to three o'clock in the morning, running on fast time, reaching the city between five and six o'clock. The barrels and hogskins are tumbled out onto the Custom House platform, the duty paid, and a hundred carts and cargadores take it to the "shops," all over the city. Pulque will not keep, and the Mexican knows it. He hurries it onto the train, and rushes it to the place of sale, drinks it and goes back after another load. From the fields to the "shops" it is not more than a day. When the plant is about to send up the long slender shoot that bears the bloom of the century plant, the bud is cut out, and in the basin formed the sap gathers, and is taken out by a man, with a long slender gourd. With his lips he withdraws the air from the gourd, and the crude pulque fills it, and is poured into the hogskin on his back, which, when full, is loaded on a burro or cart, taken to the hacienda, and after a quick process of fermentation, it is ready for the pulque train and the market.

At Soltepec all four of the great peaks may be seen in one grand sweep of the vision. At Apizaco the branch line extends south to the city of Puebla, passing Santa Ana, the station for the ancient city of Tlaxcala. Along the branch are some points of scenic interest. On the right, after leaving the station, is the Church of Santa Cruz, a little further on, on the left, the grand old mountain, Malintzi, in the distance, and near the road a little cañon and a cascade, whose waters supply the power for a woolen mill. After crossing some barrancas, the train makes a stop at Santa Ana, from whence street cars run to Tlaxcala. The towers of its churches are seen from the windows on the right, and in a little while, from these same windows, may be seen the Pyramid of Cholula, and a look ahead will show the towers of Puebla and the old forts on the hills beyond.

Buy canes at Apizaco; canes of all the woods that grow in Mexico. They are on sale on the station platform, along with the cakes, pies and pulque. You can buy one, or a cord, for it seems here is a solution of the timberless hills of the country; they have been stripped by the cane makers of Apizaco. There are large canes and small, cut and carved in designs fantastic, painted in all the colors of the rainbow and of the flowers that grow. Canes for the old man, the dude, and the small boy. It is Apizaco's admonition, that if any man passes that way, and afterward goes down to his grave caneless, it is his own fault. There is a good restaurant and buffet in the station, and there is usually time to buy canes and coffee, during the time of transfer of passengers and baggage for Puebla.

Leaving Apizaco, the course of the main line is slightly to the southeast, and in a few miles the highest point on the line, 8333 feet, is reached. The road runs at the base of old Mount Malintzi, and, passing the foot-hills, comes to San Andres, where passengers desiring to make the ascent of the volcano of Orizaba change cars. Now the scenery becomes more interesting, as the track winds in and out among the hills, a seeming prelude to the grandeur, just ahead, that no words are adequate to describe.

Esperanza is the stopping place at the edge of the great terrace of the table-land, 8043 feet above the sea, where commences the descent to the tierra caliente. At Esperanza the Mexican Railway maintains extensive yards and shops, and hence, southward, a horse-car line runs to Tehuacan. The station building combines ticket and telegraph offices, a good restaurant and comfortable hotel. It is not much of a pull for the engine to make the start out of Esperanza yards. The loosening of the brake will sometimes start the train, without the opening of the throttle. The wheels begin to turn, and the only steam needed will be to slow up, or stop the train. With only little stretches of up-grade, it is a roll from Esperanza to Vera Cruz. The drop from the yards here to Maltrata, sixteen miles, is 2493

MEXICAN RAILWAY STATION, CÓRDOBA.

feet, and from Maltrata, (5550 feet in altitude,) to Orizaba, 3943 feet. The slip down is 1607 feet in thirteen miles, making a total descent of 4100 feet in twenty-nine miles.

A seat on the right of the car is to be chosen. The incline of the train can be felt, as it moves toward Boca del Monte, the "mouth of the mountain," and here commences the grandest piece of scenery—one of the grand views of the world. On one side, the towering mountains—the road is only a little shelf hewn in the rocks—on the other, down a thousand feet or more, is a rushing stream, foaming and fretting over the rocks and boulders, at the bottom of a yawning cañon, and beyond it, mountains as high as this on whose side the train crawls along. Whether the engineers sought the spot near La Bota as the most available for a water supply, or, in commendable forethought, placed the tank here that the people might enjoy the view, while water is taken, the deponent saith not, but the thanks of every traveler are due for the placing of the tank where it is, whatever may have been the motive. Without any warning, or prelude of the grandeur, the magnificence, the surpassing beauty of the picture, it bursts upon the vision. A bridge over an awful chasm inspires awe, and a tunnel shuts the eyes to its depths, for a moment only, and then, as in the sudden lifting of a curtain, from darkness to daylight, displays the picture that no pencil paints.

Here the engine stops for water, a prosaic reason for such a poetic pleasure in the looking on such a view, and demands the traveler's gratitude.

No window is broad enough for its scope, and a doorway is all too narrow. Every passenger is out and down on the narrow space between the rails and edge of the cañon. There is Maltrata, a dozen miles away, to follow the rails, yet we look down on the red tiles of the roofs; the round tower of the village church gleams in the sunshine, two thousand feet straight down below your feet; the streets, gardens, houses, look like the toys from a child's play-box, and the people are only pigmies. The green fields are like a checker-board, spread out in the valley. You may look beyond the valley, to the other mountains, look ahead to some others, and see above them the snow-tipped peak of Orizaba; or try to follow the silver thread of the stream in the valley, or the shining rails of the track, winding down the mountain. You may for a moment traffic with the Indians for the most beautiful orchids, but the gem of the view is in the valley right under you, and your furtive glances come back to this jewel of a valley, La Joya, till it is indelibly fixed in your mind as the most beautiful picture you ever saw.

The object of the stop is accomplished, whether it was for water for the engine, or for you to see the view, and the train rolls on. Regretfully, perhaps, you think of the orchids, that you failed to purchase; surely, those very orchids were worth as many dollars in your own country as the Indians demanded in cents. And you wondered, perhaps, why they refused your offer, held them at the original price, and, unlike all the other Indians everywhere else, would not take less. Just wait a little while, and you may have another chance at these same orchids. While the train is running its dozen miles, curving in and out on the hillside, there is a rough-and-tumble scramble of these Indians, two thousand feet down the rocks, and the same orchids that you didn't buy will be at the station at Maltrata when you get there; and as that is the last chance for the Indian to sell to-day, you may be able to buy at your own price.

Crossing the little valley of Maltrata, keep your seat on the right of the car. The road enters a cañon, called "Infernillo," the ravine of the "little hell," which, barring the absence of any superfluous heat, seems to be properly named, and the railway builders must have had that sort of a time in running their lines through such a place. There is a bridge 140 feet high, with a sheer precipice above and below, with the mountain stream falling down the chasm in a roaring cascade. Through a tunnel, and out at the other end, is another beautiful valley, the Valley of the Cascades. The road runs down through the center of it, passing Nogales, and coming to Orizaba. There are fine views on either side, but the towns and villages are on the north of the road.

Orizaba is on the border of the tropic lands, and the scenery hence is unlike any left behind. The finest views are on—both sides. The rear platform is the best position, as from there nothing should be missed. Running through the palm-shaded street, the road goes into the cane and coffee fields. The volcano is in the view, and the hill on the left, overlooking the city, is the Cerro del Borrego, where a small body of French held at bay a much larger force of Mexicans, during the Maximilian war.

After six or seven miles, the line enters the Barranca de Metlac. The choice of seats is on the right, to see the deep ravine, and the Rio Metlac, nearly a thousand feet below. Here an immense horseshoe curve takes the track around the head of the valley, over a curved bridge, on the other side of which is an ascending grade to Fortin, then down hill to Córdoba. The view down the river is a pretty one indeed, the old stone bridge of the highway in the foreground, and the bluest of blue hills in the distance.

The town of Córdoba is on the north of the track. It might be seen from the cars, but for the dense tropical forest intervening. It may seem to you that all the inhabitants are at the station, dressed in their best suits of clothes—bright and clean, wide of trouser, and broad of straw sombrero, and brightly-colored

ABOVE MALTRATA, MEXICAN RAILWAY.

costume of woman's dress. Here the tropic Mexican appears, in all his pictur-
esqueness, as he is seen in pictures.

On down the hill, the road runs through coffee plantations, fields of sugar-cane
and tropic forests of palm and palmetto, groves of oranges, gardens of mangoes,
pineapples and bananas, from whence come the luscious fruits brought to the
cars at Córdoba.

Through some tunnels, and over bridges, the road drops down into the Atoyac
Valley, and crosses the river of that name, just beyond the station, and just after
leaving it. On the right, after the tunnel is passed, is another beautiful view, with
a cascade falling from the hill over the rocks, splashing the water to snowy foam,
and making a silver ribbon through the deep valley below. Passing the bridge
Chiquihuite, and that of San Alejo, the road comes to Paso del Macho, where the
mountain scenery is left behind, and with a few more twists and turns, takes a
due eastward course across the slope to Vera Cruz.

Westward Over the International.—It makes little difference at what point the traveler comes to the border, his curious
eyes will look with wonder before he crosses the bridge over the
narrow, sluggish, muddy little creek that forms the boundary
between the United States and Mexico—a creek that does not
seem to have grown a bit since it left El Paso, unless it be in mud
and murkiness, and why it was ever called the Rio Grande nobody
but the man who named it will ever know. Perhaps the discoverer came upon it unawares on a rainy day during the wet
season, certainly not on such a day as when I saw it first, when
it seemed there was hardly water enough and hardly current
enough to carry the mud along.

One does not look at the river, though, but to the hills beyond
—the bleak and barren hills that came to view when you are a
hundred miles away across the Texas prairies. And
yet one does not see Mexico in these hills—only where
Mexico is. Beyond the hills, in table-lands, fertile
valleys and old-time cities with domed and towered
churches, is Mexico.

At Spofford Junction, on the main line of the Southern
Pacific, a division of the road makes a detour to the
southwestward, and comes to the border at Eagle Pass,
where the connection is with the Mexican International
Railroad. The town on the Texas side is Eagle Pass;
at the other end of the steel bridge it is La Ciudad
Porfirio Diaz. The original name of the town, Piedras
Negras, was changed, in honor of the President of
Mexico. Since the opening of the line, in March, 1888,
and the establishment of the railroad headquarters
here, the towns have grown, till they now number about
6,000 people. The altitude is 722 feet above the sea,

AT LERDO.

and healthfulness is conceded. The higher elevations are not far away, and the
climb to them commences at the river, reaching 1,200 feet, at Nava, in twenty-
four miles, and, still on the rising grade, the road passes Allende, Leonora, Peyotes
and Blanco, places of 1,000 to 1,500 people. At Sabinas there is a branch to the
coal mines of Hondo and Felipe. The supply of bituminous coal is practically
inexhaustible. A branch line to Lampazos is proposed to be extended from the
coal mines. After crossing the Rio Sabinas, the average is up-grade to Monclova,
where the altitude is 1,926 feet. Monclova is one of the very many very old towns
in Mexico, that have made very little headway in population or advancement,

and the primitiveness of it is its novelty. Near the city is a rich mine of mag-
netic iron, and the whole region, round about, is rich in the more precious metals.
The direction hence is almost due south, to Treviño, the junction point with the
Monterey & Mexican Gulf Railway for Monterey, and the Gulf at Tampico. At
Jaral the road reaches an elevation of 3,753 feet, and runs within about thirty miles
of Saltillo, the capital of Coahuila, to which point a branch line is proposed.
There is a look of utter desolation in these hills, but there are valleys between,
where there are fertile lands, and where herds and flocks are grazing.

Now the road takes a more westerly course, runs along the table-lands and
comes to Paila, where the altitude is 3,898 feet. A few miles to the south of the
line is the very ancient town of Parras, one of the oldest in Mexico, having been
founded some three hundred and fifty years ago. The location is superb,

GUADALUPE, NEAR ZACATECAS.

renowned for its healthfulness, in the midst of a fine grape country. The wines
of Parras are sold in almost every Mexican city and are rated high. They are
made in both clarets and sauternes. When the Parras branch is completed the
old town may take a new lease of life.

ALTAR, SANTUARIO DE GUADALUPE, DURANGO.

The course is now westward, running a little north of Lake Parras, a typical Mexican lake about 3,600 feet above the sea level, and north of the line is the larger lake, Mayran. It is a level track now along the southern borders of the great Bolson de Mapimi unfil Torreon is reached, where connection is made with the Mexican Central Railway; the elevation, here, is 3,721 feet.

Torreon is near the Nazas River, the great irrigating ditch of this territory, and three miles north is the city of Lerdo in the midst of Mexico's most famous cotton regions, where 'tis said the cotton grows on trees. Proceeding westward on the International it is only five miles to the lovely San Juan Valley where the train rounds a curve and rolls into the oasis. The high point of rocks on the left forms the gateway, and to the other side of the track the valley stretches away to the north. It is a pretty valley, is the San Juan, and they have made the waters of it run around its borders on the hillsides, and through aqueducts of stone, till it is high enough to irrigate the fields. It looks as though these Indian engineers had made the water run up hill; we crossed the stream back there, and here it is on a level with our windows.

Across the valley the rows of trees show which way the river runs, and dotted here and there, little patches of white mark the village and hacienda, with the fertile fields in between and growing grain nearly ready for the harvest. They have two harvests each year in this valley, when they would not have one, perhaps, if they waited for the rains, but the blessed little river stands in the rain-maker's place.

All the mountains in Mexico are cut in fantastic shapes, but here, on this road, a freakful nature seems to have outdone herself, or perhaps, this road gives us a closer view of the rocks and crags that look like castles or a herd of some huge monsters outlined against the sky.

Some miles below there is a cave (any conductor will point out the place; a black hole in the hill on the north side), a veritable robbers' cave, where the bandits buried their dead, or came to hide themselves and count the proceeds of business in the old *diligencia* days. The robbers are not there now, but there are the relics of them in skulls and bones. The cave is high upon the almost perpendicular sides of the mountain and the opening is just large enough for a man to drop himself into a chamber twenty-five feet long, and as wide, with six or eight feet from floor to ceiling and a narrow opening to another smaller room. The darkness can almost be felt, and the dust of ages, a foot thick on the floor, makes the place uninviting. A friendly Mexican match will give a glimpse of the glittering stalactites; on the floor and against the sides of the chamber are the evidences of the robber story, and a skull or two may be added to your collection of curios from this curious country. Long drouths parch the country, but the land is fertile, even without rain, and irrigation is a science in Mexico. The stranger wonders what there is to support the haciendas that are as big as a town. "Can anything grow here?" some one asks. "Nothing is impossible in Mexico. See that palm tree over there in that hacienda; it is the only one within three hundred miles, and where the palm grows there is life in the land." This is truth, the palm is there and there is not another this side of Tampico.

ENTRANCE TO SAN JUAN VALLEY, MEXICAN INTERNATIONAL RAILROAD.

On the south of the road, a little farther on, is an extinct volcano that is near the track, some four or five hundred feet high, and if there was time for the stop, it would be worth all the climb to look down into the awful crater, with its sides and depths crusted with the lava of a thousand years, or more it may have been. You can see the volcano from the cars as you pass by, but you must climb to the crater if you would see that. I might enlarge upon this story, as the train does not stop here and there is little chance to disprove, but the truth is enough to tell of anything in Mexico.

The road now, is for the most part, across the plains; the everlasting hills surrounding it are never out of sight. There is an iron bridge across the bed of a river, now bone dry, that when you come back may be a rushing torrent. When it rains in Mexico, it rains; the showers may be few and far between, but when they come they make up for lost time. But, withal, there is life in this seemingly arid soil, else how came the trees that for miles along this plain make it look like one vast orchard? And there is water above ground, though your palace car point of observation may not disclose it, else where do they drink and how get a sustenance—these herds of horses and cattle? Across the spreading plain is the city of Durango afar off, the towers rising above the low-roofed, square-topped houses. Beyond the city, and overlooking it, is a high hill with the Church of Los Remedios on its very top. A golden sunset makes the background of gorgeous hue, and while you watch its beauties the train rolls down to the station, where the people wait your coming just as they waited for those that came yesterday.

The train comes to an anchor at the pretty stone station, and almost under the shadow of the wonderful iron mountain that was one of the objects of the building of this road. A mountain of solid iron it is, the ore ranging from 75 to 90 per cent. of pure iron, and enough of it to supply the world for a hundred years. The completion of the railroad did not help the iron industry of Durango though. The little foundry that did a land-office business for so many years got thirty-five cents a pound for iron till the railroad came, and they found they could buy in Pittsburgh and ship to Durango for a great deal less than thirty-five cents. The old foundry, with its wooden machinery and water-power, has been replaced by a million-dollar smelter, and iron is cheaper now.

A busy, bustling scene is at the station; coachmen call their destinations and fares, darting here and there to relieve some weary traveler of his baggage and, if he can, thrust him into his own particular coach, before the traveler can enter a word of protest. Private carriages are there in numbers, whose drivers, more dignified than the liverymen, assist their master, or their master's guests to transfer baggage, all the while conscious of the admiring glances cast upon them by groups of pretty Indian girls, who are there, as everybody else is, for the purpose of seeing the train come in, and catching, at the same time, a glimpse of these youths in embroidered suits and gaily tinseled sombreros. Your anticipation of seeing a city extremely primitive is not realized at the station. You stand under the shelter of a modern stone station, with its smooth grass plat, roses, green trees and graveled walks, and watch the scene before you, then glance beyond the throng, down the track over which you just passed, to see the substantial freight depots of the big stores and smelters, each one of which has its own private depot and side-track for handling freight, and wonder why they called Durango "primitive."

It was a matter of small wonder that the ancient city of Jerusalem should be so long without railroad communication with the outer world, and the completion of the line from Joppa was only the talk of a day, but a city more than three hundred years old, and with nearly a hundred thousand inhabitants, on this continent, and with a main line of railroad within a hundred and fifty miles of it, secured its first railroad since Jerusalem did. It was left to Durango to be the

ALAMEDA, DURANGO.

last of the great cities of Mexico to have a railway, and it is still such a novelty in that city that the populace wait at the station for the arrival of the train in the late afternoon, and come down early in the morning to see it pull out.

It is to see this new, old city that attracts a journey down the line of the International Railway of Mexico ; this, and to see the newest primitiveness of Mexican city life before the women exchange their lace mantillas for Parisian bonnets, and the men strip the silver bangles from their trousers, and change the ornamental, monogrammed sombrero for the silk tile. And I will be pardoned the suggestion, just here, that the primitiveness is fast fading, and he who would see Mexico as it has been written about, and dreamed of, should see it now.

THE HACIENDA WATERWORKS.

Eastward Over the Interoceanic—Leaving the City of Mexico from the handsome station of San Lazaro, the trains of the Interoceanic Railroad pass through the eastern outskirts of the city and come to the field of practice of the artillery school, with its adobe targets on the left of the track, and run along an ancient causeway that was once the high road between the capital of the Montezumas and the great city of the Tezcucans. On both sides of the track, and very close to it, are tall trees that make a shaded avenue for some miles, and such an avenue is on the roadway of no other line on earth. Looking back from the rear platform, it will be seen that the branches almost meet above the cars, and down the long vista seem to close the entrance where the train came in.

On the right is the canal of La Viga, Santa Anita, the hill Ixtapalapa, cele-brated in Aztec history, the extinct volcano of Ajusco, and, in the distance, Peñon. On the left is Lake Texcoco; on the right, the waters and marshes of Xochimilco and Chalco. Turning around the southern shore of Lake Texcoco, road comes to Los Reyes, the junction of the Morelos Division with the main line, a picturesque Indian town, where the people bring fish to the trains to sell to the pas-sengers, as something out of the ordinary of train and station ped-dlers in Mexico, or, perhaps, any-where else. Skirting the eastern shore of the lake the road enters a fertile plain, where there are haci-endas, villages and churches without number. At the station of Chapingo is the hacienda of the late ex-Presi-dent, General Gonzales, on the north of the track a group of gorgeously painted houses, bearing an oriental look of towers and bright colors; on the right, almost opposite the haci-enda of Chapingo, is the village of Huixotla, with an old church and older ruins of Aztec origin. Texcoco is the town that in the old Toltec days was the rival of Tenochtitlan, or the City of Mexico, and the capital of a powerful nation. At Texcoco Cortéz stopped to prepare his *bergantines*, with which to transport his army over the

ENTRANCE OF THE INTEROCEANIC RAILWAY TO THE CITY OF MEXICO.

waters of the lake. Tetzconcinco, or the "laughing hill," the favorite resort of Netzahualcoyotl, the Tezcucan chief, three miles east of Texcoco, may be seen from the windows on the left, and near it the trees that overshadow the Molino de Flores, and a little farther on is the aqueduct of the waters for these gardens and palaces of the chiefs of the olden times.

The course is almost due north for some miles, to make a circuit of the foot-hills of the great volcanoes that are always in the view. At the little station of San Antonio, and between there and Metepec, there is a fine view of the Texcoco Valley, the lake, and beyond it the City of Mexico, forty miles away ; and also from the north windows, beyond Metepec, in the distance, are the pyramids of the Sun and Moon, which are older, perhaps, than Cheops of Egypt.

At Otumba, Cortéz met the army of the Aztecs in 1520, and drove them in retreat before him. At Irolo are two branch roads to Pachuca, and at San Lorenzo a branch to San Nicolas; for some miles the road runs through the pulque region, then starts on an up-grade, reaching an altitude of 9,000 feet near Nanacamilca, and then down on the other side, through a most picturesque dis-trict, passing along the mountain sides, through cañons, and down to the depths of the barranca, with constantly changing scenes in every turn and curve, till it comes to the lovely valley of San Martin Texmelucan, with its streams of clear, sparkling water, shady woodlands, and boundless scenes of prosperity.

Passing San Martin and Analco, the line enters the great plain and valley of Puebla, one of the richest in all Mexico ; the great haciendas here and there and everywhere are in evidence of its wealth. At Los Arcos is the junction of

IXTACCIHUATL FROM AMECAMECA.

the branch road to Matamoros. On the right is Cholula, the greatest of the Mexican pyramids; hence the road runs across the plain to Puebla. Leaving Puebla the road skirts the eastern slope of great Malintzi, and here is a view to be enjoyed perhaps nowhere else in the world, the road running through a tropic valley in sight of four snow-capped mountains—Popocatepetl and Ixtaccihuatl to the west, Malintzi in the foreground, and Orizaba far to the east. It is a fact that, in all the miles of all the divisions of the Interoceanic road, with scarcely an exception of half an hour's run, there is a snow-capped mountain always in the view.

The route is now to the northeast, crossing the Mexican Railway at San Marcos, and coming to a well-watered plain that is just on the verge of the terrace that drops down to the hot lands. At Virreyes is a branch road to San Juan de los Llanos. On the right of the road, near Perote, is the old castle of Perote, an ancient fortress built by the Spaniards soon after the conquest, as a stopping place for rest, after the long pull up the mountain. Here was kept a large garrison of soldiers that patroled the road between Vera Cruz and Puebla in the old bandit days.

Las Vigas is on the very edge of the great terrace. If there is no mist in the valley, the view is grandly magnificent; or, you may look out over a sea of white clouds with the indescribable sensation of traveling by rail above them and through their filmy folds. The track is through an endless lava bed that is a confused mass of black rock, from a pebble to huge pieces of the weight of tons. It was a marvelous piece of engineering in the building of this road, and every crook and turn of its track seems to show greater difficulties overcome. At no place is the grade more than two and a half feet to the 100, which is remarkable, when the face of the country traversed is considered. The views are marvelous and beyond compare. There is the white-faced Cofre de Perote, white-capped Orizaba, and the lesser hills sloping away to the Gulf, the waters of which, the ships and the white houses of Vera Cruz are a hundred miles away. It is a continual drop down till the train stops in the region of the full tropics, at the picturesque station of the ancient town of Jalapa, and thence the grade is still downward to Vera Cruz.

NEPANTLA, INTEROCEANIC RAILWAY.

Between Palmar and Colorado is a beautiful piece of railroad work, in the famous Huarumbo cutting, the deepest cut in Mexico, where the line makes almost a complete loop. Near Rinconada is a sugar-loaf mountain, Cerro Gordo, where one of the hardest fights of the American war was fought. It is a wonderful track along here. There are a hundred horse-shoe curves. At one place the track you are to pass over seems a thousand feet below you, the white rock of the ballast showing through the verdure of the intervening trees. Sometimes it is hard to tell whether that is the track just passed over or the one you are coming to. In one view there is a perfect replica of the Hudson palisades.

Down at San Francisco the thatched houses of the tropics are shaded by feathery palm trees, and the straggling villages seem to have their residences designed chiefly for ventilation, with the walls of reeds and the roofs of palm leaves. Numberless streams from the mountains flowing to the sea are crossed here and there, and at La Antigua the river of the same name is passed on a steel bridge, near the place of a landing constructed by Cortéz, where there are some old cannon accredited to the conqueror, and near by some tombs and an old church, bearing date of 1526. In the approach to Vera Cruz all beauty is left behind, and but for the rolling surf of the sea, here might be the entrance to the desert of Sahara, where the sand blows in drifts like the beautiful snow, and where real snow fences are necessary to keep the sand from burying the tracks. But there is only a mile or two of this, and is not to be remembered with all the grand beauties of the hills behind us.

STATION SAN MARTIN, INTEROCEANIC RAILWAY.

The Morelos Division of the Interoceanic Railway leaves the main line at Los Reyes and runs southwest, with an ultimate destination at Acapulco on the Pacific coast. The first station of importance is Ayotla, where, like Los Reyes, the inhabitants bring fish to the trains to sell. The old adobe town on the right of the track, on the shores of the lake, is a very pretty one.

After passing Ayotla the road makes a turn around the lake, and the volcanoes come to view and are in sight through all the journey, seen first from the left windows, but as the track curves about are seen from either side.

La Compañia is a very pretty little village, where there is horse-car connection on the left for Tlalmanalco, and on the right, along a shaded roadway, to Chalco, a city on the border of the lake, whose towers and domes can be seen for some

STONE STAIRWAY, SACRO MONTE.

distance as the train moves southward. Next is the village of Cuatlenchan, on a hill on the left side; the church on the top of the hill is seen up and down the road for several miles.

Amecameca is the stopping place for the pilgrims bound for the craters of Popocatepetl and Ixtaccihuatl. The train rounds the hill and stops right at the base of Sacro Monte, the sacred mountain, one of the most picturesque shrines in all Mexico. Look from the windows on the right, or, while the train waits, step on the platform for a good view of the stone stairway, almost hidden by a dense grove of trees. The city lies spread out on a plain on the left of the track. Tourists who have no time for a longer stay, or do not continue to the end of the road, may leave Mexico on the morning train, have a few hours at Amecameca

CULVERT NEAR ACAJETE, INTEROCEANIC RAILWAY.

and return in the afternoon. The view from the Sacro Monte is superbly magnificent. No nearer view of the volcanoes is obtainable unless the ascent is made, which requires three days' time and is attended with much discomfort; but the adventure of the ascent, and the seeing of the grandest view in the world, from a height of nearly 18,000 feet, is worth any amount of fatigue. Leaving Amecameca the railway passes through one of the streets of the town and crosses the stone causeway which was built for the pilgrim processions, between the church and the shrine. At a point a few miles south of Ozumba the highest elevation of the road is reached, there having been a continuous climb from the plain of Mexico, and the down-grade to the hot country is commenced; without an engine the train would roll to Cuautla, too fast, so the engine is retained to hold it in check. From the station at Nepantla there is a magnificent view from the left windows, a view taking in millions of acres of the hot lands to the mountains, a hundred miles beyond. For miles and miles, as the train rolls down the hills, may be seen, first from one side and then the other, the dome and tower of a church. The same church may be seen for two hours; it is the Church of San Miguel, at Atlatlahutla, and near it is an abandoned monastery. Here again the tourist finds another feature of

VILLAGE OF SAN SALVADOR, INTEROCEANIC RAILWAY.

Mexico's scenery and people, totally different from all the other travels in the Republic. The houses are adobe as to walls and thatched as to roofs; the broad plains have curious trees; bands of Indians troop from one town to another in curious costumes, marching along totally oblivious to the passing locomotive and approaching civilization, and will not give away to the latter any quicker than they will to the engine if they happen to be on the track when it comes along. In fact it is hard for them to understand that the train cannot "keep to the right" when it meets people in the road, and they claim the right of way from the fact that they were there first.

Now the sugar country is reached. The train passes through a fine hacienda and backs into Cuautla on a Y, passing and crossing an aqueduct, where the natives are seen bathing and washing clothes, comes to a station that was once a church.

The train stops some minutes at Cuautla and there is time for a walk through the little alameda, just outside of the station, where there are trees and flowers, a hotel where there are good wines, coffee and lunches to be had. As the approach to the station has been through a grove of tropical trees and gardens, so is its departure, and the train continues southward through the cane country to Yautepec; the distant mountains enrich the scene, making a blue background to a lovely tropical picture that extends down to Jojutla and the end of the track.

POPOCATEPETL FROM AMECAMECA.

South Over the National—The murky, muddy, mis-named Rio Grande does not improve as it grows and goes on to the sea; it is the same insignificant little creek here, as everywhere else that a railroad crosses it, and the country of the first hundred miles of Mexico equally unattractive in chapparal and cactus-covered plains. This desolation continues only to the Salado River, at Lampazos, where the mountains begin. On the right of the track, south of the station, is *La Mesa de los Cartujanos*, a mountain with a perfectly level top, 2000 feet above the plain. A narrow path, not wider than is necessary for a man and a mule, leads up the rugged side to the wooded and watered table at the top, where once was the home of a tribe of Indians, the Cartujanos, so called from an ancient Benedictine mission, established there two hundred years ago, who, strangely enough, found wood and water on the summit, when there was none on the plain. The route of the railway is southwesterly, following what was first an Indian trail, then the King's highway, and, in later days, the line of march of the American armies, as they proceeded on an invasion that their greatest general has pronounced the most unholy and unjust war ever waged by a stronger on a weaker nation. The track crosses and recrosses the old road many times, passing Busta-mente, Villaldama and Palo Blanco. From Villaldama a branch extends to the Guadalupe mines. The mountains

TUNNEL PORFIRIO DIAZ, INTEROCEANIC RAILWAY.

are growing and closing in nearer the road, until the Saddle Mountain and the Mountain of the Mitres are in the view. These overlook the valley of Monterey, a perfectly lovely valley, with high hills on every side. At Monterey is the junction of the Monterey & Mexican Gulf Railroad and tramway lines for Topo Chico Ho Springs. South from Monterey the road runs across the plain and enters the San Juan Valley, which grows narrower and narrower, till it becomes a cañon, and the views interesting in their beauty and grandeur. Eight miles from Monterey is the village of Santa Catarina, with high mountains on either side. On the left, about two miles across the valley, high up near the top, is a hole directly through the crest, as if made by a monster cannon shot, and near Garcia are some caves, not seen from the cars, but objects of excursions from Monterey. After some miles of winding about, first on one side and then on the other of the noisy little San Juan River, the valley closes to the narrow precipitous cliffs of a cañon, and the road comes to the table-land, and at Ramos Arispe an interesting village and hacienda is seen on the right.

The wider valley continues on to Saltillo, running through fertile fields and gardens, till after the city is passed, the road enters a more barren district. Five miles south, on the left, the track runs near to the battlefield of Buena Vista. It is an up-grade to Carneros. and, just beyond, on the right, is the little *pueblo* of Gomez Farias, once the home of a band of bandits. It is a roll from here down to the plains, passing the unimportant stations of La Ventura and El Salado. At Vanegas is the junction of the Vanegas, Cedral & Rio Verde Railroad to the silver reduction works of Cedral and Matehuala, running also within a mile of the Real de Catorce, that formerly were reached only by burros from the station of Catorce, twenty miles farther on. 'At Catorce the narrow mountain path can be seen from the windows on the left. It starts up the mountain from the little village just at the foot of the hill, almost hidden by green trees. Catorce is the last stop in the Temperate Zone, the Tropic of Cancer being crossed just

THE CURVED BRIDGE ABOVE DOS RIOS, MEXICAN NATIONAL RAILROAD

before arrival at the station of La Maroma. The spot is marked by a pyramid, seen on the right of the track. The route now is across an unbroken plain, the long stretch of track being without a curve; there are deflections here and there, but no curves for nearly a hundred miles. There are no cuts or fills, and, if danger of derailment were the only consideration, trains might make a speed of a hundred miles an hour.

From Catorce the ride is still over what seems an almost endless plain, until the train reaches Bocas, where there is something to see from both sides of the cars; on the left a beautiful hacienda, looking like a walled fortress, but outside the walls are some tropical gardens, all lovely with bright flowers. On the right, almost hidden by the trees, are two white church-like towers. This place was once the property and a favorite resort of Maximilian, and nearer the track is a manufactory of *mescal* and *tequila*.

After leaving Bocas the road enters the hills again, and some pretty views are presented, but what most interests the tourists is the approach to the city of San Luis Potosí. The first view is from windows on the right, and after passing through some fertile fields and some miles of gardens, with adobe walls inclosing semi-tropic fruits and vegetables, the towers of the old-time town are in full view against a low line of hills to the westward, and when the train comes to the station one concludes it is a gala day in town, as if the entire population, resolved into a committee of reception, had come to the station to meet some distinguished guest. Leaving San Luis Potosí the road enters the rich agricultural belt of Central Mexico. The country becomes more broken and interesting, and as valley after valley is passed, it is apparent that the soil is here extremely productive. The population becomes more dense, and the vegetation increases in luxuriance. Villa Reyes is passed, with the immense hacienda of Jaral, which, during the revolution of 1810, furnished a full regiment of cavalry to assist the royalists against the armies of the patriots. The hacienda once controlled 20,000 peons. Before arriving at San Felipe a deep *barranca* is crossed, spanned by a viaduct noticeable for its height, and the engineering skill displayed in its construction. San Felipe is a town of some 6000 inhabitants, and is situated in the center of a rich farming country. Dolores Hidalgo was given its surname in honor of the patriot, Hidalgo, the Washington of Mexico, who here sounded the watchword of liberty which fired the Mexican heart, and roused the whole country to arms to repel the power of Spain. This is a quaint old town of several thousand

AT CUAUTLA, INTEROCEANIC RAILWAY.

inhabitants. It has a fine plaza, and interesting churches, and the traveler is shown many relics of the Cura Hidalgo, which are here preserved in the old house which he occupied. The approach to San Miguel is from the northeast.

VIEW NEAR DOS RIOS, MEXICAN NATIONAL RAILROAD.

The city is picturesquely located on the south side of the track, and the view from the left side of the cars is a beautiful one. The city is a mile away, but is spread out on the side of a great hill, so that it cannot be hid.

After San Miguel the road comes to the Cañon de la Laja. The best view is from the windows of the cars on the right, the waters of a little river sparkling under the trees hundreds of feet below the track. Across the cañon the hills rise up high, shutting off even the early afternoon sun; and just at a turn of the cañon, on a jutting point of the mountain, is a cross that stands out against the sky, as if it was painted there. Down in the valley, here and there, are clusters of adobe houses, with quaint little churches, making the queerest little villages imaginable; some of them are very near the track on the right side, so close that the flying tourist has glimpses of Mexican backyard life. The houses are almost hidden from view by trees and vines, among which are some oranges, lemons and bananas. There are some wonderful views all through the cañon, making it a most interesting portion of the journey. After leaving the cañon the road enters a semi-tropical region, passes the enterprising village and factories of Soria, seen from the west windows, and if the train would stop long enough, a walk through the purely Mexican town of San Juan de las Vergas would be amply repaid. The streets are hedged with giant cacti, fifteen and twenty feet high; behind, there are the adobe houses of the inhabitants, almost hidden by a luxuriant foliage of banana leaves and vines. There are forests and orange and lemon trees and some coffee trees. The people are purely Mexican, with not even a half-bred Spaniard exception.

Hence, for a while, the route is through a rich agricultural region to and beyond Celaya, which city is on the right, and for miles the domes of the churches and flat-topped houses may be seen, with a high mountain for a blue background.

The National crosses the Mexican Central Railway at Celaya, and, having left the valley of the Laja, crosses a broken country to the valley of the Lerma, the longest river in Mexico, which the road crosses after passing Salvatierra, where there are some extensive woolen mills.

At Acámbaro is the junction of the Western Division of the National Railway with the main line. The city lies on the right of the road, on a plain almost hidden by trees and at the base of a high mountain. If for any reason the train

LOS REYES, INTEROCEANIC RAILWAY.

should stop long enough at Acámbaro, a walk up town will repay. Leaving this station, the route runs more to the southeast, but follows the Lerma Valley, often running along its banks, sometimes near the water, and again high on the cliffs of a cañon.

Maravatio is a pretty little city on the right of the track, about forty miles from Acámbaro. A look from the windows shows the tower of an old church above the trees, beyond which are the low-built houses. The country now alternates between the finest agricultural lands and grazing plains, with some barren hills intervening. The Cañon of the Zopolite, through which the road passes, presents some of the finest views of wild scenery. Just before the cañon is reached, on the left is shown a high cliff from which Juan Medina, a noted brigand, leaped his horse to the death of both horse and rider, to escape the latter's capture by the pursuing soldiers. After leaving the cañon the road winds about on the barren hills in such bends and curves that the track parallels itself two or three times, and looking from either side, that part of the road passed a quarter of an hour ago, or to be gone over fifteen minutes hence, may be seen two or three hundred yards away. Along here a seat on the left of the train is best. Way across the valley is a village, down by the river Lerma, almost hidden by the trees, only the white belfry of the church rising above them. This village is not out of sight for nearly an hour. The seat on the left is best for views of the cañon, and if a careful lookout is kept, the snow-capped crater of the volcano of Toluca may be seen, the first glimpse about the hundred-and-fortieth kilometre post, and it may be seen again and again, as the train reaches the top of the grades. Coming down into the valley of Toluca the view is best from the right side, where it seems to rise higher and higher above all the hills, as the road runs nearer to its base.

The city of Toluca is in the midst of a wide, level plain, a table-land, dotted here and there with haciendas, showing evidence of great prosperity. The view of the city is from the right side of the cars. Going east from the city the route runs through the finest agricultural district, and along the broad highway that was once a paved road, with massive stone bridges, crosses the Lerma again, and comes to the base of the Sierra Madres and commences the climb up its steep

OBSERVATION CAR, MEXICAN NATIONAL RAILROAD.

sides. Looking back now, see the cities of the plain—Toluca in the distance, and the once "great city of Lerma," the home of the brigands, now a mere village. Passing the suburbs of the town of Ocoyocac, the road winds up the mountain side till it is a thousand feet above it, when, looking down on the red-tiled roofs, it looks like a toy town of playhouses. The view from the right-hand windows and the rear platform is grand beyond description; as the train crawls slowly up the steep grades the panorama spreads out wider, and the white-capped volcano seems to follow in the wake, till the view is lost behind the trees. At the foot of the mountain is the river, like a silver ribbon ; beyond, the green and fertile valley, dotted here and there with a hacienda or hamlet ; in the far distance the snow-topped mountain, and, nestling at its foot, the white walls and warm, red-

AT THE PALACE GATE, CHAPULTEPEC.

tiled roofs of Toluca. A few more turns, and the fair view is shut out, skyward ; now, along the cliffs of another cañon, the train approaches the summit. The station of La Cima is directly on the divide ; the waters flowing east go to the lake, on the Plain of Mexico ; those flowing west go to the Pacific Ocean, and the stream that rushes down the west side of the mountain, alongside of the track, is the headwaters of the river Lerma.

At Salazar, built on a plain near the summit, the train halts for some ten minutes. The air is found to have become sharp at an altitude of nearly 10,000 feet. Leaving Salazar, the train continues the ascent to La Cima. At La Cima the descent of the eastern slope begins, and the glorious beauty of the noble Valley of Mexico commences to unfold. Through gaps in the mountain wall you may catch fleeting views in the panorama, until finally it bursts like a vision full upon the sight; the glittering towers and domes of Mexico in the middle distance; a little farther, and to the left, the broad expanse of the waters of the lakes gleaming in the sunlight like burnished silver ; beyond, and overshadowing all, raising their snow-crowned heads far above, a coronal of rainbow-tinted clouds wreathing them about, stand, in majestic beauty, like guardians watching mutely over the scene, the giants of the valley, Ixtaccihuatl and Popocatepetl. Could they but speak, what a history they might unfold—the building up of cities and their throwing down; what opulence of power, what cruelty, crime and blood-

AT MONTEREY.

shed. Races have come and gone; majestic monuments, raised by the hand of man have melted into dust and are forgotten. They alone remain immutable, the hand of time dealing with them but lightly.

Passing down the east side of the backbone of the continent, in crooks and turns, through the tunnel of San Martin, the train rolls rapidly along the side of the Monte de las Cruces, called so from the innumerable crosses erected over the graves of highwaymen and their victims; then crossing a curved bridge over the Dos Rios, nearly a hundred feet high, comes down into the Hondo Valley. The village with the church, on the hill on the right, was the home of a band of robbers for many years. Just after passing the station there is shown, on the left side, an immense meteoric stone, or, "the stone that fell from the moon," as the natives call it.

Now the City of Mexico is at hand, and with a few more turns the towers and domes are in the view. As the train rolls down the Valley of Los Remedios, the sanctuary is seen on the hill to the left; Chapultepec on the right, and the town of Tacuba on the left. Again, on the left, the Church of San Esteban, and the tree of Noche Triste, and then the Colonia Station, in the City of Mexico.

Westward from Acámbaro—As the train circles the town, the view is a very pretty one. Still passing through the fertile farming lands the journey grows more interesting with every mile, interspersing rich haciendas with scenery wild and weird, and after making a quick turn from between some hills comes suddenly in view of Lake Cuitseo. Circling round through the marsh at the head of the lake, where there are some salt works, the train comes up to, and runs along the lake shore. The view is from the north side. It is a fine body of water, but very shallow, with mountain islands rising up from the water in every direction. One of these is inhabited by a tribe of Indians who have no dealings with the outside world. On a little island of a few acres they have a little world of their own, where a hardy, healthy band of contented people seem entirely oblivious to all beyond the shores of their lake. The men are strong, sturdy fellows, who go about the lakes in long canoes, and take, with a pole-net, the little white minnow-like fish on which they subsist ; dried in the sun, they are ready to be eaten. The women are fine specimens, looking as if they might be warriors too, if their little island was attacked, but seem happy in the little thatched huts that are their homes. The waters are covered with thousands of water fowl of all kinds, and there is excellent shooting. Near the station on the lake shore, on the right, see the columns of steam rising from the marshes. These are springs of hot water, hot enough to boil an egg hard in a few moments. In the thick brush near the track the Indians have made bathing pools and come here to bathe, and the fame of the cures is great. On the bushes and sticking in the ground around the pools are hundreds of little crosses, made by two sticks tied together, left there by grateful patients who have been cured of their ills by the waters. The ground all about the springs seems to be a mere crust, sounds hollow, and sinks under the weight of a person walking near the springs. There is a strong smell of sulphur, and whether this is only an upper crust of his Satanic majesty's domain may be surmised.

From Lake Cuitseo to Morelia the route crooks and turns through fertile lands, passing fine haciendas and pretty villages, crossing valleys where perpetual running streams keep the fields and gardens green from summer to winter and winter to summer. When the reaping of one crop is accomplished another is planted, and large yields of corn, wheat and barley are made.

From the right side of the cars a "saddle" mountain is seen all the way from Lake Cuitseo. It lies just north of the suburbs of Morelia, and is a landmark showing the location of that city.

The tops of the towers in the city of Morelia may be seen rising above the low intervening hills, while the train is yet some miles away. The city is on the left of the track, but a seat on the right is best. The track runs along the river bank for a mile or two, and there are hundreds of Indian women washing clothes. These with their children, and the men waiting to let their wives carry the laundry home, make an interesting scene.

The ride from the city to the western terminus of the Mexican National at Patzcuaro, is picturesque to a degree. From the left windows you see the Cuincho waterfall, where there are also some hot springs with water at a temperature sometimes reaching a hundred degrees.

The first view of Lake Patzcuaro is from the right-hand side of the cars, and after making some curves on the hillside high above the barranca, the train comes down to the shore of the lake, where there is a hacienda hotel near the station.

The city of Patzcuaro is two miles from the station, located high on the hills, from whence is a view of exceeding beauty. Miles from the lake, dotted with its dozens of islands, and the valley with nearly fifty towns and their white-domed churches, illustrate a lovely panorama.

The Mexican Northern Railway runs northeast from Escalon, on the Mexican Central Railway, to the Sierra Mojada mining district, forty miles.

South Over the Southern.—Through the south of Mexico, from Puebla to Oaxaca, runs the Mexican Southern Railroad, with an ultimate destination at Tehuantepec, or at the deep water harbor of Salina Cruz, on the Pacific Coast. The road penetrates the rich regions of one of the richest sections of the Republic, a territory with a wealth of timber and mineral resources in the mountain districts, and illimitable beds of marble and onyx. In the lowland valleys cane and coffee grow with wildest luxuriance, and all the fruits of the tropics are found in the fields of the haciendas along the line.

The products of the contiguous territory must contribute to a local traffic that will enter largely into increased earnings as mines and quarries are opened, and when all the sugar and coffee lands are put under cultivation, while the route of the road is geographically in the line that must be taken by the "backbone railroad" from North to South America, and while that plan is being promoted, this section is already built and operated, and in the near future the Mexican Southern Railroad will offer the shortest route, for through business, from the interior of the two Republics to the west coast of Central and South America.

Unlike any other railroad in Mexico the Southern does not run high on the table-lands, and along the mountain sides, but follows the valleys, and, from a scenic point of view, offers an innovation to the travelers of other lines that have looked down on the valleys below the tracks, till they came here to travel through the valleys, and through one cañon and barranca after another, looking up to the

SIERRA MOJADA, MEXICAN NORTHERN RAILWAY.

overhanging cliffs and towering peaks that close in about the roadway till it seems there is hardly room to pass betweem them. Here are the ever-running rivers to complete the innovation from the dry, rocky beds of the rainy-season rivers of other sections. The route of these rivers is the route of the road, and the two are companions, hardly out of sight of each other for many miles.

Leaving Puebla the Mexican Southern Railroad runs almost due east, parallel with the line of the Interoceanic Railway, across the plain as far as Amozoc. This should be called the Valley of Churches. Look where you will, the tiled domes rise above the plain. They are in the villages, north, east, south and west, and every hacienda has one of its own—picturesque to a degree, with the polished tiles of many colors, as in the Puebla Valley and around Cholula. Looking backward, as the train leaves the handsome station in Puebla, there is a view of the city, the forts on the surrounding hills, and beyond them, to the westward, the pyramid of Cholula; further, high against the western sky, the Volcanoes of Popocatepetl and Ixtaccihuatl; and, to the northward, old Malintzi and the Cerro del Tecolote; then, a little to the east of north, the sharp, white peak of Orizaba, rising above the hill of Amaluca. Is there a view like this, anywhere, that may be seen from the windows of a passenger car? Where?

It is a slightly ascending grade from Puebla, with an altitude of 7093 feet to Amozoc, at 7295 feet above the sea, and after leaving that station it is as constantly descending, for more than a hundred and thirty-five miles, to Quiotepec, and then it is up hill to Las Sedas, and, again, down hill to Oaxaca. Of course there are ups and downs of track, but the average ascents and descents are as mentioned. Passing the station of Santa Rosa, the first town of importance is Tepeaca, on the left of the track, with the towers of a grand old church, high above the houses and the trees surrounding it. The station of Rosendo Márquez was named for a prominent Mexican and former Governor of the State of Puebla.

Tecamachalco is a picturesque old town, lying on a hill to the north of the track. The road from it to the town skirts the hill above the intervening little valley, or, we may call it a street, since it leads from the others of the town, that wind about among the adobe houses. The picture is not exactly like any other we have seen in Mexico.

In the region around Las Animas there is a change in the cactus; the prickly-pear variety of other sections does not grow here, or, at least, not as much as elsewhere. Here it is the "organo," the full-grown plant greatly resembling the pipes of the church organ, and it is most aptly named. Here also is that variety from which the ixtle fibre is taken. It is a succession of rich valleys and nature's great terraces, the table-lands, that the road passes through along here, dropping from one to the other, by gradual descent, that is shown by the easy running of the train, and a rising temperature. Passing the stations of Tlalcotepec and Carnero, the important city of Tehuacan is next on the line. The station at Tehuacan and the city are on the east side of the track. It is a very pretty little city, its streets, with a row of trees through the center, running at right angles, and passing through pretty plazas, where there are other over-hanging trees, growing with a tropic luxuriance. It is the "Street of Democracy" that leads from the station to the Plaza Mayor. The low-walled houses on either side have their patios filled with flowers, and on the outer walls curiously curled brackets hold the old-fashioned street lamps. On one side of the plaza is the principal church of the place, on another the portales, on the others stores and residences. In the center, in the dense shade of the trees, is a handsome music stand, embowered in flowers. The outer walks of the plaza are paved with stone. There are seats on either side, and on other walks leading in and out among the trees and flowers. Near the plaza is a curious old market, and a more curious old convent-looking church with a garden behind

ABOVE THE CLOUDS, POPOCAT

the high walls surrounding it. Opposite the market is the College of Arts, and near by an abandoned church, now used as a barrack for a company of rurales.

Tehuacan is on the ridge of a great water shed from which flow the rivers to the Gulf and to the Pacific, and in the center of a rich agricultural district. It is

IN THE MOUTH OF THE CRATER, POPOCATEPETL, INTEROCEANIO RAILWAY.

the market for the surrounding villages and haciendas. This rich valley tempted the building of a tramway from Esperanza on the Mexican Railway, but it was wholly inadequate to tne traffic, and since the building of the Southern road there has been a largely increased trade.

After leaving Tehuacan, the view from the windows on the left is full of interest. The city's white walls and towers gleam through and over the trees. The plain spreads away to the mountains beyond, and not far away they break off in great cliffs of rocks some hundreds of feet high, that are in the view for miles and miles. As the track curves about the plain, the picture is constantly changing in shapes and colors, for the rocks are stained in all the colors by the oozings through of the metals of the earth coursing down the cliff, that seem cut in huge columns, as might have been in some prehistoric battlements of an ancient fortress. Here also, just below the city, is a castle-like monastery on a pyramid near a high-walled panteon. The monastery may have extracted its Pompeiian colors from the cliffs just beyond, that are so full of color.

Passing down the plain, southeasterly, the track runs near a little stream, that grows larger as it winds in and out among the hills. The stations on this table-land are La Huerta, Santa Cruz, Pantzingo, Nopala and Venta Salada. Near San Antonio the road enters the Cañon del Rio Salado, which is but the beginning of the great Cañon de los Cues, through which it runs to the town of Tecomavaca. The scenery through this cañon is grandly picturesque, resembling that of the great Marshall Pass of the Denver & Rio Grande Railroad, the track running at the bottom of the cañon, right along the banks of a rushing, roaring river. The mountains are lifted up thousands of feet, in peaks and crags, that the storms have cut into fantastic shapes. Their walled sides drop perpendicularly to the water's edge, and close in upon the river and the road till the passenger doubts, in his mind, how either will find the way out, till the train dashes through a little tunnel, that is only a wink of darkness, and the river tumbles over some high rocks, at the point of the rocks, and runs alongside again. Here is a curious freak of the scenery; we have been riding along a stream whose waters run to the south, the train passes through a cutting, across a bridge, and comes to the river again, but *the waters are running to the north.* There are two rivers; the one running south is the Rio Salado, the other, the Rio Grande. They come together behind a hill, close by, and form the Rio Quiotepec which is the head

ON THE MEXICAN SOUTHERN RAILROAD.

water of the Rio Papaloapan. And here at Quiotepec is the lowest point on the line, the altitude being only 1768 feet above the sea; the ascending grade commences, and it is almost a steady climb through the Cañon of Tomellin, along the river bank still, with high towering mountains on either side. The station at Cuicatlan is in the midst of tropical verdure. There is little of the village in view at the station, but, just after leaving it, a look back will show the picturesque little town on the hill above the track.

At Tomellin the river is crossed and left behind, and the train now begins to ascend the valley of its tributary, the Tomellin or Rio de San Antonio. The scenery of Tomellin is picturesque. The little river is very pretty, the green trees invite to cooling shades, bright plumaged birds chatter in the branches, but beyond all this, Tomellin is to be remembered—Tomellin is the dinner station. And such a dinner! Appreciated perhaps all the more, because

ON THE MEXICAN SOUTHERN RAILROAD.

so absolutely unexpected in this far-away country; for this it may be remembered, yet more than all for the very excellence of it. It could be a model for very many dinner stations some thousands of miles nearer home. If you dine at Tomellin, you'll not forget or regret it, and perhaps you will want to carry some of the dinner along for supper.

Hence, for some miles, it is an up-hill ride through the cañon still, with scenery wild and weird on either side of the road, passing the stations of Almoloyas, Santa Catarina, Parian, arriving at the summit at Las Sedas, where there is one of the grandest views of all the grand views of this scenic line. From the windows on the right the panorama extends far down the valley, and across it to the far-away pictures among the mountains, range after range rising one above the other, the deep blue of the nearer ones fading a little to those just beyond, and fading again till they seem to blend into the sky, the sun tingeing each with a different hue, and on the range near by, marking the white line of a mountain road that crosses to the valleys on the other side.

The grade is downward, and it is only a roll down past Huitzo to Etla, a pretty little village on a hill eastward from the road, showing picturesquely from the windows on the left. Etla is a town of *fiestas*, to which the pilgrims come from far and near, as they do to Amecameca and Guadalupe, and scarcely in fewer numbers. The old church is on the very top of the hill, fronting the pretty little plaza, where the *fiestas* are held, and back of it is a very ancient aqueduct of high arches extending into the mountains, bringing a supply of fresh water to the village. It is a wide, open country that the road runs through, the rich valleys extending to the hills on both sides, dotted here and there with haciendas, that, with their great houses, granaries and churches, are villages in themselves, and remind one of the principalities we have read of in the old feudal ages. Across the valley, to the west, the mountain breaks off in palisades; on the east it slopes to blue mountains. Thus the ride is, with much to see from either side, or back to the hills just climbed over. There has not been a moment of monotony in all the journey, at the end of which there are anticipations of newer novelties in this, to us, hitherto unseen city, and while we are only leaving the little town of Etla, and its outlying haciendas, just down the valley there, are the towers of Oaxaca.

South Over the Mexico, Cuernavaca & Pacific—The route is not over the old diligencia road across the Plain of Mexico, but over one equally as attractive, and while the style of travel may not be as antiquely picturesque as on the rumbling, dust-covered diligencia, the scenery is equally as fine, and there is a deal more of comfort.

Trains leave from the Buena Vista station of the Mexican Central Railway, in the City of Mexico, circling the western suburbs, running through the grounds of the Agricultural school, Nextitla, Tacuba, San Juanico, and Santa Julia, a flag station. This place will be an important one. It was a regular hacienda before, and the owners have fractioned the grounds and sold them in lots. The "Colegio Salesiano" is now in construction. This Catholic institution is devoted to poor boys, and is supported by charity of Mexican families. It is provided

CONTRERAS.

with shops of all kinds. After leaving Santa Julia the road crosses, in a straight angle, the main line of the Mexican National Railroad, and reaches the Morales flour mill, after which it runs through the grounds of "Molino del Rey," the Mexican Government's arm factory, in the surroundings of which the battle with the United States army took place in 1849. There are still some remains of the defenses built by the Mexican army. On the left-hand side, and about half a mile from the track, is the magnificent castle of Chapultepec, with its great groves and architectural solidity. It was the ancient dwelling of Aztec kings, and the present residence of the President of the Republic. From this place on the handsome views of the Valley of Mexico begin to develop, until the heights of Ajusco are reached. The next point of interest is Tacubaya. It has a population of about 20,000, and is the most important suburban town of Mexico, where wealthy men from the city have built magnificent houses and gardens for their summer resorts. From the station of Tacubaya there is a small branch to the Valdes and Santo Domingo flour mills. These mills use the waters supplying Tacubaya and the City of Mexico as motive power.

Mixcoac is a small town, but an important one of the valley, on account of its topographical situation, healthful climate, and abundant water. The principal industry of the natives is the cultivation of flowers, a great number of them being taken to the City of Mexico for daily sale. Mixcoac, as well as Tacubaya, is connected with the city by this road, by the Valley Railway, and horse cars. The passenger business is quite considerable, and there is a train of the Valley Railway every half hour, and horse cars every twenty minutes.

At 500 metres from the station the road passes by the door of "Hacienda de la Castañeda," a place of amusement, with large gardens. Balls as well as other amusements take place every Sunday.

El Olivar is the old residence of the Catholic clergy. Near the station there is another flour mill, and several factories of cotton goods and paper. The line runs through the small town of San Geronimo, devoted to the cultivation of fruit, especially strawberries. It is remarkable to see the work the natives have done in order to adapt these grounds for cultivation, as all has been formed within dry walls and filled with vegetable earth, hauled from long distances. The town is well supplied with water for irrigation. A little further on the road passes the "Lomas de Padierna," where a battle with the United States army took place. Near the track there is a small monument, erected to the memory of the soldiers who fell in that battle. In making the grading works some pieces of uniforms with buttons of the two armies were discovered.

Contreras is the oldest factory of cotton goods established in the Valley of Mexico. The greater part of the people from the town of La Magdalena are employed here. The factory is moved by the water of La Cañada River, and is situated at the entrance of a long and narrow cañon. Ever since the road was completed foreigners have chosen this place for Sunday excursions. The Cañada Cañon is one of the most picturesque of the Republic. Its vegetation is tropical, notwithstanding the elevation, and in winter, when the vegetation of the valley is dead, that of the Cañada is as exuberant as that of the *tierra caliente*.

After leaving Contreras the road passes through the lands of San Nicolás, arriving at the flag station of Eslava, situated on one side of the hacienda of the same name. A mile beyond the road enters on a tract thickly covered with volcanic stone, thrown away a long time since by the volcano of Ajusco. The grounds have a very original aspect. It has not been necessary to make any works for letting rain water run out. The ground is so porous that all the water filters in, and afterwards appears at the bottom of the mountains in a dozen crystal springs.

Near the 40-kilometre post it was necessary to make two big cuts, and one of the biggest fills in the country. To give an idea of its magnitude, it is enough to say that it may be seen distinctly from the City of Mexico, and for its construction it was necessary to remove an amount of material exceeding 90,000 cubic metres. From this point may be clearly seen the Valley of Mexico in the whole extension, the lakes of Texcoco, Chalco and Xochimilco, all the small towns of the valley, and the volcanoes with their white peaks. It is one of the most picturesque views of the road. The elevation of this place is 1,657 feet above the City of Mexico, and 9,006 feet above the sea.

The road continues ascending through the chains of mountains, and arrives at the station of Ajusco, at an elevation of 9,318 feet. The station is situated in the lower part of the town of Ajusco.

The next station is La Cima. the summit, at an elevation of 9,895 feet above the sea. This is the highest point of the line. From this place the line begins to descend, passing, at 66 kilometres, the divisory line of the Federal District and

STREET IN CUERNAVACA.

the State of Morelos. From this station to Cuernavaca, by straight line, is thirteen miles, but on account of the mountainous country the road distance is thirty-eight miles.

Fierro Del Toro, at an elevation of 9,665 feet above the sea, is situated at the entrance of the magnificent forest of Huitzilac. The road continues on one side of the mountains of Coajomulco, through the town of the same name. Before reaching this point, the small but productive State of Morelos may be seen, with the city of Cuernavaca and the numerous haciendas where they cultivate the sugar cane and tropical fruits.

After Coajomulco, the line passes San Juanico. Near this place there are some very high stone hills, in the highest of which there are some ruins called the "Gran Tepoxteco." This is a remarkable construction on account of the difficulties the Indians must have had to take up the materials to such a height, about 600 feet vertical. Some idols are still to be seen there. Access to the mountains is very difficult.

At the lower part of San Juanico Mountains, and not very far from the track, the town of "San Miguel de la Cal" is situated, where there is a deposit of

ALONG THE TAMASOPO CANON, MEXICAN CENTRAL RAILWAY.

natural lime, ready for use; it is probably the only one of such magnitude in the Republic.

From San Juanico the line runs to the west, touching the towns of Santa Maria, Chamilpa, Ocotepec and Ahuatepec, and comes to the city of

Cuernavaca, capital of the State, with a population of 7,000 inhabitants; elevation 4,937 feet above the level of the sea. It is built upon a hill between two large depressions of ground, which make two ravines that unite outside of the southern extremity of the town. From any of the culminating points of

Cuernavaca the eye embraces the territory of the State in its widest extent, its inner chains as well as its mountainous boundary. To the north is the long range of Ajusco with its ramifications, whose offshoots, known as the mountains of Tepoxtlan, rise in fantastic shapes, whilst the snowy peaks of Popocatepetl and Iztaccihuatl tower loftily in the background. The large sugar plantations and plantain farms, with which the country is filled, together with the luxuriant vegetation surrounding them, reveal the fertility of the soil of this essentially agricultural State. The town proper contains more than 500 houses, besides the cottages in the suburbs, with their orchards and gardens. It has more than sixty streets and alleys, five squares, five churches, the most important being the Parish Church, which, like that of Tula, in the State of Hidalgo, is very old and its exterior appearance that of a fortress. Among the public buildings may be mentioned the old palace of Cortéz, now occupied by the State Government, the Literary Institute, the Porfirio Diaz Theatre, the Hospital and the Barracks; the Post Office and the Telegraph Office are all that is modern.

The **Michoacan & Pacific Railway** runs west from the town of Maravatio, on the Mexican National Railroad, fifty-three miles to Ocampo, where stages connect for Ziticuaro.

The **Monterey & Mexican Gulf Railroad** extends from the station of Treviño, where it connects with the Mexican International Railroad southeast to the Gulf of Mexico, at Tampico, crossing the Mexican National Railroad at Monterey.

South from Treviño the road runs for some distance through an uninteresting district, but the barren hills and plains become verdure-clad and there are fertile valleys farther south; above Monterey the picturesque region begins and continues to the lovely valley in which that city lies, coming to it at the north and leaving it at the south side.

Approaching Monterey the best views are from the windows on the west side, showing the Mountain of the Mitres and the Saddle Mountain, on the far side of the valley, with the beautiful city at the base, almost hidden by the tall trees, only the towers showing above them. It is not all romance and antiquity at Monterey.

A NATIVE FONDA, SAN JUAN.

In every view the more prosaic chimney stack of a smelter, factory or brewery stands in line with the church tower of the olden days. Monterey has probably made greater advancement than any other Mexican city as a manufacturing centre. There are establishments of almost every branch of trade, some of the most extensive ore smelters in the country, and the brewery making the famous Cuautemoc beer from the pure waters of the Monterey Valley.

South from Monterey the Monterey & Mexican Gulf road continues through a very fertile country, passing from one valley to another, the products changing

MONTEREY & MEXICAN GULF STATION, MONTEREY.

with the climate southward, from the fruits and cereals of the temperate zone, to the cane and cotton and tropic fruits of the *tierra caliente;* from the familiar forests of our own land to the hard woods of the warmer countries. The builders of this road boast the use of ebony for ties; certainly there are some now under the rails cut within hauling distance of the track. There is merchantable mahogany, rosewood and other close-grained timber in demand for the finer uses in the arts. Another of the products of this region is a beautiful black marble, without a seam or gleam of white, or other color than its own inky blackness. This and a hard gray stone are used in the company's handsome stations, at Monterey and other points on the line.

At intervals along the plain south of Monterey are station platforms that may be used for suburban travel. At San Juan there is a picnic ground, with a dancing pavilion, in a grove of trees near a clear running stream. On the right of the track is a native "*fonda*," side by side with the "Two Republicks" restaurant ; on the other side some thatched huts, in queer contrast with the big brick kiln near by. It is a well watered country that this one, unlike the other roads of Mexico, runs through. The running streams are seen in little rivulets, creeks and rivers of more pretentious proportions than is usual in this country, and the prospect is necessarily different from most of the other railway lines.

Montemorelos, seen from the windows on the west, is a city of some 16,000 inhabitants, founded in the year 1749, about which time the first church of the town was built. The only work of art is a painting " Pensador Mexicano," by Señor Don Eduardo Lizardi. There are two Protestant churches, Presbyterian and Baptist. The former was founded by Señor Leandro Garza Mora, in 1862; the latter by Mr. Thomas Westrup, in 1869.

Linares is a flourishing town in the sugar belt, on the head waters of the Rio Tigre, sometimes called the Conchas. The sugar industry of this section has been greatly promoted by the advent of the railroad, and the importation of modern machinery. On the right, far across the plain, is a high mountain that a bright, gossipy correspondent has called the " Sombrero," and with great excuse, for no matter what its other name may be, it will be recognized at once as a "sombrero." The immense crown of the peak, and wide, spreading brim of the foothills are in sight during all the journey down to Tampico.

Victoria is the capital of the State of Tamaulipas, founded in 1750. Its population ranges from 11,000 to 12,000. The altitude of the town is 1180 feet above the sea level, and is located at the 23° 42' 54" latitude, and 0° 01' 02" longitude, east of the meridian of Mexico. The climate is almost perfect, there being neither excessive heat in summer, nor are the winters in any degree severe. Oranges, limes, bananas, pineapples, grapes, and in fact all the tropical products are grown in profusion in this locality. There are three churches in the city, two Catholic and one Protestant. One of the former is the Cathedral; its construction dates from the foundation of the town, and is still in an unfinished condition. The erection of the other was commenced at a comparatively recent date, and of the more modern style of church architecture. The Protestant church is a very unpretending place of worship, it being merely a missionary headquarters.

Among the points of interest to the tourist may be mentioned the park "Pedro José Mendez," containing many rare and beautiful plants and shrubbery. This lovely resort is situated at the southern end of the Alameda.

CAPITOL OF SONORA, MEXICO.

The Alameda is an elegant drive and promenade, with a row of fine trees on each side, extending for a distance of over two miles. The governor's residence and state house of representatives is situated on the Alameda, as are also many beautiful private residences, all of which go to make La Ciudad de Victoria a very attractive place among the comparatively newer order of cities of Mexico.

It is a descending grade with long stretches of level track across an open country, hence to Tampico, with here and there patches of tropic verdure, outlying groves of the more extended forests that are over the hills towards the coast, and in the valleys to the west of the road. The Tampico terminals of the Monterey & Mexican Gulf Railroad comprise extensive wharves at deep water, where the largest ships come alongside. The freight yards are ample and the track connections with the Mexican Central complete.

South Over the Sonora Railway—The State of Sonora is noted for its great agricultural resources. The principal staple is the famous sweet orange grown in the luxuriant orchards of Hermosillo and Guaymas. Wheat, corn, beans, alfalfa, cotton, sugar cane, tobacco and other agricultural products are cultivated in great quantities. Wheat is sometimes exported to England and to Mexican eastern markets. Flour is constantly sent to the States of Silanoa and Lower California and now and to other Mexican states. Cattle are numerous in middle and northern Sonora, are exported to Lower California and to the United States. Mines are abundant and very rich, and the mining industry is well developed all over the State. Vast amounts of rich silver ore are taken to United States smelters.

The Sonora Railway, crossing the State in a northerly direction from Guaymas to Nogales, boasts of being the first international railroad built and operated between Mexico and the United States. It is 353 miles long and standard gauge. The first tie was laid in the early part of 1880, and last spike driven in October, 1882.

There are several periodicals and newspapers published in Nogales, Magdalena, Altar, Ures, Hermosillo, Alamos and Guaymas. "*El Tráfico*," of Guaymas, is one of the largest in the Republic of Mexico and has a very wide circulation at home and abroad.

The State of Sonora is noted for the beauty of its scenery of land and sea.

Nogales, with about 3,000 inhabitants, is a thriving double town of the boundary line, half of it lying in Arizona Territory, the other portion in the State of Sonora.

CITY AND BAY, GUAYMAS, MEXICO, SONORA RAILWAY.

On the American side can be seen several fine business houses, hotels and factories, while on the other side there are some fine shops, stores and private residences. The Mexican Custom House is an imposing stone building. The town of Nogales is very enterprising, well provided with public schools, and has water works and electric light.

Just south of Nogales the tourist can admire the beautiful Casita Cañon, dotted with superb trees and shrubbery, intersected by several streams of clear water running along the route of the railroad.

From Casita south to Santa Ana the country is all under cultivation, large farms alternating with orchards and vegetable gardens. The town of Magdalena, with 4,000 inhabitants, is quite renowned, it being the rendezvous of thousands of pilgrims from Sonora, Chihuahua and Durango in Mexico, and from Arizona, California and New Mexico in the United States, all going to Magdalena to pray to San Francisco's image, on the fourth of October every year.

Hermosillo, the capital of Sonora, and the seat of the Catholic diocese, possesses a magnificent government capital, a fine new cathedral and a small but nice Protestant church, the national mint, one of the best modern flour mills, a beautiful depot and several other elegant public and private buildings. The Plaza of Hermosillo is the largest and handsomest in Sonora. The population exceeds 10,000 people. The district of Hermosillo is noted for its splendid agricultural and mining surroundings, the railroad crossing exuberant orange groves, vegetable farms and flower gardens.

Guaymas, the home of the Sonora Railway, is a city of over 8,000 inhabitants, all very enterprising and progressive. The foreign element is quite important and of high standing. Guaymas is a great commercial place and the feeder of Sonora, Lower California, Sinoloa and Colima, the Sonora Railway facilitating the imports and exports from and to the United States, Europe and Eastern Mexico.

The bay of Guaymas is the best on the Mexican Pacific coast, and one of the largest in all the Pacific Ocean. Marine trade is very important in Guaymas, and its bay is constantly visited by Mexican and foreign craft. A marine railway is being built and is nearing completion.

That the city of Guaymas is progressing rapidly, due principally to the opening of the Sonora Railway, as shown by the construction of a street-car system, two substantial brick buildings for public schools, a magnificent civil hospital, the new jail, an imposing stone structure, water-works system, a very large bonded warehouse, landings and wharves for the storage and transfer of foreign freight, protestant and catholic churches, and several other buildings, factories and private residences of modern style.

A SPECIAL CAR.

During the winter season—November to May—the temperature of Guaymas is unequaled in the world, well adapted for the invalid as well as for the tourist and sportsman. Ducks and other wild game are plentiful in the outskirts of the city, and fishing, sailing, boating and bathing in the surf, are the most enjoyable sports on the great Guaymas Bay. The Carnival in Guaymas is carried out in grand style at the same season as in New Orleans, numberless foreigners visiting the city, participating in the processions and masquerade balls.

The Tehuantepec Railroad runs from Coatzacoalcos, on the Gulf of Mexico, to Salina Cruz, on the Pacific Coast, about 145 miles.

The Hidalgo Railroad runs northeastward from the City of Mexico to Pachuca, Tulancingo and Zumpango.

The Mexican National Construction Company operates a line from Manzanillo, on the Pacific Coast, to Colima, 60 miles; also a line from Zacatecas to Guadalupe and Ojo Caliente, 30 miles.

The United States of Mexico.

The Republic of Mexico comprises twenty-eight States, one Territory and the Federal District in which the national capital is located. The State Governments are very similar to those of the United States, having a Governor, Legislature, Courts, etc. The following table gives the names, capitals, population, area, etc.

NAMES OF STATES.	CAPITAL.	Area in square miles.	Assessed value.	Population.
Aguas Calientes............	Aguas Calientes	3,080	$ 5,619,694	142,000
Campeche..................	Campeche...............	20,760	1,343,795	91,180
Coahuila	Saltillo	59,000	6,474,637	185,000
Colima	Colima	2,700	3,335,476	70,000
Chiapas	Tuxtla Guitierrez	29,600	4,430,212	309,479
Chihuahua.................	Chihuahua..............	89,200	5,653,931	298,073
Durango	Durango................	42,300	7,057,879	265,931
Guanajuato	Guanajuato	12,300	31,071,636	1,007,116
Guerrero..................	Chilpancingo...........	22,700	1,487,167	350,000
Hidalgo...................	Pachuca................	7,600	15,384,737	404,212
Jalisco	Guadalajara............	38,400	23,066,248	1,159,341
Mexico...................	Toluca.................	8,080	21,391,096	826,165
Michoacan	Morelia	23,000	22,234,279	830,923
Morelos	Cuernavaca	1,850	16,955,515	151,540
Nuevo Leon	Monterey	25,000	10,584,790	289,533
Oaxaca...................	Oaxaca................	28,400	12,741,300	793,419
Puebla	Puebla	12,600	36,682,090	866,627
Querétaro	Querétaro..............	3,800	11,560,483	213,525
San Luis Potosí	San Luis Potosí.........	26,100	14,553,656	600,000
Sinaloa...................	Culiacan...............	36,100	4,807,790	200,000
Sonora...................	Hermosillo.............	77,000	7,223,500	223,687
Tabasco..................	San Juan Bautista.......	10,000	3,859,558	115,000
Tamaulipas	Victoria...............	29,000	7,214,935	189,139
Tlaxcala	Tlaxcala...............	1,500	7,145,716	147,988
Vera Cruz	Jalapa.................	23,840	25,933,387	633,369
Yucatan..................	Merida................	28,400	4,110,455	320,000
Zacatecas	Zacatecas	25,300	16,615,651	517,000
Territory of Tepic	Tepic..................	530	550,000	120,000
Lower California	La Paz	60,000	4,355,526	35,000
Federal District	City of Mexico..........	450	58,844,421	463,646
Totals........	....	748,590	$ 392,289,560	11,908,893

For the support of the Governments of the various States there is a system of taxation on all foreign and domestic merchandise, as well as a direct tax on all classes of property, real and personal. A portion of the tax receipts are paid to the National Government.

Each State is represented in the Congress by two Senators, elected alternately every two years, and by one member of the Chamber of Deputies for each 40,000 of population, and one for each fraction of more than 20,000.

The largest State is Chihuahua, since Coahuila was shorn of that portion of the domain now called Texas. Tlaxcala is the smallest State, and Morelos the next smallest. Puebla is the wealthiest in assessed values, with Guanajuato a close second. The wealth of the former is, for the most part, in the silver mines; of the latter, in agricultural lands and onyx quarries. Campeche represents the smallest amount of wealth. The Federal District is to Mexico what the District of Columbia is to the United States, and has a similar code of laws, administered under the direction of the Federal Government.

Only five of the States and one Territory of Mexico are without railway communication, Chiapas, Tabasco, Guerrero, Sinaloa, Lower California and Tepic, but all of these have fine harbors either on the Gulf or Pacific Coast. If the next decade is as prolific in railway building as the last, every State will have its railway.

Location, Population and Altitude of Cities.

CITIES.	Population.	RAILROADS.	Dist. from City of Mexico.	Altitude. Feet.	PRONUNCIATION.
Acámbaro.............	9000	.....Mexican National....	178	6084	Ak-*kam*-baro.
Aguas Calientes	36000	.....Mexican Central.....	364	6261	Ah-*was* Cal-i-*en*-tees.
Amecameca............	12000	.......Interoceanic.......	25	7602	Ah-*may*-cah-*may*-cah.
Catorce	20000	.....Mexican National....	471	6750	Kay-*tor*-see.
Celaya...............	22000	.Mex. Cen. and Mex. Nat.	182	5816	See-*li*-ya.
Chihuahua	18000	.....Mexican Central.....	999	4718	Che-*wow*-wa.
Ciudad de Mexico.....	400000	........All Roads........	0	7875	The-u-dad day *Meh*-ico.
Córdoba..............	6500	.....Mexican Railway.....	196	2710	*Cord*-ova.
Cuautla	12000	.......Interoceanic.......	85	3556	*Kwout*-la.
Cuernavaca	13000	....Mex., Cuer. & Pac....	50	4960	*Kwer*-ne-vaca.
Durango	35000	..Mexican International..	863	6136	Doo-*rang*-o.
Guadalajara	100000	.....Mexican Central.....	381	5162	Wau-dtha-la-*hara*.
Guanajuato	90000	.....Mexican Central.....	250	6842	Wau-na-*wah*-to.
Guaymas	5000	.........Sonora.........	1674	10	Wah-ee-*mas*.
Irapuato	26000	.....Mexican Central.....	212	5890	Ir-ra-*pwat*-o.
Jalapa	15000	.......Interoceanic.......	257	4372	Ha-*lap*-pa.
Lagos	11000	.....Mexican Central....	296	6359	*Lah*-gos.
Leon	100000	.....Mexican Central.....	259	5872	Lay-*own*.
Lerdo	11000	.....Mexican Central.....	684	3844	*Laer*-do.
Linares	8000	..Monterey & Mex. Gulf..	820	1859	Le-nair-ese.
Maravatio............	6000	.. Mexican National..	139	6750	Marry-va-*tee*-o.
Mérida	35000	...Mérida & Progreso....	763	150	*Merry*-da.
Monclova	5000	..Mexican International..	1041	2000	Mon-*clo*-va.
Monterey	22000	.....Mexican National....	667	2010	Mon-te-*ray*.
Morelia	35000	.....Mexican National....	235	6226	Mo-*ray*-lya.
Morelos	5000	..Monterey & Mex. Gulf..	769	1848	Mo-*rel*-ose.
Oaxaca	30000	....Mexican Southern....	356	5065	O-ah-*hak*-a.
Orizaba	16000	.........Mexican	181	4132	Or-ry-*za*-ba.
Pachuca	20000	.......Interoceanic.......	84	8000	Pah-*choo*-ca.
Patzcuaro	15000	.....Mexican National....	274	6787	*Patz*-quaro.
Puebla	75000	.......Interoceanic.......	98	7263	Poo-*eb*-lah.
Querétaro	50000	.....Mexican Central.....	153	5963	Kay-*ret*-a-ro.
Saltillo	12000	.....Mexican National. ..	606	5342	Sal-*teel*-yo.
Salvatierra..........	11000	.....Mexican National....	197	5714	Salva-*te*-er-ra.
San Luis Potosi	80000	.Mex. Nat. and Mex. Cen.	362	5786	San *Lu*-is Po-to-*see*.
San Miguel de Allende	20000	.....Mexican National....	253	6231	San Me-*gil* day Al-*yen*-de
Silao	15000	.....Mexican Central....	238	5832	Se-*low*.
Tampico	10000	.....Mexican Central....	779	75	Tam-*pee*-co.
Texcoco	10000	.....Iuteroceanic........	20	7862	Tez-*co*-co.
Tlaxcala	4000	.........Mexican.........	97	7506	Tlaz-*cal*-ah.
Toluca	20000	.....Mexican National....	45	8617	To-*loo*-ca.
Topo Chico..........	500	.....Mexican National....	667	2010	To-po *Chee*-co.
Torreon	5000	Central and International	706	3721	Torey-*own*.
Tula	2000	.. ..Mexican Central....	50	7353	*Too*-la.
Tzintzuntzan.........	2000	.....Mexican National....	273	7000	Tzin-*tzoon*-tzan.
Yautepec............	7000	.... Interoceanic.......	98	2340	Ya-*ou*-tepec.
Vera Cruz...........	20000	.... Mexican	263	5	Vera *Crooze*.
Victoria.............	8000	..Monterey & Mex. Gulf..	975	1275	Vic-*to*-ria.
Zacatecas	75000	.....Mexican Central.....	439	8967	Zaky-*tay*-cas.

Hotels and Restaurants

NAME OF HOTEL OR RESTAURANT.	LOCATION.	RATE PER DAY.	Capacity
City of Mexico.			
American	2a San Francisco y Gante	$1.00 to $3.00	75
Bazar	Espiritu Santo	1.00 to 3.00	68
Bella Union	La Palma	.50 to 2.50	60
Comonfort	Cinco de Mayo	1.00 to 1.50	46
Continental	Cinco de Mayo	1.00 to 2.00	50
Europa	Coliseo Viejo 19	.50 to 2.00	38
Gillow	San José el Real	1.00 to 3.00	30
Gran Oriente	Monterilla No. 10	1.00 to 1.75	40
Gran Iociedad	Espiritu Santo	1.00 to 4.00	64
Guardiola	1st San Francisco	1.00 to 2.00	51
Humboldt	Calle de Jesus	1.00 to 4.00	100
Iturbide	San Francisco	1.00 to 5.00	200
Jardin	1st Independencia y Letran	3.00 to 8.00	100
Nacional	3 de San Francisco	1.00 to 1.50	40
Refugio	Refugio	1.00 to 3.00	60
San Francisco	2d Francisco y Gante	1.00 to 2.00	50
San Carlos	Coliseo	1.00 to 3.00	57
San Agustin	San Agustin	.75 to 1.25	50
Universal	Espiritu Santo	.50 to 2.50	56
RESTAURANTS.			
Café de Paris	Coliseo Viejo	A la Carte.	25
Concordia	2a Plateros	A la Carte.	200
Gillow	1a Cinco de Mayo	A la Carte.	50
Iturbide	Iturbide Hotel	A la Carte.	200
Recamier	3a San Francisco	A la Carte.	200
Rich's Chop House	Betlemitas, near Iturbide Hotel	A la Carte.	100
Teatro Nacional	14 Vergara	A la Carte.	100
Acambaro.			
Gran Hotel International	Cor. Ferrocarril and Palma Streets	Rooms .50 to .75 Meals .50	50
Mexican Nat'l R. R. Hotel	In the Station	Rooms .50 Meals .75	20
Garza Boarding House	Ferrocarril Street	Rooms .37 Meals .37	10
Aguas Calientes.			
Plaza	Plaza Mayor	$1.00 to $2.00	25
Del Comercio	Plaza Mayor	1.00 to 2.00	25
Catorce.			
Mexican Nat'l R. R. Hotel	Mexican National Station	1.00 to 2.00	10
Celaya.			
Hotel Solis	Nueva Frente 69	1.50	35
Hotel Cortazar	Calle de la Cruz 8	1.50	30
Hotel Guadalupe	Portal de Guadalupe 9	.50 to .75	26
Chihuahua.			
Palacio	Plaza Mayor	2.00 to 2.50	50
Robinson House	Near Plaza	2.00 to 3.00	50
Cuernavaca.			
Diligencia	Calle Nacional	2.00	40
San Pedro	Plaza Mayor	1.00 to 2.00	40
Durango.			
Café de la Union	5 Constitution Street	1.50	16
Central	5 Constitution Street	2.50	20
Exchange Place	6 Constitution Street	2.00	10
Santa Ana	7 Teresas	No table board.	15
Sierra Madre	6 Constitution Street	1.00 to 2.00	8
Sonora	13 Coliseo	2.00	20
Victoria	1 San Francisco Street	2.50	18

Hotels and Restaurants

NAME OF HOTEL OR RESTAURANT.	LOCATION.	RATE PER DAY.	Capacity.
Guadalajara.			
Humboldt	Near Plaza	$1.00 to $2.00	40
Cosmopolita	One square from Plaza	2.00 to 3.00	50
Guanajuato.			
Hotel de la Union	Plaza Mayor	2.00 to 3.00	40
Irapuato.			
Ferrocarril	Opposite Station	1.00 to 2.50	50
Independencia	Near Plaza	1.00 to 2.50	50
Jalapa.			
Mexicano	Plaza Mayor	2.00 to 3.00	50
Veracruzano	Half square from Plaza	2.00 to 3.00	50
Lagos.			
Progreso	Near Plaza	2.00 to 2.50	30
Leon.			
Hotel de Comercio	Plaza Mayor	1.50 to 2.00	30
Diligencias	Near Plaza	2.00 to 2.50	75
Maravatio.			
Central	Plaza Principal, Portal Morelos	1.00	10
Mesa	Real de Mexico 33	1.25	10
El Delirio	Calle Posada Nueva	.50	7
Monterey.			
Hotel Hidalgo	Plaza Hidalgo 10	3.00	50
Hotel Iturbide	Truragazu y Dromier	2.00 to 5.00	100
Hotel de la Plaza	On the Plaza	2.50	75
Hotel Topo Chico	Topo Chico Hot Springs	2.50 to 4.00	100
Morelia.			
Hotel Oseguera	Plaza Mayor	.50 to 1.00	100
Hotel Central	Near Plaza	.37 to .50	53
Hotel Soledad	Near Plaza	.50 to 1.50	30
Hotel Michoacan	Near Plaza	.50 to 1.00	36
Montemorelos.			
Hotel Plaza	Plaza Mayor	1.00 to 3.00	50
San Ygnacio	Near Plaza	1.50 to 3.00	50
Orizaba.			
Hotel Comercio	Main Street	1.50 to 2.00	40
La Borda	Main Street	1.50 to 2.00	50
Diligencia	Near Plaza	1.00 to 2.00	40
Pachuca.			
Metropolitano	Near Railway Station	1.00 to 2.00	50
San Carlos	Antigua Diligencias	1.00 to 2.00	40
Patzcuaro.			
Ibarra	Hda Ibarra	1.50	40
Concordia	Ibarra 2	1.50	30
Queretaro.			
Ferrocarril Central	Plaza Mayor	1.00	30
Aguila Roja	Plaza Mayor	1.50	25
Saltillo.			
Restaurant	Mexican National Station	2.00 to 2.50	15
Hotel San Estéban	Calle Curato	2.00 to 2.50	80
Hotel Tomasichi	Plaza Mayor	2.00 to 2.50	30
Salamanca.			
Hotel de la Union	Plaza Mayor	1.00 to 2.00	20

Hotels and Restaurants

NAME OF HOTEL OR RESTAURANT.	LOCATION.	RATE PER DAY.	Capacity.
Salvatierra.			
Hotel de la Luz	Plaza Pral	$ .50	11
Hotel de la Cruz	Zavala 2	.50	12
San Luis Potosi.			
Continental	4th Zaragoza 14	$1.25 to 1.50	30
Progreso	2d Aldama	2.50	24
Washington	Bravo	1.50 to 2.00	9
American Hotel	Alameda	2.00 to 2.50	100
Nacional Mexicano	Alameda	1.50	15
San Fernando	4th Juarez 24	2.00 to 2.50	15
Hotel de America	Plaza Principal	2.00 to 2.50	35
San Carlos	Aldama y Iturbide	2.00	24
Restaurant	Mexican National Station	1.50 to 3.00	50
San Miguel de Allende.			
Mexican Nat'l Station Hotel	Station	1.00 to 2.00	10
Hotel Allende	Plaza Mayor	1.00 to 2.00	25
Silao.			
Hotel Ridon	Near Railway Station	1.00 to 2.00	25
St. Julian	Near Railway Station	1.00 to 2.00	30
California		1.00 to 2.00	15
Restaurant	Railway Station		
Tampico.			
Hotel Robbins (Am.)	Plaza Mayor	1.50 to 3.00	50
Continental (Mex.)	Near Plaza	1.50 to 3.00	40
Tlaxcala.			
San Carlos	Plaza Mayor	1.00	10
San Francisco	Plaza Mayor	1.00	15
Toluca.			
Gran Sociedad	Matamoros, frente á los portales	.75 to 1.00	50
Hotel Central	Plaza Principal	.50 to 1.00	18
El Leon de Oro	Juarez 15	.75 to 2.00	50
San Agustin	Plaza Principal	.50 to 1.00	20
Deposito	Guerrero	.50 to 1.00	15
Texcoco.			
Restaurant	Half Square from Railway Station	1.00 to 2.00	10
Tula.			
Hidalgo	Plaza	1.00 to 2.00	25
Moctezuma	Plaza	1.00 to 2.00	25
Yautepec.			
Gran Central	Plaza Mayor	1.00	15
Vera Cruz.			
Diligencias	Plaza Mayor	2.00 to 3.00	50
Hotel de Mexico	Opposite Wharf	2.00 to 2.50	40
Vera Cruzano	Plaza Mayor	1.00 to 2.00	30
Oriente	Plaza Mayor	1.00 to 2.00	30
Victoria.			
The Central	Plaza	1.00 to 3.00	50
Navarro	Plaza	1.00 to 3.00	50
M. & M. G. Station Hotel	Railway Station	1.00 to 3.00	50
Zacatecas.			
Zacatecano	Near Plaza	2.00 to 3.00	50
Central	Near Plaza	1.50 to 2.50	40
Commercial	Near Plaza	1.50 to 2.50	50

Street Car Lines, City of Mexico and Suburban Towns.

FOR	Start From	First Car Starts	Last Car Starts	Interval between Trips	Running Time	Last Car Returning	Fare	Cars Marked	Change Cars at
Agricultural College	Plaza Mayor	5.30 am	8.00 pm	Half hour	30 minutes	8.00 pm	18 cents	Atzcapatzalco or Tlalnepantla	
Atzcapatzalco	"	5.30 am	8.00 pm	"	60	8.00 pm	18 "	Atzcapatzalco	
Batlis	Circuit	6.00 am	8.00 pm	10 minutes	15	8.00 pm	6 to 12 cents	Circuito de Baños	
Belem	Plaza Mayor	7.15 am	8.45 pm	15	30	9.00 pm	6 cents	Belem Por San Juan	
Belem	"	7.20 am	8.20 pm	20	30	9.00 pm	6 "	Belem Por Calle Ancha	
Buena Vista	"	6.40 am	8.20 pm	20	15	6.00 pm	6 to 12 cents	Buena Vista	
Castañeda, La.	"	6.30 am	6.00 pm	20	50	7.30 pm	15 cents	Tacubaya or Tlalpam	Tacubaya.
Chapultepec	"	5.20 am	10.00 pm	20	30	9.60 pm	10 "		Tacubaya or San Mateo.
Churubusco	"	6.00 am	8.00 pm	20	40	8.05 pm	20	or Tlalpam	
Coyoacan	"	6.00 am	8.00 pm	20	40	8.00 pm	20		Chapultepec.
Colonia	"	7.00 am	10.00 pm	16	25	9.30 pm	6	Colonia	
Dolores	"	7.00 am	5.30 pm	60	20	6.20 pm	12	Tacubaya	
Guadalupe	"	5.30 am	9.30 pm	20	30	9.15 pm	12 "	Guadalupe	
Guerrero	"	6.30 am	10.00 pm	10	30	10.10 pm	6 "	Guerrero	
Ixtapalapa	"	5.20 am	7.20 pm	40	50	6.40 pm	6 to 20 cents	Ixtacalco, Mexicaltzingo and Ixtapalapa.	
Jamaica	"	5.20 am	7.20 pm	40	40	6.40 pm	6 to 20 "	Ixtacalco, Mexicaltzingo and Ixtapalapa.	
La Piedad	"	6.40 am	8.00 pm	40	30	7.35 pm	10 cents	La Piedad	
La Viga	"	6.32 am	10.00 pm	15		9.30 pm	6 "	La Viga	
Los Angeles	"	6.40 am	10.00 pm	15		8.00 pm	6 "	Los Angeles	
Los Angeles y Guerrero	"	7.00 am	7.55 pm	20		7.00 pm	6 "	Los Angeles y Guerrero	
Mixcoac	"	5.50 am	9.00 pm	40	45	8.00 pm	15 "	San Angel or La Castañeda.	
Niño Perdido	"	7.00 am	8.00 pm	20	60	8.15 pm	6 to 16 cents		
Peralvillo y San Lucas	"	6.32 am	8.30 pm	8		6.00 pm	6 to 18 "		
San Angel	"	5.50 am	9.00 pm	15	65	7.50 pm	20 cents	San Angel, via Chapultepec	
San Lazaro	"	6.30 am	7.30 pm	15		7.45 pm	6 to 12 cents	San Lazaro	
Santa Anita	"	6.20 am	7.20 pm	40	40	6.40 pm	6 to 20 "	Ixtacalco, Mexicaltzingo and Ixtapalapa.	
Santa Maria	"	6.30 am	8.00 pm	10	15	8.00 pm	6 cents	San Cosme y Santa Maria	
Nantisima y Mariscala	"	7.15 am	8.00 pm	15		8.05 pm	6 "		
Tacubaya	"	5.20 am	10.00 pm	20	40	9.50 pm	10 "	Tacubaya, via Chapultepec.	
Tlalpam	"	6.00 am	8.00 pm	60	60	8.05 pm	30 "	Tlalpam	
Tlalnepantla	"	5.30 am	6.30 pm	Two hours	90	5.40 pm	31 "	Tlalnepantla	
Tlaxpana	"	7.07 am	7.37 pm	15 minutes		6.30 pm	6 "	San Cosme y Tlaxpana	
TO RAILWAY STATIONS.									
Hidalgo R. R.	Plaza Mayor	6.32 am	9.45 pm	15 minutes	15 minutes	9.45 pm	6 cents	Peralvillo y la Viga.	
Interoceanic Railway	"	6.30 am	7.30 pm	15	15	7.45 pm	12 "	San Lazaro	
Mexican Railway	"	6.40 am	6.20 pm	15	15	6.00 pm	6 "	Buena Vista	
Mexican Central Ry	"	7.00 am	8.00 pm	20		8.00 pm	6 "	San Cosme y Santa Maria via Buena Vista	
Mex., Cuer. & Pac. Ry.	"	7.00 am	8.00 pm	20	16	8.00 pm	6 "	San Cosme y Santa Maria via Buena Vista.	
Mexican National R. R.	"	7.15 am	9.00 pm	30	25	8.30 pm	6 "	Toluca y Colonia.	

SPECIAL CARS for single or round trips, or for the entire day may be hired on application to the Administrador General of the District Railways. The prices are from $3.00 to $20.00, according to the distance and time desired for the car. Rates for the day are based upon the distance the car is to travel. The cars are marked "especial" and no other passengers are allowed, or will try, to board a special car. On arrival and departure of trains special cars are run. The price for this service is, between 5 a. m. and 10 p. m., 12 cents; after 10 p. m., 25 cents.

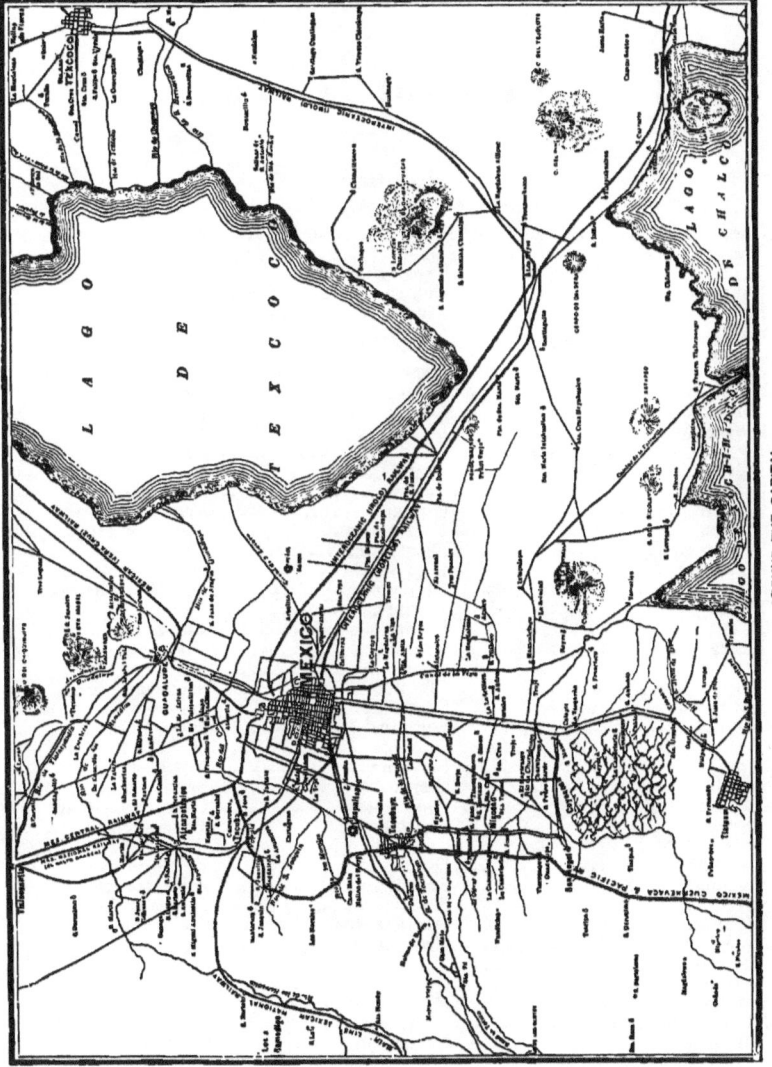

AROUND THE CAPITAL.

Table of Terms.

(Accented Syllables of Pronunciation in *Italics*.)

Numbers.

ENGLISH.	SPANISH.	PRONUNCIATION
One	Uno, una	*Oo*-no.
Two	Dos	Dose.
Three	Tres	Tress.
Four	Cuatro	*Kwah*-tro.
Five	Cinco	*Seen*-ko.
Six	Seis	*Say*-is.
Seven	Siete	See-*ai*-te.
Eight	Ocho	*O*-tcho.
Nine	Nueve	Noo-*ev*-e.
Ten	Diez	De-*eth*.
Eleven	Once	*On*-say.
Twelve	Doce	*Do*-say.
Thirteen	Trece	Tres-ay.
Fourteen	Catorce	Kay-*tor*-say.
Fifteen	Quince	*Keen*-say.
Sixteen	Diez y seis	De-*eth* e *say*-is.
Seventeen	Diez y siete	De-*eth* e see-*ai*-te.
Eighteen	Diez y ocho	De-*eth* e o-tcho.
Nineteen	Diez y nueve	De-*eth* e noo-*ev*-e.
Twenty	Veinte	*Vay*-inte.
Twenty-one, etc.	Veinte y uno, etc	*Vay*-inte e *oo*-no.
Thirty	Treinta	Tray-inta.
Forty	Cuarenta	Kwar-*en*-ta.
Fifty	Cincuenta	Seen-*kwen*-tah.
Sixty	Sesenta	Se-*sen*-tah.
Seventy	Setenta	Say-*ten*-tah.
Eighty	Ochenta	O-*chen*-tah.
Ninety	Noventa	No-*ven*-tah.
Hundred, a or one	Ciento	See-*en*-to.
Two hundred	Doscientos	Dose-see-*en*-tose.
Three hundred	Trescientos	Tress-see-*en*-tose.
Four hundred	Cuatrocientos	Kwah-tro-see-*en*-tose.
Five hundred	Quinientos	Ke-ne-*en*-tose.
Six hundred	Seiscientos	Sai-is-see-*en*-tose.
Seven hundred	Setecientos	Sai-tay-see-*en*-tose.
Eight hundred	Ochocientos	O-cho-see-*en*-tose.
Nine hundred	Novecientos	No-vay-see-*en*-tose.
Thousand, a or one	Mil	Meel.
Two thousand	Dos mil	Dose meel.
Eleven hundred	Mil ciento	Meel see-*ain*-tose.
Hundred thousand	Cien mil	See-*en* meel.
Million	Un millon	Un milyon.

Ordinal Numbers.

ENGLISH.	SPANISH.	PRONUNCIATION.
First	Primero	Prim-*mer*-ro.
Second	Segundo	Say-*goon*-do.
Third	Tercero	Ter-*sere*-o.
Fourth	Cuarto	*Kwar*-to.
Fifth	Quinto	*Keen*-to.
Sixth	Sexto	*Seks*-to.
Seventh	Septimo	*Sep*-te-mo.
Eighth	Octavo	Ok-*tah*-vo.
Ninth	Noveno, or nono	No-*vay*-no.
Tenth	Décimo	*Day*-see-mo.

Months.

ENGLISH.	SPANISH.	PRONUNCIATION.
January	Enero	Eh-*ner*-ro.
February	Febrero	Feh-*brer*-ro.
March	Marzo	*Mar*-so.
April	Abril	Ah-*breel*.
May	Mayo	*Mah*-yo.
June	Junio	*Hoo*-ne-o.
July	Julio	*Hoo*-le-o.
August	Agosto	Ah-*go*-sto.
September	Septiembre	Sep-te-*em*-bray.
October	Octubre	Ok-*too*-bray.
November	Noviembre	No-ve-*em*-bray.
December	Diciembre	De-the-*em*-bray.

Days of the Week.

ENGLISH.	SPANISH.	PRONUNCIATION.
Monday	Lúnes	*Loo*-nes.
Tuesday	Mártes	*Mar*-tes.
Wednesday	Miércoles	Me-*er*-ko-les.
Thursday	Juéves	*Whay*-ves.
Friday	Viérnes	Ve-*ere*-nes.
Saturday	Sábado	*Sah*-bah-do.
Sunday	Domingo	Do-*meen*-go.

Time.

ENGLISH.	SPANISH.	PRONUNCIATION.
Day	Dia	De-*ah*.
Morning	Mañana	Man-*yah*-nah.
Noon	Medio dia	*May*-deo *de*-ah.
Afternoon	Tarde	*Tar*-day.
Evening	Tardecita	*Tar*-day-*see*-tah.
Night	Noche	*No*-tchay.
Midnight	Media noche	*May*-de-ah *no*-tchay.
Yesterday	Ayer	Ah-*yere*.
The day before yesterday	Antes de ayer	*An*-tays *day* ah-*yere*.
To-day	Hoy	Oy.
To-morrow	Mañana	Man-*yah*-nah.

The day after to-morrow......Pasado mañana......Pa-*sah*-do man-*yah*-nah.
The night before last..........Antes de anoche .....*An*-tays day ah-*no*-tchay.
Last night....................Anoche...............Ah-*no*-tchay.
Last week.....................La semana pasada....Lah say-*mah*-nah pa-*sah*-dah.
Last month....................El mes pasado.......El mess pa-*sah*-do.
Last year.....................El año pasado........El *ahn*-yo pa-*sah*-do.
Year..........................Año.................*Ahn*-yo.
Month.........................Mes.................Mess.
Week..........................Semana..............Say-*mah*-nah.
An hour.......................Una hora............*Oon*-ah oh-rah.
Half an hour..................Media hora..........*May*-de-ah *oh*-rah.
Quarter of an hour............Un cuarto de hora....Oon *kwar*-to day *oh*-rah.
What day of the month is it?..¿Qué dia es hoy?.....Kay *de*-ah es oy?
Hour..........................Hora................*O*-rah.
Minute........................Minuto..............Min-*oo*-to.
Second........................Segundo.............Say-*goon*-do.
What time is it?..............¿Qué hora es?.......Kay *o*-ra es?
It is one o'clock.............Es la una...........Es lah *oon*-a.
It is a quarter past one......Es la una y cuarto....Es lah *oon*-ah e *kwar*-to.
It is half past one...........Es la una y media....Es lah *oon*-ah e *may*-dia.
It is a quarter to two........Son las dos ménos cuarto....Sone lahs dose *may*-nos *kwar*-to.
It is about four..............Son cerca de las cuatro....Sone *sere*-ka de las *kwah*-tro.
It is twenty minutes past ten..Son las diez y veinte minutos....Sone lahs de-eth e *vay*-inte min-*oo*-tose.
Two o'clock...................Son las dos.........Sone lahs dose.
Ten o'clock...................Son las diez........Sone lahs de-*eth*.
It is midnight................Es media noche......Es *may*-de-o *no*-tchay.
It is noon....................Es media dia........Es *may*-de-a *dee*-ah.

Seasons.

ENGLISH.	SPANISH.	PRONUNCIATION.
Spring	Primavera	Prim-mah-*vere*-ah.
Summer	Verano	Vai-*rah*-no.
Autumn	Otoño	O-*tone*-yo.
Winter	Invierno	Een-ve-*ere*-no.

Money.

ENGLISH.	SPANISH.	PRONUNCIATION.
Money	Moneda	Mo-*nay*-dah.
Money	Dinero	De-*ner*-o.
Gold	Oro	*O*-ro.
Silver	Plata	*Plat*-ah.
Paper	Papel	Pah-*pell*.
Dollar	Peso	*Pay*-so.
Cent	Centavo	Cen-*tah*-vo.
Real	Real	Ray-*al*.
Medio	Medio	*May*-de-o.
Change	Cambio	*Kam*-be-o.
Bank note	Billete	Beel-*yai*-te.

Per cent	Por ciento	Por see-*en*-to.
Bank	Banco	*Bank*-o.
Draft	Letra de cambio	*Lay*-tra day *cam*-be-o.
Check	Cheque	*Chek*-kay.
Discount	Descuento	Des-coo-*en*-to.
Premium	Premio	*Pray*-me-o.
Par	Á la par	Ah lah par.

On the Road.

ENGLISH.	SPANISH.	PRONUNCIATION.
Ticket	Boleto	Bo-*lay*-to.
First class	Primera clase	Prim-*er*-ra *klas*-say.
Second class	Segunda clase	Say-*goon*-dah *klas*-say.
Third	Tercera clase	Ter-*sere*-ah *klas*-say.
Through ticket	Boleto terminal	Bo-*lay*-to ter-me-*nal*.
Limited ticket	Boleto limitado	Bo-*lay*-to lim-e-*tah*-do.
Unlimited ticket	Boleto ilimitado	Bo-*lay*-to e-lim-e-*tah*-do.
Stop-over ticket	Boleto de parada	Bo-*lay*-to day pah-*rah*-dah.
Excursion ticket	Boleto de excursion	Bo-*lay*-to day ex-cur-see-*on*.
Round-trip ticket	Boleto de viaje redondo	Bo-*lay*-to day vee-*ah*-he ray-*don*-do.
Half-fare ticket	Médio boleto	*May*-de-o bo-*lay*-to.
Sleeping-car ticket	Boleto de coche dormitorio	Bo-*lay*-to day *ko*-tchay dor-me-*to*-re-o.
Ticket agent	Agente de boletos	Ah-*hen*-tay day bo-*lay-tos*.
Ticket office	Despacho de boletos	Des-*pah*-tcho day bo-*lay*-tos.
Telegraph office	Oficina del telégrafo	Off-e-*see*-nah del tel-*leg*-rah-fo.
Railroad	Ferrocarril	Fer-ró-car-*reel*.
Railroad station	Estacion	Es-tah-see-*on*.
Train	Tren	Tren.
Express train	Tren expreso	Tren es-*pres*-o.
First train	Primer tren	Prim-*er* tren.
Through train	Tren terminal	Tren ter-me-*nal*.
Local train	Tren local	Tren lo-*cal*.
Sleeping car	Coche dormitorio	*Ko*-tchay dor-me-*to*-re-o.
Smoking car	Coche de fumar	*Ko*-tchay day foo-*marr*.
Express car	Coche del expreso	*Ko*-tchay del es-*pres*-o.
Day coach	Coche de dia	*Ko*-tchay day de-*ah*.
Baggage car	Carro de equipajes	*Kar*-ro day ek-we-*pah*-hes.
Baggage room	Sala de equipajes	*Sah*-lah day ek-we-*pah*-hes.
Baggage agent	Agente de equipajes	Ah-*hen*-tay day ek-we-*pah*-hes.
Baggage	Equipaje	Ek-we-*pah*-he.
Trunk	Baul	Bah-*ool*.
Valise	Maleta	Mah-*lay*-tah.
Hat box	Sombrera	Som-bray-*ray*-rah.
Check	Talon	Tah-*lon*.

Dining room	Comedor	Kom-may-*dor*.
Toilet room	Retrete	Ray-*tray*-te.
Without change	Sin cambio	Seen *kam*-beo.
No transfer	Sin trasbordo	Seen trass-*bor*-do.
A. M	Por la mañana	Por lah man-*yah*-nah.
P. M	Por la tarde	Por lah *tar*-day.
Schedule	Itinerario	E-tin-a-*rair*-re-o.
Conductor	Conductor	Kon-dook-*tor*.
Sleeping-car conductor	Conductor de coche dormitorio.	Kon-dook-*tor* day *ko*-tchay door-me-*to*-re-o.
Porter	Portero	Por-*ter*-o.
Engine	Máquina	*Mack*-e-nah.
Engineer	Maquinista	Mack-in-*e*-sta.
I wish to go to —	Quiero ir hasta —	Kee-*er*-o eer *as*-tah —.
What time does the train start?	¿Á qué hora sale el tren?	Ah kay *o*-rah sally el tren?
How many miles from here to —?	¿Cuantas millas de aquí hasta—?	*Kwahn*-tahs *mee*-yas day ah-*kee* as-tah—?
When will I arrive?	¿Á qué hora llegaré?	Ah kay *o*-ra l-yay-gah-*ray*?
At what hour does the next train leave?	¿Á qué hora sale el próximo tren?	Ah kay *o*-ra sally el *prox*-e-mo tren?
How much is the cost of a ticket from here to B.?	¿Cuanto cuesta un boleto de aquí á B.?	*Kwahn*-to coo-*es*-ta oon bo-*lay*-to day ah-*kee* ah B.?
How much is the cost of a return ticket?	¿Cuanto cuesta un boleto de ida y vuelta?	*Kwahn*-to coo-*es*-ta oon bo-*lay*-to day e-da e *wel*-ta?
How long is the ticket good?.	¿Por cuanto tiempo es válido el boleto?	Por *kwahn*-to tee-*em*-po es *val*-e-do el bo-*lay*-to?
How much baggage free?	¿Cuanto equipaje es libre?	*Kwahn*-to ek-we-*pah*-he es *lee*-bre?
What is the cost for excess?	¿Cuanto cuesta por exceso?	*Kwahn*-to coo-*es*-ta por ek-*cess*-o?
Per hundred pounds?	¿Por cien libras?	Por *see*-en *lee*-brahs?
Per fifty kilos?	¿Por cincuenta kilos?	Por sink-*wen*-ta *kee*-lose?

In Town and at the Hotel.

ENGLISH.	SPANISH.	PRONUNCIATION.
Hotel	Hotel	O-*tel*.
Have you any rooms vacant?	¿Tiene Vd. cuartos vaciós?	Tee-*ai*-ne oo-*staid* kwar-tose vas-se-*osc*?
Have you a good room?	¿Tiene Vd. un cuarto bueno?	Tee-*ai*-ne oo-*staid* oon *kwar*-to boo-*ain*-o.
I want two rooms	Quiero dos cuartos	Kee-*er*-o dose *kwar*-tose.
Room	Cuarto	*Kwar*-to.
Bath	Baño	*Ban*-yo.
Another bed	Otra cama	*Oh*-trah *cam*-ah.
In the hotel	En el hotel	En el o-*tel*.
Give me my bill	Deme Vd. mi cuenta	*Day*-may oo-*staid* me cu-*en*-tah.

Give me my receipt.........Deme Vd. mi recibo ....*Day*-may oo-*staid* me re-see-bo.

Bring me some water.......Traigame agua.........Trah-*ee*-gah-*me* ah-gwa.

Bring me some hot water....Traigame agua caliente.Trah-*ee*-gah-*me* ah-gwa cal-ly-*en*-te.

Bring me some letter paper..Traigame papel de cartasTrah-*ee*-gah-*me* pah-*pel* day *kart*-as.

Bring me a pen and some ink.Traigame una pluma y Trah-*ee*-gah-*me* *oon*-ah tinta. *ploom*-ah e *teen*-tah.

Bring me some envelopes ...Traigame cubiertas.....Trah-*ee*-gah-*me* koo-be-*er*-tahs.

Towels....................Toallas ....To-*al*-yas.

Soap......................Jabon ....Ha-*bon*.

Matches ....Cerillos ....Seh-*reel*-yos.

Candle....................Candela..................Kan-*day*-la.

Lamp......................Lámpara ....*Lamp*-a-ra.

Ice.......................Hielo....................*Yai*-lo.

Beer......................Cerveza.................Ser-*vay*-za.

How much shall I have to ¿Cuanto habré de pagar *Kwahn*-to ah-*bray* day pay to the washerwoman? á la lavandera? pah-*gar* ah la lav-an-der-ah?

I want a washerwoman......Quiero una lavandera...Kee-*er*-o oo-nah lav-an-der-ah.

At what hour will you come?..¿A qué hora vendrá Vd?.À *kay* o-ra ven-*drah* oo-staid?

Street....................Calle....................Ki-ye.

Palace....................Palacio ....Pal-*as*-see-o.

Church ....Iglesia ....E-*glay*-see-ah.

Cathedral ....Catedral.................Cat-eh-*dral*.

School....................Escuela ....Es-koo-*ai*-lah.

College...................Colegio ....Col-*ai*-he-o.

Cemetery ....Cementerio ....Sem-en-*ter*-e-o.

Prison ....Cárcel ....*Kar*-sel.

Store.....................Tienda ....Tee-*en*-da.

Market....................Mercado ....Mer-*cah*-do.

House ....Casa ....*Kah*-sa.

Call me very early.........Despierteme muy tem- Des-pe-*er*-ta-me moo-e prano tem-*pran*-o.

Call me at 7 o'clock........Despierteme á las siete.Des-pe-*er*-ta-me ah lahs see-*ai*-te.

Take my baggage down ....Lleve Vd. mi equipaje *Lyai*-ve oo-*staid* me ek-abajo. we-*pah*-he a-*bah*-ho.

How much is my bill? ......¿Cuanto es mi cuenta?...*Kwahn*-to es me *coo*-enta?

I want to pay my bill ....Quiero pagar mi cuenta.Kee-*er*-o pa-*gar* me *coo*-en-ta?

What time is it? ....¿Qué hora es? ....Kay o-ra ais?

Send me a messenger.......Envieme un cargador....En-vee-*eh*-me oon car-ga-dor.

Carriage ....Coche...................*Ko*-tchay.

Coachman ....Cochero ....Ko-*cher*-o.

How much for one hour?....¿Cuanto por una hora? ..*Kwahn*-to por oo-nah o-rah?

How much to the station?..¿Cuanto hasta la estacion?*Kwahn*-to *as*-tah lah es-tah-see-*on*?

Where are you going?	¿Á donde va Vd?	Ah *don*-dy vah oo-*staid*?
Go straight ahead	Vaya derecho	*Vah*-ya day-*ray*-tcho.
Go faster	Vaya mas rápido	*Vah*-ya mass *rap*-e-do.
Go slower	Vaya mas despacio	*Vah*-ya mass des-*pas*-seo.
Stop	Párese Vd. !	*Par*-asy oo-*staid*.
Right	Derecho	Day-*ray*-tcho.
Left	Izquierdo	Ees-quee-*er*-do.
Before	Delante	Day-*lan*-teh.
Behind	Detras	Day-*tras*
North	Norte	*Nor*-tay.
South	Sur	Soor.
East	Este	*Es*-tay.
West	Oeste	*Wes*-tay.
Postoffice	Correo	Kor-*ray*-o.
Letters	Cartas	*Kar*-tas.
Postage Stamps	Timbres	*Teem*-bres.
Envelopes	Cubiertas	Koo-be-*er*-tas.
Registered letter	Carta registrada	*Kar*-tah reh-his-*tra*-da.
Have you any letters for me?	¿Tiene Vd. cartas para mí?	Tee-*ai*-ne oo-*staid* *kar*-tahs *par*-ra-me?
At what hour does the mail train leave for—?	¿A qué hora sale el tren correo para—?	A *kay* o-rah *sally* el tren kor-*ray*-o *par*-ah—?
Letter box	Buzon	Boo-*zon*.

Shop Talk.

ENGLISH.	SPANISH.	PRONUNCIATION.
Have you any	Tiene Vd.—?	Tee-*ai*-ne oo-*staid*.
I want to buy	Quiero comprar	Kee-*er*-o com-*prai*.
Have you others	Tiene Vd. otras?	Tee-*ai*-ne oo-*staid* *o*-trahs.
I want another	Quiero otra	Kee-*er*-o *o*-trah.
How many	Cuantos	*Kwahn*-tose.
Silk	Seda	*Say*-dah.
Wool	Lana	*Lah*-nah.
Cotton	Algodon	Al-go-*don*.
Linen	Lienzo	Le-*en*-zo.
Have you anything better	Tiene Vd. alguna cosa mejor?	Tee-*ai*-ne oo-*staid* al-*goo*-na *co*-sa *mai*-hor.
I want this	Quiero este	Kee-*er*-o *es*-tay.
Send this to	Envie Vd. esta á	En-ve-*eh* oo-*staid* es-ta ah.
Large	Grande	*Gran*-day.
Small	Poco	*Po*-co.
New	Nuevo	*Noo*-ev-o.
Old	Viejo	Ve-*eh*-ho.
Bad	Malo	*Mah*-lo.
Pretty	Bonito	Bo-*nee*-to.
Cheap	Barato	Bah-*rah*-to.
Dear	Caro	*Kar*-o.
Very dear	Muy Caro	*Moo*-e *kar*-o.
Narrow	Angosto	An-*gose*-to.
Wide	Ancho	An-*tcho*.
Collar	Cuello	Coo-*el*-yo.

Gloves	Guantes	*Wan*-tez.
Handkerchiefs	Pañuelos	Pan-yu-*ai*-lose.
Shoes	Zapatos	Zap-*at*-ose.
Pins	Alfileres	Al-fee-*lai*-res.
Needles	Agujas	A-*goo*-has.
Thimble	Dedal	Day-*dal*.
Thread	Hilo	*E*-lo.
Ribbon	Liston	Lees-*tone*.
Scissors	Tijeras	Tee-*hai*-ras.
Veil	Velo	*Vay*-lo.
Black	Negro	*Nay*-gro.
White	Blanco	*Blank*-o.
Red	Rubio	*Roo*-bee-o.
Blue	Azul	Ah-*sool*.
Pink	Rojizo	Ro-*hee*-zo.
Green	Verde	*Vere*-de.
Purple	Purpúreo	Poor-*poor*-ay-o.
Yellow	Amarillo	Am-a-*reei* yo.
Long	Largo	*Lar*-go.
Short	Corto	*Cor*-to.
Thick	Espeso	Es-*pay*-so.
Thin	Delgado	Del-*gah*-do.
A yard	Una vara	Oo-na *var*-a.

How do you sell it by the yard?¿Á como vende Vd. la vara? .Á *co*-mo *ven*-day oo-staid lah *var*-a?

General.

ENGLISH.	SPANISH.	PRONUNCIATION.
Good morning	Buenos dias	Boo-*en*-os *dee*-as.
Good evening	Buenas tardes	Boo-*en*-as *tar*-des.
Good night	Buenas noches	Boo-*en*-as *no*-tches.
Sir	Señor	Sane-*yor*.
Madam	Señora	Sane-*yo*-ra.
Miss	Señorita	Sane-yo-*ree*-ta.
Thank you	Gracias	*Grah*-see-as.
How do you do?	¿Como está usted?	*Co*-mo es-*tah* oo-*staid*?
Well, thank you	Bien, gracias	Be-*ehn*, *grah*-see-as.
And you?	¿Y usted?	E oo-*staid*?
Do me the favor	Hágame V. el favor	Ah-ga-me el fa-*vor*.
If you please	Si usted gusta	See oo-*staid* goo-stah.
What do you want?	¿Qué quiere usted?	Kay kee-*er*-e oo-*staid*?
What is that?	¿Qué es eso?	Kay es *ai*-so?
What do you call this?	¿Como se llama eso?	Ko-mo say *yam*-ah ai-so?
Do you know	Sabe usted	*Sah*-beh oo-*staid*.
What is the matter?	¿Que tiene?	Kay tee-*ai*-ne?
Pardon me	Perdóneme	Per-don-a-me.
As soon as possible	Tan pronto como posible	Tan *pron*-to *ko*-mo pos-*e*-bleh.
I will come again	Vendré otra vez	Ven-*dray* o-trah vace.
Which is the way to —?	¿Cual es la via para —?	Kwahl es lah *vee*-ah par-a?
Show me the way to—	Enséñeme Vd. el camino de —	En-*sane*-yai-me el cam-*ee*-no day —
What is your name?	¿Que es su nombre de Vd.?	Kay es soo *nom*-bre day oo-*staid*?

¿Or, Como se llama Vd.?. *Co*-mo say l-*yam*-a oo-*staid*?

English	Spanish	Pronunciation
I am ready	Estoy listo	Es-*toy lees*-to.
I am well	Estoy bien	Es-*toy* be-*ehn.*
Bring me	Traígame	Trah-*e*-ga-me.
Very well	Muy bien	*Moo*-e be-*ehn.*
Let us go	Vámos	*Vam*-ose.
It is late	Es tarde	Es *tar*-dy.
It is early	Es temprano	Es tem-*prah*-no.
Sit down	Siéntese Vd	See-*en*-ta-seh oo-*staid.*
Go in	Entre Vd	*En*-tray oo-*staid.*
Come in	Entre	*En*-tray.
Go away	Váya	*Vah*-ya.
Good bye	Adios	Ah-de-*ose.*
Yes	Si	See.
No	No	No.
Do you speak English?	¿Habla Vd. inglés?	*Ah*-bla oo-*staid* ing-*les*?
I speak it a little	Hablo un poco	*Ah*-blo oon po-co.
What do you say?	¿Qué dice Vd.?	Kay *dee*-say oo-*staid*?
Where is —?	¿Donde esta —?	*Don*-day es-*tah* —?
Where does he live?	¿Donde vive él?	*Don*-day *vee*-veh el?

Doctor and Medicine.

English.	Spanish.	Pronunciation.
I am sick and want a doctor.	Estoy enfermo y quiero un médico.	*Es*-toy en-*fere*-mo e kee-*ere*-o oon *med*-e-ko.
Will you go to look for a doctor.	Quiere Vd. ir á buscar un médico.	Kee-*er*-e ir ah *boos*-car oon *med*-i-ko.
I want a doctor who speaks English.	Quiero un médico que hable inglés.	Kee-*er*-o oon *med*-e-ko kay *ab*-lay een-*gless.*
Is he a good doctor?	¿Es buen médico?	Es boo-en *med*-e-ko?
Where is the drug store?	¿Donde está la botica?	*Don*-dy es-*tah* lah bo-*tee*ka?
Take this prescription to the drug store.	Lleve Vd. esta receta á la botica.	Lyai-*veh* oo-*staid es*-sta res-*ay*-tah ah la bo-*tee*-ka.
What is the matter with you?	¿Que tiene Vd.?	Kay tee-*ai*-ne oo-*staid*?
I have headache	Tengo dolor de cabeza	*Teng*-o do-*lor* day ca-*vay*za.
I have toothache	Tengo dolor de muelas	*Teng*-o do-*lor* day moo-*ai*las.
I have stomachache	Tengo dolor de estomago	*Teng*-o do-*lor* day es-*tom*ago.
I have earache	Tengo dolor de oido	*Teng*-o do-*lor* day o-*ee*-do.
I have a cold	Tengo un resfriado	*Teng*-o oon res-free-*ah*-do.
I have fever	Tengo fiebre	*Teng*-o fee-*ai*-bre.
How are you?	¿Como esta Vd.?	Ko-mo es-*tah* oo-*staid*?
I am better	Estoy mejor	Es-*toy may*-hor.
I am worse	Estoy peor	Es-*toy pay*-or.
Quinine	Quinina	Kee-*nee*-na.
Chloroform	Cloroformo	Cloro-*for*-mo.
Calomel	Calomel	Calo-*mel.*
Castor Oil	Aceite de castor	As-*ay*-e-tay day cas-*tor.*
Pills	Píldoras	*Pil*-do-rahs.

Capsules	Cápsulas	*Cap*-soo-lahs.
Salts	Sales	*Sal*-ehs.
Morphine	Morfina	Mor-*fee*-nah.
Laudanum	Láudana	*Lah*-oo-dah-na.
Porous plaster	Parche poroso	*Par*-tchay por-*o*-so.
Plaster	Emplasto *or* Parche	Em-*plas*-to *or Par*-tchay.
Mustard plaster	Sinapismo	Se-nah-*pees*-mo.
Aconite	Acónito	Ah-*con*-e-to.
Belladonna	Belladona	Bel-yah-*don*-ah.
Nux Vomica	Nuez Vómica	*Noo*-es *vo*-mi-ca.
Glycerine	Glicerina	Glee-cer-*e*-nah.
Arsenicum	Arsénico	Ar-*say*-ne-co.
Tonic	Tónico	*To*-ne-co.

Table and Meals.

ENGLISH.	SPANISH.	PRONUNCIATION.
The bill of fare	La lista	Lah *lee*-sta.
A plate	Un plato	Oon *plat*-o.
A glass	Un vaso	Oon *vaz*-o.
A teaspoon	Una cucharita	*Oo*-na coo-tchar-*ee*-tah.
Coffee	Café	Kaf-*fay*.
Coffee and milk	Café con leche	Kaf-*fay* con *lay*-tchee.
Tea	Té	Tay.
Tea and milk	Té con leche	Tay con *lay*-tchee.
Milk	Leche	*Lay*-tchee.
Cream	Crema	*Kray*-mah.
Sugar	Azúcar	Ah-*zoo*-kar.
Chocolate	Chocolate	Chock-o-*lat*-e.
Beef tea	Un caldo	Oon *cal*-do.
Lemonade	Limonada	Lee-mo-*nah*-da.
Beer	Cerveza	Ser-*vay*-sa.
Wine	Vino	*Vee*-no.
Claret	Vino tinto	*Vee*-no *teen*-to.
Ice	Hielo	*Yai*-lo.
Bread	Pan	Pahn.
Butter	Mantequilla	Manty-*keel*-ya.
Water	Agua	*Ag*-wah.
Ice water	Agua con hielo	*Ag*-wa con *yai*-lo.
Soup	Sopa	*So*-pah.
Fish	Pescado	Pes-*cah*-do.
Oysters	Ostiones	Os-te-*on*-es.
Rice	Arroz	Ar-*roce*.
Eggs	Huevos	*Wai*-voce.
Fried eggs	Huevos fritos	*Wai*-voce *free*-toce.
Hard boiled eggs	Huevos duros	*Wai*-voce *doo*-roce.
Soft boiled eggs	Huevos pasados por agua	*Wai*-voce pa-*sah*-doce por *ahg*-wah.
An omelet	Una tortilla de huevos	*Oo*-na tor-*teel*-ya day *wai*-vos.
Beef	Vaca	*Vah*-ka.

Roast beef	Vaca asada	*Vah*-ka ah-*sah*-da.
Boiled	Hervido	Er-*vee*-do.
Meat	Carne	*Kar*-nay.
Beefsteak	Beftek	Bef-tek.
Steak and potatoes	Beftek con papas	Bef-tek con *pap*-as.
Rare	Poco asado	Po-ko ah-*sah*-do.
Well done	Bién asado	Be-*en* ah-*sah*-do.
Mutton	Carnero	Kar-*nere*-o.
Mutton chops	Costillas de carnero	Kos-*teel*-yahs day kar-*nere*-o.
Cutlet	Chuleta	Choo-*lay*-ta.
Veal cutlet	Chuleta de ternera	Choo-*lay*-ta day ter-*nere*-a.
Lamb	Cordero	Kor-*dere*-o.
Pork	Puerco	Poo-*ere*-ko.
Bacon	Tocino	To-*see*-no.
Ham	Jamon	Ha-*mone*.
Fat meat	Carne gorda	*Kar*-nay *gor*-da.
Lean meat	Carne magra	*Kar*-nay *mah*-gra.
Pepper	Pimienta	Pee-mee-*en*-ta.
Salt	Sal	Sal.
Oil	Aceite	Ah-*say*-tay.
Vinegar	Vinagre	Vee-*nah*-gre.
Mustard	Mostaza	Mos-*taz*-ah.
Sauce	Salsa	*Sal*-sah.
Vegetables	Legumbres	Le-*goom*-bres.
Potatoes	Papas	*Pap*-ahs.
Fried potatoes	Papas fritas	*Pap*-ahs *free*-tas.
Beans	Frijoles	Free-*ho*-les.
Peas	Chícharos	*Chee*-char-ose.
Lettuce	Lechuga	Lay-*chu*-ga.
Cabbage	Col	Col.
Tomatoes	Tomates	To-*mat*-es.
Cauliflower	Coliflor	Col-e-*flor*.
Garlic	Ajo	*Ah*-ho.
Radishes	Rabanitos	Rah-ba-*nee*-tose.
Chicken	Pollo	*Pole*-yo.
Turkey	Pavo	*Pah*-vo.
Ice Cream	Helado	A-*lah*-do.
Cheese	Queso	*Kay*-so.
Fruit	Fruta	*Froo*-ta.
Strawberries	Fresas	*Fray*-sahs.
Grapes	Huvas	*Oo*-vas.
Oranges	Naranjas	Nar-*ran*-kas.
Bananas	Plátanos	*Plat*-a-nos.
Lemons	Limones	Lee-*mo*-nes.
Figs	Higos	*E*-gose.
Table	Mesa	*May*-sa.
Chair	Silla	*Seel*-ya.
Napkin	Servilleta	Ser-*veel*-yet-a.
Fork	Tenedor	Ten-e-*dor*.
Knife	Cuchillo	Coo-*cheel*-yo.
Spoon	Cuchara	Coo-*tchar*-ah.
Teaspoon	Cucharita	Coo-tchar-*ee*-tah.

Chronological.

ANNO DOMINI.
648—The Toltecs arrived in Anahuac.
1051—They abandoned the country.
1170—The Chicimecs arrived in Mexico.
1196—The Mexicans reached Tula.
1200—The Alcouans arrived.
1325—The Mexicans founded Tenochtitlan or the City of Mexico.
1428—Foundation of the Aztec kingdom.
1431—Enthronement of Netzahualcoyotl, King of Texcoco.
1485—Cortéz born at Medellin, Spain.
1502—Montezuma II. enthroned.
1504—Cortéz left Spain for Cuba.
1510—Great tidal wave on Lake Texcoco overflows Tenochtitlan.
1511—Turrets of the great Aztec temple burned.
   Spanish ship wrecked on the Island of Cozumel.
1516—Death of Nezahualpilli, the Tezcucan King.
1517—March 4, discovery of Yucatan by Córdoba.
1518—May 1, departure of Grijalva from Cuba for Mexico.
   November 18, Cortéz sailed from Santiago.
1519—February 10, Cortéz sailed from Habana.
   March 20, Cortéz landed at the mouth of the Tabasco River.
   April 21, Cortéz landed at Vera Cruz.
   August 16, commenced the march to the City of Mexico.
   September 23, Cortéz entered Tlaxcala.
   November 8, Cortéz entered the City of Mexico.
1520—July 1,Cortéz driven out of City of Mexico. Noche Triste, the "Dismal Night."
   July 8, battle with the Mexicans at Otumba.
1521—August 13, re-entry of Cortéz into the City of Mexico.
   Establishment by Spain of the rule over the new province by a governor.
   Cortéz established the seat of government at Coyoacan.
   Establishment of the first Christian church in the New World at Tlaxcala.
1524—First church commenced on the site of the present Cathedral.
1525—Hanging of Tetlepanquetzaltzin by Cortéz.
1526—September 19, Bishopric of Puebla established, seat at Puebla.
1528—Establishment of the government under the Audencia.
1529—July 6, Cortéz made Marques del Valle de Oaxaca.
1530—Guadalajara founded.
1531—December 9, vision of the Virgin of Guadalupe to Juan Diego.

1531—December 12, Juan Diego gathered the flowers from where the Virgin stood. The feast of Guadalupe.

July 25, Querétaro became a Christian city.

1533—Toluca founded.

1535—The first Viceroy arrived in Mexico.

June 2, Bishopric of Oaxaca established, seat at Oaxaca.

First printing press brought to the country and first book printed in Mexico.

Maravatio founded.

1536—August 29, corner stone of the Cathedral at Puebla laid.

1539—March 19, Bishopric of Chiapas established, seat at San Cristóbal.

1541—May 18, Valladolid, now Morelia, founded.

1542—San Miguel founded.

1545—January 31, Archbishopric of Mexico established, seat at City of Mexico.

1546—September 8, discovery of silver at Zacatecas.

1547—December 2, Cortéz died in the town of Castelleja de la Questa, in Spain.

1548—January 20, Zacatecas was founded.

July 31, Bishopric of Guadalajara established, seat at Guadalajara.

1550—Second Viceroy's term commenced.

1552—First inundation of the City of Mexico, and the dyke of San Lazaro built.

1553—University founded.

Silao founded.

1557—Guanajuato founded.

The Patio process for the amalgamation of silver invented by Bartolomé de Medina at Pachuca.

1562—August 15, Bishopric of Yucatan established, seat at Merida.

1568—English driven off the island of Los Sacraficios near Vera Cruz.

1570—August 16, first Inquisitor General appointed, and the Inquisition established in Mexico.

Celaya founded.

1573—Corner stone of the Cathedral laid.

1574—Twenty-one Lutherans burned by order of the Inquisition.

1576—Leon founded.

1583—San Luis Potosí founded.

1586—An English ship captured near Acapulco.

1587—Sir Francis Drake captured a Spanish ship with a rich cargo, off California.

1596—Monterey founded.

1600—The City of Monterey founded.

1603—Building of the Aqueduct of Chapultepec commenced.

1604—Church on the Pyramid of Cholula dedicated.

1607—November 28, the great drainage canal, Tajo de Nochistongo, commenced.

1615—Foundation and walls of the Cathedral completed.

1618—Córdoba founded.

1620—September 28, Bishopric of Durango established, seat at Durango.

1623—Cathedral placed under roof.

1626—First service in the Cathedral.

1629—Great inundation of the City of Mexico.

1634—Subsiding of the waters of the inundation of the Plain of Mexico.

1643—Salvatierra founded.

1649—April 10, fifteen persons burned by order of the Inquisition.
April 18, Cathedral at Puebla consecrated.

1660—A colony of a hundred families settled in New Mexico.

1667—December 22, dedication of the Cathedral.

1678—May 2, Church of Santa Maria los Angeles at Churubusco completed.

1691—Conquest of Texas.

1692—Pensacola, Fla., founded.
Building of the National Palace commenced.

1709—May 1, completion of the Church of Guadalupe near City of Mexico.

1722—January 19, opening of the first theatre in Mexico.
The first newspaper, *Gaceta de Mexico*, published in Mexico.

1724—February 4, completion of the Palacio del Ayuntimiento or City Hall.

1741—First effort to collect historical data, under a Royal Order of Philip V.,
dated June 19.

1760—The first regular army organized in Mexico.
Houses numbered in the City of Mexico.

1767—Jesuits expelled from Mexico by Royal Order, dated January 15.

1770—A fleet sailed for Spain with a cargo of thirty millions of silver dollars.

1776—February 25, establishment of the Monte de Piedad or national pawn shop.

1777—December 25,Bishopric of Linares established, seat at Monterey.

1779—May 7, Bishopric of Sonora established, seat at Culiacan.

1789—Arrival of the famous Viceroy, Conde de Revillagigedo. He appointed a
police force in the City of Mexico, lighted and paved the streets.

1791—Completion of the towers of the Cathedral.

1795—Cession of Florida, west of the Perdido River, to France.

1802—August 4, casting of the bronze statue of Charles IV., at 6.00 a. m.

1803—December 9, statue of Charles IV. unveiled in the Plaza Mayor.
Humboldt traveled in Mexico.

1810—September 16, Hidalgo sounded the *grito* of Mexican Independence.
October 30, Battle of Las Cruces.

1811—January 16, Hidalgo defeated at the Bridge of Calderon.
May 21, Hidalgo captured at Acatita de Bajan.
June 26, Allende, Aldama and Jimenez executed.
July 31, Hidalgo executed at Chihuahua.

1812—Evacuation of Cuautla by Morelos.

1813—September 14, meeting of the first Mexican Congress at Chilpancingo.
November 6, First formal Declaration of Mexican Independence.
December 23, defeat of Morelos.

1814—February 3, execution of Matamoras at Morelia.
October 22, proclamation of the first Constitution at Apatzingan.

1815—December 22, Morelos executed by order of the Inquisition.

1820—May 31, suppression of the Inquisition in Mexico.

1821—Promulgation of the Plan of Iguala and the colors of the Mexican flag.

August 2, Puebla taken by Iturbide.

September 27, Iturbide entered the City of Mexico.

1822—February 24, first Congress of the Mexican Nation assembled.

May 19, Iturbide elected emperor.

Iturbide and his wife anointed and crowned in the Cathedral of Mexico.

December 6, a Republic proclaimed by Santa Ana at Vera Cruz.

1823—July 14, Iturbide shot at Padilla.

1824—October 4, Constitution proclaimed.

October 10, First President of Mexico inaugurated.

November 7, Second Mexican Congress.

Statue of Charles IV. taken down and removed from the Plaza Mayor to the patio of the University.

1825—January 1, First Constitutional Congress assembled.

During this year the last Spanish soldier left Mexico in the evacuation of the Island of San Juan de Ulúa.

1829—A Spanish force landed at Tampico in July.

September 11, Spanish invaders defeated and captured by the forces under Generals Santa Ana and Mier.

1835—Rebellion of Texas under Sam Houston.

1836—December 28, Spain formally recognized the Republic of Mexico.

1837—August 22, first concession granted for a railway between the City of Mexico and Vera Cruz.

1840—April 27, Bishopric of Lower California established, seat at La Paz.

1846—April 24, first skirmish of the American War.

May 8, Battle of Palo Alto and May 9, Resaca de la Palma.

May 13, General Taylor crossed the Rio Grande at Matamoras.

September 26, Monterey captured.

1847—February 23, Battle of Buena Vista.

February 28, Chihuahua occupied.

March 9, General Scott landed at Vera Cruz.

March 27, Vera Cruz captured.

April 18, Battle of Cerro Gordo.

May 25, Puebla occupied by the Americans.

August 9, General Scott entered the Valley of Mexico.

August 20, Battles of Padierna and Churubusco.

September 8, Battles of Casa Mata and Molino del Rey.

September 12 and 13, storming and capture of Chapultepec.

September 13, capture of the Garita de Belem and San Cosme.

September 15, entry of the Americans into the City of Mexico.

1848—February 2, conclusion of peace and signing of the Treaty of Guadalupe, Hidalgo.

1850—June 1, Bishopric of Vera Cruz established, seat at Jalapa.

1851—President Arista inaugurated.

1852—Statue of Charles IV. placed in its present position.

1853—Santa Ana, proclaimed dictator of Mexico.

1854—August 30, Bishopric of San Luis Potosí established, seat at San Luis Potosí.

1855—Comonfort elected President.

1856—June 25, decree ordering sale of church real estate by President Comonfort.
September 16, suppression of the Franciscan monks.

1859—July 12, proclamation of the Laws of the Reform, by President Juarez.

1861—July 17, passage of the law suspending payment on bonded debt of the
Republic.
October 31, adoption of the Treaty of London by England, France and Spain.
Arrival of the allied fleet at Vera Cruz, in December '61 and January '62.

1862—January 26, Bishopric of Querétaro established, seat at Querétaro.
Bishopric of Leon established, seat at Leon.
Bishopric of Zamora established, seat at Zamora.
Bishopric of Zacatecas established, seat at Zacatecas.
February 19, Treaty of La Soledad signed.
May 5, brilliant battle at Puebla and repulse of the French by the Mexican
General Zaragosa.

1863—March 6, suppression of all religious orders in Mexico.
March 16, Bishopric of Tulancingo established, seat at Tulancingo.
Bishopric of Chilapa established, seat at Chilapa.
Archbishopric of Michoacan established, seat at Morelia.
Archbishopric of Guadalajara established, seat at Guadalajara.
May 17, Puebla captured by the French.
June 9, French troops occupied the City of Mexico.
July 10, Assembly of notables called in the City of Mexico, and the crown
tendered to Maximilian, the Archduke of Austria.

1864—June 12, Maximilian crowned Emperor of Mexico.

1865—October 3, Maximilian published a decree declaring all persons in arms
against the Imperial Government bandits, ordering them executed.
October 21, Generals Felix Diaz, Arteaga, Salazar and Villagomez shot at
Uruápam as bandits under Maximilian's decree.
November 6, the United States, through Secretary Seward, sent a dispatch
to Napoleon III, protesting against the presence of the French army in
Mexico as a grave reflection against the United States, and notifying him
that nothing but a Republican would be recognized.

1866—April 5, Napoleon withdrew his support from Maximilian.
November, Napoleon ordered the evacuation of Mexico by the French troops.

1867—The last of the French troops leave Mexico in February.
April 2, capture of Puebla by General Porfirio Diaz.
April 11, he defeated Márquez at San Lorenzo.
May 19, capture of Querétaro, surrender of Maximilian to Gen. Escobedo.
June 19, execution of Maximilian, Mejía and Miramon.

1867—June 21, capture of the City of Mexico by General Porfirio Diaz.

July 15, Juarez entered the City of Mexico and re-established his government.

1869—September 16, completion of the Mexican Railway to Puebla.

October 4, Bishopric of Tamaulipas established, seat at Victoria.

1871—December 1, Juarez re-elected President.

1872—July 18, death of President Juarez.

December 1, election of President Lerdo.

December 20, completion of the Mexican Railway in the meeting of the tracks above Maltrata.

1873—January 1, opening of the Mexican Railway between the City of Mexico and Vera Cruz.

1874—Incorporation in the Constitution of the Laws of the Reform.

1875—December 5, opening of the National Exhibition of Mexican products, in the City of Mexico,

1876—January 15, commenced the revolution under the plan of Tuxtepec.

November 24, General Porfirio Diaz entered the City of Mexico at the head of the revolutionary army and was proclaimed provisional president.

1877—May 6, General Diaz declared Constitutional President.

1878—Concession granted for the building of the Interoceanic Railway.

1879—June 24, execution of nine revolutionists against the Diaz government, at Vera Cruz.

1880—May 25, Bishopric of Tabasco established, seat at San Juan Bautista.

September 25, election of General Manuel Gonzalez as President.

Track laying on the Mexican Central commenced.

October 14, construction of Mexican National Railroad commenced.

1882—November 25, Sonora Railway opened.

1883—The "Nickel Riots" occurred.

March 15, Bishopric of Colima established, seat at Colima.

1884—March 8, completion of the tracks, and on April 5 opening of the Mexican Central Railway from El Paso to the City of Mexico.

1885—February, some Americans arrested for breaking twigs from the tree of Noche Triste.

1886—Completion of Mexican National Railroad to Morelia and Patzcuaro.

December 1, re-election of General Porfirio Diaz to the presidency.

1888—April 17, completion of the Mexican Central to Guadalajara.

March 1, completion of the International Railroad, Eagle Pass to Torreon.

November 1, completion of the Mexican National Railroad, from Laredo to the City of Mexico.

1889—Construction of the Mexican Southern Railroad commenced in September.

1892—November 11, opening of the Mexican Southern Railroad.

1893—Completion of the Interoceanic Railway to Vera Cruz.

1894—March 1, first party of American tourists visited the Ruins of Mitla, under escort of the American Tourist Association.

Completion of the Tehuantepec Railroad.

1895—Completion of the Mexico, Cuernavaca & Pacific Railway to Cuernavaca.

INDEX

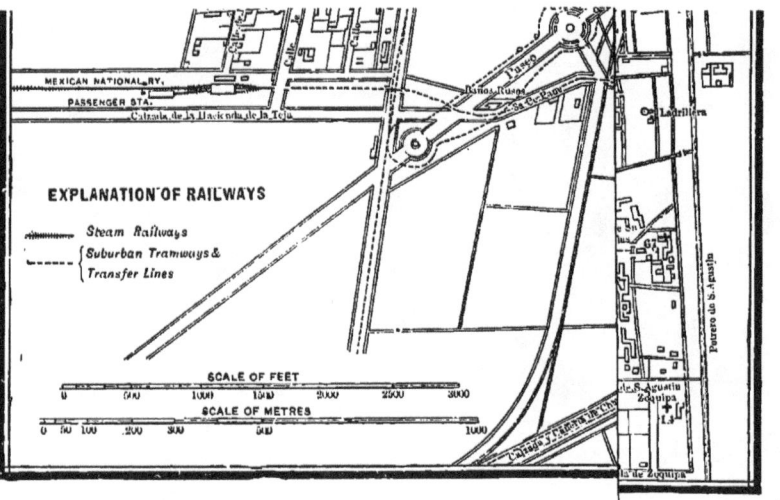

EXPLANATION OF RAILWAYS

———— Steam Railways

- - - - { Suburban Tramways & Transfer Lines

SCALE OF FEET

0   500   1000   1500   2000   2500   3000

SCALE OF METRES

0   50 100   200   300   500   1000

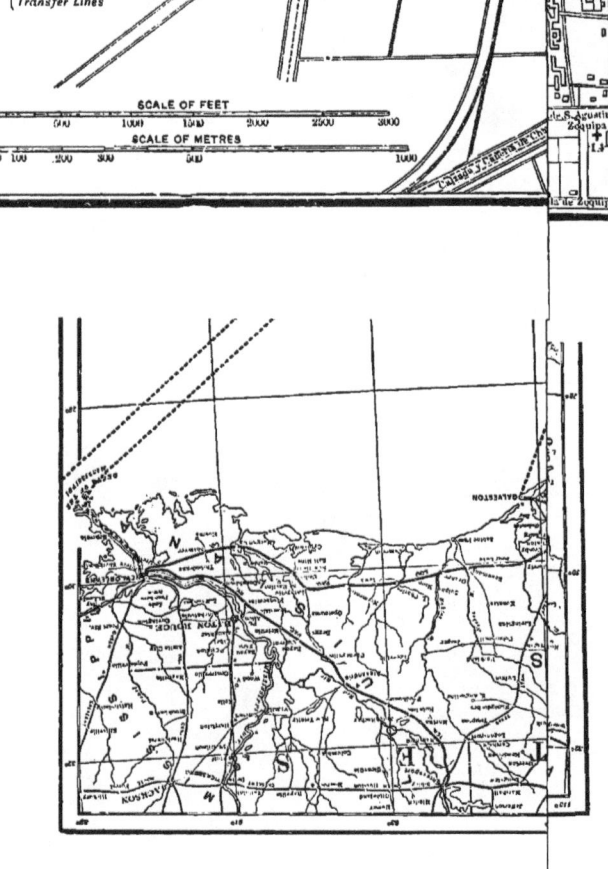

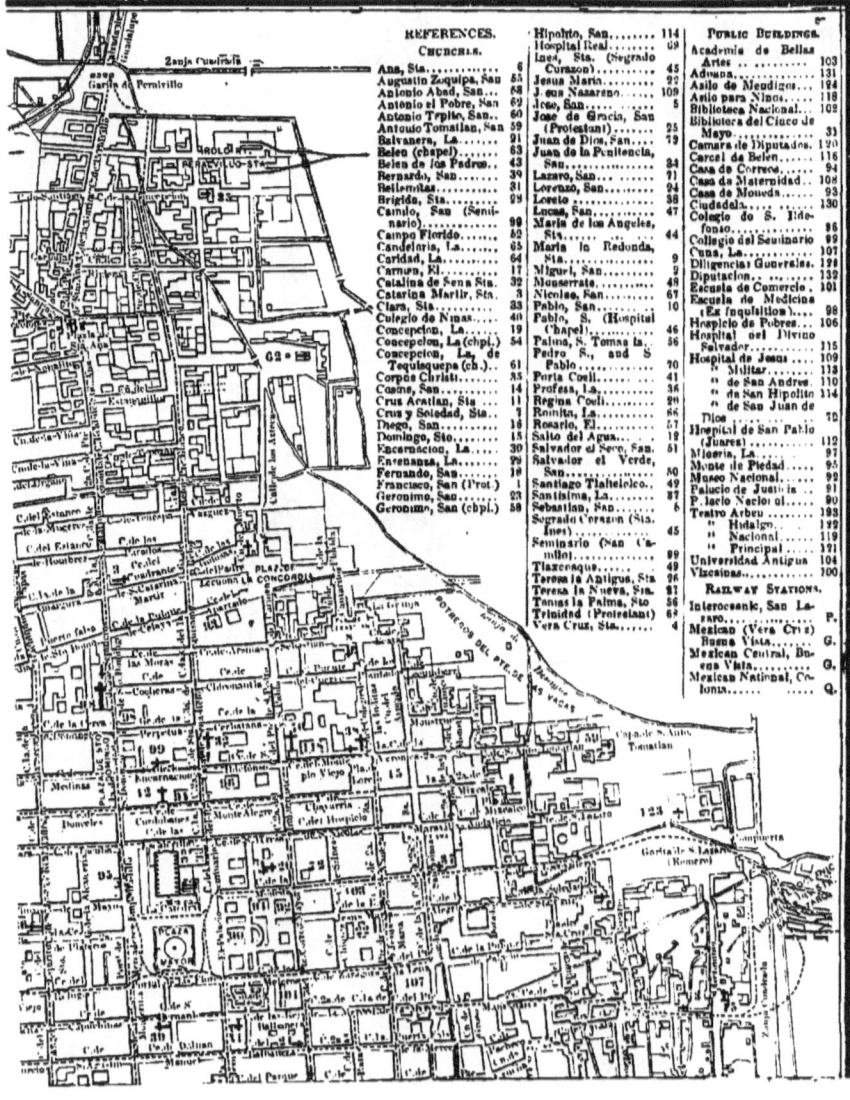

REFERENCES.

CHURCHES.

Ana, Sta.	6
Augustin Zequipa, San	55
Antonio Abad, San ...	58
Antonio el Pobre, San	62
Antonio Tepito, San..	60
Antonio Tomatlan, San	59
Balvanera, La..........	91
Belen (chapel).........	83
Belen de los Padres...	43
Bernardo, San.........	39
Belemitas.............	31
Brigida, Sta..........	28
Camilo, San (Seminario)...........	98
Campo Florido.........	52
Candelaria, La........	65
Caridad, La...........	64
Carmen, El...........	17
Catalina de Sena Sta.	32
Catarina Martir, Sta.	3
Clara, Sta.............	33
Colegio de Niñas......	40
Concepcion, La........	19
Concepcion, La (chpl.)	54
Concepcion, La, de Tequisquepa (ch.)..	61
Corpus Christi........	33
Cosme, San............	14
Cruz Acatlan, Sta.....	14
Cruz y Soledad, Sta.	7
Diego, San............	16
Domingo, Sto..........	15
Encarnacion, La.......	30
Ensenanza, La.........	29
Fernando, San.........	13
Francisco, San (Prot.)	1
Geronimo, San........	93
Geronimo, San (chpl.)	59
Hipolito, San........	114
Hospital Real........	69
Ines, Sta. (Sagrado Corazon).......	45
Jesus Maria..........	22
Jesus Nazareno.......	109
Jose, San............	5
Jose de Gracia, San (Protestant)......	25
Juan de Dios, San....	79
Juan de la Penitencia, San.............	24
Lazaro, San..........	71
Lorenzo, San.........	24
Loreto...............	58
Lucas, San...........	37
Maria de los Angeles, Sta.............	44
Maria la Redonda, Sta..............	9
Miguel, San..........	21
Monserrate...........	48
Nicolas, San.........	67
Pablo, San...........	10
Pablo, S. (Hospital Chapel).........	46
Palma, S. Tomas la..	56
Pedro S., and S Pablo............	70
Porta Coeli..........	41
Profesa, La..........	38
Regina Coeli........	20
Rosaita, La..........	68
Rosario, El..........	57
Salto del Agua.......	12
Salvador el Seco, San.	51
Salvador el Verde, San.............	80
Santiago Tlatelolco..	42
Santisima, La........	87
Sebastian, San.......	8
Sagrado Corazon (Sta. Ines)........	45
Seminario (San Camilo)............	98
Tlaxcoaque..........	49
Teresa la Antigua, Sta	26
Teresa la Nueva, Sta.	36
Tomas la Palma, Sto	56
Trinidad (Protestant)	68
Vera Cruz, Sta.......	

PUBLIC BUILDINGS.	
Academia de Bellas Artes	103
Aduana..............	131
Asilo de Mendigos...	104
Asilo para Niños.....	116
Biblioteca Nacional...	102
Biblioteca del Cinco de Mayo............	31
Camara de Diputados.	120
Carcel de Belen......	116
Casa de Correos......	94
Casa de Maternidad..	108
Casa de Moneda......	93
Ciudadela............	130
Colegio de S. Ildefonso............	86
Collegio del Seminario	99
Cuna, La............	107
Diligencias Generales.	132
Diputacion..........	132
Escuela de Comercio.	101
Escuela de Medicina (Ex Inquisition)..	98
Hospicio de Pobres...	106
Hospital del Divino Salvador.........	115
Hospital de Jesus....	109
" Militar......	113
" de San Andres.	110
" de San Hipolito	114
" de San Juan de Dios........	79
Hospital de San Pablo (Juarez)........	112
Miseria, La..........	97
Monte de Piedad.....	95
Museo Nacional......	92
Palacio de Justicia...	91
P. lacio Nacional.....	90
Teatro Arbeu........	193
" Hidalgo.......	122
" Nacional......	119
" Principal.....	121
Universidad Antigua..	104
Viscainas............	100

RAILWAY STATIONS.

Interoceanic, San Lazaro............	P.
Mexican (Vera Cruz) Buena Vista.....	G.
Mexican Central, Buena Vista.......	G.
Mexican National, Colonia............	Q.

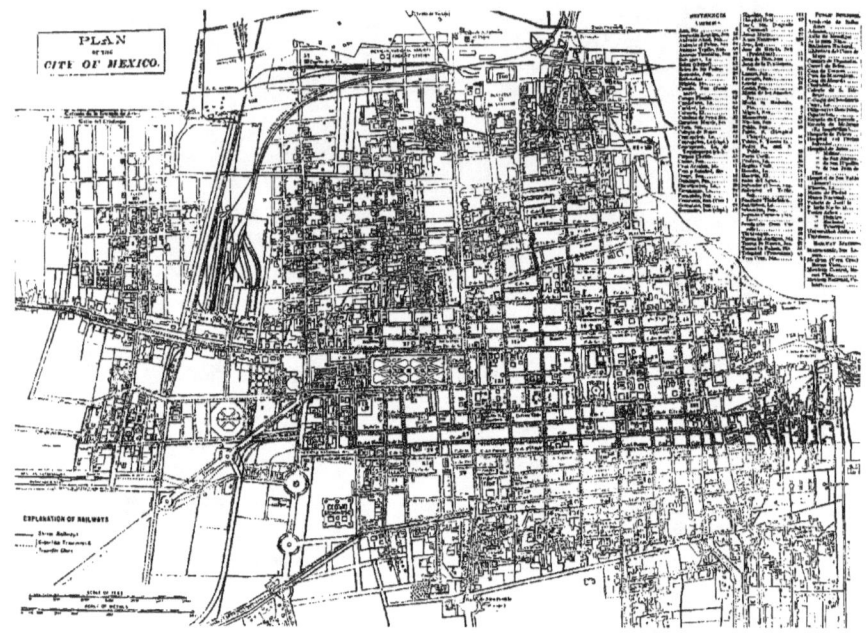